'Having read all three of Joe Ide's novels about the young Sherlock Holmes of the 'hood, Isaiah Quintabe, I am pleased to say that his third novel, *Wrecked*, is the best one yet. The stakes are higher, the suspense more intense . . . **Read it, enjoy it, and then impatiently wait around for the next one like the rest of us**' Kareem Abdul-Jabbar

'Wow! **This crime novel has it all** – a truly unusual hero, a fast-paced plot, vivid characters, great dialog, tremendous energy, acute observations, a sharp sense of humor, and a touching finale'
John Verdon, author of *Wolf Lake*

'Joe Ide [is] **the best thing to happen to mystery writing in a very long time**' *New York Times*

'He is the first new crime writer I have read in ages who truly feels like an **heir to Elmore Leonard**' *Daily Telegraph*

'**Ide writes with confidence and a sharp wit**' *Sunday Times*

'**The characters are unforgettable**, none more so than IQ himself . . . his tender intelligence and his tight moral compass are what make this series so stirring . . . and touching'
Attica Locke, author of *Bluebird, Bluebird*

'**Ide manages to combine light and dark in wholly unpredictable ways**, blending comic capering with real-life bloodletting in a manner that diminishes neither and taps a vein of deep emotion lurking amid the laugh lines and spurts of violence. Anyone who loves Thomas Perry or Timothy Hallinan needs to **hop on Ide's bandwagon while there's still room to sit**' *Booklist*

Joe Ide grew up in South Central Los Angeles. His favourite books were the Conan Doyle Sherlock Holmes stories. The idea that a person could face the world and vanquish his enemies with just his intelligence fascinated him. Joe went on to earn a graduate degree and had several careers before writing *IQ*, his debut novel, inspired by his early experiences and love of Sherlock. Joe lives in Santa Monica, California.

www.joeide.com

Also by Joe Ide

IQ
Righteous
Wrecked

RIGHTEOUS

JOE IDE

WEIDENFELD & NICOLSON

An Hachette UK Company

1 3 5 7 9 10 8 6 4 2

A CIP catalogue record for this book is
available from the British Library.

ISBN (Mass Market Paperback) 978 1 4746 0720 9
ISBN (eBook) 978 1 4746 0892 3

Printed and bound in Great Britain by Clays Ltd, Elcograf S.p.A.

www.orionbooks.co.uk

For Diane

RIGHTEOUS

Prologue

Isaiah was seventeen years old when his older brother, Marcus, was killed in a hit-and-run. Isaiah dropped out of school and spent months trying to track down the driver of the Honda Accord that left Marcus lying on the pavement smashed to pieces, his life-force draining into the gutter. His brother was his mentor, his friend, his guide through life, his only family. Everything.

Eight years later, he was at TK's wrecking yard when he stumbled upon the Accord. It was dusk. He was walking along the old race course route through the rows of abandoned cars. They reminded Isaiah of the Civil War photos he'd seen at the library. Dead soldiers on a battlefield. Crumpled bodies, chrome teeth grimacing, shattered eyes staring back at a hundred thousand miles. There was no breeze in the dying light, a lone crow atop the mountain of tires squawked plaintively, the last one on earth. Isaiah came around a corner and there it was. The sight of the murder weapon brought back a paralyzing upsurge of pain and memories: Marcus's smile that warmed and comforted, his voice, sure and soulful, the loving eyes that saw Isaiah's future, bright and full of promise. When the memories finally eased off, Isaiah blew his nose, wiped the tears off his face, and felt another surge of emotion, this one molten, made of anger and purpose. He wondered why he'd quit the search in the first place and he thought about the driver and how he was out there living his life not even caring that he'd killed the best person in the world.

Isaiah left the wrecking yard telling himself it was a long time ago and to put it behind him. The search had nearly killed him and sent his life spiraling out of control. The anguish and torment from those times were scarred over now and there was no point sticking a dagger into that old wound.

That night, he sat on the stoop sharing an energy bar with the dog. As a puppy, the purebred pit bull belonged to a hit man. When Isaiah put the guy in prison, he kept the dog and named it Ruffin after Marcus's favorite singer, David Ruffin. At ten weeks, Ruffin was cute and funny and weighed twelve pounds. Nine months later, he was a formidable fifty-seven-pound, slate-gray adolescent with amber eyes that made him look fierce and nobody thought he was cute or funny, and he could pull Isaiah down the street like a child's wagon. Isaiah realized he was fooling himself. He'd never gotten over Marcus's death. If there were ever two words that had no meaning they were *moving on*. Sorrow isn't a place you can leave behind. It's part of you. It changes the way you see, feel, and think, and every once in a while, the pain isn't remembered, it's relived; the anguish as real and heartbreaking as if it was happening all over again.

Ruffin followed Isaiah into the house, down the hall, and into the second bedroom he used as an office. A heat wave had descended on Long Beach and the room was stuffy and hot. It was so spare it looked forgotten although he used it all the time. There was an old teacher's desk, a squeaky office chair, two file cabinets, boxes of records stacked on the floor, and a six-foot folding table with nothing on it. No knickknacks or anything personal except for two snapshots on the wall. One of Marcus and Isaiah mugging for the camera. The other was of Mrs. Marquez holding up a chicken by its feet, the poor thing struggling and helpless. Isaiah had accepted the bird as payment for his services just to get it away from her. She'd named it Alejandro after her pendejo ex-husband. When the hit man came to the house to kill Isaiah, he inadvertently blasted the bird into a cloud of feathers.

Isaiah put one of the storage boxes on the table along with a folder of info he'd gathered so far. The Accord's VIN number had led to the car's owner, Fred Bellows. His Facebook page showed a paunchy white guy in his forties, with a face like an unbaked biscuit, his pants pulled up to the third button of his blue, brown, and yellow madras shirt. His wife looked like his twin sister, the three kids already showing paunches. Fred lived in Wrigley Heights, a nice area just north of Hurston where Marcus and Isaiah once had an apartment.

Isaiah took some photographs out of the file folder and spread them on the table. They were pictures of the Accord taken at the wrecking yard. The car's right front headlight assembly was smashed, the crease that ran along the top of the bumper was dented, and some paint was scraped off. It seemed wrong and impossible that a little bit of damage like that had resulted in Marcus's death. A massive bomb crater or a charred redwood split by lightning would have been more credible.

The seats and dash had been ripped out of the car's interior but Isaiah had found things on the floor. There were four smashed cigarette butts, Marlboros, four empty Carta Blanca cans, a crumpled white food bag, and a balled-up sandwich wrapper. Isaiah laid the items on the table. He opened the wrapper. Part of the sandwich was still there, shrunken and mummified, along with a few shriveled jalapeño circles, bread crumbs in the crinkles of the paper. The wrapper was from Kayo Subs. Their logo was on it: a target of rainbow colors with a fist punching through it holding a sandwich.

Isaiah had a Google Earth map of East Long Beach inside his head with landmarks for every gang turf, crack house, flophouse, bar, dance hall, pool hall, drug corner, hooker stroll, murder scene, sex offender, abandoned building, liquor store, and park in the area. Any locus of criminals, crime, or potential crime. Isaiah placed Kayo's on his map. It was right across the street from McClarin Park. He and Marcus had played basketball there just before the accident. Isaiah heard a single faint *ping* on his internal sonar.

The white bag was generic. It held unused napkins, a packet of mustard, and a receipt for one twelve-inch sub and a bag of chips. It was dated the same day as the accident at 5:02 p.m. Marcus was killed around six. *Ping ping.* Fred was no doubt capable of knocking back four Carta Blancas but he looked like a Budweiser or Coors man, and he wouldn't leave the cans in the car, not with a family. They belonged to the driver. A&J Liquor was two doors down from Kayo's so the driver gets his sandwich, buys some beer, then sits in the car eating and drinking and smoking—but for *an hour?* A Grand Slam breakfast at Denny's might take you that long but this guy didn't even finish the sandwich. More likely, he was waiting for something, eating because Kayo's was there, taking a few bites and leaving the rest; more interested in smoking a cigarette and drinking a beer every fifteen minutes, which meant he was either an alcoholic chain smoker or he was nervous. Really nervous. *Ping ping ping.*

After Isaiah and Marcus finished their basketball game, they walked north on McClarin until it ended at Bethesda, made a turn onto Baldwin, and walked two blocks to Anaheim, where the Accord hit Marcus as he was coming off the curb. Isaiah's sonar was *ping*ing like a torpedo was fifty feet away and closing fast. The Accord was going from west to east when it ran down Marcus. To come from that direction the driver would have had to leave Kayo's and take a circuitous route *around and away* from the brothers to get west of them, and why would he do that unless he was setting up to run Marcus over?

This was no accident. *This was a hit.*

CHAPTER ONE
Grace Period

The dance floor was a street riot under a disco ball, hands sprouting out of the crowd waving green light sticks and six-hundred-dollar bottles of Ciroc, go-go dancers in fur bikinis and fishnet body stockings writhing like tentacles of smoke, the air warm and close, soggy with the smells of alcohol, musky colognes, and pheromones.

It was Saturday night at Seven Sevens. The DJ was dropping a dubstep, the bass deep and pounding as the earth's pulse, a nasal whine snaking through the syncopated beats while a Buddhist monk on speed chanted *The world is mine the world is mine the world is mine,* the music accelerating, synthesized strings spiraling upward, keening into what they called *trance,* the breathy beat driving faster and faster, the dancers frenzied as warring ants, the energy so extreme it threatened to crack the walls, and then mercifully, a break, the keening winding down, the beat decelerating into a thumping, head-bobbing tom-tom.

An Asian girl was on the DJ stand, held in a column of vaporous light like Scotty had just beamed her down to work the turntables.

Her gleaming black hair thrashed like a horse's tail, a yellow star on her red belly shirt, her denim shorts so short Benny said he could see the outline of her junk. She shouted into the mike, jubilant and fierce: "Whassup my people! This is your queen kamikaze, the heat in your wasabi, the gravy train in the food chain, the champagne in the chow mein, I'm DJ Dama, baby, that was my set, and I'm gettin' up outta heeerre, PEACE!"

Janine Van came down from the DJ stand and moved through the crowd. She loved this part, people woo-hooing, whistling, clapping, high-fiving her. A group of drunk college boys howled at her like love-struck coyotes, the brothers checking her out, leaning back with their hands on their chins. Hey, being a hottie never hurt. DJ Young Suicide was up next, not even looking at her as he went by. Prick. Like she was a scrub, not worth acknowledging. Yeah, that's aight, he'd wake up one day and be Old Suicide and she'd be headlining at the Marquee club.

Janine had chosen Dama as her DJ name because it was different and the Chinese word for *weed*. She had a following in LA and San Francisco but especially here in Vegas, her hometown. The club gave her the early set, opening for Suicide, DJ Twista, and DJ Gone Viral, but that wouldn't be for long. Chinese tourists were discovering her. They loved seeing one of their own do something besides play Ping-Pong and solve math problems. You'd think Jeremy Lin invented noodles the way they carried on.

The pay was good, seven hundred and fifty bucks a set, not bad for a twenty-one-year-old who'd only been mixing professionally for eleven months. She played two sets a week, enough for most people, but the slots and blackjack tables were disappearing her paychecks as fast as she could cash them, and now Leo had her and Benny by the Ben Wa balls. They'd only borrowed five grand but they hadn't paid the twenty percent vig in four weeks and now the five was nearly nine; fourteen hundred for the vig alone.

Once in a while they tried to stay away from the tables; kick the monkey off their backs and focus on their careers. Janine on her DJing, Benny a rising star on the motocross circuit. For two or three days they'd have a lot of sex and smoke a lot of weed until the monkey came back like a silverback gorilla, and they'd be off to the casinos pledging to manage their stake more professionally this time, which made no sense if you were going to spend it all no matter how big you won or how fast you were losing. A few months back, Benny's sponsor dropped him because he hadn't shown at a couple of meets. He couldn't afford the maintenance on a sophisticated racing bike so to solve the problem he and Janine gambled *more,* and didn't even talk about quitting. They played whenever they had money. On Christmas Day, they both had pneumonia and twenty-seven dollars between them but they played nickel slots at the Rio until security threw them out for coughing up loogies fat as slugs and spitting them into plastic cups.

Janine loved Benny. God, she loved him. He was funny and sweet, and an Olympian in the sack. He wasn't especially smart but he listened to her and was good to her, hard-to-find qualities these days. But Benny was also a lousy gambler, more than half the debt was his. Janine resented it, Leo considering the two of them as a single deadbeat unit. He was diabolical like that, knowing Benny would never leave Vegas, and if she did she'd be leaving him with the debt and breaking both their hearts. She hoped Benny was lying low. Leo was a mean son of a bitch. If he had you down he'd hurt you and smile while he was doing it.

* * *

Leo had snitches all over town. Lots of people owed him money and were happy to rat out their friends for a little extra time. Leo caught Benny at the Siesta Vegas Motel going to the vending machine for a Mountain Dew. He took Benny's key and they went back to the room, Balthazar trailing to make sure Benny didn't bolt.

"Do you have my vig or don't you?" Leo said. "And don't bullshit."

"Soon, Leo, I swear, really soon," Benny said, shaking his head at the same time. "My grandmother's estate is out of probate and the lawyer says he'll have a check for me in a few days, a week tops."

"You told me that one already," Leo said. Leo couldn't have been anything else but a loan shark. Large rose-tinted aviators perched over a rodentlike face and a permanent smirk, his long, greasy hair swept back over his ears. His fashion sense tended toward paisley disco shirts with jumbo collars; nobody telling him that seventies retro was not now and never had been in. Leo was a gold-medal asshole, giving you shit even when you paid him off, and he didn't seem to care that everybody, including the people he called friends, would rather hang out at the morgue than have a drink with him.

"All I need is a little more time," Benny said. "You know, like a grace period."

"Grace period?" Leo said. "Who do you think you're dealing with, the Stupid People's Credit Union? *Grace period?* That expression is not in my daily lexicon, and in case you haven't noticed, I'm a criminal. A dedicated, lifelong, unrepentant, lawbreaking motherfucker and I play by no one's rules but my own and rule number one is *Pay me my fucking money.*"

"You know I don't have it," Benny said. "Look around." The motel room that Benny and Janine rented by the month was a dump to begin with, but with all their damp, random, unlaundered shit piled up everywhere the place was hardly livable. Benny used to park his motocross bike inside, but he kept it at Ray's now so Leo wouldn't take it. Janine stored her DJ equipment in Sal's garage.

"Gimme what you've got on you," Leo said.

"Aww, come on, Leo," Benny said. "That's my rent money."

"Give it," Balthazar said, "or I'll break your fucking neck, eh?"

Balthazar was from Saskatchewan, right across the border from Montana, the difference being Montana grew brown trout and buffalo instead of terrifying freakazoids. Balthazar was seven feet tall with a jutting chin and comatose eyes set under a Frankenstein forehead; his body cobbled together with parts from an orangutan and an office building. Benny wondered where he got his clothes. He'd joked about it, asking Balthazar if the guy who made his pants also made circus tents. Balthazar swatted him with a hand that was more like a foot. "Don't be a smart-ass, eh?"

Benny gave up his wallet, his last eighty-three dollars in there, money he'd won at the Lucky Streak, a dive over in Henderson. He liked to play there when he was bummed or stressed out. The casino was smoky as a forest fire, frayed felt on the blackjack tables and lots of senior citizens in Hawaiian shirts shuffling around on walkers. Sign up for the comp club and get a free six-pack of Pepsi, but you could play craps for a dollar, even in the morning, and for $3.99 you got two eggs, two slices of bacon, two sausages, toast, and a Belgian waffle.

"Take your clothes off," Leo said.

"What?"

"You heard me. Do it or Zar will do it for you."

"Hey, wait a second, you're not gonna—you don't want to do that, Leo, I've got diarrhea!"

"Don't be disgusting, and leave your boxers on. I don't want your corn hole smelling up my car."

"I know I owe you but you don't have to humiliate me."

"Yeah, I know. I'm doing this for fun."

As Benny stripped, Leo said, "Look at you, you fucking loser. Don't you believe in doing your laundry? Your socks don't even match. You and your plastic wallet and your fucked-up haircut and that stupid-ass puka shell bracelet. Why Janine hooked up with a dud like you is one of the world's great mysteries. One of these days in the not-too-distant future she's gonna realize she could pick a better boyfriend out of a lineup and leave your ass flat."

"My wallet isn't plastic," Benny said.

Benny rode in the backseat of Leo's white Mercedes, more like a limo than a car and quieter than the motel room at four in the morning. They drove out of Vegas proper and through North Las Vegas, a Whitman's Sampler of housing developments, all of them different but the same. Now they were in the desert, so dark you could only see what the headlights saw, not even a gas station out here.

"Where we going, Leo?" Benny asked for the fifth time.

"Like I told you five times already," Leo said, "you'll see when we get there. Where's Janine?"

"Playing a gig at the War Room."

"Can't you open your mouth without telling a lie? She's at Seven Sevens, her name's on the fucking sign."

"Come on, Leo, be reasonable. If you mess me up I won't be able to pay you back."

"Not from the tables, not the way you play. Like I told you before, you need to get the money from someplace else."

"I will, Leo, I swear on my little sister. Did I tell you she's got cancer?"

"Your sister is older than you and she *died* of cancer. Remember we went to the hospital to hit her up for a loan?"

They made a turn and drove through a parking lot, vast and empty, ominous in the yellow floodlights; the place where the girl looks back, sees the killer, and starts to run. They stopped at the end.

"Get out of the car," Leo said.

"You go, I'll wait here," Benny said.

Balthazar reached back with his orangutan arm and smacked him. "Get out of the car, eh?"

As soon as Benny smelled garbage he knew where he was. He'd come here on a school field trip when he was eleven years old. A dork who looked like SpongeBob in orange coveralls gave them the tour. "The Apex Regional Landfill is one of the biggest in the world," he said, like it was the Grand Canyon. "The pit covers three hundred and sixty acres, it's two hundred feet deep, there's five hundred million tons of refuse in there so far, and when it's filled to the top it'll be a billion! That's right, kids. A billion tons of trash! What do you think of that, young man?"

"I think it stinks," Benny said.

Balthazar pushed Benny toward the landfill, Leo leading the way with a flashlight. Benny felt the air pressure change; gases from the moldering garbage creating its own atmosphere of heat and rot.

"Don't, Leo, please don't do this," Benny said. "I'll get the money someplace else, I swear on my—"

"Swear on your what?" Leo said. "Your two-year-old niece that's got syphilis? Your mom that's dying from ass tumors? Shut the fuck up."

Benny remembered the huge pyramids of trash and garbage, the valleys so deep they could swallow you up, and all of it splattered with seagull shit and crawling with a million rats.

"I could die down there, Leo."

"Yeah, if you're lucky."

"Please don't do this," Benny said. He could see the edge of the pit, the smell was so strong it was almost gelatinous. He was crying now. He tried to backpedal, but Balthazar grabbed him by the neck, lifted him like he was hanging him on a coatrack, and walked him forward. "Don't do this, I'm begging you," Benny said. "I'll rob a bank, I'll go to the bus station and suck dicks in the men's room." He was blubbering like a child, the words so wet they were barely words. "No, please, Leo, please, ple-ee-eese."

"The vig by Friday," Leo said, "or tell Janine she's next."

"Okay, now that's over the line—"

Leo nodded and Balthazar shoved Benny into the blackness, his scream cutting in and out as he bumped and tumbled down the slope, hardly making a sound as he landed wherever he landed. Leo waited for Benny to groan or call for help but he couldn't hear anything except garbage bags flapping in the breeze. Leo wondered if Benny had broken his neck.

"I warned him, didn't I?" he said, a pinhead of regret in his voice.

"He's lucky, eh?" Balthazar said. "We could have shot him first."

CHAPTER TWO

Citrus and Cypress Trees

Isaiah was in Beaumont's store buying a cranberry juice when his cell buzzed. He didn't recognize the number. "Hello?" he said.

"Isaiah, is that you?" A woman's voice.

"Yeah, this is Isaiah."

"It's Sarita."

Isaiah's heart seized up. His tongue stuck to the roof of his mouth. "It is?" he said.

"Yes, it is," she said, laughing. "It's been so long. How are you?" Her voice was happy and relaxed and confident. It was breathtaking.

"I'm fine," he said. "How are you?"

"I'm good, Isaiah, but listen, I'm sorry I don't have time to talk right now, but I'd like to get together and catch up. Would that be all right?"

He had to clear his throat before words would come out. "Yeah, sure, that'd be great."

"I know this is short notice but how about tomorrow night, around eight? I'll be at the Intercontinental Hotel in Century City. Do you know where that is?"

"No," he said, "but I'll find it."

Dizzy with excitement, Isaiah hurried out to his car, wishing he didn't have so much on his plate. Somebody broke into Miss Myra's house and stole, among other things, a brooch her mother had given to her when she was on her deathbed, honeycombed with cancer, a rattle in her throat as she hummed an old spiritual about going home. The brooch was a flimsy thing; painted metal and colored glass, not even pawnable, and nobody but Miss Myra would wear it. Any self-respecting thief would have tossed it away. Finding it would mean searching the storm drains, dumpsters, and alleys near her house. Then there was Doris Sattiewhite, a checkout clerk at Shop 'n Save who was being stalked by her ex-husband, Mike. He'd show up at her work, get in line, and pay for something with pennies and nickels so she'd have to count it while he said *I'm coming for you, bitch. You hear me? I'm coming for you.*

Raymond Marcel, aka Rayo, was thirteen years old, and lived in a foster home with a woman who kept a padlock on the refrigerator and a crowbar under her pillow. Rayo was built like Shrek and was three times the size of anybody in his class; a lifetime of abuse and a passion for bullying festering in his angry, broken spirit. His favorite victims were members of the Carver Middle School Science Club. A delegation from the club showed up at Isaiah's door and pleaded with him to do something about Rayo. They were afraid to go to school, afraid to leave school, afraid all the time. Unfortunately, the club president said, as she tried to get her backpack off while she held on to her tuba case, the club could not, at the present time, afford Isaiah's per diem. However, they could offer him a promissory note, payable when their startup went public, or, the club president went on to say as she tried to extract some hair from her braces, the club could act as Isaiah's eyes and ears around the neighborhood. Operatives, as it were. Isaiah said he'd consider it and the meeting adjourned.

He wasn't looking forward to any of it. The problems were important but mundane, as challenging as cleaning the stove, and now Sarita called out of the blue. He'd experienced a lot of anxiety during his cases but in those situations he could figure a way out or solve the puzzle and end whatever it was that was making him anxious. This was different. He didn't understand the situation or even if there was one, and if there was a puzzle to solve he couldn't identify it.

A '66 Dodger-blue Chevy Nova rolling on chrome twenties pulled up in front of the store, the engine loping at idle, a 327 small-block by the sound of it. Rap music was pounding like it was trying to break a window and get out of the car. Isaiah wasn't a fan of rap to begin with but this had accordions and trumpets in it and sounded like some pissed-off Mexicans shouting over a polka band.

Two members of Sureños Locos 13 and a girl named Ramona got out of the car. Isaiah'd had a recent run-in with them and they warned him they'd fuck him up if they caught him on the street. Ramona was fifteen or sixteen. She had pink streaks in her blue-black hair, her stark, penciled-in eyebrows angled over young eyes, pink lipstick outlined in plum, sleeve tats crawling up her arms into a white tank top, her pants called fifties because they were fifty inches wide, the hems stapled to her fridge-white sneakers so she wouldn't step on them. Her vibe was different than her male colleagues. Hard as them to be sure, no doubt she'd stab you with a bottle so she wouldn't break a nail, but there was something desperate about her, like she had something to prove and was in a hurry to do it.

"What's up, motherfucker," she said. "Remember me?"

One of the fellas wore wraparound shades and a Raiders cap. The other guy, Vicente, was smiling and cocky, a hairnet over his bald head. "Are you stupid?" he said. "Shit, if I was you, I'd be long gone. This is Loco soil, ese." He swept his arm across Chuck's Check Cashing, Lo Mejor Jewelry and Loans, Carlita's Bridal Shop where all the dresses were piñata colors, and Z&Z Trading; racks of handbags, sweatshirts, and stuffed animals in front of the store.

"Are you ready for a beatdown, motherfucker?" Ramona said.

Vicente stepped in close. "What about it, bitch," he said. "Are you?"

Beaumont was looking between the Bud Light sign and the Red Man poster, watching the Mexicans mess with Isaiah. Damn hooligans. Think they can intimidate everybody and take what they want. It really pissed him off and he was afraid for Isaiah too. Beaumont went back to the cash register, reached under the counter, and brought out the .45-caliber Colt Commander he'd brought home from Vietnam. There was rust around the end of the barrel, and rice paddy mud still encrusted on the grip. He wondered if the damn thing would fire.

"Look," Isaiah said, trying to buy time. "I messed up, okay? I meant no disrespect."

"You came into my house, you fucked with my brother," Ramona said.

"If it was up to me?" Vicente said. He made his hand into a gun and pointed it at Isaiah's head. *"Pow."* Vicente was leaning back on his right foot and lowering his right shoulder, about to throw a punch. Ramona and Raiders Cap were fanning out, caging him in the vestibule. Nothing else to do but get off first. The main thing:

Stay off the ground. You could fight off your back with one opponent but not three.

Isaiah dropped the cranberry juice, the bottle shattering on the pavement, Vicente's eyes going with it. Isaiah stepped into him with a slashing right elbow, catching him across the nose, the sound like ice cracking. Isaiah brought the elbow back the other way, the point of it hitting Vicente in the temple. His eyeballs froze and he fell over like a tree but Ramona was coming at Isaiah with a wild roundhouse. Isaiah blocked it with an inside-out forearm and punched her in the solar plexus. She fell to her knees, gasping. But Isaiah was off-balance now and couldn't block Raiders Cap's hammer fist, the blow coming down on his forehead and knocking him back into the door. Raiders Cap jammed his forearm into Isaiah's throat and pushed like he was trying to move a wall, teeth clenched and growling, sweat squeezing out of his pores. Isaiah could feel his trachea buckling. He stiffened his fingers into an adze and stabbed Raiders Cap in the left eye. Raiders Cap screamed, turning his head and backing away. Isaiah hit him where his jaw met his temple and kneed him in the balls. Raiders Cap collapsed, but Vicente and Ramona were on their feet now and charging Isaiah. They bulldozed him into the door and dragged him to the ground.

"Kill him," Ramona said. "Kill this fucker."

Beaumont watched, feeling helpless and stupid, the heavy pistol in his arthritic hand. Firing an M16 at little guys in black pajamas you could barely see wasn't the same thing as shooting a gangbanger at point-blank range with a gun that might or might not fire. He was fumbling for his phone when another car pulled up next to the Nova. A Chevy Caprice, a '95, around in there, black with a blacked-out grill and black wheels. Darth Vader's car if he was a cop. A Mexican man got out. He was older than the others and dressed nice. Khaki chinos that fit him like regular pants, black polo buttoned at the neck. He looked tired and irritated, but he had a nobility about him, like that Indian chief on the buffalo-head nickel.

"Okay, that's enough," Manzo said. He moved the three gangsters aside like he was parting curtains. "Get up," he said. He put his hand out and pulled Isaiah to his feet.

"The fuck, Manzo?" Ramona said. "He's the one that came to my house and fucked with Frankie."

"You don't think I know that?" Manzo said, giving Isaiah a look. "We already talked about it." Manzo still had the welts and bruises from their *talk*.

"What's talking got to do with it?" she said.

"You better shut up, chica," Raiders Cap said.

"I don't see why he gets off without no punishment. That's bull-shit."

"Did you hear what happened to Néstor's daughter?" Manzo said.

"Néstor? Who's Néstor?" Ramona said.

"She's my goddaughter, and do you remember when that crazy white boy was setting fires all around the neighborhood?"

"I don't know, I guess so."

"And remember when somebody broke into the school where my son Nikki goes and stole all the computers?"

"Yeah, I remember, but—"

"And remember when Jorge who brings in our weed got busted for distribution and was looking at fifteen years?"

"The fuck we talkin' about, Manzo?"

"We're talking about Isaiah. He stopped the guy that was going to rape Néstor's daughter, and he caught the guy that was setting

21

the fires and he got the school's computers back, and he busted the cops for entrapment so they had to let Jorge go."

"Who gives a shit, Manzo?" she said. "You can't go soft just because—"

Manzo backhanded her so hard her head did a Linda Blair, and she collapsed like somebody had yanked out her skeleton. The blow was so sudden and violent Isaiah and the other Locos made *ooh* faces.

"Listen to me, Ramona," Manzo said, standing over her. "I'm telling you again. You can't just do shit because you feel like it. You gotta think about consequences. You gotta weigh the pros and cons. If you fuck Isaiah up and he leaves the neighborhood who would be better off? Néstor's daughter that didn't get raped? The people who didn't get their houses burned down? And what about you? If Jorge was in the joint there wouldn't be no weed to sell and you'd be working at Taco Bell." Ramona was lying on her side with her hands over her face, blood seeping through her fingers. Manzo nudged her with his foot. "Are you listening?" he said. "This shit is important. If you want to get somewhere, like in the hierarchy? Then you gotta be more than a soldier. You gotta be smart. You gotta have foresight. You gotta use your fucking head. In other words, think, bitch, and if you ever call me soft again I'll kill you." He looked at Vicente and Raiders Cap. "And that goes for you assholes too. Didn't I tell you about shit like this? Don't you pendejos understand anything? We're businessmen now, okay?"

"Okay," Raiders Cap replied meekly.

Manzo shifted his eyes to Vicente. "Are you hearing me, Vicente?" he said, demanding a response. Vicente looked at him, sneering and defiant. He drew the moment out, deliberately testing Manzo's patience.

The tension was about to boil over when Vicente said, "Sure, Manzo. Whatever you say."

Manzo glanced at Isaiah, went to his car, and drove away.

"What a fucking asshole," Vicente said. He and Raiders Cap picked Ramona up by her armpits, her head lolling like a baby's.

"When you gonna learn, chica," Raiders Cap said. "You don't get no slack because you're Frankie's sister."

She looked at Isaiah with half-open eyes, blood bubbling from her lips. "I'm not finished with you, motherfucker."

Isaiah lay back on the sofa, held a bag of ice to his head, and took another ibuprofen on top of the three he'd already swallowed. He had bruises and abrasions all over his body. It hurt every time he inhaled but there were no broken bones. He thought about Manzo. A week ago, they'd had a fight that could have ended up with one of them dead. He was surprised the gang leader hadn't joined in the beatdown. And what was all that stuff about rescuing Néstor's daughter and the stolen computers? Why was Manzo making excuses for him? There had to be something else behind it, some kind of Michael Corleone calculated agenda. Manzo had a rep for that, thinking three steps ahead of the pack, plotting for the long run.

Isaiah wouldn't be meeting Sarita for another three hours, but he started getting ready anyway, a cauldron of anticipation bubbling inside him. She was Marcus's girlfriend back when Isaiah was in high school, and he'd always had a crush on her. Soft and mink-slinky, the color of coffee with two creams and smart enough to go to Stanford Law on scholarship and pass the bar on her first try. Thinking about her eyes was corny, but Isaiah couldn't help it. Shining like buffed copper, knowing and kind, seeing past your outside and into your heart. That was why she didn't care that Marcus was a handyman and never went to college, she saw him for the good man he was. When she came over to the apartment, Isaiah had to leave the room, afraid he'd give himself away.

He took a shower and dressed. He didn't usually look at himself in the mirror unless he was brushing his teeth, but he wanted to see what Sarita would see. He went into the bedroom and checked himself in the full-length mirror. He looked his age, twenty-six; six feet tall and slim, maybe an athlete, maybe not. You'd choose him third for pickup basketball. His face surprised him, so watchful and serious. A girl once told him he looked like he was waiting for bad weather. He thought his nose was too broad, and his lips were too thick. It embarrassed him to think like that. He looked okay but just.

He took Anaheim to the freeway, trying to keep to the speed limit. It was a short but depressing drive, the city fathers and mothers having no use for trees or green strips. He went past Pronto Auto Body, where he'd had a dent fixed with filler so cheap you could dig it out with your fingernail, and Bed Time Furniture, where they sold reconditioned mattresses as new, and the Clean King coin laundry, where you had to wait for a machine on Saturdays, and the strip mall where Looney Hopkins was shot and the empty lot where Luis Delgado was shot and the barbershop where Isaiah had his hair cut and old men played dominoes and Tristar Liquor Mart, where the cash register was behind bulletproof glass and the clerk had an assault rifle.

The Intercontinental Hotel was in Century City, a moneyed enclave of shopping, office buildings, and luxury condos right down the road from Beverly Hills. The hotel's Grand Salon was teeming with suits, the din so loud you couldn't pick out an individual voice. Isaiah made his way through the crowd, everybody holding a drink, talking over the noise or waiting for their turn to speak like somebody'd said *On your mark.* Nobody noticed him, but he was embarrassed anyway. If he hadn't been so nervous he'd have thought to wear something better than jeans and Timberlands. He posted up near the bar and looked for Sarita, hoping he wasn't too late or too early or on the wrong side of the room or in the wrong place altogether.

A tall black man in a sharp navy blue suit and caramel-colored shoes came toward him. Thirties, fit, condescending eyes and so well groomed he could have been airbrushed. "Excuse me," he said, "but you don't belong here, now do you?" He had the confidence of success, charm just short of pretentious and a wide Billy Dee Williams smile. "You thought you'd wander in here off the street and help yourself to champagne and jumbo prawns and no one would call you out?"

Isaiah considered telling him he was waiting for Sarita but didn't. This was one of those guys that screamed at his assistant, wore handmade shirts and only drank French wine. "I haven't had anything to eat or drink," Isaiah said, "and how do you know I don't belong here?"

"I know everyone that was invited to Arthur's birthday party and that didn't include you," the man said. He straightened his already straight tie, leaned in, his voice confidential but the volume the same. "Can I give you a piece of advice?" he said. "If you're going to pretend to be something you're not, the least you could do is dress the part."

"You mean like your watch?" Isaiah said.

"What? What are you talking about?" the man said.

Isaiah had investigated employee theft at the Jewelry Bazaar and learned to tell the difference between platinum and rhodium plating, diamonds and cubic zirconia, 18K gold and polished 70/30 anodes, and real versus counterfeit watches. "Your watch is pretending to be a Rolex," he said.

"You mean it's counterfeit?" the man said. "That's ridiculous." He looked at the fat gold disk like it was turning into a frog.

"Check out the second hand," Isaiah said. "It's ticking. On a real Yacht-Master, it sweeps, and the date should be magnified two and a half times and yours is closer to two. Can I give *you* a piece of advice? If you're supposed to be a big-time attorney? Buy yourself a real watch."

They looked at each other, the Billy Dee smile pulled tight as a garrote.

"Leave now or I'm calling security," the man said.

A faint scent of citrus and cypress trees arrived before she did. Sarita was making her way through the crowd. She looked like a champion Thoroughbred coming through a herd of plow horses even in her dark suit and her hair pulled back. "Isaiah?" she said. She gave him a big hug and held on. "It's so good to see you!" She leaned away but kept her hands on his shoulders. "My God, you're the spitting image of Marcus."

"I don't think so," he said. "You look great, Sarita."

"Oh, have you two met?" she said. "Isaiah Quintabe, this is my colleague, Kevin Marshall."

"How do you do," Kevin said, like he was about to draw his weapon.

"I'm doing just fine," Isaiah said.

"Will you excuse us, Kevin?" Sarita said. "Isaiah and I need to talk."

"Sure," Kevin said. He huffed dismissively and walked away.

"What was that all about?" Sarita said.

"It was nothing."

"I'm sorry about this, but I had to be here. One of the partners is having a birthday. Let's go someplace and talk."

They went outside and walked south on the Avenue of the Stars, a wide clean street with a strip of manicured drought-resistant plants running down the middle and a water feature that sparkled like bobbled ice cubes. They apologized to each other for not staying in touch and reminisced about Marcus and the old apartment and the neighborhood and all the people they had in common. Sarita had read about Isaiah's exploits. Since the article had come out about him in *The Scene,* others had appeared in *Vibe* and the *Long Beach Press-Telegram.* Isaiah wouldn't do interviews, but his clients were eager to talk about the quiet, unassuming young man who took on their problems when nobody else cared and got paid with live chickens and blueberry muffins.

"Marcus would have been so proud and happy for you," she said. "He was the only person I ever met who could be unabashedly joyful. God, I miss him."

"Me too," Isaiah said, whispering so he wouldn't choke up.

They walked past a high-rise looming like a sentry, wearing its hundreds of reflective windows like shields. Beyond that, there was nothing on either side of the street except tall hedges fronting tall iron fences, the tops of the bars bent outward, the rooftops of places you couldn't afford peeking over the top.

"When Marcus died I was devastated," Sarita said. "Every place I went I waited for him to stop messing around and show himself. I was crying all the time, and when I wasn't doing that I was sleeping. But then law school started, and I couldn't afford to drop out.

It was a struggle but a good thing too. Studying kept me from throwing myself under a bus."

Isaiah was content to let her talk; it was a good excuse to look at her. She was as beautiful as ever, but the shining, unstoppable enthusiasm he remembered was gone, and in its place was a tension, a guardedness, like, *I'm in the real world now and they don't mess around.*

She'd grown up near MacArthur Park, on the other side of Cambodia Town, a hood like any other. She worked two jobs while she made the dean's list at Long Beach State. Then she went to Stanford Law and did a semester abroad before she graduated with honors. She was hired immediately by a small firm in San Francisco. It was a good place to get started, but after a couple of years she was ready to paint on a bigger canvas. When she got an offer to join the two hundred and twenty-one lawyers at Edgars, Mehlman, Cross and Severeid in LA for almost double the money, she jumped at it. She'd only been there a year, but it felt like forever. The workload was crushing, sixty–seventy hours a week; a relentless grind of client meetings, reading the fine print, redlining contracts, taking depositions, court appearances, filling out process documents, making a thousand phone calls and answering a thousand emails with nothing to look forward to except more of the same. Seven years minimum to be a partner. Five if you were on the fast track.

"I'm a cog in a machine that cares nothing about me except my billable hours," she said.

They crossed over an overpass, Olympic Boulevard, a traffic jam even at this hour, brake lights extending into the horizon.

"What are you going to do?" Isaiah said.

"Stay for a while, get some experience, have something high-profile on my LinkedIn page, and then—I don't know. Work for a nonprofit, be a prosecutor. Do something meaningful." Isaiah wondered when she was going to talk about whatever she came to talk about. All this chatter was a prelude to something but that was okay. If she wanted him to do something that was fine with him.

The Avenue of the Stars ended at Pico Boulevard, the Hillcrest Country Club across the street, Fox Studios around the corner. They stopped there, Sarita turning to him, nervous. "There's something else," she said. "It's about my sister."

"I didn't know you had a sister," Isaiah said.

"Half sister. Same father, different mothers. Janine lives in Vegas. She's a great kid and I love her to death, but she's a gambling addict, always getting herself into one situation or another. I kept loaning her money until I realized I was feeding her habit and cut her off. My dad did too. Both of us were waiting for her to hit rock bottom and get some help. Well, be careful what you wish for. She's hit rock bottom, and she definitely needs help. Her and that idiot boyfriend of hers."

"What can I do?" Isaiah said, eager to find out so he could go do it, come back and tell her. Sarita's chin fell, her eyes closing in despair. Isaiah wanted to hug her but didn't know if he should.

"Oh, Isaiah," she said, "Janine is in so much trouble."

"What did you say?" Janine said.

"I said Bears and Packers," Benny called out from the shower. He'd been in there for twenty minutes scrubbing himself with vinegar and baking soda to get the garbage smell off. "We take the dog and the points for two bucks. If we push it's only five percent juice if we get it down with Shelton."

"We're off the boards with Shelton," Janine said. She picked up Benny's underwear with two fingers, put it in the wastebasket, and put the wastebasket outside.

"What we do is we spread the bets around," Benny said. "I got a tip from Nate, the handicapper, the guy that bets at Caesars? The seventh at Belmont. We put down two—no, make it three bucks, we key the six horse and wheel the rest for second. Angelo's laying down big."

"Isn't Nate the guy who told you Gary's Gone Girl was a sure thing at the Santa Anita Cup?"

"The horse stumbled out of the gate, happens all the time."

"The horse stumbled out of the gate because it broke its leg *before* the fucking race," Janine said. "And where do we get these bucks you're talking about?"

Benny came out of the bathroom drying his hair and smelling a little like salad dressing. "Didn't you get a paycheck?"

"I took an advance from Sal the last time I played there."

"You got nothing?"

"I owed him more than my check. He said he'd give me a hundred if I let him look at my junk."

"A hundred to let him *look?*"

"He's such a perv. He said he wanted to find out if a Chinese vagina really went sideways."

"You should have done it," Benny said.

"I did," Janine said.

Benny stopped short, nodding, trying to be adult about it. "Sure, sure, okay, we need the money."

Janine wondered if Benny really believed she'd show her junk to Sal and watched him rummage around for some boxers he'd only worn two or three times. She loved how he looked. The child's trusting brown eyes and the sweet doofy face. The haircut needed work. Too Jesus Christ-ey but his body more than made up for it, his muscles smooth and rounded like a suit of armor for a skinny guy with a big penis.

Benny got the milk out of the midget fridge and drank it straight from the carton. "I think I swallowed a rat turd. What about your dad?"

"No chance," Janine said, reminding herself not to drink milk or kiss Benny. "He won't even speak to me until I go back to GA and get a sponsor."

They'd met at a Gamblers Anonymous meeting in the Sunday-school room at All Saints Methodist Church. Between the two of them they knew most of the people there. Benny said all they needed was a deck of cards and they could play Hold 'Em. That made her laugh. They sat at the back and made dollar bets on whether the speaker would say *I hit rock bottom, I ruined my life,* or *I destroyed my family.* Benny won two out of three. After the meeting they went to the Venetian and played a little, just messing around, wanting to see if the other just gambled too much or had a full-on jones. It takes a junkie to know a junkie. When they hit a blackjack on the same hand they knew it was destiny. They had sex in Janine's VW bus and almost got married at the Golden Moments Wedding Chapel, but the ceremony cost a hundred and twenty-nine dollars and they needed the money to gamble.

"Leo's right," Janine said. "We're in a slump. We're not gonna make the vig by the weekend. We need to get the money some other way."

"See, that's a fucked-up attitude," Benny said. "That's why we've been losing. You think we're gonna lose so we do."

"Check yourself, dude. You lost most of the money."

"Remember at Bally's, I was playing that progressive machine over by the sports book? I was up three bills until you came along and jinxed me with that story about crapping out five times. I lost the three bills and three more after that."

"Fuck you, Benny. You just don't know when to quit."

"Oh, and you do?"

They were arguing more lately, the stress of owing Leo getting to them. The squalor didn't help. When her dad threw her out, and she moved into the motel room, Benny was happy about it but she was secretly horrified. The room looked more like a re-cycling station than a place to live, the smell of weed and dirty laundry part of the decor, the bathroom like it was the only one in the men's dorm.

Benny was searching for his pants now, pawing through the rub-ble of their lifestyle, kicking shoes out of the way. "Where's my fucking pants?" he said. "They were right fucking here!"

Janine could sense his edges unraveling, threads of his psyche coming loose. A night in the landfill must have been horrible and humiliating. The slope was too steep to climb so he had to hike out. She imagined him clomping over and down the shifting, crunch-ing, slippery peaks of trash and garbage, his bare feet plunging into rotting chicken bones, fish heads, coffee grounds, and little blue bags full of dog shit. He said the smell was so strong, he puked over and over again. By the time he got to the access road the sun was coming up. Leo had taken his phone away so he had to borrow one from a backhoe driver.

"You should camp somewhere else, buddy," the driver said. "You could die out there."

"Camping?" Benny said, standing there, slop dripping off him. "You think I was camping?"

Benny found his pants hanging on a doorknob. "Who do we know with money?" he said. He was still wet from the shower and couldn't yank them on, hopping around like he was in a potato sack race.

"We know a lot of people with money," Janine said, "but none of them are gonna give us a loan."

"There's gotta be somebody!" Benny said. His voice was gravelly and strangled, his pants puddled around his ankles, the child's eyes spilling tears. Janine looked away. Nobody wants an audience when they're having a breakdown.

"What about your dad?" Benny said.

"You already asked me that. He won't loan me money, Benny. We talked about this a hundred times."

"What do we owe Leo now? Three weeks' vig?"

"Four."

"That's only what, fourteen hundred? Your dad's rich. What does he care?"

"Then you ask him, Benny. You have such a great relationship."

Her dad hated Benny but he would have hated anyone who wasn't a nice Chinese boy with a backpack, a bad haircut, and a scholarship in chemistry. The gambling made him crazy. He told her he'd played high-stakes mah jong when he was younger and had screwed up his life. How exactly he didn't say. But the shit really hit the roulette wheel when she told him she was dropping out of college to be a DJ. She thought he would have taken it better if she'd said she wanted to be a cabdriver or a cowboy.

Benny got the vodka out of the cupboard. He unscrewed the cap and took a long glug, wiping his mouth with the back of his hand. Janine looked at him.

"I'm getting wasted, okay?" he said. "I fucking deserve it."

"Yeah, I guess you do," she said softly.

Benny swatted the motorcycle magazines off the couch and sat down, the cushions so dirty the lines on the plaid were blurred.

"I'm so fucked up," he said, crying now. "I'm sorry, Janine. I'm sorry I can't do better."

She sat down beside him and put her arm around him, her head touching his. "It's all right, Benny. You're having a bad run, that's all. Everybody does."

Benny took another long glug, not bothering to wipe off his mouth, his lips loose and glistening. "It's gotta be your dad. There's nobody else."

"Dad's not an option, okay?" She got up and hugged herself, more afraid than angry, the man she loved falling apart. "Seriously, Benny, lay off."

Benny sat there, staring like the blackness of the landfill was staring back at him. He guzzled the rest of the vodka and dropped the bottle on the floor. "I'm going to the store," he said. "Want something?"

"No, I'm good," Janine said, pretending to do something with her phone.

Benny got up and went to the door. "Leo said you're next."

"Next? Next for what?"

"The landfill. Sure you don't want something?"

CHAPTER THREE

Whale Fat

They walked back to the hotel, Sarita telling him about Janine, the story pouring out of her. It never occurred to him that her last name, Van, was Chinese.

"It's crazy, isn't it?" Sarita said.

"Hard to believe," Isaiah said. He never ceased to be amazed at the messes people got themselves into. This one was in his top ten. "Do you want me to go to Vegas? Check it out?"

"Yes. I do. Janine is a serial liar, and hopefully it's a story she made up to get money from me. She's done it many times before. On the other hand, she might be telling the truth and if she is, she'll need help—oh, I'm sorry, Isaiah, I'm just assuming you'll drop everything you're doing and go."

"I'm not doing anything," he said, even though he had cases and was in the middle of investigating Marcus's murder. He'd tell her about it when he brought the killer to justice. Surprise her. Impress her. Make her forget the difference in their ages.

"And there's something else," Sarita said. She hesitated, filling the moment with a deep breath. "As soon as my sister asked me for

35

help I was bound by attorney-client privilege. Anything she tells me has to stay between the two of us. If I go to the authorities about this now or later it's breaking that confidentiality, and I'll probably get fired."

"Why?" Isaiah said.

"Attorneys keep secrets, that's what we're paid to do. If it's made public that I broke confidentiality, the firm's other clients might wonder if *their* secrets were at risk—and I could be prosecuted."

"Prosecuted? For what?"

"Aiding and abetting. Bringing you into it could be seen as part of a cover-up, which I am *not* asking you to do."

But she was, Isaiah thought. At least she was thinking about it. It was understandable, her loved ones at risk. He'd have done anything for Marcus and vice versa. The law wouldn't have mattered. "That's no problem," he said, "and if anything happens it's all on me. You and I never spoke."

"I feel terrible about this," Sarita said.

"Don't."

"It's a lot to ask."

"If you hadn't asked I'd have volunteered."

"I want you to know there's the real possibility of reprisals."

"Don't worry about it," Isaiah said, happy there was a heroic aspect to it.

The night was warm and clear. She took his arm, and he felt a live current sparking where her skin met his. It seemed so obvious and unnatural Isaiah thought she had to be feeling it too—didn't she? He was sensitive to emotional vibes in his cases, but this was a whole other magnetic field.

"We have to see each other more often," she said.

"Yeah, that'd be good," he said. Wait. Was it his imagination or was she slowing down? He kept the same pace to see if it was really happening and it was. *She's stretching this out.*

"Are you going to stay in Long Beach, Isaiah?" she said.

"I don't know, maybe," he said, thinking she could be living in a luxed-out condo on the other side of those walls.

"You don't have to stay there, you know. There's people with problems everywhere."

"Yeah, I know," he said. Was she saying she didn't want to be stuck with someone who lived in the hood? That if he lived somewhere else he'd have a shot?

Sarita held on to his arm and relaxed a little. "I'm so glad to see you," she said. He didn't know what to say and nodded. This was turning out way better than he'd hoped. He wished he could enjoy it, but the sense of betraying Marcus was pounding in his head like that Mexican polka band.

They got back to the hotel, Isaiah sorry it wasn't someplace farther like Pasadena or Glendale. Sarita put her arms around him and hugged him tight, the feel of her body and the smell of citrus and cypress trees making him woozy, thoughts of Marcus vanishing into the starless LA sky.

"Thank you, Isaiah," she said. "Thank you so much." She leaned her head back and looked at him, her eyes full of—was that *longing?*

"I've got to go," she said, stepping away. "Call me, okay?"

Isaiah was at once deflated and hugely relieved. The pressure of being with her was like a test of personality and social skills. He thought about saying goodbye, but somehow that seemed lame. She turned and went back inside. Isaiah watched her through the hotel's tall windows, the cascading chandeliers casting mood lighting on the lobby. She walked quickly, heels clicking on the marble floor. She turned a corner and was gone.

*   *   *

He drove home kicking himself for all the things he did and didn't say. He'd heard women liked men who made them laugh, and he hadn't done that once, not that he knew how. What did you do, tell a joke? Marcus would have made her laugh. He could find something funny at a funeral, and he'd have put his arm around her, comforted her. He could do that without sending out the wrong vibe, and he would have been wise and helpful and given her sound advice. Even now, Isaiah couldn't think of any. Instead, he'd nodded and spoken in monosyllables, couldn't even carry on a conversation. Another mystery. What were you supposed to talk about? The weather? Afghanistan? Taylor Swift, whoever that was? And what was that he'd said? *That'd be good?* She was inviting him to spend more time together, and all he could think of to say was *That'd be good?* He'd cringe about that for all eternity, and then there was that look, that last longing look. Was that for him or Marcus? How were you to know? Maybe she was telling him she wished he was more *like* Marcus. Big shoes to fill. *Shaq's* shoes to fill. He knew he had a long way to go, and rescuing Sarita's sister was a good way to start.

The next morning, he sat in his easy chair, drinking an espresso and listening to Segovia, the music as warm and yearning as he'd been last night. His phone buzzed. A text from Sarita. She was insisting on paying him. Her father had started a college fund when she was a child, which she hadn't touched because she'd always been on scholarship. Interest and dividends had been compounding all this time and she was loaded.

No arguments. I'm paying you and that's that.

Doesn't paying me make you more involved?

I'll pay you in cash.

Can't do it. If I needed a lawyer would you charge me?

That's different.

No it's not. It's exactly the same.

Isaiah, for the sake of my conscience, you must let me pay you.

Isaiah thought a bit before he replied.

I won't take your money but you can pay my partner.

You have a partner?

After her argument with Benny, Janine went to the MGM Grand to play video poker. She dreaded seeing her dad and needed time to not think about it. The Chinese considered red a lucky color so she was wearing her red panties. She had a dozen pairs and wore them whether she was gambling or not. The ancient fêng shui masters had put a curse on front entrances so she entered the MGM from the New York New York side and took the walkway. You used to have to go through the mouth of a gigantic gold lion to get in until management found out a Chinese gambler would rather crawl through a ventilation duct. Washing your hands was part of the regimen and no bumping shoulders, hard to do at the crap tables.

Books were never mentioned because *book* sounded like the Chinese word for *lose*. The west side of the casino where you could see a door was more auspicious, and eight was a lucky number so she always chose the eighth machine from the end. *Eight* in Chinese sounds like the word for *prosperity*. Fours of any kind were to be avoided. *Four* sounds like *death*. Benny said by the time you got through all that you forgot why you were there.

She played some but couldn't get into it so she went to the pub and had a couple of beers. She thought about hurtling into the land-fill and getting sucked into a black hole of rotting garbage and rat turds. Cold fingers spidered up and down her spine. She had to go see her dad.

Ken Van lived in the Red Rock Country Club, an exclusive community with a golf course, private lakes, and McMansions distinctive as Quarter Pounders painted Band-Aid beige. It was late when she pulled in the driveway and parked behind his Lexus. He'd be working now. There was a twelve-hour time difference with Hong Kong and Macau. She let herself in and went down the hall. She could hear him in the study, talking on his cell.

"No, I'm afraid there's been a mistake," he said, like it was probably his fault. "I was expecting four parcels, not three—something happened? Oh, I see, of course." This was how he usually sounded, apologetic or like the problem was tiresome and you were in this together. "That's understandable," he said. "Yes, okay, no, please don't worry, I'll make some adjustments." For once she wished he'd say What's your problem, you fucking moron? But he had that Chinese thing about avoiding confrontation. That, and he was a wimp. Tommy Lau, supposedly his partner, walked all over him, and he never said a thing. "All right then," her dad said. "We'll talk soon."

He hung up and muttered like the caller might be able to hear him, "You lying son of a bitch."

Janine approached the door and peeked in. Her dad was at his desk, hunched over his laptop like he couldn't read the fine print. She'd always thought he was handsome; trim in that chestless, bootyless Asian man way, fifty-six years old and not a wrinkle on his face or a trace of gray in his jet-black hair. She thought he looked like that guy who hosted *Iron Chef* and did kung fu moves while he shouted *Pork bellies!*

"Hey, Pop," she said.

He was startled and then annoyed. "What are you doing here?" he said.

"Good to see you too."

"You want a loan, don't you?"

"What? No, I don't want a loan. I just came to get a few things. God."

She left and went outside. A sandpaper breeze was rasping through the palm trees and rippling the surface of the swimming pool. She thought about going back to the study and telling her dad she owed twenty-seven large to Leo, and that he was going to throw her in a landfill if she didn't have the vig. He wouldn't believe her, she'd lied to him too many times before and even if he bought the story he wasn't going to give her fourteen cents, let alone fourteen hundred. He'd say *It serves you right* or *It will teach you a lesson* and then he'd be pissed that any daughter of his got talked into paying twenty percent. Why didn't she bargain harder, didn't she know she was Chinese?

She only had two options. One, she could buy a hazmat suit and wait for Leo to find her. Two, she could steal from her dad. It was almost life or death, wasn't it? The problem was he never kept cash in the house. Once he tried to pay for a fifteen-dollar pizza with his American Express Black Card. The delivery guy refused it, saying there was no such thing as a titanium credit card.

She went back to the motel, parked in the lot, and sat there awhile. The radio was on, music and chatter fading in and out of her consciousness. When she left the apartment, Benny was sitting on the sofa, limp like he'd been shot, too drunk to wipe the snot off his upper lip, his eyes clouded over with doom and hopelessness. What would she tell him? She couldn't ask her dad because it was too humiliating? He'd say, *Oh yeah? Try spending a night in the landfill.* She thought about coming up with a lie, but he'd know. They watched each other lie to people all the time. They even lied as a tag team, one of them starting some bullshit about getting money from a lawsuit and the other finishing it without even a look passing between them.

Her brain was tired of grinding and switched its attention to the radio. The same guy who did the voice-overs on action movies was talking about an identity theft protection service; going on and on about how thousands of people were being victimized and how you were next and how the thieves were making billions of dollars.

Identity theft. Now there's an idea.

Her dad's clients weren't just fat cats, they were *whale* fat. The kind of fat the casinos flew in on a private jet and comped a suite bigger than a big house with an infinity pool on the balcony and a private butler with room service from Nobu twenty-four seven because they knew you could drop a half mil playing baccarat and not even call your accountant. If you're going to steal identities, Janine thought, you couldn't do better than the people on her dad's laptop.

*　　*　　*

Isaiah was excited about his mission to Vegas. He couldn't have imagined a better way to advance his relationship with Sarita. He could show off his detective prowess and be the knight in shining armor. What could be more emotionally charged than saving her sister? He couldn't wait to get started.

It was 10 p.m. on the first Friday of the month, a cool mist in the air. Isaiah drove past a dozen food trucks parked end to end on Abbot Kinney, a funky, narrow street in Venice Beach. Art galleries, clothing boutiques, upscale restaurants, and grain-fed food stores mingled with dive bars, auto body shops, and graffiti-scarred apartment buildings. It was a place to go when you wanted to feel edgy and hip. The street was crowded, long lines of people waiting to get a Korean fusion taco or a slice of Uncle Tetsu's cheesecake. Isaiah tried to think of a dish he'd stand in line for and the only thing he could think of was a can of Alpo for Ruffin. He spotted the truck he was looking for, D&D'S DOWNHOME BUTTERMILK FRIED CHICKEN. Now all he needed was a place to park.

"Kelly?" Dodson called out. A blond girl in white cutoffs and a USC sweatshirt came up to the service window.

"I'm Kelly," she said. "I forgot to ask. Is your food gluten-free?"

"Free as the last day of our probation," Dodson said, knowing that wasn't true. The whole gluten-free thing was a scam, and he admired whoever'd thought it up; telling people something natural in your bread and breakfast cereal messed up your immune system and then selling them food without it. That was like selling cars without wheels so you wouldn't get into a crash.

"What about the chickens?" the girl said. "Are they cage-free?"

"Cage-free?" Dodson said. "Our chickens live in a condo with a farmyard in the back. Did I tell you they've never seen a hormone shot?" Dodson bought the chicken on sale at Vons. Getting busted didn't seem too likely unless the girl had a chemistry set in that Whole Foods shopping bag. He gave her a warm Styrofoam box and plastic utensils. "Y'all have a nice evening now, and if you enjoy your meal please like us on Facebook."

"Stop talking to everybody and hurry your ass up," Deronda snapped, poking at the chicken bubbling in the fryers, her head scarf dark with sweat. I'm two plates ahead of you."

"What I'm doing here is called public relations," Dodson said. "Something you wouldn't know about."

A brand-new food truck would set you back a hundred grand, but the eighteen-foot 2001 GMC Workhorse with a hundred and sixteen thousand miles on the odometer that smelled like baked-on grease and burnt tortillas had cost sixty-eight nine, Dodson talking the owner down from seventy-two five. Deronda, who was working at Rite Aid at the time, emptied her 401(k) and got a loan from her dad. Dodson sold his portfolio and borrowed from every person he knew who wasn't terminal or under the age of twelve. He wished he hadn't put all the burglary money into Flaco's condo. Cherise would never let him hear the end of that.

The truck came fully equipped except for the paint job. The partners argued about it, eventually settling on canary yellow with D&D'S DOWNHOME BUTTERMILK FRIED CHICKEN on the side in big brown letters and two crossed drumsticks like a coat of arms. They both had their own thoughts about which D was who.

"Here you are, sir," Dodson said, handing out another box. "If you enjoy your meal please like us on Facebook. What's that? Free as the last day of your probation. Did I tell you our chickens never had a hormone shot? You hope it's what? As good as your mother's?

Give your mother a taste of that and see if she don't show up asking for the recipe."

"Goddammit, Dodson," Deronda said. "Just give out the box and go on to the next person."

They'd decided by mutual consent that Deronda would stick to cooking and stay away from the service window. One customer wanted a refund for his order because it was too salty.

"Ain't no refunds up in here," she said. "The hell you think this is, Walmart? You bought it, you eat it." Another customer complained that the mac and cheese was too greasy. "Cheese *is* grease," she said, like he was a moron. "The macaroni don't do nothin' but *hold* the grease—what? Yeah, you write a bad review and see if I don't come lookin' for your ass." Which the guy quoted word for word on Yelp.

People were getting tired of waiting, leaving for a mahimahi taco or Vietnamese sandwich. "What'd I tell you?" Deronda said. "That's cash out the window right there."

"You see I'm hurrying, don't you?" Dodson said. "Shit. I need the money more than you do."

The overhead on the truck was a backbreaker and the baby was due next week. Dodson had tried to convince Cherise to hold off getting pregnant until business was doing better, showing her an article in the *Star* about a woman in Appalachia who had a baby when she was sixty-seven years old. There was a picture of her wearing a shawl and a frontier dress holding a baby wrinklier than she was. The father, who had a scraggly beard and a three-tooth grin, was giving the camera double thumbs up.

"See there?" Dodson said. "Ain't no need to rush into it."

"Don't be stupid, Dodson," Cherise said. "That baby belongs to the woman's granddaughter and you know it. Now get over here and do your duty."

*   *   *

The crowd had dwindled to a handful of foodies, bikers, and people with the munchies. Dodson was exhausted. He leaned against the fridge and wondered if going legit had been a mistake. He'd questioned himself about the decision a hundred times, but in the end he knew he was too old to keep hustling. It was undignified and not worthy of his talents. That, and Cherise threatened to leave him if he didn't get his shit together. Compared to adulthood, selling crack was easy.

"Why you standing there?" Deronda said. "Let's clean up and go home." For security's sake they parked the truck in Deronda's backyard, right under her bedroom window where she slept with her dad's Kel-Tec fourteen-round pump-action tactical shotgun.

Deronda scraped the flattop thinking she'd be making more money at Rite Aid and with benefits too. But she could never go back there, stocking shelves all day, customers asking you stupid questions, cameras all up in your business, a half hour for lunch. Her boss was a white boy named Brian who had more zits than face and began every sentence with "As your supervisor—." She could always go back to stripping at the Kandy Kane. Alonzo, the manager, called her from time to time saying her booty was a national treasure and why wasn't she out there sharing it with the world? But she was done with that. She never understood how a whole group of men with hard-ons could sit in the same room together. Another reason was her son, Janeel. He was almost ready for kindergarten, and she didn't want one of his classmates saying his daddy saw Janeel's mama buck-ass naked. Her dad had taken the boy to the San Diego Zoo for the weekend, and she was looking forward to having the evenings to herself.

"Look what the cat dragged in," she said. Isaiah was looking in the service window.

"Am I too late for a three-piece?" he said.

"How you doin', Isaiah?"

"I'm doing okay. You?"

"I'd be doing fine if it wasn't for Dodson."

Dodson came around to the window. "What's blazin', son?" he said, smiling. "What you been up to?"

They sat on a bus bench, Isaiah with his three-piece that Deronda insisted he pay for, not even a discount.

"This is really good," Isaiah said. "Whose recipe?"

"Deronda's grandmother. See how crispy it is? After you got the coating on you let it sit 'til it gets doughy."

"I'll remember that," Isaiah said, knowing he never made anything more complicated than a steak.

"Yeah, customers love it, but making that nut is a bitch. We gotta pay off the loans too. Working with Deronda—you might as well have Bigfoot in the kitchen."

Dodson looked like he always did; a cool, casual featherweight with ropy arms and an attitude that would make you think twice about messing with him. But Isaiah heard a glint of regret in his voice, like I've missed the turnoff and all I can do is keep driving.

"When's the baby due?" Isaiah said.

"Soon," Dodson said. "Cherise looks like Jabba the damn Hutt. I might have to hire a crane to lift her ass out of bed, and that thing about cravings ain't no lie. You know last night she ate Cheez Whiz on a pork chop?"

"Pick out a name yet?"

"If it's a boy I wanted to name him Tupac, but Cherise copped

47

an attitude, talking 'bout, yeah, let's name him after a dead rapper. How about Eazy-E or L'A Capone or Ol' Dirty Bastard? Can't you just hear me? Oh, Bastard, come in for supper now."

Dodson had run into Isaiah a couple of times since the Black the Knife case. They small-talked but neither of them knew how to go forward or what forward was, and they lived in separate worlds. Dodson with his food truck, Cherise, their circle of friends, and now the baby. Isaiah with his cases, a circle of one.

Isaiah finished the chicken and closed the box. "Best I've ever had," he said.

"Glad you liked it but you didn't come all the way out here from Long Beach to eat fried chicken," Dodson said. "What's on your mind?"

Isaiah explained how Sarita had reached out to him and how her sister was in serious trouble and that he had to go to Vegas to see about it. "I could use some help," he said. "If you could come along I'd really appreciate it."

Dodson hesitated, not sure he'd heard right. Not too long ago Isaiah wouldn't have asked for help if his arm was stuck in the deep fryer, and since when did he *appreciate* anything? Something strange was going on here. "Can't do it," Dodson said. "Deronda will go crazy if I leave her here by herself, and if the baby comes while I'm away, Cherise will choke me to death with the umbilical cord."

"You'll get the whole per diem," Isaiah said.

Dodson stared at him, then looked back at the truck. "Let me see what I can do."

Janine couldn't believe she was doing this. Crawling on her hands and knees across the Italian broadloom, her dad sleeping twenty feet away, his snore like dragging a table over a cement patio. Her mistake was telling Benny about identity theft and the fat cats. He went nuts, shrugging off his hangover, dancing around the room and singing *We're in the money, we're in the money.* He was such a little kid. He didn't hear her when she talked about how smart her dad was and how she could get caught and that he might call the cops. Then Benny really got into it, making plans, drawing indecipherable diagrams and going over the moves step by step like he was Brad Pitt in a heist movie, and now here she was, smelling her failing deodorant and so scared she could barely hold back the pee.

Her destination was the bedside table and her dad's cell phone blinking in its charger. The password to his laptop was in there. He was supposed to keep it in his head so it couldn't be hacked, but he cheated. He'd explained it to her when she was his darling daughter getting straight As in middle school, and he was eager to prepare her for a complicated world. He had two very important passwords. One for encrypted business files, the other for encrypted email. Both were twelve digits long, hard to remember with all those numbers, letters, and symbols. He showed her what he did.

"First I go to my contact list," he said. "Then I pick someone innocuous—innocuous means not standing out." Ken scrolled through hundreds of names and found Laura Vincent. "She's the woman who cuts my hair. I use her name because V is the first letter of our last name. Easy to remember, right? Okay, see the phone number? That's the first seven digits of the password. And the address? That's the last five. Can you guess who has the other password?"

"Somebody whose last name starts with A-N," Janine said.

"Right, very good. Martin Anders is my insurance man. So you see, if my phone is stolen no one would think to look there and I still have my passwords handy."

*　　*　　*

The chemical smell from the carpet was making Janine nauseous. She felt ridiculous, dressed all in black including a ski mask. Benny's idea—he was into ninjas. He volunteered to do the job himself but if her dad woke up he'd shoot him with the gun he kept in the bedside drawer whether he recognized Benny or not.

Her dad stirred. He smacked his lips and snorted. Janine felt her entire body congeal. She held her breath, wondering what she'd say if he woke up. She could just see herself lying on her back like a submissive puppy saying It's me, Pop, and him saying What the hell are you doing, Janine, and her saying—what exactly? She lost a contact lens? She'd decided to drop the DJ thing and become a ninja?

She started to move again, but her dad's breathing changed and he yawned. *He was awake.* She was in the middle of the floor, and there was no place to hide. She curled up like one of those armadillos that tiptoed through the backyard; the black clothes were a good idea after all. She peeked under her arms. Her dad was sitting on the edge of the bed. She could see his feet and his fish-white calves. Was he looking at her, letting his anger swell? It would be just like him, let her sweat it out, wait for her to crack.

Her dad cleared his throat and stood up.

Highway 15 to Vegas. Eighty miles an hour through the parched, unending desert, the road straight as a yardstick but not as interesting, power lines running parallel against a background of barren browns and dusty grays.

"How did you work it out with Deronda?" Isaiah said.

"I'm giving her half the per diem, and that's more than she makes working at the truck," Dodson said. "Her sister's helping out."

"What about Cherise?"

"Doctor said the baby's not due 'til next week, and Lord have mercy I'm glad to be out of there. Cherise's mama is over all the time and she hates my ass. Every time she sees me she says *Oh, it's you* like I'm not supposed to be in my own damn apartment. Did I tell you Cherise made me sit through the baby shower? The fuck we gonna do with a li'l biddy pair of pajamas got a seahorse on 'em? The goddamn baby don't even know what water is."

"Are you worried about being a father?"

"No, I'm worried about being broke. For what it's gonna cost me to raise that baby I could buy a KFC. I tried to convince Cherise to adopt. You know, get a young buck from Somalia or the Congo, eighteen–nineteen years old, somebody grateful who could go get a job right away."

"It's that bad?"

"I sat down and worked a budget out four or five times, and it always came out the same. If the food truck don't start doing better the Dodson family's gonna end up living in my car."

Isaiah had never seen Dodson like this, stressing about an unpredictable future just like everybody else. "Come on, you must be a little excited," Isaiah said.

"Yeah, I suppose. I can see myself doing things with a kid. Teach him to shoot craps, roll a dub, help him pick out a gang to join— don't tell Cherise I said that."

They crossed the California-Nevada border and sped past Whiskey Pete's, a casino for people who couldn't wait to lose their money in Vegas or spend what little they had left. The place looked bizarre out here in the desert all by itself like a giant Steve Wynn had dropped it out of the sky.

"What you been up to?" Dodson said.

"Cases," Isaiah said.

"You got an ol' lady yet?"

"No."

"I heard Vatrice Coleman wants to go out with you."

"Yeah, she called me up and told me as much. Not my type."

"Not your type? *Nobody's* your type, and that girl is fine, went to college too."

"Beauty school."

"Still an uppity li'l nigga, ain't you? Well, in case you don't remember, you dropped out of high school, you ain't even got a GED. Compared to you that girl's an Einstein."

"I still don't want to go out with her."

"Cherise wants to set you up with her friend Kalina," Dodson said. "You know her? Looks like Halle Berry but darker?"

"Yeah, I know her. We don't have anything in common."

"Hard to have something in common with an abnormal muthafucka like you. You know what your problem is? You too damn particular. What are you waiting for? Some girl with a PhD likes to stay home all the time and play with that damn pit bull?"

No, Isaiah thought, I'm waiting for Sarita. Much of the guilt he'd been carrying around for years had lifted and feelings were surfacing that he'd always ignored. He was lonely. He wanted friends, he wanted to go out and be with people. He wanted to have fun, not that he knew how. Inviting Dodson to come along was a bold step for him. He felt vulnerable, as if his need was a weakness.

Isaiah had been to Vegas on cases and was less impressed every time he came; the Strip's kaleidoscopic walls of neon signs losing their appeal, the colors so bright and starved for attention they all ran together. He wondered if the tourists had a meeting and decided to look more or less the same. The beer-bellied men in Bermuda shorts, golf shirts, and running shoes, their top-heavy wives in white capris and flowered pregnancy tops. The Luxor sphinx must have been built by somebody who'd only done sand castles before. Lady Liberty looked stranded like she'd wandered into an amusement park and couldn't find her way out. The canals at the Venetian were the same color blue as toilet water dyed with an automatic cleaner, the Eiffel Tower lit up like Elton John at a New Year's Eve party. Everything was a spectacle. Too bright, too loud, too colossal. Once, Isaiah bought a hot dog for ninety-nine cents and it was as big as a cat.

Isaiah didn't gamble much, the gaming odds were ridiculous, but occasionally he played poker. He was good at it, instantly calculating the odds and reading bluffs like the *LA Times,* but he didn't like sitting around for hours and hours. Other than that there was nothing to do except look at things. *Look* at the water show, *look* at the light show, *look* at the New York skyline and the giant Coke bottle tall as a nuclear missile. The Ansel Adams photographs at the Bellagio were just wrong. Like Pavarotti at the MTV awards or a family of gazelles running down the Avenue of the Stars.

"Where we going?" Dodson said.

"Janine's DJing at a club," Isaiah said. "She left our names at the door."

Seven Sevens was like the Tokyo subway at rush hour. You couldn't lift an arm without putting somebody's eye out. Isaiah sidled through the crowd saying excuse me a hundred times, Dodson somewhere behind him. The music, if you could call it that, was a barrage of cell phone beeps, tin cans, sirens, whistles, Morse code, panting dogs, buzzing hornets, foghorns, cannon fire, and fragments of songs he didn't recognize set to a beat as fast as a drum roll.

Isaiah surveyed the dance floor, the fellas moving their shoulders and bobbing their heads, looking past their dance partners like there must be a hotter babe in here somewhere; a few holding liquor bottles like they were strangling a goose. Isaiah hadn't seen so many gold chains since the Jewelry Bazaar. The girls danced with their hands over their heads, snaking their bodies around, laughing and grinning at their friends. *Look at us! We're here!* Isaiah wondering why you'd wear a miniskirt if your thighs were like two Beluga whales swimming side by side. Kanye West and an oil sheik must have gotten together and decorated the lounge area, people in there drinking and trying to be cool; not easy when you were sunk down in a plush pink sofa so soft your knees were above your waist. Was this the fun Isaiah had heard so much about? He felt old and out of it and wished he was home playing with Ruffin.

"I ain't been to a club in a long damn time," Dodson yelled over the music. "It's a trip, ain't it? Reminds me of my wayward youth."

Janine was on the DJ stand. A fantasy woman in a halo of gauzy light, fluid and rhythmic, her arm extended and pumping up and down, her long hair moving like it was underwater, her music commanding the crowd to speed up, slow down, go berserk.

"Girl got some skills, don't she?" Dodson said.

The beat decelerated into a head-bobbing tom-tom. "Whassup my people!" she shouted into the mike. "This is your queen kamikaze, the heat in your wasabi, the gravy train in the food chain, the champagne in the chow mein, I'm DJ Dama, baby, that's my set and I'm gettin' up outta heeerre, PEACE!" The crowd let loose with a raucous cacophony of cheers, applause, woo-hoos and offers of sexual release.

"Damn, that girl got it going on," Dodson said.

"She's showing off her good side," Isaiah said, "before she shows off her stupid one."

They went back to the motel room and talked. Sarita had told Janine all about Isaiah, assuring her he could be trusted and to tell him everything. Isaiah already knew the story, but he wanted to hear it from her, fill in the blanks. He didn't want to sit down in all the mess so he stood with his hands in his front pockets. Dodson had the same idea and leaned against a wall. Janine sat on the couch looking at the floor and shaking her head. She'd changed into sweats and a T-shirt and didn't look like a fantasy woman anymore. She looked like a kid who'd thrown a rock at a window and accidentally killed somebody. She talked about Leo and the vig and the landfill and how desperate she and Benny were and stealing her dad's records.

"Everything went okay at first," she said. "Dad was so sleepy he didn't see me and went to the bathroom. I switched his phone for mine, went downstairs and downloaded his records onto a flash drive. Then I waited until he was asleep again, switched the phones and got out of there. When I got back, me and Benny took a look at the records. God, I wish I had a joint."

"Keep going," Dodson said.

"They were business records, account records." She blinked angry tears out of her eyes. "For brothels and massage parlors. Lots of them. Here, Henderson, Reno, San Diego." She found her laptop in the junk on the coffee table, typed something and turned the screen around. "Look," she said.

There was a gallery of photos. Chinese girls, in their late teens and twenties, their names and places of origin written in black marker.

MEI—FUJIAN
JIAO—HUNAN
LIJIANG—GUANGXI
AH KUM—FUJIAN

There were dozens of them. No models or starlets or hooker types. Just ordinary girls. Janine scrolled through page after page of photos. "I can't even imagine it," she said. "Fucking strangers all day." Her expression turned hard and bitter. "My dad," she said. "He's the head pimp. That's why he's always on the phone, supervising employees, making sure everybody's on their toes. You know what they say, the customer's always right."

"Does your dad own the business?" Dodson said. Isaiah looked at him. It was a logical question but it was beginning to seem like Dodson was in charge of the case.

"No," Janine said. "He works for a triad. 14K. *Thousands* of members. They're vicious dudes. They're into sex trafficking, dope, kidnapping, all kinds of fucked-up things."

"How do you know it's 14K?" Dodson said, stepping on Isaiah's line.

"My uncle, Tommy Lau—he's not really my uncle. He used to be their Mountain Master, sort of like the president. He and my dad talk all the time. Tommy told me he'd quit when he got into currency trading, but I guess that was a lie."

"I don't understand something," Isaiah said, feeling like he had to hurry. "If you knew the records belonged to the triad why didn't you just get rid of them?"

"I wanted to," Janine said. New tears were seeping out of her eyes. "It's Benny," she said. "We had a huge argument. He took the flash drive and left. Now he won't answer my calls. He's disappeared."

"What's he going to do with it?" Dodson said.

Janine wiped her face with the back of her arm, sat up straight, and took a breath. She was setting up for the punch line, Isaiah thought.

"Benny's going to blackmail them," Janine said. "He's going to blackmail the 14K Triad."

CHAPTER FOUR
Seb Habimana

Isaiah's office was so stuffy it was hard to breathe. He opened a window and let in a breeze that was warmer than the room. The discovery that Marcus had been murdered enraged him. The hit-and-run had fractured Marcus's skull, broken both his legs, smashed his rib cage, collapsed his lungs, caused cardiac arrest and massive internal bleeding. He died at the hospital after six hours of surgery.

Isaiah put away the Kayo's bag and the photos of the Accord. He tried to calm himself. He needed his brain to work unencumbered by emotion. After Marcus had passed, some functionary gave Isaiah a big plastic tote bag containing his belongings. He had never looked inside. The whole idea made him feel ghoulish and afraid. He took it out of the storage box, breathed deeply, and opened the bag. Wafting out were smells of leather, paper, musty ballistic nylon, and another scent that made him close his eyes. A lot of people said it smelled like your hands after handling coins but the smell didn't come from metal. It was a variety of organic chemicals and amino acids that gave blood its distinctive coppery odor.

The wallet first. Driver's license, a few business cards, an expired

Visa card, a discount coupon for Nestlé's Quik, a shopping list, and seventeen dollars in cash. Isaiah recognized every key on the key ring. There were also some change and a folding knife. It had belonged to their father. He said it was an antique but it might have just been old. Six inches long, a nicked blade with a bone handle and sharp as a box cutter. Pieces of Marcus's crushed cell phone were also in the bag.

Marcus's backpack was a JanSport, gray in color, limp from use, a billion of them out there. Isaiah remembered the paramedic cutting the straps off with a scissors so he could slip the backpack off Marcus's shoulders. There was a large black bloodstain shaped like a desert island. Inside was a copy of *The Known World* by Edward P. Jones. Isaiah thought he'd take a look, see why Marcus chose it. There were also a dented tape measure, a multitool, safety goggles, a rolled-up windbreaker, an empty thermos, a little box of earplugs and a package of surgical masks. Marcus did a lot of construction and the work got loud and dusty.

The stain overlapped the small zippered pocket. There was some dried blood in the teeth of the zipper that hadn't flaked off. The pocket hadn't been opened. Isaiah unzipped it and another familiar smell drifted out. Most people said it was from the paper or the ink, but Isaiah thought it was the funk from a million dirty hands. Used twenty-dollar bills were bundled neatly with a rubber band. Three thousand dollars. There were also a package of oral syringes and, most disturbing, sixteen plasticine envelopes of white powder. It didn't numb the tongue so it wasn't cocaine. There was a faint vinegary smell, a by-product of converting morphine to heroin. The quantity was enough to get you busted for distribution. No way to tell the purity. The cops on TV who dabbed their finger in a Baggie, tasted it, and said *Yeah, this is the good stuff* were full of it. The only way to measure the purity of heroin was in a lab. This stuff could be cut with anything from vitamin B and quinine to crushed-up Tylenol to Fentanyl. Fentanyl was popular these days. It was a synthetic painkiller, fifty times more powerful than morphine. Mixed with heroin they called it flatline.

The implications were unimaginable. Marcus a heroin addict? A drug dealer? Beyond ridiculous. No way could he have hidden that from Isaiah. The oral syringes gave Isaiah a moment's pause. Junkies used them as a suppository, mixing up a heroin solution and injecting it into the rectum or vagina. No needle marks and more efficient than shooting up. Still, the whole idea that Marcus was in any way involved with drugs was too farfetched to think about. This had to be a plant. A setup. The motive was unknowable at this point, so the question for now was, who had access to the backpack? The plant couldn't have happened in the apartment so it had to be when Marcus was at work.

It was late September, but fall was slow in coming. The hot, dry breath of the Santa Anas rippled off the asphalt, burned up dashboards, and drove up the attendance at movie theaters because their air-conditioning worked. Isaiah went to Marcus's storage locker for the first time in eight years. Dread and foreboding writhed around inside him like pythons in a burlap bag. He unlocked the padlock and lifted the roll-up door. The trapped air was hotter than the heat wave, stale as an underground parking garage, and heavy with the smells of dust, cement, and the rubber-tire stink of cardboard. There were memories in the locker. Marcus making a cherry wood rocking chair for Mrs. Barnes, singing Motown even as the band saw sprayed sawdust on his safety goggles. Marcus showing Isaiah how to miter corners, use the drill press, the router, and a hundred other things, always patient and painstaking. Isaiah saw himself and Dodson prepping for a burglary, hyped as tightrope walkers. He saw them gloating over their stolen booty and arguing about money and merchandise and control, every issue momentous and critical but absurd in retrospect. The most excruciating memory was of who he was back then. A boy. Confused and lonely and grieving, constantly in motion, Marcus's ghost dogging him, pissed off and ashamed.

Isaiah let the heat dissipate and stepped inside. Trash on the floor, cobwebby boxes and bins lining the metal shelves. The battering ram was standing in the corner, crusted with ashy oxidation. The standing tools looked abandoned like they were too heavy to carry out before the enemy troops arrived.

Marcus kept his work log in the top drawer of the big red toolbox. He was scrupulous about his jobs but record keeping wasn't a strong suit. Like his little brother, he was able to keep vast amounts of information in his head. The work log was a jumble of notations, reminders, job descriptions, estimates, and supplies to pick up. The only thing that kept them organized was the dates. In the days leading up to the accident, Marcus had jotted down a number of names and numbers. Stores, tradesmen, people Isaiah knew or knew of. The only one that stood out was Seb Habimana. A neighborhood character with a shady reputation. There was a circle between Seb's name and the one written above it. Inside the circle was a note: *ISLANDER CHALET 8-47 BAM LT GRY.* Whether it applied to Seb or the name above it was hard to tell.

Isaiah asked around. Seb was known to hang out at the Nyanza Bar, a place so unwelcoming it was hard to believe it was open to the public. The front of the shack-like building was scaled with cedar shingles so old and black they looked blowtorched. Gold stick-on letters spelled NYANZA BAR on a window covered with tar paper, a single string of dead Christmas lights strung across the top. The vestibule looked like a cave even in the daytime.

It was cool inside, a welcome relief from the heat. Isaiah let his eyes adjust to the dark. The only light came from around the edges of the tar paper and the neon Tusker sign. Two men and a woman were hunched over their drinks at ten-thirty in the morning. Music was playing, an African woman wailing like she'd lost her whole family. The bartender was a twist of beef jerky in a chartreuse polo shirt. He was sitting on a stool looking up at a TV, a soccer game on.

"What you want in here?" he demanded.

"I'm looking for Seb Habimana," Isaiah said, wondering why the guy didn't say good morning or what will you have to drink.

"He don't come round dis place," the bartender said.

Isaiah looked down the hall. Through an open door he saw part of a room and a pool table. Voices back there. "I'm going to shoot pool," he said.

"You don't go back dere, boy."

"Don't call me boy."

As Isaiah approached the door he saw Seb. He was a small, fastidious man, almost aristocratic in the way he carried himself. He was leaning lightly on a cane and wearing a three-piece glen plaid suit, squares and lines in muted mustard, brown, and green. His shoes were old-fashioned wing tips, but they were lustrous and expensive and matched the darker browns in the suit. Hard to tell his age. Thirties? Forties? His face was surprisingly warm and generous, his eyes yellowed like old piano keys. Seb was talking to Laquez, a neighborhood hooligan. Isaiah had busted him twice for burglary. Isaiah took a step back into the shadows, he wanted to hear this.

"Come now, Laquez," Seb said patiently. "Enough of your lies and diversions, let us be truthful for once." Seb had an accent like Nelson Mandela; African by way of colonialism.

"Swear to God, Seb," Laquez said. "I'm telling you straight up. I wouldn't take no money from you." Laquez was goggle-eyed and puffy-cheeked; a black goldfish in a big white T-shirt.

"Tell me what you did today," Seb said.

"Okay, no problem. Like first I went to Wells Fargo, then B of A, Citibank, Republic, Chase, and then the other Wells Fargo, the one on PCH—no, that's wrong. I went to Wells Fargo and *then* I went to Chase," Laquez said, as if correcting himself made him more credible.

"And what were the amounts?" Seb said.

Laquez frowned. "Well, let me see—don't worry, I got it, I got it. Yeah, it was fifteen hundred, twenty-five hundred, seven hundred— shit, Seb, I can't remember all that."

"Fifteen hundred, twenty-*six* hundred, seven hundred, thirty-one hundred, fifty-five hundred, twelve hundred, and twelve hundred," Seb said. "That comes to fifteen thousand eight hundred dollars but only fifteen thousand *seven* hundred was loaded onto the debit cards. You kept a hundred dollars because you didn't think I would check."

"Naw, naw, naw," Laquez said, smiling and shaking his head, "y'all can't put that on me. This is bullshit, Seb, I mean like, maybe *you* made a mistake, like when you was countin' the money."

"I do not make mistakes counting money," Seb said. The fatherly warmth had fallen away, leaving in its place an Easter Island monolith with yellow eyes. "You took the money, Laquez, and if you continue to lie to me it will go hard for you."

"Come on, Seb, that ain't even logical. Sheeit. If I was gonna take your money I'd take the whole thing." Laquez did jazz hands. "Naw, naw, naw, I'm just playin'. I'd never do you like that. You my boy, Seb. Me and you is tight."

Seb rapped his cane on the floor like he was quieting a rowdy classroom. The cane was made of dark wood, scars and dents on the shaft, the finish worn through in places, a brass ferrule, the head shaped like a cabinet knob crudely carved from some kind of white stone, smooth with age. Sentimental value, Isaiah thought, Seb could afford better.

"I am losing my patience, Laquez," Seb said. "I will ask you one more time. Did you steal my money?"

"Naw, Seb, I told you, man, I wouldn't do you like that."

With surprising quickness Seb stepped forward and slashed Laquez with the cane. Laquez spun around, holding his face and saying *Oh fuck oh fuck*. He staggered away, Seb going after him, whacking him twice more, the boy dropping to the floor and curling against the wall.

"I'm sorry, Seb," Laquez said, holding a hand up to protect himself. "It won't happen again, I promise. Please forgive me, Seb, gimme another chance."

Seb limped rapidly back and forth, going in and out of Isaiah's view. "Did I ever tell you how I lost my leg?" he said. "It was during the genocide. My tribe, the Hutus, were killing Tutsis, slaughtering them by the thousands. Don't ask me why. There are no explanations for such things. One afternoon, I was visiting a friend in the neighboring village when a Tutsi man captured me. He used a machete to cut off my leg and with every blow he called out the name of a loved one he had lost." Seb slashed Laquez and screamed like the militiaman, "Ariche! Farelle! Bijoux! Brihanna!" He was trembling, his face bunched up with rage.

He took a moment to calm himself and found a square pack of English Ovals cigarettes in his coat pocket. He put one in his mouth, and another man appeared. He'd been in a different part of the room. The man was tall, lean, and striking, his eyes patient and intelligent; a Zulu warrior in a cranberry-colored Members Only jacket. His pants were too short, two inches of white sock showing between his cuffs and his cheap sneakers. He had four deep scars on the side of his head. It looked like a bear had attacked him, its claws scooping out creek beds of flesh; suture marks left by someone with a knitting needle and kite string. Without a word he produced an old Zippo, lit the cigarette, and snapped the lighter shut like a mousetrap.

"Thank you, Gahigi," Seb said, twin streams of smoke jetting out of his nose. "Would you like one?"

"No, Seb," Gahigi said, sounding a little annoyed. He leaned back against the pool table with his arms crossed. Neither he nor Seb gave any notice to Laquez's crying and whimpering.

"I understood the man's anger," Seb went on, "but I did not forgive. Many years later I went looking for him. I asked the people in his village if they knew a man who had four children who were killed in the genocide, and I named them. For a small fee, they told me he was in Kigali selling vegetables by the side of the road. I searched all the roads leading in and out of Kigali until I found him. He did not remember me, but I refreshed his memory. Do you see the handle on my cane? I fashioned it from the man's—what is it called? Oh yes. The tibia."

Laquez didn't know what a tibia was, but he knew it was bad. "Come on, Seb, I won't fuck up no more, swear to God I won't." Laquez had his knees pulled up to his chest, his hands over his head. He looked pitiful, something about that making Seb's anger rise again. Maybe that was how he looked as the machete came down on his leg. Seb raised the cane to strike him and Isaiah stepped into the room. Gahigi got up quickly like he'd left his gun in the car. Seb lowered the cane, the rage vanishing in a millisecond, replaced by the warm fatherly smile.

"Hello, Isaiah," he said. "May I offer you a cup of tea?"

They went to the bar and sat down in a booth, apparently set aside for Seb's exclusive use. In stark contrast to the rest of the place, the table and vinyl seats smelled of disinfectant and were so shiny they looked shellacked. In front of Seb, some items were arranged in a grid. Lined up nearest him was a beautiful porcelain tea set. Sugar bowl and spoon to his left. Teacup and saucer directly before him. Teapot on his right. In a row above that: a new gold foil ashtray, a gold lighter, and a pack of English Ovals.

"Yes, I am somewhat exacting at times," Seb said, catching Isaiah's look. "A form of OCD, I am told, but harmless enough. Will you have some tea, Isaiah? It's Taylors of Harrogate."

"No, thanks," Isaiah said.

Gahigi was watching from a bar stool, nearly invisible, a panther in a thicket of shadows and liquor bottles.

"How do you know my name?" Isaiah said.

"Come now," Seb said, lifting the teapot and pouring himself a cup. "Everyone knows your name and what you do. Let us not pretend you are unaware of this. Now tell me, Isaiah, why have you come to see me?" Seb shifted in his seat and winced. "Gout. Another indignity. It would be better to fall apart all at once, don't you think?"

"Do you remember my brother doing some work for you?" Isaiah said.

66

Seb put sugar in his tea and stirred it with the small silver spoon, the sound like a glass clock ticking. "You make it seem like an accusation," he said. "Please remind me, who is your brother?"

"Marcus. Marcus Quintabe."

"When was this?"

"Eight years ago."

"Eight years ago? My goodness, Isaiah, do you really expect me to remember something like that?"

"I'm asking you if you do."

Seb took a slow sip of tea. "No, I'm afraid not. My memory does not serve me well these days." He sighed. "Age, as they say, is not for sissies, but I suppose there are some advantages. What was the line? Ah yes. *The afternoon knows what the morning never suspected.* I believe it was your Robert Frost who said that. I once took a class on American poets. A bit too optimistic and sentimental for my tastes." Seb nodded at the bartender. "Sahid," he said. "Was my booth cleaned?"

"This morning, Seb," the bartender said.

"Well, please clean it again."

"Okay, Seb."

Seb lit a cigarette, putting the lighter and cigarettes back in their places. "Would you like a cigarette, Gahigi?" he said with a mischievous smile.

"No, Seb," Gahigi said sternly. "You know I am quitting."

"Someone told him smoking was bad for his health," Seb said, amused. "Gahigi, will you see to Laquez? Tell him if he does not return the money he will be punished."

"You have already told him, Seb."

"Tell him again—and make sure he understands." Gahigi unzipped his jacket and brought out a pair of leather gloves. He pulled them on and went down the hall flexing his fists. "I'm sorry, I interrupted you," Seb said to Isaiah. "Please continue."

"I asked you if Marcus did some work at your house."

"And this was eight years ago?" Seb said. Isaiah nodded. "Not likely. I was living in an apartment then. Upkeep was the landlord's responsibility."

"Your name and phone number were in his work log."

Seb took another slow sip of tea. "It is possible your brother did some work for me at my office, but I do not keep track of who did what or what their names might be."

"Do you know how three thousand dollars in cash and sixteen grams of heroin ended up in my brother's backpack?" Isaiah said.

Seb carefully squeezed some lemon into his cup, Isaiah wondering why he hadn't put it in before. "I don't know what you're trying to suggest, Isaiah," Seb said, unruffled, "but I will let the innuendo pass for the moment. However, if I do not remember your brother, how would I know if he had a backpack or anything else?" Seb huffed through his nose. "Heroin," he said. "Filthy stuff. A professor of mine was an addict. The last time I saw him was at the Drummer Street bus station. He was dressed in rags and sleeping on the sidewalk, poor man."

"The drugs and money were put in Marcus's backpack while he was working for you," Isaiah said.

Seb smiled, patient and patronizing. "But you haven't established that your brother worked for me at all. Perhaps I asked for an estimate or advice. It is impossible to say. And really, Isaiah, suspicion is one thing but paranoia is quite another. Have you considered the possibility that your brother was an addict? Or a dealer, perhaps?"

"He wasn't involved in drugs. I'd know."

"Forgive me, I did not mean to offend."

"You can't offend me."

That smile again. "You are bright and tenacious, Isaiah. I think you will do well in the world assuming your rudeness is held in check. But I'm afraid your argument rests on the assumption that your brother was unaware the contraband was in the backpack. Perhaps he placed it there himself for reasons he chose not to confide."

"If Marcus knew that stuff was in his backpack he wouldn't have left it on a bench while we were playing basketball."

"If I may ask," Seb said, "where was your brother the day *before* he allegedly worked for me?"

"The day before?"

"Yes. According to you, he was unaware that the money and heroin were in the backpack, and if that is true, then the items might well have been placed there the day before your basketball game or two days before or a week before. How is one to know?"

Isaiah hesitated. This was new to him; a mind as agile as his own.

Seb went on. "Surely, others have come in contact with the backpack, perhaps while it was left on the bench while you and your brother were playing basketball. No, I'm sorry, Isaiah, but I'm afraid your logic leaves much to be desired." A note of amused contempt had crept into his voice. "Now, I have enjoyed our little discussion, but I'm afraid I have other matters I must attend to. Please stop by anytime. Perhaps we can talk about subjects more pleasant and productive."

Isaiah drove home, thinking about what happened in the bar. What Seb and Laquez were talking about was a money-laundering technique called smurfing. Cash was taken to the bank and loaded onto debit cards, the amounts always under ten thousand dollars. More than that and the IRS would get involved. The card money was now effectively clean, no paper trail, and you could use the cards to go shopping, pay a debt, or withdraw the money in cash, Seb taking his fee off the top. But did the money-laundering have anything to do with Marcus's murder? Too soon to say. But Seb *was* hiding something. He said he had gout but that didn't prevent him from going after Laquez, and as soon as he saw Isaiah he leaned more heavily on his cane and his limp got worse. Why pretend you were more handicapped than you actually were? Ask him a direct question and he rambled on about aging and Robert Frost, trying to get your eye off the ball. Those leisurely sips of tea, squeezing the lemon, the asides to Gahigi about cigarettes were delaying tactics; give him time to think, come up with his next move.

Seb also claimed his memory was bad but he quoted a poem from his college days, knew the dollar amounts for the seven debit cards and the face of the Tutsi man who had cut his leg off when he was a kid, bleeding profusely and screaming in pain. No, Seb had a very good memory. Isaiah resisted the urge to equate deception with guilt. The genocide in Rwanda would make anyone wary of revealing themselves. And Seb had a point. It *was* possible for someone else to have put the contraband into Marcus's backpack, and Seb had no apparent motive to kill him.

Isaiah got online and ran a background check on Seb. Eight years ago, he was living in a seedy building on Seminole. He was there for three years and moved to a rented condo in El Segundo. That part of his story held together. Neither was the kind of place you'd remodel at your own expense.

Seb's office was a small storefront wedged in between a shoe repair shop and a dry cleaner's. There was a CLOSED sign in the window, the sill a graveyard for flies and moths, the blinds clamped shut. Dust had accumulated on the top edges of the inset door panels and on the doorknob. If Seb went in and out it wasn't through this door.

Isaiah went around to the back. The doorknob was dust-free, the keyhole worn from use. The dead bolt was an ordinary Schlage. Not a lot of security for a money launderer. Isaiah bought a blank at the locksmith's, went home, and made a bump key. That night he came back and let himself in.

The smell of Lysol permeated the place. A calculator was set on a cheap fiberboard desk along with a gooseneck lamp, a container of hand sanitizer and a couple of unused gold foil ashtrays. There was nothing in the desk drawers, not even dust or cobwebs. A brown vinyl couch was polished to a high shine, no footprints on the gray linoleum floor. A floor-to-ceiling bookshelf was set against one wall, dog-eared tax code manuals on the shelves. The wastebasket was empty and clean. The file cabinet was empty too. Nothing on the walls but a Tusker calendar from 2006. A cupboard held Styrofoam cups, tea bags, plastic spoons, spare toilet paper, and an electric kettle. The bathroom was spotless, a bar of soap and a roll of paper towels on the sink. Isaiah checked every inch of the place and concluded that no remodeling work had been done before or since eight years ago. Marcus hadn't worked here.

Isaiah wondered why Seb kept an office with no office supplies, landline, or internet connection. Meetings, he decided. Seb didn't want them at his condo, his hangout, or anyplace he couldn't control.

The next night, Isaiah came back and set up a spy cam. It was motion-activated and recorded sound as well as color video. He hid it above the line of sight in a narrow space between two tax manuals. The cam's receiver was the size of a flip phone. Isaiah hid it on the same shelf. The odds the camera would capture something important were low, like photographing a snow leopard, but you couldn't follow Seb around all day and night. Like with most things, you'd need a little luck.

CHAPTER FIVE

Red Poles

Ken Van talked on the phone with Liko about the three new arrivals, two from Fujian, one from Guangdong. The Guangdong girl was sick and had to be tended to. A doctor with a suspended license was on the payroll, but the girls only trusted Chinese medicine. He'd have to bring in an herbalist and the massage parlor would stink of wolfberry and dang gui for a week.

He thought about Janine and wondered why she turned out the way she did. He'd given her every advantage. Private school, music school, piano lessons, her own horse, trips to Europe and Asia. It was depressing. All that time and money had no effect. *He* had no effect. Love a kid to death, and all she wants to do is throw her life away. He remembered that terrible night when she told him she wanted to be a DJ.

They were in his office. She'd come to borrow money, saying she needed to invest in DJ equipment.

"You want to be a DJ? Like on the radio?" he said, knowing that wasn't what she meant.

"No, not that kind of DJ," Janine said. "It's more like—remember Kerri's wedding, there was a guy there playing records?"

"*That's* what you want to do?"

"No, it's on a much bigger scale, Pop. DJing is really huge now. Have you heard of Tiësto?" She kept talking before he could give her a look. "He's a really famous DJ. I mean he fills up whole fucking—sorry, whole arenas. Thousands of people come to see him, and you know how much he makes? Two hundred and fifty grand a set, that's over sixty thousand dollars an hour, Pop!"

Ken had his elbows on the desk, rubbing his temples with both hands. A migraine was coming on. You could almost see it, like you were the head pin and the bowling ball was coming straight down the lane. So much bullshit to deal with, so much self-loathing, so much impatience to get away from Vegas and now this. "A fantasy, Janine," he said. "The whole idea is ridiculous."

"No it's not, Pop. It's totally legit. Hip-hop is like a whole culture."

"Wearing your cap backwards, and listening to rap music is not a culture, Janine. Once and for all, you're not doing this."

She looked at him like she was stopping herself from saying *Fuck you*. "Try to understand, okay?" she said. "I *have* to. It's the only thing I'm good at—it's my passion."

"So what?" Ken said. "Who gets to live their passion? You need a real career, Janine. Something to be proud of, not this silliness."

"You mean like Sarita?"

"*Yes,* like Sarita." Ken felt the migraine taking over. His hands and feet were cold, a pounding in his left temple was getting louder. "There are things I could have done—accomplished, but there were practical considerations."

"I don't get it," she said. "Your dreams get smashed so mine have to get smashed too?"

"Janine, you're *not* going to do this," he said.

"Dad, I'm going to be a DJ," she said, getting flip. "You might as well get used to it."

Ken stood up and felt his body swell. He felt like a wolf, defending the last shreds of flesh on a rotting carcass. "I paid for the best private schools," he said. "I paid for tennis lessons and art lessons and piano lessons. You were playing Beethoven when you were eleven years old. We went to concerts and museums. I took you to London and Paris and all over the world. You've seen the Forbidden Palace and the Ganges and the goddamn pyramids and do you want to know why?"

"So I could be more like my sister?"

"Do you want to know why?" he shouted. He was shaking, the pounding bashing through his eardrums.

"Sure," Janine said. She looked frightened and thrilled, her aloof, self-contained father going ballistic.

"So you'll never have to face the fact that you've wasted your life and there's nothing you can do about it. One day you'll wake up and realize you're fifty-six years old and all you've done is...nothing."

"What are you talking about, Pop? You're doing really great."

"Be silent, Janine. For once in your life be silent!" Ken screamed. He came toward her, his trigger finger pointed right between her eyes. He wanted to hit her, beat her, exorcise his helplessness. "You will not do this, do you understand? You will not throw your life away! You will stop your gambling and you will forget this DJ nonsense as of now, this minute!"

"I can't, Pop," she said.

"YOU CAN AND YOU WILL! I'M YOUR FATHER AND YOU WILL DO AS I SAY OR GET OUT OF THIS HOUSE!"

Ten minutes later, she had a suitcase and a duffel bag packed, and he heard her get in her car and drive away.

Ken called the herbalist to attend to the sick girl from Guangdong. Then he went to the wet bar and poured himself a baijiu, a habit he'd picked up playing fan-tan and mah jong in one of Tommy Lau's gambling dens. The drink was made from sorghum fermented in mud pits and aged in earthenware jugs for a year or two or thirty. People thought it was wine, like sake, but it was fifty to sixty percent alcohol, smelled like a hamper on laundry day, and would knock you on your behind if you weren't used to it.

Ken had been a heavy gambler when he was younger. He wondered if it was genetic, Janine's habit driven by some errant chromosome. She'd borrowed a small fortune from him, telling him lie after lie. Tuition was going up, her car broke down, her bag got stolen, her friend was in trouble, she needed a new computer and a bunch of other ones he couldn't remember. If anybody else had even *thought* about scamming him he'd have known immediately, but not his daughters. They had him wrapped around their fingers, wrists, arms.

Ken never thought he could love Sarita, a product of an affair with a hooker named Angela who was half black and half Hispanic. It went on for a year until he got tired of her wanting things and the smell of marijuana in the house. He gave her two thousand dollars and told her it was over. A few weeks later she showed up at the house, pregnant. She told him how she'd set him up and stopped taking her birth control pills and showed him the test and said she'd soak him for child support, reminding him that it would go on until the kid was eighteen years old. Wouldn't it be better to make a onetime payment now?

Ken said no, leaving the twenty-two-year-old airhead who liked to party, get high, wear expensive clothes, and swim naked with her friends in Lake Powell, with the prospect of getting an abortion or being a mom. Even if she carried the pregnancy to term and wanted child support she'd still be stuck with the baby. No, she'd get an abortion, he was sure of it.

Ten months went by and one Sunday morning Ken came home from his golf game and the housekeeper showed him a cardboard box. A baby was nestled inside, wrapped in a towel. She told him somebody had rung the bell and left it on the front porch. There was a note that said *Leaving Vegas. By the way, my real name isn't Angela. The baby's name is Sarita. Fuck you.* But Angela or whatever her name was must have had a branch of superior DNA growing on her family tree because Sarita was a dream child. Smart, motivated, loving. Ken was glad when she went away to college. It was getting harder and harder to shield her from the business. If Sarita found out it would crush her, and he'd hate himself more than he already did.

Ken's phone buzzed. An email alert. Tommy Lau. There was no one else on their private network. What's the greedy old bastard want now? If Tommy owned every dollar in the world, he'd send Ken to Mars to steal some from the Martians. Ken opened up his laptop and typed his username and twelve-digit password. Everything going in or out was encrypted with 256-bit SSL software, the same kind the banks used. In the unlikely event he was hacked, the hacker couldn't decrypt the data unless he had a couple of supercomputers and a century or two to spend. The password was the only way to read the files.

Tommy's message said he was coming to Vegas and to pick him up at McCarran at 8:15, an hour from now. That was unusual. Why was he coming on such short notice? Why was he coming here at all? What couldn't be said in an encrypted phone call or email? Ken poured himself another shot of baijiu. Did Tommy know he was quitting? That he'd finally had enough and was walking away, the consequences be damned? Whatever the case, Tommy wasn't coming to Vegas because he was happy. He only came to town when there was trouble.

Benny would no doubt be gambling so Janine took Isaiah and Dodson to his favorite casinos. The Palm for dollar slots. The Four Queens for the five-dollar minimum Let It Ride, the Mirage for single-zero roulette, the Casino Royale for the hundred-times odds at the crap table.

"You bet a dollar, you win a hundred?" Dodson said.

"No. Tourists make that mistake all the time," Janine said. "A hundred times odds means that after the rollout, you can put up a hundred times whatever you put on the pass line. Bet on the pass line by itself and the house has about a percent and a half edge. On an odds bet, the edge is about two tenths of a percent."

"Damn, you know your shit, girl."

"Yeah, I guess. But if the dice are cold, the dice are cold."

Isaiah interrupted. "Did you make me a copy of the records?"

"Yeah," Janine said. "I emailed them to you."

"Delete your copy. We don't want anybody finding them on your computer."

As they drove, Isaiah thought about the girls in the photo galleries. They looked like college students or factory workers or food sellers at an outdoor market or straight off the rice farm.

Most of the photos were bleak as mug shots, taken against a wall with cracks in the plaster. Others were probably shot for a marriage site, the girls hoping a nice man would take them away to anyplace but here. Some posed like girlie photos from the fifties; hair lacquered with hair spray, too much makeup and a vamped-up look that was supposed to be seductive. You could almost hear them batting their eyelashes. Others smiled brightly with a fish market or a canal in the background. One girl was standing demurely in a field of flowers wearing a traditional embroidered Chinese dress. Isaiah imagined the kind of men who would be attracted to them; resentful, unable to control their wives or girlfriends, telling themselves American women were spoiled and too demanding and had abandoned traditional values; fantasizing about a submissive Asian wife who would see them as a savior and be grateful and let herself be bossed around and not talk back and fuck whenever they wanted. Isaiah's throat tightened. These were ordinary girls, naïve and hopeful, trapped in poverty or abuse and wishing for a decent life. Not a luxurious life or even a happy one. Just decent. Their only mistake was trusting someone and now they were locked in a dirty windowless room reeking of semen, their pies in the sky turned to horror and degradation.

"Keep calling him, Janine," Isaiah said, "let him hear your voice."

"Tell him how worried you are," Dodson said. "Put some tears in your voice. The boy'll break down sooner or later."

Janine had already left a dozen plaintive messages, telling Benny she was sick with worry and begging him to call. "I already called all his friends," she said. "No one's heard from him."

They stopped for coffee and looked at Benny's Facebook page. No recent posts; lots of photos of his motocross races and shots of Janine in a bikini, a micro-mini, or short-shorts, or in some other way semi-naked.

"I look good, huh?" she said.

"Yes, you do," Dodson said.

There were other pictures of Janine and Benny in casinos, standing next to a slot machine where they'd won a jackpot or at a craps table raking in a big stack of chips.

"Are any of these places unfamiliar to you?" Isaiah said.

"No, I know them all," Janine said.

"Who's his best friend?" Dodson said.

"Me."

"Would he hide out with his motocross buddies?" Isaiah said.

"No, they don't gamble."

"What about his parents?" Dodson said.

"They live in Pennsylvania."

"How is Benny getting around?"

"His bike," Janine said.

"Well, it's gonna be harder for us or anybody else to catch up with him."

Dodson *was* trying to take over the case. They looked at each other, Isaiah incredulous, Dodson with an expression that said *It's game on, son.*

Dodson had been thinking about the Black the Knife case and how he'd been relegated to sidekick. He'd felt dumb and useless, Isaiah figuring everything out and telling him what to do. Dodson hated being led. When he was a teenager, he'd been in a gang, submitting himself to groupthink, but that was for survival. Those times were long gone, and he'd be damned before he'd let Isaiah dominate the action again. This time he'd contribute, be part of the investigation. He was smart. He could figure shit out too.

Janine's phone buzzed. "He texted me!" she said. There was a selfie of Benny smiling uneasily at the camera. The message said: Don't worry babe. Got it under control. I love you.

"Look at him," Janine said, "he's scared out of his mind. He won't call because he knows I'll talk him into not doing it."

Isaiah went still, staring at the selfie. Dodson stared at it too, like he was straining to see what Isaiah saw.

"What?" Dodson said, annoyed.

"Behind him," Isaiah said. Over Benny's shoulder, you could see a BIG CASH machine; three reels showing different kinds of fruit, coin slot on the lower left, spin button on the right, aluminum payout tray at the bottom. "They don't use those anymore, do they?"

"You're right," Janine said. "That's an old-school slot. I haven't seen one of those in a long—oh my God, he's at the Lucky Streak! How did you see that?"

"It's my job," Isaiah said. He took a last sip of espresso and shot a look at Dodson. "Let's go."

Ken picked up Tommy at the airport and they drove back to the house. Tommy had all the style and flash of the Chinese prime minister. Dark gray suit, red tie, rimless glasses on an almost-featureless face, and an old-guard haircut, Brylcreemed and parted on the side. If you had to tell a police sketch artist what he looked like all you could say was *an Asian guy wearing a suit.* Only those who knew him would notice the faint ruthless smile and the eyes like a dozing crocodile's, open just enough to see who was stepping into the water.

They'd been driving for fifteen minutes and Tommy had only commented on the weather in San Francisco. This was what he did, keeping you in suspense, showing you who was boss, as if you didn't know already. Like when they spotted his suitcase on the carousel he didn't move, expecting Ken to get it, and when they got to the car he stood there until Ken opened the door for him. It was bad form to ask him anything so Ken just drove.

When they got to the Red Rock house Tommy walked straight through the great room to the sliding glass door and went outside, Ken right behind him. Tommy never spoke where there was the slightest possibility he'd be recorded.

"What's going on, Tommy?" Ken said.

Tommy stood near the pool, hands clasped behind his back, reflected light wobbling on the suit, the rimless glasses like silver dollars. He got a cigarette out of his platinum cigarette case and lit it with his platinum lighter. He didn't like gold, too flashy, too low-class, he'd said. He took his time, tucking the lighter away, taking a couple of long drags while he stared at the water like it was a crystal ball; Ken waiting, his punishment for asking a question.

"This is a very serious matter," Tommy said. He spoke with a Cantonese accent, the syllables going up and down. *Dis is a waydee seriose madda.* "On Friday, at two thirty-two in the morning, someone downloaded our business records," he said.

"No, that's impossible," Ken said. "I never download anything, that's an ironclad rule. All the records stay in the cloud."

"Apparently not."

"How do you know this?"

"Zhi checks the event log every day."

"You keep tabs on me?"

Tommy looked at him, surprised he'd asked. "I keep tabs on everyone that works for me. It was not a hack, Ken. The person responsible used the password."

"No, that can't be. The password only exists in my head and yours."

A balloon full of ice water burst in Ken's gut. *Janine.* He'd forgotten he'd told her about the contact list back when she was a kid. Why did he do such a stupid thing?

"The only two people in the house are you and your daughter," Tommy said.

"There's no way she could know the password, Tommy. I didn't tell her, why would I?" Ken hoped that didn't sound like a lie. Tommy could smell bullshit if it was a hundred years old and buried under the Mirage.

"There are no other suspects," Tommy said, "unless you count the housekeeper." Tommy had referred her. An elderly Guatemalan woman who barely spoke English. She called Ken *meester* and Janine *she-lady.* "Goo morneen, meester," she'd say. "Is she-lady okay?"

"Isn't Janine a gambling addict?" Tommy said. He turned his back and walked alongside the pool, forcing Ken to talk louder.

"I wouldn't call her an addict," Ken said.

"Well, she has borrowed a lot of money from me for a recreational gambler."

"She's borrowed from *you?*"

"Yes. You didn't know?" Tommy said, as if this was a sign of bad parenting.

"Tommy, she wouldn't do something like this."

"Do you know where she is?" Tommy said.

Tommy was barely audible, Ken had to walk after him. "I have no idea," he said. "She could be anywhere. I don't even know where she lives."

"She lives at the Siesta Vegas Motel," Tommy said. "Zhi found her." Zhi was Tommy's internet whiz. If you were mute, illiterate, and living in the Gobi desert, Zhi could find out what rock you were sleeping under and what kinds of scorpions you ate. "My men went to the club where she was working tonight," Tommy said. "Her friends said she left with two black men. Do you know who they are?"

"No, I don't. I've only met the boyfriend." Ken wanted to warn Janine, tell her to get out of town. Even if she turned over the records and hadn't copied them she still would have *seen* them. She was as good as dead, and if he had the slightest objection, so was he. "Look, how about I call her and straighten this out?"

"No, I don't want her to be on guard," Tommy said.

"Be on guard? Tommy, this is ridiculous."

"It's far from ridiculous. Would you like to calculate the prison term for operating the largest human trafficking ring on the West Coast?"

"What are you going to do?" Ken said.

"Find her, talk to her," Tommy said. "We've already located the boyfriend."

"You have? How?"

"14K has hundreds of friends all over Vegas. Not just Chinese— Vietnamese, Filipino, white. Some we do business with, the rest know who we are and want to be on our good side. We spread the boyfriend's picture around and a blackjack dealer called us. Benny is gambling at a casino in Henderson."

Ken wondered why he wasn't told about these *friends* and what else he didn't know. Tommy turned around, his blank face like a mask of a blank face, the crocodile eyes watching you pull on your swimming trunks.

"Has she contacted you?" Tommy said.

"No, we hardly speak."

"If you have the slightest idea, tell me now. You don't want the Red Poles to find her."

The Red Poles were Tommy's enforcers, recruited from Hong Kong's rooftop slums. Thousands of people who couldn't afford two grand a month for an apartment the size of a one-car garage lived on the roofs of old buildings; six or seven families crammed into a shack made from corrugated tin and scrap lumber; one toilet, no ventilation, sleeping on newspapers, infested with rats and white ants, sweltering in the tropical heat, drenched during the rainy season. Survive there and you're a hard remorseless motherfucker. *Chosen* from there and you're loyal as a robot.

"Help us and things will go easier," Tommy said.

"No they won't," Ken said.

Tommy took a moment. "No," he said, "they won't."

"I'm calling her," Ken said, reaching for his phone. He felt something cold and hard pressed against his neck. He could smell the cordite. He didn't have to turn around to know it was Tung, Tommy's personal bodyguard. He should have known the old bastard would do something like this, pretend he was alone until Ken showed his hand.

"Tung," Tommy said. "Lock Ken in a room somewhere, please. If he makes the slightest bit of trouble gag him and tie him head to toe."

Leo and Balthazar were driving back to the crib, tired after a long day of chasing down deadbeats. Leo thought he'd call Renee and Misty Love, have a little party. Renee was the only hooker in Vegas who would have sex with Balthazar. She didn't seem to mind, saying all she had to do was close her eyes and pretend she was lying under Kevin Durant. It was a pain in the ass, but you had to go through their manager, Charlie O. He was an old-school pimp; canary-yellow Borsalino, matching Superfly double-breasted overcoat worn rain or shine, white alligator loafers, and enough bling to make everybody at Bad Boy Records happy. Once, Leo had asked Charlie what the O in his name stood for.

"The O stands for *Oh my God, you must be crazy,*" Charlie said.

"What kind of name is that?" Leo said.

"Ask my bitches," Charlie said, puffing on a cigarillo. "That's what every one of 'em said the first time they saw my dick."

Leo was about to ring him up when Nate called and told him Benny was gambling at the Lucky Streak.

"You hear that, Zar?" Leo said. "That little turd says he's broke and what's he doing?"

"Gambling," Zar said. "Isn't that what Nate said?"

"That was a rhetorical question, it didn't really need an answer."

"Oh."

"I believe Benny needs a second trip to the landfill. What do you think?"

"Sure," Zar said.

Crowds of seniors had come in on buses and were roving around the Lucky Streak Casino with their sun visors, fanny packs, and free six-packs of Pepsi, looking for their lucky machines. *That's not it, Edith, it's over there.* Chandeliers made of spangly rectangles bounced light off the slot machines; the smoky air-conditioned atmosphere congested with sounds. Alarm bells ringing, screams of *I won I won,* clattering roulette wheels, coins clanging in the payout trays, a stickman shouting *A natural winner, a natural winner,* the crowd cheering and woo-hooing.

Benny didn't notice any of it. He was so nervous he'd chosen the wrong video poker machine, an eight-five instead of a nine-six. A nine-six paid nine coins for a full house and six for a flush. An eight-five paid eight and five. Play six hundred hands an hour, slow for Benny, and you'd lose sixty-six dollars of potential winnings. That shit added up.

"Jesus I'm stupid," he said. He cashed out, the voucher for seven dollars and fifty cents, all he had left from twenty he'd borrowed from Nate. He stared at the piece of paper like it was a breakup note from Janine. Today was Friday, vig day, and he hoped she was at Seven Sevens and not on her way to the landfill. He felt like an asshole. He couldn't protect her, and he couldn't pay the vig. Leo was right. Janine could do better, way better, but Benny loved her and he'd fight for her and do whatever it took to keep her. He might be a loser, but he wasn't a wimp.

He went over what he'd done so far. He'd gone to Kinko's and used one of their computers to set up an email account. Then he sent Janine's dad a ransom note, demanding a hundred thousand dollars for the return of the records. Her dad could afford it, and there was no sense getting greedy. By the time Benny got the money, the added vig would bring Leo's tab up to ten or eleven grand. Pay him off and the rest for him and Janine. He hadn't gotten an answer to his email yet and hoped the demand note wasn't stuck in a spam folder. He had the exchange all worked out. He'd tell them to drive somewhere on I-15 and throw the money out of a moving car. Then he'd swoop in on his Yamaha, grab it and take off into the desert. *Nobody* could catch him on his bike.

Still, he was scared. Janine had told him about the Red Poles and how they were smart and brutal and had no conscience. The sanctity of life might as well be a vegan restaurant. He knew the danger was real but leaving town wasn't even a consideration. They'd talked about it a couple of times, Janine wanting to get away from Leo, start over somewhere else, change their luck. Go to LA maybe. Lots of Indian casinos. Pechanga, San Miguel, Harrah's Rincon; play cards at the Bicycle or Hollywood Park. It wasn't Vegas, but it wouldn't be so bad, and maybe they could rein it in a little, save some money, settle down. Have a kid. Benny said sure, sure, he'd think about it, but he only said that to please her. Vegas was his world—or more like his natural environment. If he left he'd be like one of those killer whales at SeaWorld that goes berserk because it's not in the ocean.

Shit, man, he was *known* here. Dealers, pit bosses, bartenders, busboys, waitresses, working girls, cabdrivers, parking valets, housekeepers, security guards. The whole understructure of the city knew him by name. Nobody cared that he was small-time, that he was a loser. He was like one of those Mafia guys who knows there's a contract out on him but can't leave his neighborhood. The smiles, hellos, jokes, claps on the back, free coupons for drinks, comped rooms so he could get Janine out of that fucking motel—those things were like body parts or blood cells. Without them holding him together he was nothing, and that was what he feared most. Being nothing.

Benny hated Leo for making him afraid. He couldn't wait to throw the money in his face and tell him to fuck off. Seeing that in his head bolstered his courage, and he imagined himself showing up at the motel room in a limo and taking Janine to dinner at Gordon Ramsay's, where an eight-ounce filet cost a hundred and eighty bucks, and then casino-hopping without worrying about money. Yeah, he'd show her he wasn't such a loser after all.

The video poker machines were grouped on a raised area, three steps above the casino floor. Benny was about to leave when he saw four young Chinese men in black suits, sunglasses, and skinny black ties. They looked like the bad guys in *The Matrix*. *No, it couldn't be,* he said to himself. *You're being paranoid.* The men were weaving their way through the rows of machines and tables, rubbernecking, searching. Benny could feel their intensity; like snakes slithering through the underbrush, their tongues flicking, tracking a helpless mouse. No, these guys weren't looking for their lucky machines, they were *hunting*. People said Benny was slow on the uptake, and maybe that was happening now. Benny stepped behind a row of slots, got low and made his way toward the exit. As he came around a corner, he saw a fifth guy at the end of the aisle. They looked at each other. Benny turned and broke for the exit.

The Audi entered the Lucky Streak parking lot and Isaiah drove around, looking for a parking space.

"That's Benny's bike!" Janine said, pointing at the bright blue Yamaha parked next to a light pole. "He always does that so it won't get hit by a car." A black BMW 750i with chrome turbine rims was parked in a striped no parking zone. "The Red Poles," she said. "We're screwed."

Isaiah parked the Audi in the next row over. He gave Janine his Harvard cap, Dodson gave her his hoodie, and they jogged to the casino entrance. They were about to go in when Benny came sprinting out, blowing right past them, not even noticing Janine.

"Step back, and look the other way," Isaiah said. *"Now."* Janine did as she was told as five Chinese guys stampeded by.

"They're gonna kill him!" she said. Isaiah gave her his car keys. "Get in the car, and stay there," he said.

By the time Isaiah and Dodson caught up with the Red Poles, they were gathered near the Yamaha, beating Benny to the ground.

He lay there, groaning, cheek smushed into the asphalt. One of them, as skinny as a number two pencil, seemed to be the leader. He was angry and punched one of his colleagues. "You hit him too hard," he said. "Tommy want him awake."

Isaiah and Dodson slowed as they approached, the five guys turning to face them. Not another fight, Isaiah thought. He couldn't take it.

"Who are you?" Skinny said. He looked like an anorexic limo driver. His peg-leg pants made his pointy shoes look like kayaks.

"Hey, how you doing?" Isaiah said, trying to keep his tone light. "Benny's a friend of ours."

"This not your business. You go away now."

Another guy with ears big as satellite dishes reached under his jacket. "No gun," Skinny said. "They got video here." He turned back to Isaiah. "Look, my fren," he said. "You go way now or we fuck you up bad."

The guy with the big ears got in Dodson's face. "You too," he said.

"Damn, man," Dodson said. "They ever do a remake of *Dumbo* I believe you got the part."

"Look, we don't want any trouble," Isaiah said, holding his palms out. "We just want to take Benny home."

"That's all, huh?" Skinny said. "Fuck you, okay? You go way now."

Janine drove up in the Audi and saw Benny on the ground. "Benny! Are you all right?"

"Stay in the car," Isaiah said.

"What did you do to him?" she said.

"You coming too," Skinny said.

"Fuck off, dickhead," she said. "Are you one of Tommy's flunkies?"

"She called 911," Isaiah said, not knowing if that had occurred to her. Skinny had a moment's pause until he saw Janine fumbling for her phone. He smiled.

"Oh yeah?" he said. "I don't think so."

Skinny threw a big right hook. Isaiah was waiting for it. He stepped toward him, into his chest, the punch going around him, in the same instant ramming the heel of his hand into Skinny's upper lip, snapping his head back. Skinny spun away screaming and bleeding from the mouth.

Dodson was bouncing around, shadowboxing. "Come on, Dumbo," he said. "Get some of this." Dumbo rushed him. Dodson rat-tat-tatted him with two lefts, a right, and another left. The guy stopped, touching the blood pouring out of his nose, not believing he'd been hit four times in two seconds. "What's up, son?" Dodson said. "You want some more?"

The other three Red Poles rushed in to join the fight, one going for Dodson, the other two for Isaiah. Isaiah backed up, no attacks from behind. A guy with a pockmarked face and big hands walked toward him, casual, confident; the other two staying back, grinning, waiting for the show to start. *This guy's got skills.*

"What," the pockmarked guy said. "You don't want fight?"

Isaiah kept his weight on the balls of his feet and tried to relax, get too tight and you can't react. He kept his hands open, one in front of his face, the other guarding his left cheek; his opponent was right-handed, his punches would likely land there. The guy kept coming, smiling, his knees bent, hands like he was about to catch a basketball. He feinted a charge, Isaiah leaning forward, ready to step in and counterattack. The front kick came so fast he didn't see it, the spinning back fist right behind it grazing his chin. Isaiah stumbled back, the pain like a cramp in his chest. All three Red Poles charged. He put up his guard. *Stay off the ground.*

Dodson was doing his Muhammad Ali impression, dancing and dodging and ducking, two opponents now. He hit Dumbo with a couple of stiff jabs, enough to slow him down, and rat-tat-tatted the second guy, giving him a few extra tats, the same combination that knocked out Ernesto Rodriguez for the flyweight title at Vacaville State Prison.

"Come on, bitches," he said. "Where you at?" They came at him, yelling in Chinese. These guys were street fighters, throwing wild punches, trying to overwhelm. Dodson made them pay, busting a cheekbone, loosening a tooth, but they wrapped him up and slung him to the ground.

The three Red Poles swarmed Isaiah, windmilling punches, too many fists to block, and he was reeling from the front kick. He had to defend and couldn't attack. He caught a glimpse of Dodson, rolling across the asphalt to keep from getting stomped. Janine was blasting the Audi's horn to attract attention, but the Lucky Streak was light on security guards. Isaiah was getting punished, absorbing blow after blow, his knees buckling. *Stay off the ground.*

Leo drove the Benz into the parking lot and spotted Benny's Yamaha parked under a lamppost, a bunch of guys fighting over there. Benny was lying on the ground. Two black guys were getting the shit beat out of them by a bunch of dudes in black suits. Janine was in a car, yelling and honking the horn. Leo drove over there, and the fighting stopped. He got out of the car and looked at all the Chinese faces. His mother used to call them *those squinty people*.

"What are you motherfuckers doing here?" he said. "Somebody order too much takeout?"

A skinny guy, bleeding from the mouth, said: "Look, my fren, this none of your business, okay?"

"Who gave you permission to be my friend?" Leo said. "You need to get on the waiting list like everybody else. And could you wake Benny up? We need to have a talk."

The guys who were beating up the black guys came over and re-grouped around Benny.

"You go away, nobody get hurt," Skinny said.

"Me get hurt?" Leo said. "By who? You and them other Jackie Chans? The last time I got hurt was at the Pimp and Ho softball game. I was sliding into second, ran into El Romeo and twisted my ankle. Now maybe you didn't hear me the first time so I'll say it again. I need to talk to Benny." Leo thought about pulling the Sig Sauer, but there were surveillance cameras everywhere. Show a gun near a casino, and you wouldn't get out of jail until you were eating soft foods.

"You say goodbye now or we fuck you up," Skinny said.

"Say goodbye now? Who do you think you're talking to, your ugly, stupid girlfriend? Benny owes me and rule number one is *Pay me my fucking money*." The whole group moved toward him. Leo sighed. "Bad idea, fellas," he said. "Maybe you should go have an egg roll and think this over."

"Okay," Skinny said, "you get beat down now."

Balthazar got out of the car. It was like watching somebody un-fold a card table, his arms and legs coming out one at a time. The Chinese guys tried not to react but couldn't help it, staring like they were trying to make out what species he was. Balthazar lumbered right at them, reaching out with a telescopic arm and clamping a massive hand around Skinny's neck. "Fuck you, eh?"

Skinny's eyes bulged. "Geh him," he croaked.

*　　*　　*

Isaiah picked himself up off the ground, Dodson coming over to help him up. "You okay?" he said.

"Not really," Isaiah said, wincing with every movement.

"Who the fuck is that?" Dodson said.

Some big giant dude was fighting off the Red Poles like King Kong swatting at single-engine airplanes. Another guy who looked like an extra in *Saturday Night Fever* was banging on the Audi's windshield and yelling at Janine.

"Benny," Isaiah said. Benny had risen from the dead. He was mounted on his bike, starting the engine. The fighting stopped.

"Hey, don't let him go!" Skinny said.

"Benny!" Janine shouted, her voice trapped inside the car. "Benny, wait!"

Benny wheelied out of there, the bike pluming blue smoke as it raced across the parking lot, disappearing into the night. Skinny was red-faced and rubbing his neck.

"See what you do?" he said to Balthazar. "You fuck up everything."

Balthazar ignored him. "Too bad, eh?" he said to Leo.

Skinny turned and punched Dumbo. "Why you not watching him? That's your job!"

Security guards were running out of the casino, sirens coming. Everyone broke for their cars.

Isaiah drove away from the Lucky Streak; police cars with their lights flashing whipping past the other way. He was running on pure adrenaline, the onslaught of pain just beginning. To take his mind off it, he thought about Sarita.

He was fourteen when he met her. Marcus was being secretive

but seemed happy about it; taking his phone calls in the bedroom, going out more than usual, freshly shaven, wearing his best clothes and coming home late. A girl no doubt, but that was okay. Like all the rest, she'd last a few weeks, they'd argue, and she'd disappear.

The brothers were having breakfast, Marcus with his coffee and Shredded Wheat, humming "Sugar Pie Honey Bunch" between bites. "Met a girl," he said, trying to keep his smile from turning into a grin.

"Who is it this time?" Isaiah said. "Wait, let me guess. A sales associate at Home Depot? A dog walker you met at the park?"

"Are you finished? She happens to be a student at Long Beach State."

"How did you meet her?"

"Remember Dewey Patterson, the contractor? Doesn't matter. He owns an apartment building over by the college. Gave me a job doing some work in an apartment. There was water damage, and I was putting up new ceiling tiles and replacing some drywall. The tenant was away on some kind of foreign exchange program, but then she came home early. She had nowhere to go, and I had to finish the job. We got to talking, and one thing led to another."

"What does she see in you?" Isaiah said, smirking.

"For your information, women find me very attractive."

"They do? Then why don't they stick around?"

"I'm the one that doesn't stick around, and this girl is different. This girl is special. You'll see."

It worried Isaiah, seeing Marcus so excited. He could already feel his brother's affections splitting in two. The energy that used to be all his was lessening with every phone call and date and fell off alarmingly when Marcus started staying out all night. Marcus tried to remain attentive, doing the things with Isaiah they always did.

Watching movies together, playing basketball at the park, walks around the harbor talking about everything and nothing. But then Marcus started begging off, saying he'd make up for it but he never did. A month went by. Isaiah waited for the breakup, but it never came. He got resentful; this usurper horning in on what was his. He imagined her as an undernourished bookworm with an eating disorder and big thick glasses, nappy hair and a bulky cardigan that went down to her knees. He started sulking and cold-shouldering Marcus, speaking when spoken to, pointedly ignoring him, but he hardly seemed to notice, and if he did he didn't say anything.

It was a rare chilly day when Marcus brought Sarita back to the apartment for the first time. He wanted to get her a jacket before they went out to lunch. Isaiah could only stare as she came in, slender and lovely, kidding around about something, her laugh full and genuine, a face that brought light into the room and cemented Isaiah's feet to the floor. She was wearing jeans, suede ankle boots the color of a lion's mane, a designer field jacket, and a dark scarf that made her look sophisticated.

"Isaiah," Marcus said. "This is Sarita Van."

She smiled, the buffed copper eyes warm as a space heater. "Hello, Isaiah," she said. "I've heard a lot about you."

It took a moment for him to find his voice, and when he did, it came out hoarse, almost like a cough.

"Uh, hi," he said.

"I'm so glad to meet you," she said, like she'd been waiting a long time to say it. She gave him a hug, Isaiah rigid and starting to sweat. He didn't know what to say and paused for so long Sarita's smile began to fade.

Marcus looked at him. "Are you going to say something?" he said.

"I'm, uh, glad to meet you too," Isaiah said.

"I have an idea," Sarita said. "Why don't you come to lunch with us?"

Isaiah scrunched up his face like he'd suddenly lost a hundred IQ points. "Lunch?"

"Yeah, lunch," Marcus said. "You know, when you sit down and eat a sandwich?"

"Stop, Marcus," she said. "Please come, Isaiah. We'd love to have you."

They went to lunch at Thai Tastes and sat in a booth; Marcus and Sarita sitting next to each other. They chatted about her parents and her trip to Cambridge and her plan to go to Stanford Law. They teased each other about something Isaiah didn't understand, but it felt so intimate he had to find something interesting to look at in his pad Thai. When she gave Marcus a spontaneous kiss, the first stab of jealousy pierced Isaiah's heart, went out the other side, turned around and stabbed him again. What was it like to have her look at you like that? To spend time with her, talk to her, listen to her. And Marcus got to have *sex* with her? Oh my God. What was it like to see her with her hair down? To see her *naked?* He could hardly stand to think about it.

"Marcus tells me you're a real scholar," she said.

Isaiah blinked, not a single coherent thought in his head. "What?" he said.

"I'm sorry, Sarita," Marcus said. "My brother seems to have taken too much cold medicine."

"Marcus, *stop,*" she said. She seemed to sense what was going on. "We'll get to know each other soon enough. Won't we, Isaiah?"

Isaiah smiled like he was half in pain. "Yeah," he said. "That'd be great."

Marcus and Sarita were going to the movies. Isaiah said he had too much homework and came back to the apartment. He was worried. This girl *was* special. What if she and Marcus got married? What would happen to him and Marcus? He'd have to see her all the time. How could he stand it?

He imagined Marcus joining the Peace Corps, leaving Sarita alone and lonely. She leaned on Isaiah for support and couldn't help falling in love with him, but there was Marcus to consider so a relationship was out of the question. They stayed away from each other, chaste and pining, but then Marcus called from Haiti and broke up with Sarita, and she immediately rushed over to the apartment and fell into Isaiah's arms, and they were together at last, and then they heard Marcus was marrying a Haitian girl so everything worked out perfectly.

Over the next few months, Sarita came over to the apartment more and more, her presence so disturbing he avoided her. She'd greet him warmly; he'd mumble a hello, make an excuse and leave, sometimes lurking outside the apartment building and looking up at the window, wondering if they were making out or had gone into the bedroom. Then he'd come back later and smell her perfume and see something like fairy dust floating in the air. Marcus would be smiling like he was about to burst out singing *The Sound of Music*.

At breakfast one morning, Marcus was pensive, worried. "Are you okay with Sarita?" he said.

"What?" Isaiah said. "What do you mean?"

"I mean you're always avoiding her. She comes in, and you act like she's got the plague."

"No, no, everything's okay, I like her, I do. I just, you know, want to give you privacy."

"When I need privacy I'll let you know." Marcus put his spoon down. "Look, Isaiah, she's it for me. She's the love of my life. It's important that everything is okay with you two."

"Everything is okay. Really," Isaiah said, but he avoided her anyway.

Marcus and Sarita were inseparable, no question they'd share a future together. Sarita graduated with honors, a bachelor's degree in international relations, and she got a scholarship to Stanford Law. A week before her departure, Marcus was brooding and short-tempered, snapping at Isaiah for little things, getting into a fender bender, throwing a fit when a job got canceled. Mysteriously, college brochures started showing up in the bathroom and on the coffee table. Marcus had long phone conversations with her; out on the balcony, pacing, his voice intense and combative like he was being sent on a suicide mission. The day before Sarita was to leave, Marcus was killed in the hit-and-run. When she heard the news she came to the apartment and banged on the door, but Isaiah was dealing with his own pain and didn't answer. He didn't see or hear from her again until their meeting at the Intercontinental Hotel. He'd thought about her frequently, her image and the sound of her voice becoming almost mythical, a princess in a story told many times and long ago.

Isaiah had a massive purple hematoma on his chest where the Chinese guy had kicked him. He also had a headache, and his cheekbones were swollen; bruises and abrasions pretty much everywhere. They stopped and bought first aid supplies and got a room at the Travel Inn. Dodson put ice packs on Isaiah's worst injuries and antiseptic on the abrasions. It made Isaiah uncomfortable; somebody tending to him that wasn't Marcus. Someone tending him at all. Janine went out and brought back a bottle of Vicodin, not saying where she got it.

"Janine's gotta leave town," Isaiah said. "The question is how."

"Why don't we just put her on a plane or a bus?" Dodson said.

"No, she might be spotted."

"You guys know I'm right here, don't you?" Janine said. She'd taken some Vicodin herself and was pretty relaxed.

"Look at her. She's high," Dodson said. "She ain't fit to drive nowhere."

"Can you drive, Janine?" Isaiah said.

"No problem," she said. "Once, me and Benny drove to Miami on acid."

"We'll check out the motel," Isaiah said. "If the Red Poles aren't watching it she can take her own car."

Dodson persisted. "But where's she gonna go? Another motel?"

"No. If they found the first one, they'll find her again."

"Then send her to LA. She could stay with Sarita."

"Too obvious."

"How 'bout this?" Dodson said, getting testy. "We get her a seat on a satellite and put her ass in orbit."

"Give me your phone," Isaiah said.

"What for?" Janine said.

"So any calls will come to me."

"I'm not gonna give you my phone."

"Oh yes you are."

"That's stupid," Dodson said. "What if she needs to call *us?*"

"We'll get her a burner."

Dodson looked out the window and sulked.

"Are you guys on the same side?" Janine said.

There was nobody watching the motel so she grabbed a few things and threw them in her VW bus. Isaiah took away her phone. She cried but he wouldn't give it back.

"You know, my whole life is in there," she said, Isaiah wondering how that could be. He only made calls and text messages on his.

Dodson gave her directions and called ahead to make the arrangements. "This is crazy," he said as they watched her van putter out of the lot. "She might be in more trouble there than if she stayed here."

"Best we can do," Isaiah said.

"Well, what now?" Dodson said, hoping Isaiah didn't know. Isaiah had gone into a trance again, that look on his face like he was trying to see something faraway and in the dark. *Damn,* Dodson thought. Isaiah was racing ahead of him, thinking about how to find Benny. That fool could be anywhere. Janine had already checked with his friends and relatives, and Benny wouldn't be gambling in a casino anytime soon. He could be camping out in the mountains or driving to Alaska. No, let Isaiah zone out all he wanted to. There was no way in the world to locate that dumb-ass white boy.

"I know how to find Benny," Isaiah said.

Dodson heaved a sigh that was almost a groan. He was in for it now. Isaiah would no doubt mess with him, not telling him the plan until he asked, torturing him, making him draw it out little by little. No, fuck that. If Isaiah could figure it out there was no reason why he couldn't too. *Put your mind to it,* he told himself. *Do one of them brainstorming things and throw out some ideas to yourself. Cogitate, son.*

CHAPTER SIX

PTSD

Seb was wearing his favorite suit. A three-piece glen plaid, this one brown with threads of bone and beige running through it. It was uncomfortable in the hot weather, but appearances were important, especially now. He let himself into his office, turned on the lamp and carefully made a cup of tea. He inspected the desk and chair for cleanliness, then sat down and arranged the Styrofoam cup, a package of English Ovals, his lighter, and an ashtray into a grid, concentrating, like he was moving chess pieces. Gahigi was outside in the dark, keeping watch like he was waiting for Tutsis.

A few minutes later, Gahigi led Manzo and Ramona inside, the Members Only jacket zipped up to his neck. He had his hand in his pocket, something heavy in there. Manzo was carrying a Trader Joe's shopping bag. He seemed weary and exasperated. Ramona looked like she'd been called into the principal's office.

"It's good to see you, Manzo," Seb said. "I hope you are well and prospering."

"It's all good, busy, you know. I could use some help," Manzo said, glancing at Ramona, "but people don't want to change, adapt to the new environment." Ramona sighed and leaned her head to one side. Gahigi gave her an amused look and her eyes fired back a *Fuck you.*

"How's my money?" Manzo said.

"Yes, down to business," Seb said. He dabbed at his phone. "Your last deposit was distributed as we discussed. Eighty percent in large-caps, the rest in an Oppenheimer ETF, which can also serve as ready cash. You should be able to see the buy orders online."

"I have."

"Of course," Seb said. He lit a cigarette and held out the pack to Gahigi. "Cigarette, my friend?" he said, smiling. Gahigi took one grudgingly. "What do we have in our shopping bag?" Seb said.

"Fifty-five grand," Manzo said, putting the bag on the desk.

Ramona was still eye wrestling with Gahigi. "You got some kind of problem?" she said.

"No," Gahigi said like he didn't want ketchup for his fries.

"What's happening with the house on Latimer?" Manzo said.

"The seller says he will take forty percent in cash but no more," Seb said.

"Okay. Make the deal."

"What's the house on Latimer?" Ramona said, meandering over to the Tusker calendar.

"I told you, but you didn't listen. Pay attention, okay? I didn't bring you along to look at calendars."

"Oh yes, a small matter," Seb said. "A hundred dollars was missing from one of the debit cards today."

"I wondered if you were going to bring it up," Manzo said, the two men exchanging a brief smile.

"I can replace it or credit your account, whichever you prefer," Seb said.

"Put it in the account. Do you want to count the money?"

"No, it's not necessary. We are men of honor, are we not?"

"Hey, where'd he go?" Ramona said. Gahigi had slipped away unnoticed.

"Yes, he has a way of disappearing," Seb said. "But you may rest assured, he is around."

When Seb first arrived in Long Beach, he hung out with the shadier elements of the small East African community. Broke and without a lot of options, he started selling weed for a local distributor. He earned enough to rent a small shabby room and keep his clothes clean, but that was all. He needed an occupation. Something to use as a front, a way to be presentable to the straight world. Nothing nine-to-five, of course, and an endeavor where his background in economics and finance would be useful. He saw an ad in the paper. TRAIN TO BE A TAX PREPARER. There were courses and licensing and such, but it was a long and drawn-out process. Instead, Seb studied the tax forms, learned some vocabulary and put up flyers. EXPERT TAX PREPARER. LICENSED AND BONDED. Who would check? There were dozens of practitioners in Long Beach.

There were only a few customers at first. He met them in their homes and reassured them with his fancy suit, his warm smile and lilting educated accent, and his rates that were less than H&R Block. If there was a tax issue Seb didn't understand, he read up on that specific item. Who had time to read all nine thousand pages of the tax code?

More and more customers sought Seb's services. He opened an office and started giving financial advice, patiently teaching his working-class clients about mutual funds, ETFs, and municipal bonds. He advised them on buying property and businesses, negotiating for them, always learning just enough to do the deal. All the while he looked for a way to exploit his position. Ponzi schemes were a shortcut to prison, stealing was hard to hide, and people around here wouldn't call the SEC, they'd bust down your door and beat you with a tire iron.

His break came when Manzo walked into the office. He wanted to buy a house for his mother and needed a cutout, a straw buyer. He didn't want anything in his name or his family's name that the government could take away. Could Seb help him out? Seb used his corporation in Kenya to buy the house. Then he quitclaimed the property over to Manzo, who held on to the deed but didn't file it. When Manzo's mother died, Seb sold the house at a profit and gave the money to Manzo less his commission. The process took a fair bit of trust, and when it was done a new business relationship was born.

They went on to money-laundering. Small amounts were smurfed. For bigger amounts Seb set up shell companies and made investments in them, the money coming back to Manzo as profits. Seb's shell companies sold nonexistent Porsches to other shell companies, the money recorded as sales. The money was wired to a holding company Seb had created in Mauritius, an island nation and tax haven seven hundred miles off the coast of Madagascar. Some cash was held there. The rest was wired back to a shell corporation as foreign investments, which, Seb liked to point out, were tax-exempt. Seb paid retainers to corrupt attorneys that were returned less a processing fee or got the money back as proceeds from nonexistent litigation.

Seb invested the Locos' money in the market and in real estate, the enterprise operating like a mutual fund. Gang members could buy shares, collect dividends, or let them accumulate. In the beginning, they'd demand meetings at all hours, wanting to know where their money was, cashing in shares just to be sure, threatening Seb with death and worse if he was fucking with them. Things settled down after a while, Manzo ordering them to chill, personally guaranteeing their money back if things turned to shit.

Presently, the gang owned four houses, an apartment building, two laundromats, a tire and muffler shop, a check-cashing store, and a Mexican grocery store. There were no loans to service so profit margins were better than most. Manzo encouraged membership, but a lot of the homies were skeptical and didn't like getting their money in such small increments. Owning equities required a belief in the future. Other criminals heard about Seb's services and signed on as clients; corrupt politicians, drug dealers, bookies, burglary and car theft rings. Seb was instinctively thrifty, an outcome of growing up with nothing, and a shrewd investor. He was a wealthy man now.

After the meeting with Manzo, Seb and Gahigi left the office and stopped at an Ethiopian restaurant. Seb thought the food was boring, and he'd eaten enough goat stew to last several lifetimes, but it made Gahigi happy and that was reason enough. Seb was optimistic. He'd made an offer on a house in Brentwood and was waiting to hear back from the broker. The house was just below Sunset, a three-bedroom Tudor, a million two, with an expansive lawn, mature maples and oak trees, the neighborhood crawling with doctors, lawyers, and show business types. It was time he left Long Beach and lived somewhere more suited to his new persona as a legitimate investor who was doing well. He imagined his grand entrance and thought about what he'd say and how he'd say it. The defenses would go up at first, but they'd come down soon enough.

He was a charming man, was he not? The only thing holding him up was how to make that first contact. A delicate matter. It had to appear absolutely random. A contrivance would be seen as dangerous and obsessive. He was close, though. All that was needed was that perfect point of convergence, and everything would fall into place.

Isaiah sat in his easy chair and watched the tape of Seb and Manzo on his MacBook three times. They'd obviously been doing business together for a while now. They were comfortable with each other and trusting to a degree. Isaiah wondered what Manzo and Ramona's relationship was all about. They weren't related and yet Manzo seemed to be mentoring her, and not enthusiastically.

Isaiah needed to think and took Ruffin for a walk. He was a strange dog. An anomaly among guard dogs but especially pits. He had no aggressive instincts, and he wasn't protective. He was also indifferent to people and had an aversion to kids. If he saw a squealing four-year-old tottering toward him he'd quickly leave the area. He shied away from conflict. Isaiah was sitting on the stoop one afternoon, resting after trimming the azalea bushes, Ruffin just waking up from his fifth nap, yawning and stretching, maybe wondering what to do now. Should he go for his sixth or eat some grass and throw up? Two pigeons started squabbling six feet from his nose, one chasing the other round and round. Any other dog would have at least been curious, but Ruffin got up, crossed the yard, and lay down under the lemon tree.

Another time, Isaiah was in his easy chair, reading, the dog lazing on the floor beside him. An argument broke out next door, Mrs. Fielding was yelling at her husband to get his lazy ass up off the damn sofa and do something useful, Mr. Fielding saying why didn't she shut her fat mouth and go make him his supper like a good wife was supposed to. Ruffin listened a moment like he was waiting for them to stop. When they didn't, he got up, sighed wearily, and trotted off into the bedroom. Isaiah wondered what the dog would do if he was ever attacked. The dog was unruly too. He pulled on his leash, obeyed commands sporadically, and if he deigned to like you, he put his paws up on your clean shirt and nearly knocked you over.

Isaiah's friend Harry Haldeman had been the supervisor at the Hurston Animal Shelter for seventeen years and knew everything there was to know about dogs. He'd warned Isaiah about pit bulls, how they were a high-energy, potentially dangerous animal.

"He's not like other dogs, Harry," Isaiah said.

"So I gather," Harry said. "But all you need is one accident with a pit. If they bite you they don't let go."

"I know, Harry," Isaiah said.

"You don't know crap, and just because this dog is a sweetie doesn't mean the other dogs are. You've got to socialize him. Get him out with other dogs while he's still a pup; let him learn what he can and can't do, learn the signals, when to play, when to back off, what a growl means; get him out with people so he'll get used to them and not be so damn goofy."

"Okay, Harry."

"Don't say *Okay, Harry,* just say you'll do it."

"I'll do it."

"And obedience training every day."

"Right."

"Screw *right,* just do it."

"Okay, Harry, okay."

"Don't disappoint me, Isaiah, or I'll put you in the idiot column with the rest of the world."

But the dog lived like Isaiah; isolated, with few outings except their long walks and with little contact with other people or dogs. Pedestrians crossed the street to avoid them, cops looking at them as they drove by. Isaiah didn't like that part, people thinking he was one more gangsta with his big bad dog. Training went by the wayside. As long as the dog was on the leash, he was fine, Isaiah telling himself he was too busy to go through all the exercises.

Isaiah thought about the tape again. The house on Latimer Seb and Manzo were talking about was another way to wash money. Say the seller wants a hundred and fifty thousand for the house. Manzo gives him fifty thousand in cash, and the seller agrees to list the price at a hundred thousand on the closing documents. Just like that, Manzo's money is equity in the house, and even if he sells the house at the original hundred and fifty thousand he still has fifty thousand dollars of sparkling-clean money.

But what kind of gangster buys real estate and Oppenheimer mutual funds? A smart one, Isaiah thought. Gangsters usually spend their money as fast as they make it. On cars, clothes, weed, big-screen TVs, and whatever else. If they have cash they carry it, nothing like flashing a big roll of bills when you're buying a pack of Juicy Fruit. But Manzo was taking the gang's money and investing it. Must have taken some convincing to make that happen.

All that was interesting but not on point, the point being, did any of this have anything to do with Marcus. Maybe. The three thousand dollars in used twenties had to be drug money. Nobody but dealers had cash like that, and the Locos sold cocaine, crack, weed and heroin as well. Were the Locos somehow mixed up in the killing? At least there was a connection there, however vague. Eight years ago, Frankie Montañez was the shot caller. He would have been the one who ordered the hit, but that was all supposition. Isaiah needed real information. He needed to talk to a Loco who was around back then. None of the current membership would talk to him. They'd kick his ass for asking. He was watching the dog pee when it came to him. *Néstor*.

Néstor González had a successful plumbing business, and he owned a house in Wilmore, raising a family there. His wife, Lucy, was always sending Isaiah homemade biscochitos and tamales, grateful to him for saving their daughter, Teresa, from rape and death. Néstor was surprised and pleased to see Isaiah on his front doorstep.

"What's up, Isaiah? Long time no see," he said, clasping hands and bumping shoulders.

"I need to talk, Néstor," Isaiah said.

"Sure, whatever you want. Let's have a beer."

It was hot outside but hotter inside the house. They sat at a picnic bench in the backyard under the shade of a shaggy eucalyptus tree. Néstor's three-year-old daughter, Isabel, was toddling around the swing set waving a stick and singing a song about mice.

"Why does Manzo use Seb to wash his money?" Isaiah said. "The Locos must have their own connections."

"Why are you asking me this?" Néstor said.

"Because you used to be a Loco, and I need to know."

Néstor considered that, took a swallow of beer. "Manzo uses Seb because he knows more about investing than putting money into your cousin's body shop. He's smart too. I think it was his idea to set up trust accounts."

"Trust accounts?"

"Okay, say like you're in the joint, right? Well, you can set up a trust account and transfer money from there into your commissary account for like cigarettes, chips, shit like that. But the thing is, there's no limit on how much you can deposit. So say like somebody on the outside owes you money for something. All he's gotta do is deposit the cash in the trust account. Shit, man, there's some home-boys who got twenty, twenty-five thou in there. And check this out. You can write checks to anybody you want. You could pay for drugs, bribe a guard to get you a cell phone, whatever, and the pigs can't do nothing about it—hey, Isabel, don't eat the stick, what's wrong with you?" Néstor shook his head. "Whatever you do, man, don't have daughters. You gotta watch them every second."

"What about boys?" Isaiah said.

"Who cares what they eat? I used to eat stuff that would put me in the hospital now."

"Tell me about Frankie."

"El Piedra? Shit, man, Frankie was like the Mexican General Patton. If we were going to war he was like, *the man*. All that strategizing stuff, getting intelligence, figuring out the best way to attack. If they had him in Iraq, Fallujah would be part of the US right now."

"What happened to him? I don't see him around anymore."

"Remember the war between the Locos and the Violators?"

"Yeah, I remember."

"He got wounded, and then right after that he got shot during a robbery. That was like the fifth or sixth time. He couldn't take it no more so he stepped down. Everybody thought Manzo would just take over, like a smooth transition, you know? But then some bull-shit happened with Vicente."

"Who's Vicente?"

"That crazy vato with the hairnet. You seen him around. He was like the gang's enforcer, you know? If somebody had to be taken out, he was always down for it. That motherfucker *liked* to kill people. I stayed away from him and so did a lot of people."

"What was his problem?"

"Vicente wanted to be shot caller. He thought he was the most badass so he should get the job, saying shit like Manzo wasn't a real gangsta, like implying he was soft. Manzo heard about it and they got into it."

"They had a fight?"

"Yeah. It was like legendary. You remember in *Lethal Weapon* when Mel Gibson and Mr. Joshua threw down on Danny Glover's front lawn? Same kind of shit. They beat the hell out of each other. You couldn't believe it, man, they were all busted up and bleeding, but at the end of it, Vicente kind of gave up. Manzo had more heart, that's all. After that, Vicente lost all respect. He's kind of an outcast now—hey, Lucy? Isabel won't stop eating the stick."

Lucy was in the kitchen, noisily washing dishes. You could see her through the window screen. "Then take it away from her, estúpido," she said. "If she chokes I'm going to cut you."

Néstor groaned, got up, took the stick away from Isabel and threw it in the bushes. She immediately started bawling. Néstor found another stick and gave it to her. "Here, okay? Don't eat this one." Delighted, Isabel gurgled and went back to singing about mice.

Néstor sat down again and finished his beer. "That fucking Manzo is like revolutionizing gangbanging," he said. "He like changed the whole culture, man. Like he started by getting everybody off the street. Like no more business out in the open. They do everything indoors now. I mean like, at the time that was some radical shit."

"I still see the Locos hanging in front of the Capri," Isaiah said as Néstor came back to the picnic bench.

"Yeah, but to socialize, not to deal," Néstor said. "Nobody's carrying and have you noticed there aren't any drive-bys anymore? At least by the Locos. Manzo decreed that shit is over. No more banging just to bang. You can't even do little stuff no more. No fighting, jacking somebody, stealing a car. Nothing that's bad for business, nothing to bring the cops down here. The Locos are more like a corporation now. Oh, they'll shoot you if you mess with them, but other than that it's all about capitalism."

"What about the other gangs?"

"Manzo made alliances with all our enemies. The Violators, Pimpside Family, Boulevard Mafia, and those fucking Samoans—hey, Lucy? Could you bring us a couple more beers?" Lucy didn't answer and slammed the window shut.

"Did you know Manzo buys real estate?" Néstor said. "Like at first, everybody thought he was crazy. The first one was this fucked-up place on Del Orto, over by the wrecking yard? The plumbing was leaking, wires hanging from the ceiling, rats and roaches everywhere."

"Who was living there?" Isaiah said.

"Mostly junkies and hookers. Manzo gave them a hundred bucks each to move out. There were a few people who didn't want to go, but the homies put guns in their mouths and threw their shit out the windows."

Néstor said Manzo hired neighborhood people like him to repair the building, bring it up to code, and make the apartments nice.

"And not just Latinos," Néstor said. "He was like an equal opportunity employer. He wanted everybody in the hood to be cool with us. Smart, huh?"

There was a green lawn in front of the building now and a playground with a fence around it in the parking lot. Manzo rented the apartments out to families and installed his brother, Jacinto, as the property manager. Jacinto weighed two hundred and sixty pounds and had a spiderweb tattoo that covered his whole face.

"It's like the best apartments in the hood," Néstor said. "Like there's no graffiti, nobody drinking outside, no loud music, no screaming kids running around in the halls—and *nobody's* late with the rent. I know a guy that sold his car so he wouldn't have Jacinto knocking on his door. And if you invested in the building? You get a check every month like clockwork. You know what they call Manzo now? El Empresario."

Isabel had lost interest in the second stick and was sitting in the dirt, picking up little rocks and throwing them down again.

"Hey, Isabel, don't eat the rocks, okay?" Néstor said.

"Do you remember when my brother Marcus was killed in that accident?" Isaiah said.

Néstor wasn't ready for that, his forehead screwing up like he was trying to see something on the end of his nose. "Uh, yeah, maybe. Wasn't that like a long time ago?"

"It wasn't an accident, Néstor. It was a hit."

"No shit? That's messed up, man," Néstor said a little too earnestly. He took a swig off his empty beer bottle. "Say, you want something to eat? We got some leftover cholorio. Lucy's a mean old bitch, but she can cook her ass off."

"Do you know anything about it? The hit?"

"Me? Why would I know something about it?" Néstor was talking fast now. "I was just a soldier back then. You had to be in the upper echelon to know about that stuff."

"I didn't say anything about the gang, Néstor. I just asked you if you knew anything."

Isaiah looked at him a long moment. Néstor groaned. "Come on, Isaiah, I took an oath," he said. "Once a Loco always a Loco. I can't betray my brothers—goddammit, Isabel, get the rock out of your mouth."

Isaiah was sorry he had to break out the hammer. "I saw Teresa the other day," he said. "She was playing soccer at the park. She looks good, all healthy and happy. Is she planning to go to college? You must be very proud of her."

Néstor looked like he was holding four kings and still lost the hand. "This is fucked up, Isaiah. And you're not gonna like what I tell you. Hey, I'm thirsty, I need another beer. Could you do me a favor and take the rock out of her mouth?"

Néstor went in the house, and Isaiah gently pried the rock out of Isabel's mouth. Before she started crying again he picked her up, put her in the swing. She smelled like baby powder and candy. Isaiah swung the little girl back and forth while she squealed and laughed. He liked doing it, wishing he could be that happy playing on a swing.

Néstor came back with two beers and a bowl of peanuts. "Okay, you asked for it," he said, sitting down. "So like Frankie was going to a money drop at Seb's and somebody robbed him. That's when he took the bullet that made him quit. Your brother had something to do with it."

"I don't understand. *My* brother had something to do with a robbery?" Isaiah picked Isabel up, set her down on the picnic table and gave her a peanut. She put it in her mouth but didn't seem to know what it was. "Something to do with it like what?"

"I don't know, I swear, Isaiah, that's all I heard."

"You must know more than that, Néstor."

"Look, I was going with Lucy back then, and she wanted me to quit the gang. I didn't want to, but she was giving me sex all the time so what could I do? I started pulling back, you know? I mean, shit was happening but I wasn't really paying attention."

"Quit messing around, Néstor," Isaiah said, getting angry. *"I need to know."*

"Okay, okay, calm down, man." Néstor took a sip of beer and ate a handful of peanuts. "See, the homies were talking about somebody named Marcus, and then—don't get pissed at me, okay? I heard they put a hit out on him."

"A hit on my brother?"

"That's what I heard."

Isaiah stood up. "Did they? Did the Locos kill my brother?"

"I don't know, I swear to God, I don't know." Néstor put his hands up like Isaiah was aiming a gun at him. "Hey, don't look at me like that. I didn't have nothing to do with anything—could you sit down, man? You're scaring Isabel."

Isaiah thought a moment, then sat. "How do I talk to Frankie?"

"You don't," Néstor said. "He's like a fucking hermit. He don't talk to nobody, he don't even answer the phone. Some of the homies think he's dead—that's a peanut, Isabel, you're supposed to chew it." Isabel grimaced and showed her teeth like a chattering chimpanzee, peanut gravel falling out of her mouth. "Will you look at this?" Néstor said. "She'll eat sticks and rocks but not food."

Isaiah sat in the car, turned on the air-conditioning, and tried to absorb the new information. The Locos had put a hit out on Marcus? Why? Obviously, they thought he was the one that robbed Frankie, but that was impossible. Marcus wouldn't take a dime from Donald

Trump if he was starving to death. The robber had set Marcus up, but who could identify him except Frankie? Maybe he could remember some clue, some detail that would put Isaiah on the scent.

Néstor had given him the address, and he drove over to Frankie's place, a crumbling stucco house not far from Isaiah's. A crinkled blue plastic sheet had been tied over a lowrider spotted with rust, the axles up on cinder blocks. Flyers were stuck in the chain link fence, beer cans and cigarette butts on the patchy lawn. Dos Equis, not Carta Blanca. Newports, not Marlboros. A number was missing from the address, the ghost of a 5 in the empty space. Without drug money rolling in, the gang leader had fallen on hard times. Isaiah thought about that. He drove over to Beaumont's store and made a stop at Raphael's house before returning to Frankie's.

When the door opened, Isaiah almost didn't recognize the man behind the security screen. The proud, fearless ex–shot caller for the Locos, nicknamed the Stone because he was a hardhearted motherfucker, was frail and gaunt and looked like an XXL T-shirt hung on a wire coat hanger. He was wearing an old gray bathrobe, nubs worn off the terry cloth, his shearling slippers flattened with wear and too big for his feet. Frankie was in his thirties, but his hair had gone the color of the bathrobe, white stubble on his concave cheeks, his dark eyes empty like the life behind them had vacated.

"Yeah?" Frankie said. His voice sounded sticky and he smelled like old people and vitamins.

"Frankie, my name's Isaiah," Isaiah said. "I live in the neighborhood, you might have seen me around. They call me IQ."

"IQ, huh?" he said. "I might have heard of you. What do you want?" He took a quick glance at the six-pack of Dos Equis Isaiah had picked up at Beaumont's.

"Something happened a long time ago. I need some information. Manzo said I should talk to you."

"Manzo?" Frankie said, like he was trying to remember who that was.

"He can vouch for me. I can call him right now," Isaiah said, thinking, *Don't make me call him. Please don't make me call him.*

Ever the gangster, Frankie turned belligerent. "Look, I ain't got no time to talk, okay? So fuck off." He started to close the door. Isaiah pulled a bag of weed out of his pocket.

"Trip Diesel," Isaiah said. "Got it from Raphael. Let's have a beer and light one up."

The living room was clean, neat, and crowded. The shelves and end tables covered with knickknacks and souvenirs. Ashtrays from Mazatlán, Acapulco, and Disneyland, a snowball with a grass shack and palm trees in it, glass figurines of horses, cats, and the Little Mermaid. Votive candles. Two teddy bears in matching Santa hats. A white porcelain statue of Jesus, prayer beads hung around his neck. Lots of family photographs.

"Sit anywhere, relax," Frankie said.

Isaiah's eyes were still adjusting to the clutter. There were throw rugs with red and orange Mexican designs on them, embroidered arm covers on the moss-green velvet couch and a serape thrown over the chair back. A Raiders banner hung on the wall next to a carved wooden plaque of the Virgin Mary and a clock with different kinds of birds instead of numbers. Frankie went into the kitchen and opened a beer.

"You want one?" he said.

"No, thanks."

Isaiah sat on the couch and immediately started rolling a joint. Frankie took the chair across from him. He drank half the beer, then put his head back like he was tired of holding it up. He kept his eyes on the weed.

"I wanted to talk to you about something that happened eight years ago," Isaiah said. "After the war with the Violators."

"Eight years ago?" Frankie frowned. "I don't remember too good. Yeah, I got that post-traumatic stress. Doctor said it was because I been up in too much violence, like them soldiers from Iraq. Is that a trip or what? Can't sleep without a whole bunch of drugs. Shit. I can't do nothing without a whole bunch of drugs."

"I'm sorry to hear that." Isaiah carefully sprinkled weed on the rolling paper, making sure it was evenly distributed, expertly rolling the joint back and forth between his thumb and forefinger. Isaiah also knew how to cook cocaine into crack, smoke a bowl of meth, prep a syringe for shooting up heroin, and a dozen other drug addict skills. When your job is chasing criminals it helps to know their recreational habits.

"Yeah, I get these flashbacks," Frankie said. He'd perked up some, like he was remembering that talking felt okay.

"There was this homie named Oscar," he said. "He welched on a deal. Shit like that happens all the time. I coulda just kicked his ass but I fucked him over good. Stabbed him a bunch of times. I didn't have to do it but that was my rep, right? So yesterday—was it yesterday? Yeah, yesterday, I'm watching TV, and out of nowhere I see it happening all over again. You know, blood everywhere, Oscar screaming, his ol' lady screaming. I got all shaky and shit. I had to take some more pills." A profound bewilderment filled the void behind Frankie's eyes like the life he'd lived was beyond his imagining. "That shit is fucked up, man."

Isaiah used the eraser end of a pencil to tamp down the weed spilling out of the end. Raphael had given him a pad of filters; strips of paper the size of a stick of gum. He folded the serrations on one end into an accordion, then rolled it up from the other end to create a tiny tube, the accordion folds inside it. It was unnecessary but it gave him more time.

"That's kinda cool," Frankie said. "I never seen them things before."

A short wide woman in an apron looked in like she expected to see a cop. "Toda está bien, Mom," Frankie said. The woman disappeared. "Yeah, I know some other homies that are messed up like me," he went on. "Miguel, Mateo, Esteban. Everybody thinks they got Lyme disease or something, but it's the stress thing. I guess it's like karma, huh? The bad shit you've done comes back to bite you in the ass. Fuck man, if that's the case I might as well kill myself."

Isaiah inserted the filter into the tamped-down end of the joint. It was as neatly formed as a Newport fresh out of the pack. He gave it to Frankie. He lit up, took a hit and nodded appreciatively. "The draw's a lot smoother," he said. He offered the joint to Isaiah.

"No, thanks, I smoked at Raphael's," Isaiah said. "I get any higher I won't be able to drive." Isaiah waited until Frankie had finished his third hit. "There's something I wanted to ask you about," he said.

"Oh yeah?" Frankie said, blissfully blowing out a cloud of smoke.

"I heard you were making a money drop to Seb and got robbed."

Frankie was still a moment, his mind thumbing through a fat photo album of deadly encounters. "Yeah, I remember," he said. "I was getting out of my car and some motherfucker sticks a gun in my face. He says gimme the money and I tell him I'm not giving you shit and I try to grab the gun, right? So the gun goes off, the bullet goes through my—" Frankie started to lift his shirt but stopped like he couldn't expend the energy. "My gut, the worst place to get shot. Ruptures all kinds of organs and shit. I fucking almost died. I shoulda just gave him the money."

"Do you remember anything about him? The guy that robbed you?"

Frankie stared through the window like the memories were backing out of the driveway. He didn't move or blink for what seemed like a long time, Isaiah wondering if he'd drifted off completely. A goldfinch whistled from the bird clock. Suddenly, Frankie sat up with a lurch and glared like he'd been blindsided. "The fuck you want to know for?" he said.

"Whoever robbed you might have killed my brother, Marcus."

"*Marcus?*" Frankie said.

Isaiah nearly gasped. "You knew him? You knew my brother?"

Realizing the beer and weed were a ruse, Frankie stood up. "Hey, motherfucker. It's time for you to go."

Isaiah couldn't believe it. There was only one reason for Frankie to react like this. *The Locos had killed Marcus.* Isaiah got to his feet, the hate coiling inside him. He stared at this mess of a human being who had ordered his brother's death. "You put out a hit on him, didn't you?"

Frankie was about to reply when the front door swung open. A girl came in. She was sixteen or so, pink streaks in her hair, dressed in a long pink sweatshirt and black tights. The set of her eyes and the shape of her face were just like Frankie's. His sister. A guy came in after her, a hairnet draped over his shiny bald head. Vicente.

"Manzo's always bossing me around, you know?" the girl said. "I'm tired of that shit."

"You should tell him to fuck off, Ramona," Vicente said. "Thinks he's jefe of the whole fucking world." The pair saw Isaiah and Frankie, obviously some shit going down.

121

"Who's this?" she said.

"Some asshole asking too many questions," Frankie said.

"Oh yeah?" Vicente said. "About what?"

"Marcus."

"What Marcus? You mean the guy from—" Vicente was immediately pissed. He pulled a gun from the back of his pants, racked the slide, walked quickly toward Isaiah, his arm held straight out, aiming at Isaiah's heart. "You know what happens to people who stick their noses into Loco business?" he said. "They end up in the fucking grave."

"You come into my *house,* motherfucker?" Ramona said. "You mess with my brother?"

"Wait. Let me explain—" Isaiah said.

Vicente was red-faced, his mouth in a snarl. He was more enraged than Ramona and she lived here. He pressed the barrel into Isaiah's forehead. "We don't need no explanation, cabron." Isaiah thought, *This asshole's actually going to shoot me!*

It was so over-the-top, Frankie said, "Are you crazy, Vicente? You're gonna shoot somebody in my fucking house?"

"Don't be stupid, Vicente," Ramona said. "What's wrong with you?"

"Okay," Vicente said, lowering the gun. "I'll take him someplace else and shoot him."

"No," Frankie said wearily. "*No more shooting.* Just get him out of here."

"You heard him," Ramona said. "Get your ass moving."

Vicente and Ramona ushered Isaiah out of the room. They got to the door and Isaiah opened it. He felt Vicente's Converse All Star in the small of his back, and in the next instant, he was catapulted down the stoop and on to the cement walkway, banging his knees, catching himself with his hands, nearly buckling his wrists.

"Mind your own business, cabron," Vicente said. "I see you in our hood your ass is mine."

"We're gonna fuck you up," Ramona said.

Frankie came and stood in the doorway with the other two, his hand on his sister's shoulder. "It was your brother that robbed me," he said. "Your fucking brother shot me in the gut."

Isaiah hobbled away. Those sons of bitches had murdered Marcus, and sooner or later they'd pay the price. But the idea that his brother had actually stuck a gun in Frankie's face, stole his money, and then shot him was unthinkable. Isaiah couldn't conceive of a scenario where his rigidly moral brother would be desperate enough to do something like that. So if Marcus didn't rob Frankie, who did?

Vicente was a possibility. According to Néstor, Vicente had suffered a bitter loss to Manzo in the leadership battle, and when Manzo assumed leadership he banned old-school banging and started his program to remake the Locos into a conglomerate. That left Vicente the enforcer disrespected and useless. Did Vicente harbor enough resentment to stage the robbery? He was a hothead, eager for violence, just the kind of personality who'd take revenge on the man who passed him over, and why not make a profit at the same time? But where would Vicente have had the opportunity to plant the money and drugs in Marcus's backpack? Did he tail Isaiah and Marcus to the park that day, slip the stuff into the backpack, and then rush to get into the Accord so he could run Marcus over? No, too complicated. If Vicente wanted you dead he'd just shoot you.

Seb was another possibility. The money was being delivered to him so he knew the time and place, and if Marcus had worked for him, he would have had the opportunity to plant the contraband. Okay, so maybe he sent Gahigi to do the robbery. Then he tells Frankie that when Marcus was working for him, the sneaky bastard eavesdropped on their phone calls. It made sense but it didn't. Seb was from a country where a kid could get his leg hacked off with a machete. A bullet in the head or slitting your throat was more in keeping with a survivor of a genocide, and Gahigi's accent would have surely given him away. Not a lot of East Africans running around in the Locos' hood. Then there was the backpack. Seb had plenty of opportunity to plant the contraband, but what would have been the point? He had no reason to give away three thousand dollars in cash and sixteen grams of heroin. Okay, yes, Seb's phone number was in Marcus's work log, but it could have been as innocent as Seb suggested, and he was too smart to risk robbing his biggest client for a onetime score, especially given the consequences if he was caught. It was depressing to think of how many other people might have known about the drop. Other Locos, Seb's criminal clients. But that didn't feel right. Nothing felt right.

Isaiah drove home, thinking about the robber. He'd never experienced hate before. It was like an ulcer growing on a tumor, festering and stinking. Late at night or between dreams and sleep, he'd get into it, bathing in the venom, wallowing in thoughts of revenge. In a way, the hate felt good. You were righteous, godlike, the dispenser of justice. Hate dispelled your fears and forged every disappointment, setback, loss, humiliation, and failure that ever happened to you into one massive steel sledgehammer of rage, poised to obliterate, and for one brief, purifying moment, give you relief.

CHAPTER SEVEN

I Don't Know

Tommy Lau drank Ken's Glenfiddich while he waited in the study. The sooner this whole thing was over the better. Vegas was like standing in the middle of a Chinese New Year's parade, too much going on. Tommy thought about Janine, his favorite niece until this happened. She reminded him of himself. Independent, spirited, going her own way no matter what her father said, and she was the only Chinese girl Tommy had ever seen who didn't put her hand over her mouth when she laughed.

When Ken came to San Francisco on business he'd bring Janine along, and Tommy would take her to lunch in Chinatown. There was no place to park down there so they'd take the cable car and walk the three blocks to Grant. Tommy's favorite restaurant was the China Moon, where everybody knew who and what he was. As soon as he walked in the door there was a chorus of *ni haos,* nervous smiles, and head-nodding. Three waiters would appear to serve the two of them. Tommy always ordered in Chinese without looking at the menu, Janine saying wait, wait, I might want something else, Tommy saying sorry, no cheeseburger today.

Tommy liked to regale her with stories about the triads, always preceding them with a reminder that he'd quit 14K when he was quite young because he was disgusted by their activities. At one lunch he told her about human trafficking.

"The business really boomed under George W.," Tommy said, trying to hide his nostalgia. "The triads should have thrown him a party. He gave an executive order. If you said you were persecuted because of China's one-child-per-couple policy all you had to do was get here and they would let you stay."

"I guess a lot of people wanted to come," Janine said. She was thirteen, fidgety, drumming her chopsticks on the table.

"Thousands of them, most of them from Fujian. They called the US the Golden Mountain. The triads saw it as a business opportunity and they all got involved. There was a huge market for counterfeit passports. 14K charged thirty thousand each."

"Wow, that's a lot," Janine said. She looked at a waiter. "Could I get a fork, please?"

"You get what you pay for," Tommy said. "We—14K—only sold quality. The passports were made in Bangkok by a family of counterfeiters. Four generations. An acquaintance of mine used their passports to get a hundred and fifty-three Chinese on a three-hundred-and-seventy-seat plane going to JFK. Pretty good, huh? And the risk was low. If he got caught smuggling in one hundred and fifty-three people, the maximum sentence was eighteen months, but he didn't get caught and made four and a half million dollars in one day. If he was caught with four and a half million dollars' worth of heroin he would have gotten twenty-seven years."

The waiter brought Janine a fork. "Thank you," she said, beaming.

"After a while, there were not enough counterfeit passports to go around," Tommy said, "and many people could not afford them. They had to come by ship. Horrible conditions. I heard some people were locked in a pigsty with the pigs until their boat arrived at Fuzhou."

"Eeeuw, yuck," Janine said.

Tommy liked to tell her horror stories. Watch her eyes get big like she was going downhill on a roller coaster. It was good for her. Learn there was more to the world than the Red Rock Country Club and private school. "The ship was usually an old freighter," he said. "Built who knows when, everything barely running. It's a miracle they could stay afloat. The people were kept in the hold and they had to stay there for the whole trip. Forty, fifty days. It was dark, filthy, full of diesel fumes. You could suffocate and some people did. Or they starved to death."

Janine made a face. "I'm losing my appetite, Uncle Tommy."

"I remember one ship that foundered near San Francisco Bay," Tommy said. "The authorities found the people ankle-deep in feces, no water, and most of them had a serious illness. Hepatitis B, even cholera. I remember another ship had engine trouble off the coast of North Carolina. All the passengers were infected with a mutant strain of German measles."

"Uncle Tommy, you're making me sick."

"Nowadays, most of the people come in with visas," Tommy said, like another old tradition had gone by the wayside. "Student visas, work visas. You have to pay off the right people, of course. Some fly to Thailand with a forged passport and pay off an official there to let them in. At the airport in Bangkok you can always tell which officials are on the take—their lines are the longest. Then the people fly to Central America and make the rest of the trip overland. The cartels provide the transportation. Very dangerous. Assaults, rape, extortion. In Mexico, the coyotes take over. People die of thirst and heatstroke coming across the desert. On the US side of the border they have beacons set up for people who get lost. The signs are in three languages. English, Spanish, and Chinese."

"Three, huh?" Janine said, still drumming her chopsticks.

"Stop that, Janine," Tommy said.

The waiters brought drunken prawns, steamed pigeon, five-spice short ribs, and a whole fish curved like the wok it was cooked in. Janine reached for a serving spoon.

"No, stop, do this first," Tommy said. He put the ends of his chopsticks in his teacup and poured hot tea over them. "See? You warm your chopsticks this way. Do the same with your bowl. Pour in some tea, swish it around—yes, like that, and then put the tea back in your teacup. The waiter will bring you another."

"All I want to do is eat," Janine said.

"The smugglers' costs are very high," Tommy said, like he was talking about Apple. "The bribes, the documents, travel costs. That's why they charge sixty, seventy, eighty thousand dollars and then another five hundred or so to the coyotes."

"I thought they were poor. How can they afford it?"

"Families and relatives pool their money, send the male with the most potential for success. Once he's here he pays them back. Hard to do if you're a dishwasher or a busboy. They have to live like animals."

Janine was trying to stab a short rib with a fork but couldn't pierce the bone.

"Don't use a fork," Tommy said. "You see how the rib is cut small? Perfect for chopsticks." The ribs were about the size of a nine-volt battery. Tommy picked one up and held it close to his mouth while he sucked and chewed off the meat. "The last bit of rice is always the best, has all the juices." He used the bone like a snow shovel, pushing the rice on his plate into a lump. Then he picked up the plate and used the bone to sweep the rice into his mouth. "You see?" he said. "Chinese way is always best."

"I bet you couldn't do that with a cheeseburger," Janine said.

"For girls wanting to come to America it's quite a different story," Tommy said. "Many are duped into believing they'll get good jobs, but when they get here they are forced to be prostitutes to pay off their debt."

"God, that's awful," Janine said.

"There's even a new market trafficking girls from Vietnam *into* China."

"Why?"

"There is a one-child policy in China, and the enforcement is very strict. Forced abortions, sterilizations. Everyone prefers sons so if they have a daughter, many people get rid of them. Leave them somewhere to die, throw them down wells, turn them upside down in a bucket of water. Millions of them."

"Oh my God. I'm glad I wasn't born there."

"The result is, there aren't enough marriageable women in China, and they have to come from somewhere. The other reason is financial. If a man wishes to get married he is expected to put on an expensive wedding and buy a new house for his bride. Marrying a Vietnamese girl is a big money-saver."

"Do the girls want to be married?"

"Oh no," Tommy said, chuckling. "They are kidnapped. Some of them are as young as you."

"Don't the triad people feel bad about what they're doing?"

Tommy picked up another short rib and chewed off the meat. "No," he said. "They do not."

*   *   *

Tommy was immune to suffering. He'd watched his father eat half a fish while the other half was still alive. He'd been there when Chongqing police inspectors beat a man to death with hammers for illegally selling a watermelon. He'd seen a baby girl stuck in a laundry sack and thrown in the Yangtze River, and he'd been to the Yulin Dog Eating Festival. Ten thousand dogs slaughtered, some of them boiled alive. If that was what you grew up with, cruelty wasn't cruelty, it was a fact of life. Same as the weather or working for a living. Americans liked to say the Chinese were *like that* as if brutality was a cultural characteristic instead of a characteristic of the destitute; people who have to fight for every morsel, drop, bite, breath. People did such things everywhere, not just in the third world. It was happening in America, where poverty wasn't an excuse. Teenagers set fire to homeless people, soldiers raped their subordinates, guards let prisoners out of their cells to kill other prisoners, police shot the mentally ill. It wouldn't be long before they were eating their Labradoodles and throwing their unwanted children off the Bay Bridge. Yes, Americans should mind their own business, clean their own house.

Tommy poured himself another Glenfiddich and went outside to smoke. Tung was there, seated in a patio chair, not an inch of space left between the arms. Tung was built like a refrigerator made from beef and bone, his eyes were dull and implacable, a perpetual scowl on his face like he'd found a cockroach climbing over his toothbrush. Tommy liked to say Tung could kill you with a finger flick.

"Where is he?" Tommy said.

"Upstairs," Tung said. "He won't cause trouble. He's Ken."

*   *   *

Ken agonized and paced, wondering if there was any possible way to get out of this. He heard a car arrive in the driveway. Did the Red Poles have Benny? A part of him wished they did. He had to contact Janine, but Tung had taken away his phone and pulled the landline out of the wall. He could climb out the side window and climb down the drainpipe but he was afraid he'd get stuck or hurt or caught. The idea of being tied up and gagged terrified him.

He heard voices and went to the window overlooking the pool. Tommy was upset, yelling at the kid who needed to eat more. His head was bowed, hands clasped in front of him. He was scuffed up, his mouth swollen, dirt on that ridiculous undertaker's suit.

"How could this happen?" Tommy said. "How could you let him get away? I knew you would fuck it up. I should have sent Tung."

"Some men came," the skinny kid said. "Got in way. We had to fight them."

"What men?"

"Two black guys. Janine was with them."

"So? There were five of you, weren't there?"

"Other man came. Big. Like giant."

"You were attacked by two black men and a giant?"

"Yes, Tommy."

Tommy looked over at Tung as if to say *Do you believe this asshole?* "Who were the black men?" Tommy said.

"Don't know," Skinny said. "We got license plate number. Zhi say he work on it."

"All right," Tommy said, exasperated. "I don't have a choice so unfortunately you're 438."

Triads used number codes for the different ranks that were based on the I Ching. 438 was the Vanguard, like a field general. 489 was Tommy, the Mountain Master. Red Poles were 436. 415 was White

Paper Fan for business and financial. 49s were ordinary soldiers. 425 was a traitor. Like Janine.

"The boyfriend is dangerous," Tommy said. "I want him dead or alive. We'll find out what we need to know from Janine."

Zhi came scurrying out of the house. He was a nervous, intense little man who reminded Ken of a gerbil running around in an exercise wheel.

"What is it?" Tommy said. Zhi said something inaudible. "Blackmail?" Tommy said. "Those fools are blackmailing *us?*"

Ken stepped away from the window. *How could they do it?* he thought. *How could they be so stupid? I'll kill that fucking Benny.* He hoped Janine had enough sense to get out of Vegas. Tommy would send the Dragon Boyz after her, a local gang. There were gangs like them in many of the cities where 14K operated, hired to do the dirty work and keep the Mountain Master safe on his mountain.

Ken couldn't get over it. Janine and Benny blackmailing 14K? What were they thinking? Didn't they know the triads' reach extended to practically every place in the world? He felt like he was going to throw up and went to the bathroom and stood over the bowl. If Janine wasn't dead before she was sure as hell dead now. He could only hope they wouldn't torture her and would kill her fast, two bullets in the back of the head. He wished the same for himself.

Another wave of nausea washed through his gut, and he vomited into the toilet. How could this have happened to him? he wondered. How could this possibly be his life? He came from a good home, he was educated, intelligent, and personable when he wanted to be. He thought back to the beginning.

He was a graduate student in business. It was his final semester and the pressure was unrelenting. His parents had always expected him to be the best in everything he did. It was number one or nothing, and Ken was consistently nothing, even if he was second or third. It was why he quit the university tennis team; the two of them sitting in the stands like disappointed gargoyles, muttering to each other every time he hit an unforced error and leaving altogether if he was losing. His fiancée was a med student who *was* number one in her class and looked like she was studying even when she was riding a bicycle or having sex. Her father had a job waiting for Ken at his hedge fund and had already bought a condo for the couple in Pacific Heights. Everyone said Ken was fortunate, but he didn't feel that way. He felt manipulated and coerced. To let off steam, he'd go gambling at one of Tommy Lau's places in Chinatown. A basement, a back room, or a storefront with no signage and the blinds drawn, the entrance in the back. There were mismatched chairs around folding tables, a pall of cigarette smoke under the humming fluorescents. The clientele were mostly old men; liver-spotted, jowly, receding hairlines, senior citizen pants, and cheap sneakers. Lots of noise. Mah jong tiles clacking, cards shuffling, coins clinking at the fan-tan tables, the incessant choppy chatter of spoken Chinese.

Though he'd be loath to admit it, Ken believed, like his parents, grandparents, and ancestors before him, that luck, destiny, and chance controlled your life more than you did. Ken put his faith in auspicious objects and numbers and fêng shui. These things could be manipulated, maybe bending your fate a little, giving luck a better chance to find you.

Ken played pai gow and fan-tan but mah jong was his favorite. A draw-and-discard game like gin rummy, it required skill and calculation as well as an element of luck. While Ken had the former in spades, he had very little of the latter. As his finals approached and the pressure had him at the breaking point, he played obsessively, running up an enormous tab, thousands of dollars. Tommy didn't seem too concerned about it, extending Ken credit whenever he asked, Ken telling himself he could pay it back when he was working at the hedge fund. And then one day, for no apparent reason, his credit was cut off, and a Chinese man who must have been a tree stump in his previous life asked him to leave.

The next day, the tree stump man showed up at Ken's door and introduced himself as a friend of Tommy's. He asked if Ken could pay the vig on his debt and Ken said no. The man punched him in the stomach and while he writhed around on the floor struggling to catch his breath, the man smashed every single object in the apartment including the TV and Ken's laptop. When Ken asked if he could keep his bicycle so he could get to class, the man stomped it into scrap metal and threw it off the balcony.

"Tommy want to see you," the man said. "Tomorrow, one-thirty, China Moon."

When Ken entered the restaurant, Tommy was already seated and working his way through a lobster with black bean sauce. Tung was at a separate table, a napkin tucked into his shirt, his square jaws crunching whole shrimp with their shells on, the carcass of an entire duck in front of him.

"Please, sit down," Tommy said. "Would you like something to eat?"

"No, thank you," Ken said. "I'm fine."

"Nonsense," Tommy said. "Eat."

Ken picked at a plate of char siu while Tommy asked him questions about his studies. What classes did he take, what were his grades like, what was he planning to do.

"Do you know accounting?" Tommy said.

"Some," Ken said. "But I'm not an accountant. Why do you ask?"

"It's rude to ask a direct question. Don't you know that?"

"But you just asked me a question."

"I am your elder."

They'd finished the meal and were drinking their tea when Tommy said: "Let us talk about your debt."

"I'll pay you back, Tommy," Ken said. "As soon as I'm working. I promise."

"The vig is twenty percent a week."

"A *week?* But that's..."

"Ten thousand percent a year," Tommy said. "Give or take."

"I'll never be able to pay that off."

"No, you won't. A shame, really. What will you do when your family finds out, not to mention your future in-laws? Did I tell you I know your fiancée's father? A very principled man, very conservative. They will be disgraced, you know. They will never forgive you and neither will your parents."

"Please, Tommy," Ken said. "Tell me what you want me to do."

Tommy said he had a growing operation in Las Vegas and he needed someone to run it; someone smart and trustworthy who knew numbers and could manage a business. He was vague about what kind of business it was. "You can graduate or not, up to you," Tommy said.

"And my parents?"

"Yes, they will be shocked at first but when they see how much money you are making they will come around."

"Can I have time to think about it?"

"Certainly. You have until we finish the meal. Would you like something else?"

"Yeah, I guess I would."

Somewhere between the char siu and the steamed frog legs on lotus leaf, Ken realized his parents would be disappointed with him no matter what he did or how hard he tried. As for his fiancée—well, if he never saw her rigorous, goal-oriented face again that was okay with him. And working at a hedge fund? He couldn't think of anything he wanted to do less. Actually, it would be something of a relief, escaping a life he'd never asked for or wanted.

So Ken went to Vegas and worked for Tommy. He was repelled at first, almost quitting any number of times, but he was still in debt and there was nothing for him in San Francisco. Despite what Tommy had said, he was disowned, disgraced, and blacklisted by his family, his former future in-laws, and seemingly the whole legit Chinese community. The work itself wasn't so bad. He was on the business and financial end, Liko did the work on the ground. As the years rolled by, Tommy didn't talk about the debt anymore but it was implicit that Ken could never quit. He had the affair with Angela, and Sarita entered his life. Then he married a stewardess from Hong Kong, and Janine was born. The stewardess missed her family and went back home to Hong Kong, thank God, and now he was a very wealthy pimp under a death sentence, locked in his own bedroom, afraid for his daughter's life but more afraid of climbing down a drainpipe.

Ken wiped the vomit off his mouth, flushed the toilet, and went back into the bedroom. *Tommy,* he thought. Fucking Tommy. That greedy, evil old man, arrogant and contemptuous, enslaving him all these years. He didn't think enough of Ken to tie him up or search the room and find the gun he kept in the bedside table. After all, Ken was a weakling, a coward, no one to be concerned about. Ken was overcome with hurt and humiliation. Why should he go down without a fight? Why shouldn't Tommy pay a price? Why should that asshole get to live while his daughter died?

"Fucking old man," Ken said. He went to the bedside table, yanked open the drawer, and found the Glock. They would come for him sooner or later; use him as bait to bring in Janine. No, he wouldn't let that happen. Ken sat on the bed, taking deep breaths, rehearsing what he would do and what he would say, mouthing the words and pointing the gun at the mirror. He heard footsteps coming down the hall and stood up, facing the door. His hand was sweaty and he wiped it off on his shirt. "Here we go," he whispered.

Tung came into the bedroom first, Tommy right behind him. Ken aimed the gun at them. "Stop right there!" he shouted. They stopped but didn't look afraid. "Okay, turn around and put your hands up."

They did neither.

"So," Tommy said, "you've grown a pair, is that it?"

Ken's face was terrified and trembling. "Turn around, I said!" Tommy was expressionless. Tung looked puzzled, like the cockroach had started to sing. "I'm not kidding!" Ken said. He knew he sounded pathetic. *Don't back down, don't back down like you have your whole life!*

"Are you going to shoot me, Ken?" Tommy said mildly.

"Fuck you, Tommy," Ken said, his voice losing volume, a note of mewling creeping in. Tung was coming toward him. "Stay back," Ken said. "Stay back, Tung!" But Tung kept coming. *Shoot him, Ken! Shoot him!* "I'll shoot, Tung, don't come any closer!" But he'd waited too long and knew it. Tung slapped the gun aside and hit him with what felt like a flying anvil, bouncing him off the wall and into another flying anvil. Tung kept at it, punch after punch, crunching and crushing, Tommy watching, the crocodile smiling as it dragged the kicking body underwater.

*　　*　　*

Despite his injuries, Isaiah had insisted on driving. They were heading west on Charleston Boulevard. He hadn't told Dodson his plan, a game they played when they were the Battering Ram Bandits, a way to stay in control. Dodson was pretending he didn't care about where they were going and was busy texting Cherise. That was fine with Isaiah. He could hold out forever, Dodson would break down sooner or later. He wanted to call Sarita and it took him a few minutes to work up his nerve. He hit the speed dial.

"Hello?" she said.

"It's Isaiah," he said.

"What's happening? Is Janine okay?"

"I sent her to LA. She's not safe here."

"Not safe? Well, she can stay with me."

"No, you might be watched."

"You're scaring me, Isaiah."

"Everything will be okay."

The fear in her voice was thrilling but he didn't know why.

"What about my dad?" she said.

"He's probably all right for now. They'll use him to find Janine." He hesitated a moment. "He works for the triad." He was talking in short, clipped sentences like a cop. He hadn't planned it that way but he liked it. He thought he sounded more in charge this way.

"I don't know what to say," Sarita said. "I'm so disappointed and angry at him I—excuse me a moment, Isaiah." He heard her talking to someone. He couldn't make out the words but it sounded like she was explaining and then arguing. She got back on the line. "Sorry about that," she said. "What should I do, Isaiah?"

"Nothing. Just be careful. "Keep your doors locked. If you go out have someone with you."

"Is it really that dire?"

"Precaution."

"What will you do now?" she said.

"Find your dad, find Benny."

"How?"

"It's better you don't know," he said. There was no reason why she *couldn't* know but that sounded resolute, like he was on top of it.

"Isaiah, I feel so bad about this. You're not in danger, are you?"

"I'll be fine."

"Thank you, Isaiah. Thank you so much. You'll call me, won't you?"

"I will," he said. He didn't say goodbye and ended the call. *Perfect. At least you didn't sound like a bumbling idiot.*

Dodson looked up from his phone. "That's who you into, Marcus's ex? She's a little old for you, ain't she?"

"What? No. I'm just helping her out."

"Who you think you talking to? I know the fever when I see it."

"I don't have any fever."

"Really? Then why was you talking like you was on *CSI*? I almost got out the car and put my hands up."

"I was just telling her what's going on."

"You told her just enough so she'd worry about you, and I like how you said *I'll be fine* like you knew some shit was coming down but you was ready for it. I couldn't have done better myself."

"Could we change the subject, please?"

"Let me give you some advice, son. Don't never front with a woman. Be who you are, and if you ain't sure, be not sure. They way ahead of us anyway. Don't matter what you do, they'll find out your true shit sooner or later."

139

Isaiah drove on. The Vicodin made him dreamy and he imagined himself with Sarita; how they'd live in one of those Century City condos with the cool furniture and hardwood floors and marble countertops and stainless steel appliances and a sparkling view of the city that went all the way to the ocean. He imagined Sarita returning home from a day at the Justice Center and then coming into his study, where he was sitting at a desk made from some kind of Scandinavian wood working on a case about industrial espionage. Then they'd curl up together on a leather sofa the color of heavy cream and have a glass of wine, a subject he'd have to brush up on, and talk about what she was doing and how she was helping people and what he was doing and the problems he was having with the case. Then they'd have dinner; get some steaks from Gelson's where a rib eye was thirty-two dollars a pound, maybe cook it up for her with some fresh vegetables, make her laugh while she sat at the counter and ate some snacky things from Italy or Spain and had another glass of wine. Then they'd go have a drink with their friends at a fancy bar somewhere and talk about global warming or the humanitarian crises in Europe or North Korea exploding another nuclear bomb. Then they'd go home and have crazy sex and when they woke up in the morning she'd serve him espresso and a warm croissant and on Sundays they'd have brunch, whatever that was, and when they came home they'd have crazy sex again and—

"Hey," Dodson said. "Wake up. If you're going to the Red Rock Country Club you missed the turn."

Isaiah looked at him. How did Dodson know they were going there? He hadn't told him the plan yet.

"The triad can cover Vegas better than we can so why not let them do all the work?" Dodson said. "Didn't think I figured that out, did you?"

"Wasn't that hard to do," Isaiah said, without much behind it. He made a U-turn.

"You know what I'm thinking?" Dodson said. "What if the skinny dude ain't the one that finds Benny?"

"What?" Isaiah said.

"What if the skinny dude don't find Benny and somebody else does? What do we do then?"

"He looked to be in charge," Isaiah said like it was obvious. "If something happens he'll know one way or the other."

"Okay, suppose them Red Poles catch Benny. Then what we gonna do? Strong-arm 'em? I ain't got a strap, do you?"

Isaiah thought a moment. Dodson was putting everything on him like he always did. Why should that be?

"Well?" Dodson said.

"I don't know," Isaiah said.

Dodson looked at him sharply. "*I don't know?*" he said. "Is that what you said? *I don't know?*"

"I don't know. What's wrong with that?"

"Long as I've known you I never heard you say that."

"Well, I'm saying it now, and so what if I don't know something? If something needs to be known why don't *you* know it?"

"But you *always* know," Dodson said, sounding a little alarmed.

"And you always don't. Why is that? You're always complaining about my freakishly large brain. Well, how about we use yours for a change, or is that too much to ask? Now, I brought you along to help so why don't you, instead of sitting there complaining like a bitch?"

Dodson had no comeback, Isaiah enjoying an inward smile. *Challenge me at your own risk, son.*

They waited near the entrance to the Red Rock Country Club for an hour before the black BMW with turbine wheels came out of the gate, the skinny guy and Dumbo in the front seat.

"There's our boy," Dodson said.

Isaiah followed him, staying out of the BMW's mirrors, wondering what they'd do if they caught up to Benny. Separating him from the Red Poles wouldn't be easy. They followed the BMW to a public park. About thirty young Chinese guys were milling around on a floodlit basketball court. Baggy jeans, white T-shirts, and gold chains were apparently mandatory. Could have been a tattoo convention. Their gleaming dubbed-out, tricked-out cars were parked on the grass. A few bony girls were with them. Dark glasses, painted-on jeans, and heels. They looked like assassins in a James Bond movie.

Isaiah parked.

"Damn," Dodson said. "Are all them dudes in the triad?"

"Affiliated. They're a gang, the Dragon Boyz."

"How do you know?"

"The graffiti on the sidewalk, the stop sign, and the bus bench right outside your window."

"Fuck you, Isaiah."

Skinny got out of the BMW, the other Red Poles remaining inside, the engine running, windows down. No doubt there was an arsenal in there, the safeties clicked off. Skinny went over to a guy who was probably the gang's shot caller. Same uniform, heavy-lidded and sullen, arms folded across his chest. Isaiah wondered what made him so special. Maybe he had a good personality. Behind him was a massive Hummer the color of French's mustard, his three-man personal crew leaning on it.

Skinny talked to the shot caller in Chinese, demanding, even threatening, but he could have been elevator music for all the reaction he got, the guy smoking and looking bored. At one point he yawned. When Skinny finished talking, the guy took a last drag off his cigarette and flipped the butt to the ground, orange sparks landing on Skinny's pointy shoes. Then he exhaled wearily, his cheeks puffing out like it was time to mow the lawn. He said something and the whole group got into their cars. They must be loving this part, Isaiah thought, starting their engines together like a scene from *Fast & Furious,* thirty throaty roars blasting the night apart with power and menace, tires fishtailing, leaving squiggle marks on the grass as they took off in different directions, Skinny left in a cloud of exhaust.

"They'll post up around town," Isaiah said. "When somebody in their network spots Benny they'll have people close by."

"You don't think I know that?" Dodson said.

Fed up with the arguments, Isaiah said, "What's your problem, Dodson?"

"I don't have no problem. I'm just letting you know it's not like the old days. I got my own thinking cap. You ain't the only one that can work shit out."

"And you think you're in *my* league?" Isaiah said. "Be serious."

"No, I'm not in your league—not yet."

"Not yet? You're not even close and you never will be."

"Yeah, well, I just might surprise you. Besides, why the fuck did you bring me here if I'm so damn useless?"

Isaiah had no answer to that. He *did* tell Dodson to be more helpful, but he hadn't anticipated it would feel like an intrusion, like someone was trespassing on his domain. He'd worked long and hard to be *IQ,* and he wasn't sharing that title with anybody.

They followed the Red Poles to a Chinese restaurant, where they ate dumplings and Skinny took calls. Dodson kept sending Benny texts on Janine's phone. Red Poles are after you. Leave Vegas. You're in danger. Leave Vegas. Leave Vegas. Whole town out looking for you. Leave Vegas. Forty-five minutes later, Skinny got a call that made him stand up. He said something to the others and threw some bills on the table and the group ran out to the BMW.

"They found him," Isaiah said. He looked at Dodson. "I know you know that, okay?"

They followed the BMW to a commercial street in Summerlin, a nondescript suburb south of Vegas. There was a blue-and-white neon sign over a shop that said RAY'S YAMAHA, a tire store on one side, a towing yard on the other. At the near end of the block, some of the Dragon Boyz were arriving in a parking lot. The Red Pole who had kicked Isaiah in the chest was talking on his phone like a commando calling in air support. He said something to the crew and a few of them broke off and headed for an alley.

"They're going around to the back," Isaiah and Dodson said at the same time.

There was light traffic. Isaiah got behind a delivery truck and drove past the gangsters, parking across the street from Ray's. A scissor-type security gate extended over the front window, a roll-up garage door next to it. At the far end of the block, the BMW, the Hummer, and a white Denali were parked; Skinny, the shot caller, and a few other Dragon Boyz were down there. If Benny managed to run, he'd be trapped no matter which way he went.

"Are you texting Benny?" Isaiah said.

"No, I'm playing Angry Birds," Dodson said. Red Poles know you're at Ray's. Go now. Go now.

Benny texted back, thinking it was Janine. What are you doing here? How did you find me?

Go. Get out. Red Poles surrounding you. Dodson stopped texting. The Red Pole and three gangsters were jogging up the block toward the Yamaha store. They had tools. A fire axe, a sledgehammer, a bolt cutter.

"Shit, it's game over now," Dodson said. "What do we do?"

"I don't know."

"I liked you better before."

The gangsters gathered at the security gate, the guy with the bolt cutter cutting off the padlock. As the Red Pole yanked the gate open, they heard the whine of an electric motor and a chain clanking. The garage door was starting to rise. You could hear an engine grumbling at idle, revving now, getting louder.

"He coming out!" the Red Pole shouted. "Geh him! Geh him!" The gangsters dropped their tools and went for their guns. The door was four feet off the ground, the gangsters ready to rush in, when Benny's bike exploded out. Benny was wearing leathers, lying flat over the gas tank, his head behind the handlebars, the top of his helmet grazing the underside of the door. As soon as he hit the street, he made a hard turn, planting a foot on the pavement, the rear wheel skittering out wide. The gangsters got off some shots but missed, a moving target hard to hit with a handgun. Benny straightened the bike up, cranked the gas, and rocketed down the block, the gangsters running out in the street to shoot. They fired off a salvo but Skinny and his crew were at the far end of the block, directly in the line of fire. Some dived to the pavement, others scattered, bullets zinging past them.

"The fuck you doing?" Skinny screamed. Benny kept accelerating, charging directly at them. They started shooting. "Kill him! Kill him!"

"Benny's gonna get his ass shot to pieces," Dodson said.

Benny swerved sharply, standing on the pegs and bumping over the curb, getting low again as he sped down the sidewalk, the parked cars shielding him from the gunshots, the barrage blowing out windows, puncturing tires, and shattering storefronts. In seconds he was by them and gone. "What you waiting for?" Skinny screamed as he ran for the BMW. "Geh him!"

The speed limit on Wyatt Avenue was forty-five miles per hour, the Audi going seventy, following the Denali, the Hummer, and the BMW, Benny too far in front to see. It hurt to work the gears and pedals, but Isaiah tried to ignore it. The problem was the Vicodin. He had to shake it off. Fortunately, Wyatt was a long straightaway, apartment buildings and businesses were on either side, the only obstacles were other cars. It was dangerous weaving around them when you were going that fast but the Audi's sports suspension was made for it, no body lean, stuck to the road like a slot car.

"Why is Benny going straight?" Dodson said. "Why doesn't he turn, try to shake them loose?"

"He must have something in mind," Isaiah said, blinking hard as he braked, swerving around a Volvo station wagon and a FedEx truck, downshifting, the pain in his chest throbbing as he rocketed off again. "Check your GPS. See what's ahead."

Dodson got out his phone. "There's a big turn up there. Nothing after that but desert."

"That's it," Isaiah said. "He's going to go off-road and disappear. No way to catch him out there."

Isaiah changed lanes and got a quick look at Benny. He was well ahead, but the BMW was powerful and closing the distance. "They're gonna run him off the road," he said. He downshifted and stomped on the gas, the big V8 WAAAAHing, the sound so loud

Isaiah had to shout over it. "The BMW is faster than the bike. We've got to get in front of it, slow it down." The Denali was at the rear of the pack. Isaiah caught up and passed it, the gangsters' eyes popping as they surged past.

"Bye-bye, muthafuckas," Dodson said, giving them a little wave.

The Audi's speed hit eighty-five as it approached the Hummer. The driver started zigzagging back and forth, trying to block his path.

"He's a fool," Isaiah said. "He's gonna tip over."

The driver zigged a little too sharply, the three-ton vehicle rocking back and forth, skidding sideways, nearly rolling over as it slammed into a curb.

Isaiah could see Benny clearly now. He had his head tucked low, elbows out, going full throttle, the engine screaming. Motocross bikes were built for mobility on dirt, not top speed, and Benny had topped out, the BMW a few car lengths behind him. Both braked hard to get around a traffic island and Isaiah caught up, all three getting back on the straightaway, Benny with a slight lead. Just ahead of them, a minivan blocked the right lane, a tiny Fiat blocked the left. Benny shot right between them but the BMW had to slow down, Skinny leaning on the horn, riding the minivan's bumper, the kids in the backseat making faces and giving him the finger. Isaiah pulled up behind the Fiat and even with the BMW. The Fiat couldn't move over and neither could the minivan, one had to pass the other. With aching slowness the Fiat sped up, the Audi a foot behind it, the driver's terrified eyes in the mirror.

"Let's go! Let's go!" Dodson shouted. The Audi edged ahead of the BMW by half a length. "Isaiah?" Dodson said.

"I see him."

Dumbo had an Uzi, somebody in the backseat handing him a clip.

"Hurry up, hurry your ass up!" Dodson shouted at the Fiat; its engine straining like a mosquito in a headwind, the tiny car passing the minivan an inch at a time. "Oh shit," Dodson said. The window of the BMW was coming down, the barrel of the Uzi sticking out. "HURRY UP! HURRY THE FUCK UP!" he screamed at the Fiat. Dumbo was leaning out of the window, trying to get an angle. "HURRY UP, MUTHAFUCKA!" Isaiah was about to slam on the brakes and let the BMW go by but the Fiat moved forward just enough for the Audi to slip in front of the minivan. Isaiah downshifted, winced at the pain, and blasted off after Benny.

"Thank you Jesus!" Dodson yelled.

The BMW came around the minivan and in moments caught up with the Audi. Dumbo had the gun stuck out of the window, his arm in a semicircle. He started shooting but it was harder than it looked in the movies. If your aim is off even slightly with a short-barreled gun, the bullet strays wider the closer it gets to your bull's-eye. Dumbo's rounds were hitting parked cars, buildings, and streetlamps. Skinny screamed at him and yanked him back in the car.

Benny was a quarter mile ahead now, approaching the big turn. Beyond it the fences and guardrails stopped, and there was nothing but wide-open desert on either side of the road.

"He's gonna make it," Dodson said.

"He's going too fast," Isaiah said. "His tires won't hold."

"Don't jinx the boy!"

"Slow down, Benny, slow down!"

Benny slowed but it didn't seem nearly enough. He leaned over so steeply he could almost reach down and touch the pavement.

"Go, Benny, go!" Dodson shouted. Benny made it through the turn, and you could almost hear him yell *Yahoo*. "What'd I tell you?" Dodson said, whacking Isaiah with the back of his hand. "That's my boy—*oh shit!*" Benny hit a patch of gravel, the bike skewing sideways. He tried to correct it, turning into the slide, but the knobby tires let go, the bike landing on its side. Benny slid off and tumbled into the brush, the bike whirlybirding across the asphalt in a shower of sparks, going another hundred feet before it stopped.

Isaiah sped past Benny and then the bike, its wheels still spinning. "We can't stop," he said.

"You don't think I know that?" Dodson said. "That muthafucka had an Uzi."

"Dammit," Isaiah said. He pulled over, and they looked back. The BMW had stopped, the guys running into the brush where Benny had disappeared. Dumbo saw them and Isaiah took off again.

"What do you think?" Dodson said. "Fifty-fifty that Benny's still alive?"

"Yeah," Isaiah said. "Fifty-fifty." The whole mission was falling apart. To console himself, he said, "Well, at least Janine is safe."

"Where is she now?" Tommy said.

"She's still on I-15," Zhi said, his MacBook set up on Ken's desk. "She should be in LA in three hours." Zhi was smart, having the guys attach a GPS tracker to Janine's bus. Zhi said that sooner or later everybody comes back for their car.

"What type of tracker?" Tommy said.

"It's the same one the FBI uses. Motion-activated, battery lasts a hundred hours, operates up to a hundred and forty degrees Fahrenheit, military standards for shock and vibration, four-G network. We'll know where she is within three meters."

Tommy didn't understand half the things Zhi said but asking a question made it sound like he did. "What about the black guys?" he said.

"We have nothing on one of them," Zhi said. "The other is Isaiah Quin-ta-bee. He's some sort of neighborhood detective. Quite well known and by all reports very good at it. They call him IQ."

"Who works for us in LA?" Tommy said.

"The Chink Mob. They're reliable. Hard to keep them in check, though."

"Once Janine reaches her destination they are to approach her and bring her back, by force if necessary. Tell them to do this quietly. Small team, in and out, no police."

"Yes, Tommy."

"And keep digging on this IQ and find out about his friend. I want to know more about them."

"Yes, Tommy."

Ken woke up, his eyes crusted shut. Opening them was like peeling off a Velcro strip. Everything hurt. Every movement made him wince and groan. He was in a windowless room lit like night vision through a red lens, the air sluggish with the smells of disinfectant, garlic, and baby oil. A folded towel was on the massage table, plucked minor notes playing through a scratchy speaker.

When Ken first started working for Tommy he'd done a quick walk-through at a brothel near the Rose Parkway, not really looking around, afraid he'd remember something that would keep him up nights. Since then, he hadn't visited a single facility. If there was trouble, he handled it on the phone. He didn't know what any of the mama-sans looked like and he'd never had a conversation with one of the girls. He couldn't imagine coming in here, taking off his clothes, and lying naked on a table where hundreds of men had grunted and ejaculated. He thought if he had a UV light the whole room would glow. He wondered how this was even sex. Some anonymous girl unlovingly rubbing your dick until you got off and leaving you using the towel to wipe the cum off your stomach. What did you think afterward? *Ooowee, that was hot!* What the girl thought was too awful to contemplate.

Ken heard a groan. There was somebody else in the room. "Benny?" he said.

"Who's that?" Benny said. Ken could barely make him out, curled up against the far wall, knees pulled up to his chest.

"It's Ken Van."

A silence like Benny had stopped breathing. "What are you doing here, Mr. Van?" he said at last.

"What do you think I'm doing here, you fucking idiot?"

"I'm sorry. I'm so sorry."

"Good for you." Ken wanted to crawl over there and kick him to death.

"Is Janine okay?" Benny said.

"I don't know, Benny," Ken said. "I don't know how she is. She could be in the next room getting the shit beat out of her. She could be dead."

"Oh God," Benny said. "Don't say that."

"How could you do this, Benny? How could you be so stupid?"

"I don't know," Benny said, tears in his voice.

"If my daughter is hurt in any way, I'll kill you, Benny."

"That's okay. You won't have to."

There was an argument out in the hall. Ken recognized the skinny guy's voice. He was arguing with the mama-san. She wanted the room back, she was running a business here. A minute later,

Skinny returned with a couple of other guys and they hauled Ken and Benny into the back room.

Three girls were sitting on an old car seat. They were all wearing cheap shorts, tank tops, and mules. No makeup, blunt haircuts, and bad acne; not used to eating a diet of fast food and Coca-Cola. They were watching TV. A Chinese boy band with their caps on sideways were doing a herky-jerky dance. The girls looked like they were waiting for a train that wouldn't arrive until tomorrow. They could have been in the third world someplace, the room painted that bilious green you only see in prisons and aging hospitals. There were a pile of dirty dishes on the sink and a microwave with greasy fingerprints all over it. Hunks of drywall were torn out of the walls, no covers on the harsh fluorescents. The one window was painted over, chicken wire inside the glass. Bras and panties hung on wire racks, aluminum pie pans full of cigarette butts were scattered around.

The girls didn't say a word when Ken and Benny were shoved down on the floor. The skinny guy and his buddies resumed playing cards on a rickety Formica table, smoking, drinking Tsingtaos, talking in Cantonese, their guns in front of them. Above them on wall brackets were two worn-out surveillance monitors. One showed the reception area, the mama-san at the desk. The other showed the hallway leading to where they were now.

The skinny guy glanced at his watch and then looked at Ken and Benny. "Not long for you," he said, smiling. "Everything over pretty soon."

"You're letting us go?" Benny said.

The Red Poles laughed. "Yeah," Skinny said. "We let you go."

Benny looked at Ken like that was cause to be hopeful.

"How did you get to be so fucking stupid?" Ken said.

CHAPTER EIGHT

Ascension

The morning after the confrontation at Frankie's, Isaiah went out for an espresso and a Danish at the Coffee Cup. He was still grinding on the identity of the robber. He'd come up with nothing and was burning himself out. He needed a break. He hadn't been to the gym in a while. It'd be good to scrape the mold off his reflexes, refresh the memories his muscles had forgotten. But take it easy, just work up a sweat.

If Ari was glad to see him he didn't let on. "Where have you been, Isaiah?" he said. "Did you gain some weight? Yes, definitely. Four pounds at least." It was Ari's gym. He was thick like a pillar and made from the same concrete, a wary unyielding look in his eyes, his silver crew cut matching the tangle of hair on his chest, his fists like cannonballs studded with knuckles. Ari had fought in the first and second Intifadas and the war in Lebanon. He'd emigrated to the US seeking peace and safety but never seemed to be convinced that he'd found either.

"Go change," Ari said. "Let's see how you are doing."

Isaiah changed his clothes in the locker room, remembering his first lesson in Krav Maga. He was nineteen. He was walking back to his apartment from the hospital after seeing Flaco. He dreaded the idea of going back to the depressing one-room hovel that was dingy no matter how many times he cleaned and scrubbed. He was wondering what he could do to fill the hours and passed a place he'd been by numerous times. KRAV MAGA SELF-DEFENSE TRAINING.

He went in, stood at the edge of the mat, and watched other people work out. They were doing exercises and sparring but the movements were different from the martial arts he'd seen in the movies. No posturing or grace, everything quick and brutal.

Ari approached him. "You want to learn Krav Maga?" he said.

"I don't know what it is," Isaiah said.

There were old black-and-white photos on the wall, many of a balding man with a mustache and soldier's fatigues. He was a rugged-looking brawler. A Sean Connery type. He was demonstrating moves to other soldiers. Choking one out, taking away a knife. A hip throw, bringing a man to the ground, one hand clamped over his mouth, a knee in his back, the man bent like a horseshoe.

"Krav Maga came from Czechoslovakia, the 1930s," Ari said. "A terrible time. The fascists were attacking the Jewish quarter, beating people, killing people, but it was against the law for Jews to have guns. A man named Imi Lichtenfeld wanted a way for the Jews to defend themselves. He came up with a combination of aikido, judo, boxing, and wrestling."

"Like MMA," Isaiah said.

"Yes. This was MMA before there was MMA. He went on to teach the Israeli military, tough guys, believe me. Take off your shoes." Isaiah removed his sneakers and Ari led him onto the mat. "Okay," Ari said. "First principle. We defend and attack at the same time. Here, I show you. Throw a punch at me. A good one. Right here on the chin. Go on. You can't hurt me."

Isaiah was hesitant. He'd seen martial arts demonstrations before; the guinea pig trying to clock a black belt and ending up on the floor wondering what happened. But he'd always thought those demos were rigged, the guinea pig telegraphing the punch, the black belt knowing what was coming.

"Okay," Isaiah said, and with no hesitation he threw a punch straight from the shoulder with his off hand. What happened next went so fast Ari had to explain it to him afterward. Ari blocked the punch with his left forearm. Simultaneously, he threw a straight right that stopped a paper cut away from Isaiah's nose, the left hand coming off the block, grabbing Isaiah by the back of the head and pulling him down into what would have been Ari's face-smashing knee.

"Damn," Isaiah said.

"You see?" Ari said. "We never defend with both hands, always one to attack and always aggressive." Ari threw a blizzard of punches and kicks that ended with Isaiah in a wristlock and forced to his knees. "This is real fighting," Ari said, helping him up. "Street fighting. Not pretty to look at, but effective. Okay, second principle. We focus our attacks where the opponent is weakest. Groin, throat, eyes, temple, pressure points. There's a fissure on top of the skull that comes together as you grow up. Hit your opponent there with enough force and you could kill him."

"I don't want to kill anybody," Isaiah said.

"Maybe not now," Ari said. "But you never know."

Isaiah came out of the locker room and onto the mat, thinking he shouldn't have eaten that Danish. The heat wave had turned the gym into a convection oven and he was already sweating under his clothes. There was a class of grade school kids being taught by a woman about Isaiah's age. She wore a light blue head scarf, no makeup, and was pretty in an uncompromising way. Her kicks and punches were so sharp Isaiah had no doubt she could beat his ass. Maybe some of those kids could too.

Ari put Isaiah through his paces, holding a punching pad that looked like a human head, Isaiah doing repetitive sequences of kicks, punches, elbows and knees, breathing hard after the first ten minutes.

"Embarrassing," Ari said. "Have you forgotten everything? Are you washed up already?"

"Maybe so," Isaiah said.

"Try to remember. You throw the jab at *one* eye. See, like this. If you throw it in the middle he lowers his head, you break your fingers."

"Right," Isaiah said, hoping Ari would keep talking so he could catch his breath.

"Okay," Ari said, "so now he is turning his head to protect his eye and you see what happens? He exposes a pressure point. Here, where the jaw meets the cheekbone. Boom. You hit him there, he goes down. If he doesn't it's because you are punching too soft, like you are today. Then it's left, right, elbow, elbow, knee to the balls. Okay, do it again."

They practiced until Isaiah's sweats were soaked through and his lungs were scorched. They practiced a new move: disarming someone with a gun. It seemed like a relevant thing to learn given what happened at Frankie's house. Ari gave Isaiah a toy gun and demonstrated. It involved a series of movements, but Ari did them so quickly it seemed like a single motion. The gunman had to be an

arm's distance away, the gun held in front of him. With no hesitation, you turned sideways, out of the line of fire, at the same
time grabbing your opponent's gun hand by the wrist, your other
hand turning the gun barrel upward and twisting it away. Ari made
it seem easy. In one instant, the toy gun disappeared from Isaiah's
hand, and in the next, it was aimed at his chest. If there'd been a
puff of smoke Isaiah wouldn't have been surprised.

"Okay. You try."

They switched places. Isaiah's first efforts were clumsy and slow,
Ari instantaneously taking the gun back and putting Isaiah in an
armlock or a choke hold or flipping him over his hip and slamming
him to the mat.

"Come on, Isaiah," Ari said. "Quicker, smoother."

After another half hour of constant motion, Isiah got better but
he couldn't breathe without bending over with his hands on his
knees. He raised his hand. *No más.*

"You need more cardio," Ari said. "Look at you, breathing with
your mouth open. Are you a fish? If you were in better shape you
could be a P4 by now."

"No ... thanks ... couldn't ... take it," Isaiah said between wheezes.

"I will tell you your problem," Ari said.

"That's okay," Isaiah said. "I don't want to know."

"You are holding back," Ari said accusingly. "You are afraid of
hurting your opponent. But remember, he wants to kill you. Do
you understand? He wants to take your life and *you must not let him.*"
Ari had turned indignant, like Isaiah was refuting him.

"Okay, Ari," Isaiah said, taken aback. The woman instructor and
the kids had stopped their exercises and were staring.

"You must fight, Isaiah," Ari said. "Fight with everything you
have. No quitting, no quarter! Do you understand?"

"I understand, Ari, I really do," Isaiah said, trying to calm him down.

"Okay, we start again."

"I can't. Really. I'm beat."

"Beat?" Ari said. "This is not beat. This is nothing. *We start again!*"

"Papa," the woman instructor said like she'd said it before.

"Look, Ari, I'm done for now, okay?" Isaiah said. "I'll come back tomorrow."

"Tomorrow? What tomorrow?"

"Take it easy, Ari," Isaiah said, but Ari got more adamant, like he couldn't get it through Isaiah's thick head.

"You must do whatever is necessary to win!" he shouted. "You win or you die!" He came forward, his jaw hard set, the muscles in his neck bulging, his big hands ready to grab and destroy.

"Okay, Ari, we'll start again," Isaiah said, retreating with his palms out. Ari kept advancing, his eyes big and horrified, sweat pouring off him. The woman was running toward them.

"Papa!" she screamed.

"YOU WIN OR YOU DIE!" Ari bellowed.

Stumbling backward was the only thing that saved Isaiah from the full force of Ari's punches. The straight right nearly ripped his ear off. The left knocked the wind out of him, the side kick missing as he fell to the floor. In an instant, Ari was on top of him, one hand clamped around his throat, the other in a cannonball fist about to smash his face.

"PAPA, STOP IT! STOP IT! STOP IT!" the woman screamed. She tackled Ari's arm and held on. He half-turned, ready to strike her. "Papa, it's me! It's me!" she said. "Stop fighting. It's me." Ari hesitated a moment, looking as if he'd just now recognized her.

Then his entire body went slack. The woman was crying now, hugging him, stroking his head as he wept into her shoulder. "You don't have to fight anymore, Papa," she said. "The fighting is done. All the fighting is done."

Isaiah wondered about Ari, what had happened to him. There were consequences to violence. Like grief, it changed you, eroded your core, exposing and desensitizing at the same time. So many things were not like they happened in the movies. The hero shooting the bad guy in the face or throwing him off a rooftop and in the next scene he's sipping a martini with a babe in a tight dress. No night sweats, nightmares, anxiety attacks, or flashbacks. No kids cowering in the closet because you're drunk again. No weeping in the psychologist's office, or attacking a student you've known for years, your screaming daughter the only one who can bring you back to reality.

When Isaiah got home, he took a shower and put on some music. There were a lot of Marcus's old jazz albums, the covers probably hip at the time. Men in shiny suits and dark sunglasses in a haze of blue sepia; a cutout of a horn player against a background of mod triangles and psychedelic flowers. Isaiah put on Coltrane's *Ascension,* forty-five minutes of improvised pandemonium and musicianship. Music helped Isaiah bear down and think, his neurons forced to overcome the sounds, the notes filling in the blank spaces between thoughts, keeping more pleasant diversions out of his head: having an espresso, reading, walking the dog, tinkering with the car. He lay down on the sofa with an ice pack on his ear, his middle aching where Ari punched him. Ruffin trotted over. He mewled and rested his head on Isaiah's knee. "It's okay, boy," Isaiah said. "Everything's okay." It was common knowledge that dogs could sense your emotional state, but nobody ever said how a species that bears no resemblance to humans, doesn't speak English, and was bred to herd sheep, retrieve dead birds, or ward off predators knows that you're upset and comes over to comfort you. Most humans weren't nearly that sensitive.

Frankie said, *It was your brother that robbed me. Your fucking brother shot me in the gut.* Ridiculous. Isaiah was restless and decided to go for a drive, Ruffin in the passenger seat, wearing his seat belt like anybody else. He had his head out the window, enjoying the night air laden with a thousand scents. They drove past Dodson's apartment, shadows moving across the curtains. Isaiah thought about calling him and talking things over but he couldn't work up the nerve. Dodson and Cherise were expecting their first child. They were probably shopping online for bassinets and baby carriages or fixing up the nursery. He wondered what that would be like, sharing a future with someone you love.

He kept driving, past Deronda's house and the animal shelter where Harry Haldeman worked and Hot Dog Heaven where the gang war had started and the taquería where Flaco was shot. Isaiah ended up at the Del Orto, the building Manzo had rehabilitated. Something had drawn him here but he didn't know what. Just as Néstor had said, it was definitely the best apartments in the hood, with its crisp white paint unmarked by graffiti. The steel-framed front door and the intercom had been expertly installed. The Spanish tiles in the vestibule had been laid by a craftsman, the grout lines straight as arrows. The burglar bars looked new, as did many of the window frames. Something inside him twitched. *What?* he thought. *What is it?*

That night, he slept fitfully, waking up numerous times. Theories and possibilities tumbled in his head like laundry in a clothes dryer. He got up at dawn, exhausted. He played some music, walked Ruffin, and had three espressos but still nothing came to him. He decided to go to TK's wrecking yard and get a replacement cruise control module for the Audi. At least he'd be accomplishing something.

He parked in the lot next to a spotless Volkswagen GTI, five or six years old, gleaming white, eighteen-inch wheels and a six-speed manual. Fast car, handled great. A driver's car. It would be good to see TK, something reassuring about his timelessness. Way back when Isaiah met him, he was bony and decrepit, wrinkled as crackled varnish, a fuzz of white whiskers on his drooping hound-dog face. He was wearing coveralls, black and waxy with layers of grease, the STP cap so filthy you could only see the S. Eight years later, absolutely nothing had changed except you couldn't see the S either.

"How you doin', Isaiah?" TK said, squinting as he lit a Pall Mall, a crust in his voice. "Been a while."

"I've been busy," Isaiah said. "You know how it is. How are you?"

"Old and slow," TK said. "But I'm hangin' in." He looked at the dog and said: "You ain't gonna say hello, you ungrateful fleabag?" Ruffin jumped up and put his paws on the old man's chest. "You know the best thing about people?" he said, scratching the dog's ears. "Their dogs." TK gave Ruffin a treat that had probably been in his pocket for months or maybe wasn't a treat at all. With some trepidation, Isaiah left the dog here when his cases took him out of town. Ruffin loved the wrecking yard, roaming the bleak twelve acres, sniffing, peeing on things, and chasing ground squirrels.

"Say," TK said, "did you know they buildin' one of them Jewish churches right down the street?"

"You mean a synagogue?" Isaiah said. *"Here?"*

"Uh-huh. They callin' it Beth You Is My Woman Now."

Isaiah looked at him and shook his head. "That's the worst joke you've ever told."

"That's all right," TK said with a chuckle. "More of 'em where that came from."

Isaiah told TK about his investigation into Marcus's death, about Seb and Frankie and Manzo and how his hatred was keeping him up nights and how he wanted revenge.

"Careful, boy," TK said. "Go down that road too far and you might never get back."

"What do you mean?"

"Oh, this was a while ago, when I was still married to Etta. There was a pal of mine name of Jimmy Truitt, we was in the army together." TK said Jimmy used to come over to the house, play cards, watch TV, and drink. Sometimes they'd go out on an overnight charter boat and catch rockfish, lingcod, and yellowtail off San Clemente Island. Then they'd have a fish fry, wives and kids partying in TK's backyard. TK fixed Jimmy's car for free and when he lost his job, TK loaned him money. When Jimmy's wife kicked him out, he crashed on TK's couch. "We was buddies," TK said. "Good buddies. But then I found out he was messin' around with Etta. You believe that? Bonin' my woman in my own damn bed? Stabbin' me in the back like that? Well, I worked up a real hatred for the man, that's all I thought about night and day. Got to a point where I couldn't stand it no more, so I go over to Jimmy's place, drag his ass out of his house, and beat him black and blue. Left him lying on the lawn like the sack of shit he was."

"He deserved it," Isaiah said.

"Yeah, I think so too. But you know what? I felt bad about it."

"What? Why?"

"Getting my revenge didn't make the pain go away and didn't make Etta love me again. Jimmy got over his beatin' soon enough, but all that hatred made me crazy and turned me into somebody I didn't want to be. So who got the worst of it? Me or Jimmy?"

TK said he didn't have an Audi on the lot but a cruise control module wasn't vehicle-specific. Maybe Isaiah could find one in the German section that would work. "I got a customer to tend to," he said. "Go on and look for yourself. You know where everything is."

Isaiah took his toolbox and wound his way through the yard. Strange being here again; so quiet, not even sparrows chirping, walking through row after row of abandoned cars. Cars that took people to work, families on vacations, couples on dates, kids on joyrides, pregnant women to the hospital. He could hear them laughing and talking and making love. He could hear their anger, heartbreak, and joyful celebrations. He could hear the life he'd never had.

Ruffin had wandered off, probably chasing a ground squirrel. Isaiah thought about what TK had said. It made sense but it had no effect on how he *felt:* furious and savage. Some murdering son of a bitch had not only taken Marcus's life away, he'd stolen Isaiah's future. He could have gone to Harvard; studied, achieved, fulfilled his own dreams, and made Marcus proud. Instead, he was here in the hood with no family and a career chasing cockroaches like Frankie. Isaiah would get his revenge and what happened after that didn't matter. As he came around the mountain of tires, he saw that the Accord was gone, a rectangle of dead grass the only evidence it had been there at all. TK probably removed it so Isaiah wouldn't think about Marcus every time he came here. Nice of him but it didn't help.

When Isaiah reached the German section he saw someone leaning under the hood of a battered Passat. A white girl, muttering to herself, body tense, struggling with something. She had on jeans with authentic holes in the knees; an old chambray shirt over a faded gray T-shirt that said ROYAL & LANGNICKEL. Royal & Langnickel made paintbrushes; Isaiah had come across the name in a case. There were different-colored paints splattered on her work boots, the faint smell of turpentine coming off her. No great leap to figure out she was an artist.

"Need some help?" he said. The girl didn't look up or answer. She was fussing with a length of the wiring harness, trying to remove the terminal ends from one of the connectors. She already had the secondary lock off but was stuck there, frustrated, staring at the intricate plastic widget, wires coming off it.

"You need a depinning tool," he said.

"I don't have one," she said.

"Hold on."

He went into his toolbox, found what looked like a tweezer with a handle like a screwdriver.

"Oh," she said. She took the tool, looked at it a moment, and without waiting for instructions inserted it in the pin slots and slipped out the terminal ends. "Yeah. That works. Thanks." She continued depinning more connectors, a quiet confidence about her but a sadness too. Isaiah recognized it right away. Like things had happened to her she was trying to forget.

"Are you trying to take out the whole harness?" he asked.

"Yeah," she said, like it was obvious.

Isaiah got some more tools and for the next twenty minutes, the two of them removed a myriad of bolts, screws, and connectors. The girl was focused, not seeming to mind the heat, the stink of oil and gasoline or the sweat dripping off her nose. Her blond hair was tied back in a ponytail. She wore no jewelry, little makeup, a tattoo of an antique pocket watch on her forearm, secrets behind the pale green eyes.

"Water?" he said, offering her his bottle of FIJI.

"Got my own," she said.

The girl went on working like he wasn't there. He wondered if he'd done something to offend her or if she saw something about him that put her off. Now she was stuck again, pulling on the harness and moving wires aside, looking for a way to detach the section she was working on. She seemed in a hurry, like she wanted to find it before he said anything. He thought about letting it pass but couldn't help himself. He went and stood next to her, lifted some corrugated tubing out of the way, his hips touching hers, but she didn't seem to notice. "There's a bolt," he said. "See it?" She shook her head and sighed like she was stupid for missing it.

"You a mechanic?" she said.

"No. I used to work here. Took apart a lot of cars."

Isaiah was skeptical of artists generally, not that he knew anything about art. He'd been to the Getty, LACMA, and MOCA. He had no real interest in art. A lot of the things he saw were in a language he didn't understand. Smeared concentric circles. Big letters stenciled on a canvas. Coiling scribbles of white on a gray background that looked like a fourth grader had doodled on a chalkboard. Were they supposed to *be* something? *Represent* something? Make you *feel* something? They should at least give you something beautiful to look at, something that required some skill, some craftsmanship. The Rembrandt portraits Isaiah saw at the Getty had faces that jumped off the canvas and talked to you, and you could feel the wind and smell the grass coming off the Van Goghs.

When they'd finally gotten everything loose, they wrestled the harness out like a length of seaweed made of wire and plastic.

"It's in pretty good shape," he said. "Should work fine. That GTI out there yours?"

"Yeah, it's mine."

"What year?"

"Oh nine."

"Nice car. They switched to a turbo that year."

"Yeah, they did," she said, not impressed.

And then, amazingly, she smiled at him, big and warm and glad, like she was just realizing how incredible he was. He was wondering what the hell had happened when Ruffin bounded up to them. She was smiling at the dog.

"Hello, friend," she said, a laugh in her voice. "Aren't you beautiful." Ruffin jumped up, his paws on her chest.

"Ruffin, get off her," Isaiah said. "Get off her, Ruffin." But the dog didn't obey. The girl calmly turned her back, forcing the dog to get down. "Sorry, he's bad about that," Isaiah said.

"It's not his fault," she said, turning around again. "Dogs don't speak English. Get off her doesn't mean anything to him."

"Right," Isaiah said, stung.

Most people were wary of the powerful slate-gray pit bull with fierce amber eyes, but she got down on one knee and scratched Ruffin's neck and stroked his head. "How are you, huh?" she said, looking at him like parents look at their sleeping babies. Ruffin was usually standoffish with people but this was like old home week, the dog wagging his tail, reveling in the attention. "What's his name?" she said.

"Ruffin."

"After David Ruffin? Cool. He looks to be what, a year?"

"About that."

"How come you haven't trained him?"

"I just started," he mumbled.

"At a year? You should have started when he was a puppy."

Isaiah was used to asking the questions, backing other people into corners. He tried to turn it around. "You know a lot about dogs," he said. A statement, get her talking about herself. Instead, she shut down in an instant, her whole self going still. Isaiah got the same way when somebody tried to manipulate him.

"He's not neutered, is he?" the girl said.

"No," he said. "Haven't gotten around to it." *Dammit. You're still on defense.*

"That's really messed up, you know. It's hard on the dog." She gave the dog one last flurry of scratches, beamed at him for a moment, then slung the wiring harness over her shoulder and picked up her toolbox, so heavy it made her tilt to one side. Isaiah thought about giving her a hand but that didn't seem like a good idea.

"Thanks for the help," she said, like she was sorry she had to say it.

"Sure. Anytime."

As she walked away, she half-turned, smiled, and said, "Bye."

"Bye," Isaiah said, not expecting that, a moment later realizing she'd been talking to the dog again. "Great," he said to himself.

He felt more intrigued than attracted. This girl who drove a fast car, had a pocket watch tattoo, wasn't afraid of pit bulls, and knew about David Ruffin. Yeah, she was rude, but she was alone in a wrecking yard. He could have been anybody, and okay, she'd given him a hard time but that was because she cared about the dog. As he packed up his tools, he wondered why he was making excuses for her. Maybe because she was a little like him. Removed, prickly, never acknowledging you needed help, and if you saw something you didn't like, you said so and not politely.

When Isaiah got back to the warehouse, TK was leaning against the hoist and drinking a beer.

"Want one?" he said.

"No, thanks," Isaiah said. "Who was that girl?"

"*Who* is she? I don't know, but she's a lezbo." TK's word for lesbian.

"How can you tell?"

"She got that hard look like you 'bout to grab her titty. She's a lezbo all right."

"What's her name?"

"Name? Hmm, lemme think, it was on her check. Tracy or Macy or something like that. Why you asking?"

"No reason."

A customer arrived and wanted suspension parts for a '76 Cutlass. TK said maybe he had them, maybe he didn't. He asked Isaiah, "Can you look after things 'til I get back?"

"Sure," Isaiah said. As soon as TK and the customer were out of view, he hustled into the office and opened the cash register. There was only one check. The account holder was Grace Monarova, an address on Linden right off Seventh. Okay, so now that he knew that, what? He thought a moment but nothing came to him. He put the check back and left.

The 1995 Caprice had 1995 air-conditioning that hardly made a dent in the sweltering heat. The black paint didn't help either. Manzo cruised along Magnolia, wondering who gave out the zoning permits and how much they got paid. A mattress company next to an apartment building next to a church next to a house next to a pain clinic next to another apartment building next to an auto body shop. He thought about Isaiah. He was a relentless dude. All these years later looking into what happened to his brother, and then he's got the cojones to show up at Frankie's house? Why the hell did Frankie let him in? Isaiah was smart. And fierce in his own way.

A homeboy named Stacks had a beef with Isaiah for busting his brother, a bubble-eyed idiot named Laquez. Stacks decided he'd get back at Isaiah by killing his dog. He took a potshot at Ruffin with his .22 and fortunately for him, he missed. Isaiah was beyond pissed but it wasn't like him to get physical. He found out Stacks was a baggage handler at LAX. Then he went to an auction and bought a dozen pieces of lost luggage. After he removed all the ID tags, he broke into Stacks's house and piled the stuff up in the basement. He used a burner and sent Stacks texts: Got any more iPads? Jewelry you sold me was shit. Drop by the crib 2night with $$. Keeping Armani suit for myself. Stacks had no idea what they were about and ignored them. Then Isaiah called the airport police. He said he worked alongside Stacks and he was stealing. No, he didn't want to give his name. The police paid Stacks a visit. He didn't think he had anything to hide and let them search the place. He got five years because he wouldn't give up his partner. No, Isaiah wasn't anybody to mess with, but there were limits, even for him.

Manzo drove past the elementary school. A low wall ran the length of the playground, a mural on it in bright fiesta colors. Daisies, clowns, flamingoes, a village with happy campesinos working in the fields, a doctor examining a patient, a man in a spacesuit landing on the moon. Was a kid from the barrio supposed to look at that and want to be an astronaut? There should be warnings instead. A homie behind bars or dead on the sidewalk or looking at his food stamp debit card.

There was graffiti on the mural. LIL GENIUS SL 13 ELB. Lil Genius, Sureños Locos 13, East Long Beach. SL13 →. Go in that direction and you're in Loco territory. ANGEL ~~CPV~~. Angel killed a Crip Violator. FREE JUAN KVSP. Free Juan from Kern Valley State Prison. Fans of Lil' Wayne had started that bullshit when he went to Rikers for eight months. LKSRKC. Locos, Kimball Street set, Ramona, kill Crips.

Manzo felt sorry for her, trying to get respect by going heavy into the gangsta thing. People made fun of her behind her back, and nothing he could say would convince her to relax and be a regular chola, like Pilar and them weren't crazy enough already. He had a feeling something bad would happen to Ramona but he didn't know what he could do about it.

There was more graffiti on fences, street signs, sidewalks, and bus benches. Manzo had told everybody to cut that shit out. It pissed people off, seeing their property all messed up, and it helped cops focus in on them. Motherfuckers stuck in that barrio mentality. They couldn't wrap their heads around change.

Manzo got the idea for a new kind of gang from *Godfather II* when Michael Corleone bought the casino in Vegas and told Kay that in five years, the family would be completely legitimate; legitimate another way of saying you'd be free. Free from the cops and people trying to kill you and spending half your life in the joint. Manzo's goal was to dominate East Long Beach, not because the Locos were feared and sold the most drugs, but because they owned real estate and businesses and had a serious portfolio. Manzo wanted to get his homeboys off the street and stop dooming themselves to a life of crime and death. Lots of holdouts. Jorge, Popeye, X Ray, and Vicente to name a few; Vicente with that stupid fucking hairnet. And Ramona. One of the worst decisions of Manzo's life was when he agreed to be her mentor. Not that he had much choice. Frankie asked him and he couldn't refuse. Frankie had mentored him when he was coming up; gave him responsibility, grooming him, teaching him how shit worked. Nine years old and Manzo was delivering dope from the stash to the street dealers. He carried money and guns for the gang, the cops less likely to stop and search a little kid. He did surveillance on the Violators and Pimpside Family and those fucking Samoans who didn't notice a scruffy Mexican kid riding through their hood on a beat-up bicycle. He played lookout when there were meetings at the park and when the homies hung out at the Capri. He got jumped into the gang when he was fourteen, the shit beat out of him in Jorge's backyard. Frankie joined in.

Frankie was the one who recognized Manzo's ability to see the big picture, learn from it, and figure out how to do things better. Hard to say where that talent came from. His dad maybe, a city planner in Mexico City before he died from lung cancer and left the family with nothing. Manzo figured out ways to improve the gang's operations. If a big reup was happening, he sent out a decoy courier to test the waters. Then he split the real package between the real couriers so if there was a bust, the cops would only get part of the dope. And no more dealing on street corners. Better to do business in alleys where there were multiple escape routes; passageways, garages, back doors, and courtyards, everything mapped out in advance. Even if the cops entered from both ends of the alley all they'd catch were beer cans, weed ashes, and footprints. And always sell the best shit available at the going rate. No rip-offs. If the dope was iffy, sell it off to the unaffiliated dealers, let them fuck up their reputations. Let it be known: If you buy from the Locos you get the good shit every time. Eventually Manzo brought everyone indoors. No more police taking pictures of you dealing and the prosecutor showing them to a jury and telling them you were poisoning a whole generation of children.

Manzo encouraged secrecy. Most of the big busts happened because somebody was looking at a long jail term and snitched. Manzo said only Frankie and his top lieutenants should know what shit was coming down when, and only issue orders to specific people at the last minute. Manzo gave free dope to dope fiends for spying on each other; to give him a heads-up if somebody was released from custody too early. He decreed that drugs weren't to be sold from stash houses and to move the locations so they'd be harder to raid. He encouraged everybody to get a medical marijuana permit and only carry small amounts to avoid a felony charge. He told everybody to keep their guns outside the house so a search warrant would come up with nothing. If you *have* to have a Glock on the coffee table while you watch TV then get your mom to buy it, and get a separate gun to use on the street. If you shoot somebody with it, sell it or throw it away. Simple shit but it kept you out of the joint.

Manzo said extorting protection money wasn't worth the trouble. Take cash from some guy with a hot dog cart who's making forty dollars a day and maybe he tells the cops and you get busted and then what happens? You and the fellas take revenge, beat the guy up, which somebody records on their phone, and everybody's busted for aggravated assault and you get the max sentence because you've got a record. Better to protect the neighborhood, get people on your side. Some thug fucks with the hot dog man? Kick the thug's ass, make him pay a fine, and give the money to the hot dog man. Some kids burglarize an old lady's apartment? Make them give the shit back, cut the old lady's lawn, and apologize. A junkie sticks up a neighborhood store? Take his dope away, lock him up somewhere, and let him get sick. The next time he wants to rob somebody it won't be in the Locos' hood. Manzo told the fellas to be Robin

Hood, be Pablo Escobar. People were less likely to call the cops on you and take videos and be witnesses. Because of Manzo's policies, gang arrests went down and profits went up, along with Manzo's stature in the gang. When Frankie decided he wanted out there was no question Manzo would take over. Vicente held a grudge but so what? Manzo didn't like violence but he wouldn't run from it. If Vicente wanted to start some shit, he knew where to come.

He pulled over and parked. He pried a panel off the door, exposing the secret compartment Diego at the body shop had installed. Velcroed neatly in place were a Glock 9mm and an extra clip. More than once, the hiding place had saved him from a prison term. He let his anger rise, then loaded the gun and stuck it in his belt. The Audi was parked in the driveway. Isaiah was home.

CHAPTER NINE

A Real Man Does the Right Thing

After the car chase, Dodson drove. Isaiah was in a lot of pain. He had the seat back and his eyes closed. Dodson wondered if he should be taking all these chances. He was going to be a dad in a few days. *A dad.* The last thing he ever thought he'd be. Despite all his complaining, he was excited about it. He wondered what it would be like, watching Lil' Tupac grow up, guiding him, protecting him. There was no way in hell the boy would be running the streets. It was college or death. Cherise had made it possible. She made everything possible. That he'd hooked up with her at all was nothing short of a miracle.

Dodson met Cherise just after he was released from Vacaville, in there on a variety of charges, all of them under the general definition of hustling. He was broke, living with his Auntie May again. Her house smelled like fried food and potpourri, the furniture like sleeping elephants in the rooms of her dark house, a million knick-knacks with doilies under them.

One Sunday, Auntie May's rheumatism was acting up and she

couldn't drive herself to church. Dodson took her. He hated her car, an old Dodge Fury. It drove like a freighter, with a plastic steering wheel the size of a Hula-Hoop and a bench seat covered in the same kind of polyester mesh you'd find on a beach chair. Punch the gas and it sputtered, backfired, swallowed three gallons of gas and took off about as fast as Auntie May answering the phone.

The United in God Baptist Church was an unimpressive pink stucco building with stained-glass windows that looked like colored cellophane and a steepled roof with a cross at its peak that used to light up but didn't anymore. Dodson had nothing to do so instead of waiting around, he went to the service with Auntie May. As they took their seats in the chapel, Dodson noticed a woman stationed at the very back. She must have been in her eighties, withered as a dead vine, her owlish eyes behind glasses big as ski goggles. She was wearing a crisp white nurse's uniform and a matching cap with a red cross on it.

"What's a nurse doing here?" Dodson said.

"Oh, that's Celia Mayfield," Auntie May said. "She's not really a nurse." Auntie May explained that sometimes parishioners got moved by the spirit to the point of falling down on the floor and bucking like they were being electrocuted. "Celia's supposed to keep people from hurting themselves but I don't know how," Auntie May said. "She can barely see her hand in front of her face."

Reverend Arnall came to the pulpit. Dodson was in elementary school the last time he'd seen him, dragged to church by his mother and forced to sit still or get pinched to death. That his father was at home watching the game with a cold beer and a big bowl of Doritos didn't make it any easier. The Reverend's hair had gone white, he had more wrinkles, and he moved a little slower but the dignified, upright posture and upraised chin were the same, and so were the eyes that understood, forgave, and expected better of you. People said he looked like the actor Sidney Poitier. One of his dad's favorite movies was *In the Heat of the Night*. Poitier played a detective from New York who was forced to work a case in the Deep South. Dodson's dad would always fast-forward to the scene where Poitier was slapped by a rich old redneck and in the blink of an eye slapped him back. "Pow-pow," his dad would say with a chuckle.

The Reverend was wearing what he always wore. A dark suit with a crisp white shirt, and a silver-blue tie with a pattern of loaves and fishes. His wife, Sylvia, had to tie it for him or it came out looking like a fist. Not a glint of gold anywhere on him except his wedding ring.

"Welcome, my friends," he said, his warm smile a blessing in itself. "We are gathered here today to worship our Lord Jesus Christ and reaffirm our faith, that in Him we are refreshed, renewed, and born again." The Reverend surveyed the congregation with a pride and compassion even a card-carrying atheist would feel. "I see familiar faces," he said, "but I also see someone who hasn't been here since he was a boy. Juanell Dodson, stand up and be greeted by the congregation."

Dodson wondered who he was talking to. Was there someone else here named Juanell Dodson? Auntie May elbowed him.

"Stand up, Juanell," she said, more than a little amused.

Dodson felt like he'd been called on to sing the national anthem at the Super Bowl. Slowly, he got to his feet. Why was everybody smiling at him? Was his zipper open? Did he have a weed stem on his teeth?

"Welcome, Juanell!" the congregation said in unison. It startled him and he flinched. There was a pause, everybody looking at him expectantly.

"Say something," Auntie May said.

"Uh," he said. He swallowed hard. "Hello."

"We're glad to have you, Juanell," the Reverend said. "The Lord is always pleased when one of his children returns to the flock. I hope to see you more regularly from now on."

Dodson didn't want to lie in church. "You never know," he said.

"The Lord does," the Reverend replied, a wink in his smile. "Now let us join hands and pray."

Dodson joined hands with Auntie May and a little girl in a yellow dress and yellow ribbons in her hair. The Reverend spoke of God's grace and how we are His instruments of peace and justice, and he asked for understanding between men of all creeds, colors, and races. He said when we help others, even our enemies, we are serving His holy name. He asked for guidance as we navigated the perils and temptations of our temporal lives, and he gave thanks for God's enduring love. Familiar lines, but the Reverend said them as if the Holy Spirit had whispered them in his ear that morning.

Dodson couldn't relate, but when he glanced around he saw that the congregation was deeply affected. Some looked in agony, their eyes closed or turning to the heavens and waving a hand as if they hoped God would notice them. But most seemed happy or relieved, like this was what they'd come for, this feeling like a hot shower after a long day or climbing into cool, clean sheets after a longer one. He envied them. Nothing in his life made him feel that way.

When the prayer was over, the organist began to play an old spiritual Dodson had heard many times as a child, "Oh Mary Don't You Weep." The choir came in from the back, their white robes trimmed in gold, doing a time step as they moved down the center aisle singing like angels from the hood. Dodson liked old-school gospel. No dance moves or rapping, no beatbox or theatrics, just pure, divine voices making a joyful noise unto the Lord. The little girl in the yellow dress was singing, not understanding the words but with a sound so pure and beautiful it gave Dodson the chills. We are all God's children, he thought, but some of us get more blessings than others.

As the choir went by him, he saw a girl who made him blink a couple of times. Head erect, a posture like she knew who she was, a passionate face and you knew there was a body underneath that robe. She moved through the light from the stained-glass windows, now gold, now red, now blue, like heaven's police car was pulling her over for being too fine. The girl was an alto, singing harmony right on key, her voice as smooth as butterscotch pudding, a little too sexy for a choir. I need to meet her, Dodson thought.

After the service, Auntie May stopped to talk to the Reverend and Dodson went outside and waited for the girl. She was in street clothes and walked past him without a glance. He followed her to her car, a late-model Prius. When she chirped off the alarm, she turned around, her expression like she was late for work and he was a detour sign.

"Can I help you?" she said.

"Good morning," Dodson said with his best smile. "I'm Juanell Dodson." If he was wearing a hat he'd have tipped it. "I don't believe I've had the pleasure."

"A pleasure for who, you or me?"

"Can you tell me your name or is that too personal?"

"Cherise Johnson. I don't think I've seen you in church before."

"I haven't been in here since I was eleven years old."

"Maybe that's why you fell from grace and ended up in Vacaville."

"How do you know about that?"

"Deronda is a friend of mine."

"Well, that's unfortunate," Dodson said. "Perhaps if we spent some time together I could introduce you to a better class of people."

"Deronda has enough class for me and it's you that's got the problem."

"Problem? What problem?"

"You were in Vacaville. Did you go there voluntarily?"

"I was incarcerated on a technicality."

"A technicality? Is that what you call writing bad checks, running a Ponzi scheme, and selling counterfeit Gucci bags out the trunk of your car?"

"Yes, I've had some legal difficulties but I'm a free man now and I intend to resume my career as legitimate businessman."

"How can you resume a legitimate career when you've never had one?"

"I know my past is checkered but that's all behind me now."

"Yeah, well, you better keep moving," she said, getting into her car. "At the rate you're going it might catch up." She drove away, hitting the gas hard enough for the tires to squeal. For some reason, Dodson was drawn to her even more, and he wasn't discouraged in the least. She could have said nothing or told him to get lost instead of talking to him. She liked him, he was sure of it.

The following Sunday, he waited for her again and followed her to her car. She walked so fast he had to lengthen his stride.

"Could you slow down, please?" Dodson said.

"Why would I want to do that?" she said.

"It's hard to have a conversation when you're breathing so hard."

"Don't you have anything better to do, like cleaning your assault rifle or meeting somebody at the crack house?"

"I left the drug business a long time ago and I think it's very insensitive to bring that up now."

"You're going to tell me about insensitivity while you're following me to my car? What is it you want from me?"

"What I want is to have a conversation. I have qualities that might surprise you."

"Is that what you told your parole officer?" she said. "And what makes you think I have any interest in your qualities?" She reached her car, got in, and rolled the window down. "Leave me alone, do you understand?"

Dodson got her number and email address from Suki and he called or emailed Cherise every day.

I'm sorry to distract you from your busy life but your failure to respond to my messages is very disappointing. I don't recall doing anything that would call for this kind of treatment. I believe you owe me an explanation.

Owe you an explanation for what? Rejecting your advances that I never asked for and certainly don't desire? All you're doing is getting on my nerves and filling up my spam folder. You might have been in prison when they passed the law so perhaps you weren't aware that your behavior is called stalking.

I'm not stalking you. I'm merely persistent, which most people would consider a virtue. I believe we have a connection that transcends the ordinary. I felt it when I first saw you singing in the choir.

Maybe what you felt was my general hostility toward crime and criminals. Now will you please leave me alone? Don't make me

get my brother Jerome involved. He plays arena football and his
bicep is bigger than you.

Dodson kept calling and emailing. Cherise's brother Jerome
came by the house, his bicep as she'd described it. Dodson sent
Auntie May out to deal with him. An elderly churchgoing black
woman can back down anybody. She hit Jerome with a broom and
told him to scat before she really got mad and got her pistol.

Another Sunday. Cherise had slowed her pace some so they were
walking side by side. "For your information," she said, "I am not
like Suki, Loretta, Laeesha, or any of those other tramps you've
dated. Perhaps you'd have more success finding somebody suitable
on Long Beach Boulevard where the prostitutes congregate, and
you can socialize with every other jobless scalawag around here."

"Nobody said you were like those other girls, and I have never
paid for sex in my entire life," Dodson said, almost telling her that
there were girls he knew who would pay *him* to have sex. "All I'm
asking for is a conversation; an opportunity to reveal my true character and gain some understanding of yours. Is that too much for
you?"

"You will never in your life be too much for me."

"Well, then. Have a cup of coffee with me. What harm could
that do? And despite the fact I'm a jobless scalawag I'll even pay for
it."

She got in her car, rolled the window down, and looked at him
like he was trying to sell her a mountain-view lot in Arizona. "One
cup or ten minutes," she said. "Whichever comes first."

They met at the Coffee Cup later that day. She told him she
worked as a paralegal, ate healthy food, drank sparingly, and only
went to clubs on somebody's birthday. She gave money to her par-

ents, tutored her younger sister, went to night school, had been to Europe, wore clear polish on her nails, calling all that sparkly nonsense a waste of money. She'd only had two boyfriends, one of whom turned into a fiancé whom she broke up with when he asked her for a loan.

"And you?" she said. "What are you doing with yourself?"

"I am presently evaluating my career options."

"And in the meantime you're sponging off your Auntie May even though you know she's on Social Security and wouldn't be getting by at all if it weren't for her children, who are responsible adults and live productive lives."

"This is one of the worst conversations I have ever had in my entire life," Dodson said. "Usually on social occasions, people don't go out of their way to denigrate and disrespect you. I'd say you need to learn some manners and maybe take a class in civility while you're at it."

"I'm sorry if I've offended you," she said, not looking sorry at all. "But how do you expect to be treated with respect when there's nothing I can see to respect you for?" She got up and slipped her handbag over her shoulder. "Are you sure you can pay for the coffee?"

"Yes, I'm sure," Dodson said.

Despite the fact that she made him feel like a bum, he kept asking her to go to coffee and she kept saying yes. Dodson told her about his father, a marine sergeant, who gave orders instead of love. He was deployed overseas six months at a time. He'd missed all of Dodson's birthdays except the fourth and the sixth. When he retired he stayed by himself a lot, drank all the time, and had a temper like a landmine. Dodson told her about selling crack and being homeless and living in Keenya's car and meeting Isaiah and their run as the Battering Ram Bandits and the gang war and the kid named Flaco who got shot in the head. He told her about hustling and going to the joint and how he always knew he was meant for something better but survival always came first.

What struck him about Cherise, aside from her looks, was that she listened. Really listened. Like she was taking each word and turning it over in her mind, checking it for truth before she went on to the next. As their conversations continued, he felt like she saw something in him: his potential, who he could be. A disturbing thing to be measured against yourself, and it made him curious. Who, in fact, *could* he be?

"I know I should have something going by now," Dodson said. "But an opportunity will come along. It always does."

"See, that's your problem, Dodson."

"You mean I've got another one?"

"Oh, I have a list, believe me."

"You were saying?"

"I was saying that one of your problems is that you have no initiative. Nothing's gonna *happen* for you."

"Yeah, I know," Dodson said, irritated now. "I gotta go *make* something happen. Shit. That ain't nothing but a damn cliché. I dropped out of high school and just got out the joint. I ain't got nothing to make something *with*."

"And that ain't nothing but a damn excuse," she replied. "Let me ask you something."

"What? Do I know I'm a lazy bum, I have a criminal nature, and I lack initiative? I believe you answered that yourself."

"What are you good at?"

"Good at?"

"Yes, good at. Don't make me repeat myself. You must have some kind of skill set besides selling stolen goods and illegal drugs." Dodson thought a moment. And then another.

"You mean you have none?" Cherise said. "There is nothing legitimate you know how to do? And talking doesn't count."

Dodson's entire life fast-forwarded through his head but he couldn't think of a single thing. It was humiliating. He leaned back in his chair. Maybe it was time to cut this off. This girl was never gonna come around, and he was tired of getting his ego hacked to pieces. Now she was looking at him over her coffee cup. "What," he said, expecting more abuse.

"I know you don't like Deronda, but she's having a birthday party for her niece. She's turning six. Would you like to go?"

"Go? You mean with you?"

"Yes, with me. There won't be any liquor, weed, or hoochie dancing, but Deronda's grandmother is cooking and you haven't tasted anything until you've had her fried chicken."

"That's 'cause you ain't tasted mine."

Deronda couldn't believe Dodson was Cherise's date and neither could any of the other people there, including the girls Dodson had gone out with.

"All of the men that want to take you out and *that's* who you bring?" Deronda said. "Girl, you need to raise your standards."

"What do you know about standards?" Dodson said. "Your last boyfriend couldn't even read."

"He had dislex—dismex—he had that thing Tom Cruise had."

"Tom Cruise? That boy ain't got nothin' in common with Tom Cruise except hands and feet."

"Maybe, but he don't have a criminal record."

"That's 'cause he's too busy learning the alphabet." Dodson looked around. Cherise had disappeared. "Where'd she go?"

"Away from you," Deronda said.

Dodson found her helping Deronda's grandmother put food on the table. "Why'd you leave?" he said.

"So I could do something besides listen to you and Deronda run your mouths." She stopped what she was doing and looked at him. "Dodson, there's something you need to understand. If we're together, *I* am the center of your attention, and if something ever happens between us? I promise you, you'll be the center of mine."

They sat on the stoop and ate Deronda's grandmother's fried chicken off paper plates.

"What do you think?" Cherise said.

"Best I ever had," Dodson said.

She wouldn't go out with him on a one-on-one date until he got a job. After filling out twenty application forms and getting no callbacks, he finally got a position driving a delivery truck for a meat-packing plant. When she opened the door to her apartment, he was, for the second time in his life, speechless; the first time was when he walked in on Auntie May having sex with Carter Samuels, a police officer who patrolled the neighborhood and was twenty years her junior. Cherise was wearing a nice black dress, the hem two inches above the knee, heels, and a thin gold chain with a cross around her neck and some kind of perfume that was sexy and sensible at the same time. They went out to dinner, an Italian place in El Segundo, Dodson thinking she'd appreciate it, having been to Europe and all. As the hostess led them to their table, he felt something else he'd never felt before; proud of his date. He wished he could introduce her to his parents, see their faces when they saw she wasn't another ho.

Dodson thought he'd had sex before but that was patty-cake compared to Cherise. Making love to a beautiful woman was one thing. Making love to a beautiful woman who wasn't high and didn't scream at you like a personal trainer who wanted one more push-up and whose eyes were like the sun and you were ice cream melting all over the pillow; who moaned like the moment was too good to let pass without an acknowledgment and who made it clear with every wet kiss and warm caress that she cared about you and wanted good things for you—was the closest thing to the Holy Spirit he'd ever felt.

About two months into the relationship, he delivered some boxes of steaks to a supermarket and discovered there was one box left over and it wasn't on the invoice. He took a couple of T-bones over to Cherise's, looking forward to cooking her dinner.

"No, I don't want them," she said.

"Why not?"

"Because you stole them."

"They don't even know they're gone and even if they do there's no way to trace it back to me."

She looked at him like he was cooking the steaks in the microwave. "Dodson," she said simply. "A real man does the right thing."

He took the steaks back but kept one for himself and ate it without pleasure. At some point, he realized he was being trained, like the tomato vines that grew on trellises in Auntie May's backyard. Every time his hooligan tendencies led him astray, Cherise wouldn't have it, and in their absence, Dodson discovered another side of himself and felt the pleasures of being a real man. Bit by bit, he became a person she could fall in love with.

*　　*　　*

Isaiah was on the bed at the Travel Inn, staring up at an ancient map of water stains on the popcorn ceiling. Losing Benny to the Red Poles was a major setback, and he had no idea what to do about Sarita's father. Okay, he'd saved Janine, but he wanted to ace this, slam-dunk it, come back the all-conquering hero. If he didn't, what else could he offer her? What he was, how he lived, and where he was going surely weren't enough.

Dodson was walking in circles, talking on the phone with Cherise. "I said I'll be there. How many times do you want me to say it? What? I better be? See, this is what I was trying to tell you. The baby ain't even here yet and got us squabblin'. By the time that li'l nigga's in the house we might be broke up already—what? Don't call him nigga? What do you think he's gonna be, Polynesian? Okay, okay, I'll call him something else." Dodson turned his back to Isaiah and lowered his voice. "You okay? Course I love you, I *been* loving you. You know you my boo." Isaiah could hear a grin in Dodson's voice. "Say something nasty for me, Cherise—yes, now. Ain't nobody here but me. Come on, just for me?" Dodson listened and chuckled. "Damn," he said. "I can't wait for that baby to vacate the premises. Aight, I'll see you in the morning. Y'all take care now."

Isaiah was envious. Dodson had someone who needed him, someone who wanted him to come home. There was no one waiting for Isaiah except Ruffin, who might or might not be missing him.

"You're leaving?" Isaiah said.

"Baby's dropping early and I ain't missing Lil' Tupac's coming-out party for nothing," Dodson said.

"Okay," Isaiah said with an indifferent shrug.

"Okay? What's that supposed to mean?"

"It means you're leaving in the middle of the case."

"I guess you didn't hear me about the baby," Dodson said.

"I heard you," Isaiah said, with another shrug. He knew he was being childish but couldn't help himself.

"The fuck's wrong with you, Isaiah?" Dodson said. "If you think a damn per diem means more to me than Cherise, then you have lost your tiny little mind."

Dodson went to take a shower. Isaiah sulked. And felt ridiculous. Was he really going to give Dodson a hard time for going home to his pregnant wife? He dozed, waking up when Dodson came out of the bathroom with a towel around his waist. He put on his clothes in silence.

"I'm glad about the baby," Isaiah said at last.

"Thanks," Dodson said.

"When you get back, will you check on Janine?"

"Yeah, I'll check on her," Dodson said. "I'm surprised she ain't called you already and said get me the fuck outta here."

Janine wondered if loving Benny was worth the trouble. Just thinking about it felt like a betrayal, but here she was, hiding three hundred miles from home and in danger for her life, the adrenaline and fear a lot different than putting your last money on the pass line. She had to get out of here, go back to Vegas. Maybe she couldn't do anything but at least she'd be close to Benny. Deronda was talking again. The girl had an opinion about everything, even stuff nobody ever thought about.

"This ain't no racism, okay?" Deronda said. "But black people done a whole lot more than the Chinese ever have."

"That's crazy," Janine said, wiping the gravy off her mouth with a napkin. "Black people are cool but achievement-wise they're not even in the same ballpark."

"Achievement-wise or any other kinda wise, we got y'all beat by a country damn mile." They were sitting at the breakfast table in Deronda's kitchen, everything a mess from making side dishes for the truck. "Where you think rap music came from?" Deronda said. "Not from you people. Your music sound like a broke-down banjo and a church bell."

"Yeah, and what do you play that rap music *on?* An iPod made in Compton? Half the stuff in your house comes from China."

"You people didn't *invent* the damn iPod. They just make it over there 'cause y'all work for ten cents an hour—and what about food? Fried chicken, macaroni and cheese, biscuits and gravy, all that stuff."

"You know who invented macaroni? The Chinese. And we were frying chicken while you guys were still in Africa. I'll give you the biscuits and gravy. Can I have some more?"

"Is your leg broke? Go on and get it yourself," Deronda said.

Janine got up, got another biscuit off the tray and gravy out of the pot. "Tell me something," she said. "What's up with black people and conspiracy theories? I mean, you guys come up with some crazy shit."

"Why? I'll tell you why. We *know* more than you. Did you know that before 9/11, George Bush *hung out* with Bin Laden? They did some business together, had him up to the ranch and everything. Barbara gave Osama a horse for a birthday present."

"Seriously?"

"Do a Google on him. Got a million pictures of him riding around on that thing. And I'll tell you something else, and I know this one for a fact."

"I can't wait."

"There's a chemical in government cheese that makes black folks late for work."

Janine choked on her biscuit. "Get out of here," she said.

"It's true," Deronda said. "I was forty-five minutes late for every job I ever had 'til I started eatin' Velveeta. Shit. You think we ain't got alarm clocks?"

"Damn this stuff is good. I could eat this all day."

"Wait'll you taste the chicken. You'll never eat that Kung Pao shit for the rest of your life."

There was a stuffed animal on the floor. A cow. Janine picked it up and gave it a squeeze and it mooed. "That's funny," she said.

"You think that's funny?" Deronda said. "Try listening to that thing moo fifty times in a row and you might change your mind."

"You've got a kid?"

"Janeel. He's four. I love that boy. Nothing I wouldn't do for him but I'm glad as hell he's in San Diego. You want kids?"

"I don't know. Maybe."

"Look before you leap, girl. It's the hardest job you will ever have in your life." Deronda got up and started clearing away the dishes. "You must be in a whole bunch of trouble," she said. "Got to run all the way to Long Beach."

"You don't know the half of it," Janine said.

"Y'all can relax. Ain't nothing gonna happen to you here."

Three members of the Chink Mob rode in the silver '99 Integra, the car lowered, black rims, dual exhausts chugging, a turbocharger sucking air. Wing drove, worried about the job. Kidnap a girl from a house? What kind of bullshit was that? What if her boyfriend was with her? What if she had a piece? Fucking Tommy was crazy. This shit was going to get him busted. He was twenty-one and already had two strikes. One more and he was off to San Quentin, share a cell with his brother in there for murdering a South Side Maravilla.

"Shit, we made a wrong turn," Huan said. He was in the backseat shaking his phone like it was the problem. "Go back—no, make a right."

"Damn, Huan," Wing said. "All you gotta do is look at the blue dot. What's wrong with you?"

It was a little after eleven. The businesses on Anaheim were closed except for the Shell Station and the 7-Eleven.

"I'm hungry," Huan said. "Let's get something to eat."

"You're always fucking hungry," Gerald said, the cigarette in his mouth bobbing up and down. He took the Glock out of his pants and popped the clip in and out for the tenth time.

"Put it away, okay, Gerald?" Wing said.

"Yes, sir, Mr. Boss Man," Gerald said, popping the clip in with a little extra snap.

They came to a stop at an intersection, Gerald reading the graffiti on a road sign. "Who the fuck are the Locos?" he said. "I bet they ain't shit. Fucking Mexicans got numbers, that's all. Motherfuckers breed like rabbits. Man to man we'd fuck them up." Gerald was like that, always talking shit, starting shit. You'd never know by looking at him; bald, soft, potbelly, nerd glasses. He looked like a nearsighted Buddha with an attitude.

"We're early," Wing said.

"Early for what?" Gerald said.

"We've got to wait for people to go to bed. Not so many witnesses."

"You're a pussy, Wing. The fuck are we gonna do, just drive around?"

"Up there," Huan said, "the burrito place is open."

Frankie was having nightmares again. Ramona gently dabbed the sweat off his face with a towel and made him change his T-shirt.

Then she gave him another couple of trazodone and waited until he fell asleep. She and her mother had been taking care of him for years now, but she still couldn't believe that this was her big brother. He'd been her idol. She was proud of him. He looked out for her and protected her and gave her status. *Don't mess with Ramona, ese, she's Frankie's sister. You touch her and Frankie will kill you for real.* She wondered if you could love somebody and feel sorry for them at the same time. She wondered if she loved him for himself or the respect she got from being his sister and now that he was a nobody if she loved him at all.

With Frankie gone from the scene, Ramona had become an outcast. Nobody calling her or texting her or asking her to go places. Most of that was her fault. When she was on top she was a bitch; starting arguments, fights, spreading rumors, talking down to people. Now the homegirls had dropped her completely, paying her back. Lately, she'd been hanging out with the fellas, thinking if she got their respect the girls would take her back, but that wasn't happening. That bitch Pilar had taken over the crew. Everybody looked to her to see who was in, who was out, where they should go, if they should have a party. Get in good with her and maybe she'd get a second chance. The problem was finding her; Pilar liked to hang out at different places. It was humiliating, driving around looking for somebody to be her friend, but she was lonely and she had to do something before she went crazy. That fucking Pilar had to be somewhere.

Ramona took her mom's Sentra and drove around for an hour. She finally found the crew in front of the Capri where she should have looked in the first place. When she drove up they were standing around like they always did, hands in the pockets of their hoodies, smoking, drinking, restless. It always struck her as weird that the whole group of them couldn't think of anything better to do. Pilar was talking louder than anyone else, her laugh a piercing, high-pitched cackle like something you'd hear at the zoo. Somebody should have told her you don't wear supertight clothes if you're built like a heavyweight fighter, and your boobs weigh thirty pounds apiece. If it wasn't for the chola makeup her face was a dead ringer for Santa Claus.

Ramona stuck her head out of the window. "What's happening?" she said.

"Well, look who's here," Pilar said. "Manzo's mascot."

"Yeah, that's funny," Ramona said.

Everybody looked at her like what's *she* doing here. She used to be that way, on the inside, looking for a reason to keep you out.

"Say, do you have to ask him to go to take a piss or can you just go?" Pilar said. The other girls laughed, made faces at each other.

"I don't have to ask him nothing," Ramona said.

"Are you guys doing it?"

"I'm not doing it with nobody."

"I'm not surprised. Who would want to do it with you?" More laughing, the girls grinning like Halloween pumpkins, Ramona's insides shriveling with embarrassment. She could feel her face flush. "Well, what are you doing here?" Pilar said. "How come you're not home with your big bad brother?"

"Fuck you, Pilar," Ramona said. Suddenly it was quiet, the girls making *uh-oh* faces and saying *oooh*. Pilar smiled like she was hoping this would happen.

"Oh yeah?" she said. "Come on out here and say that, bitch."

"She's not gonna do nothing without Frankie," that puta Margo said. Somebody threw a beer bottle and bounced it off the Sentra's fender, the girls high-fiving the one that did it.

"So come on, Ramona," Pilar said. "What are you waiting for?"

Ramona hesitated. How did she get into this? How could she get out?

"I told you she's not gonna do nothing," that puta Margo said. The girls were yelling now, calling her a pussy and a bitch and telling her to put her money where her mouth was.

No choice. Ramona got out, the girls eager for violence, something to break up the boredom.

"Yeah, come on, Ramona," Pilar said, gesturing like she was helping her park the car. "Come on and do something."

Ramona walked toward her, adrenaline and shame pushing her forward, not seeing the girls or hearing their yelling as she threw a punch that caught Pilar on the cheek and drove her back a few steps.

"Ohh shit," somebody said. "You fucked up for real."

Pilar's face changed from Santa Claus to serial killer. Screaming, she charged, bulling her way through Ramona's punches. She grabbed her by her hair with one hand and hit her with the other, the cholas egging her on like men at a cockfight.

"Let go of me!" Ramona screamed.

Pilar slung her to the ground and sat on her like a donkey, pushing her face into the grass, mashing and grinding, Ramona screaming *Get off me get off me,* dirt and grass in her mouth. She thought she was going to suffocate, but Pilar dismounted, kicked her a few times, and spit on her. "Bitch. The next time I won't go so easy on you."

Ramona stayed still, too humiliated to get up, the girls talking as they moved away. *Way to go, Pilar, teach her a lesson, put her in her place, stupid little bitch, she ain't nothing without Frankie.*

"Let's go to Tito's," Pilar said.

"Okay," that puta Margo said. "See you there."

*   *   *

When they were gone, Ramona stood up, spit the grass out of her mouth, and got in the car. She looked in the mirror. Bleeding scratches, bloody nose, pebbles embedded in her skin, one eye fat and closing. A clump of hair torn out. She started to cry. "Fucking bitches, fucking bitches." Tears cut paths through the dirt on her face. Her anger was an electric chair, sizzling voltage crackling through her veins. She'd get them back. Those bitches would be sorry for this. She'd walk up to that fucking Pilar and put a bullet in her head and spit on her and ask those other bitches if they wanted some and watch them back away. *Shit, Ramona, you're fucking crazy. Shit, Ramona, you ain't fucking around. Shit, Ramona, you're just like Frankie.* She'd go home, get her piece, go to Tito's, and put that fat bitch in the ground. Yeah, Pilar's brothers would retaliate and she'd go to jail but she didn't care. She'd get her respect back and people would know: *Ramona Montañez is on the block.*

They all ordered the Supreme, Gerald taking giant bites, his mouth so full he could hardly chew.

"Damn, man," Wing said. "Can't you eat like normal people?"

"Fluck foo," Gerald said, beans and rice falling out of his mouth.

The burrito place was small and warm. Red-checkered plastic tablecloths, straws in a jam jar, bottles of Tabasco and sriracha. Wing couldn't taste the food, eating because he was nervous. The GPS said they were only four or five blocks away from the girl they were supposed to kidnap. Google Earth showed a fucked-up house with a chain link fence like every other crib in the hood. The main thing was to be cautious, no cowboy shit. Case the place. Not go in all at once, have Huan wait in the car with the engine running. That's about all he was good for. Look at him, sitting there chewing and nodding like he'd eaten the burrito in a dream and the real thing was just as good.

"East Long Beach ain't shit," Gerald said. "You see them Mexicans on YouTube? Got the guns, got the ink, talking all bad. It's bullshit, man."

Just like our videos, Wing thought.

A Mexican girl came in. "Hey, Tito," she said to the guy behind the counter. "Did Pilar and them come in?"

"They just left," he said.

"Did they say where they were going?"

"No."

"Fucking beaners try to rap," Gerald said. "That shit is lame, man. You can't understand that shit, it's all in Mexican."

"Could you give it a rest?" Wing said.

Gerald didn't hear him, talking with his mouth open, like a tree shredder full of garbage in there. "Them punk-ass Locos should come to Arcadia, see how the real niggas do it. They'd get their asses smoked."

"Or maybe *you* would," the girl said.

"You talking to me?" Gerald said.

"Yeah, I'm talking to you," the girl said. "Who'd you think?"

Wing wondered what this girl was so mad about. She just *got* here.

"You down for the Locos, is that it?" Gerald said.

"Uh-huh. Who the fuck are you?"

"The Chink Mob, bitch. You wanna get dominated, come on down to our hood."

"Never heard of you, and you ain't dominating nobody around here."

"Come on, Gerald," Wing said. "Don't start no shit."

"She's the one that started it," Gerald said. He wiped his mouth with the back of his hand, stood, and walked over to her, Huan still eating, not even raising his head. "What happened to you?" Gerald said, looking the girl up and down. "Your old man beat you up?"

"Fuck you, asshole." The girl had some spine, not acting scared, not backing down.

"Let it go, Gerald," Wing said. He could see THIRD STRIKE written on the girl's forehead.

"What's your problem, bitch?" Gerald said. "You don't think I'll fuck you up just 'cause you're a girl?"

"Well, come on and do it then," the girl said, her hands out, palms up.

This girl was crazy, Wing thought. Gerald was a head taller and outweighed her by fifty pounds. Did she *want* to get her ass kicked?

"What are you waiting for, cabron," she said. "Stop talking and do something."

"Gerald, don't be stupid, man, come on," Wing said.

Gerald went nose-to-nose with the girl and grinned. "I'm gonna fuck you up, you wetback bitch."

"Get out of my face, motherfucker," she said.

Gerald walked into her, forcing her to back up. "Or what bitch? Or what?"

The girl retreated a few steps, reached behind her, and found the gun stuck in the back of her pants.

"She's strapping!" Wing shouted.

The girl tried to pull the gun out, but the sight got stuck in her waistband. Gerald gave her a hard two-handed shove, putting his weight into it, sending her crashing into the salsa table. She slid to the floor, pico de gallo, pickled carrots, a napkin dispenser, and plastic utensils crashing down on her. She tried to get the gun out, but Gerald kicked her a couple of times. She doubled up, groaning.

"You got anything else to say, bitch?" Gerald said.

"Let's get out of here," Wing said. The guy behind the counter was dialing his phone.

"I want to take her gun," Gerald said, pushing salsa around with his foot.

"Fuck that, let's go!" Wing shouted. He grabbed Gerald and yanked him toward the door. He looked back at Huan. "Put the fucking burrito down and LET'S GO!"

Ramona sat in the mess, dripping vinegar, cilantro leaves stuck to her face. "FUUUUCKK!" she shrieked. She shot a glare at Tito, who disappeared into the kitchen. On her hands and knees, she searched around for her gun. "Motherfuckers, mother*fuckers*!" She found it, scrambled to her feet, and ran out the door.

They were in the living room with the lights off, the music turned down. It sounded like Kendrick Lamar was rapping from a block away. Janine was sitting in the Barcalounger with her feet up. Deronda was lying on the sofa, her head on the armrest. It was mellow, not seeing anything but the glowing tips of their joints. Janine thought about Benny; where he was and what he was doing and why had he had to be such a fuckup. "You got a boyfriend?" she said.

"No I ain't got no boyfriend," Deronda said. "Ain't had one in a long damn time, unreliable muthafuckas."

"You gotta meet Benny," Janine said. "Unreliable is his middle name."

"But it don't matter and you love him, right?"

"Yeah, I guess so," Janine said. She really did love Benny, even if he was unreliable and a loser. She was unreliable and a loser too, and he loved her back. "He's really nice, really sweet."

"Ain't none of them kind around here," Deronda said. "Believe that. I been looking everywhere for a good man, ain't found a one yet."

"Isaiah's a nice guy."

"Back in the day, he was on my list but not no more. He need to get himself some social skills, learn how to have some fun."

"Yeah, he is kind of weird. What's wrong with him?"

"I don't know. He's always been like that. Maybe when he was a baby his mama dropped him on his head."

Janine saw the tip of Deronda's joint get brighter, smoke rising ghostlike and hovering over the sofa.

"My daddy's a good man," Deronda said. "Don't get drunk, go to work every day. Been married to my mama for twenty-six years and ain't played around once."

"I don't know anybody like that," Janine said.

"What's wrong with men today? Bunch of damn control freaks, always bossin' you around. *Get down on your knees. Bend over. How come the house ain't clean?* Makes me wanna do as little as possible. Then the relationship ain't nothin' but one long negotiation. Tit for tat. You want something from me, you gotta give something up. Buy low, sell high, and you don't never get but half of what you wanted. How 'bout this for an idea? You take care of me, I take care of you. I give you everything, you give me everything. What's wrong with that?"

"Not a thing," Janine said.

Deronda sat up abruptly and stared at a window, the one on the side of the house. "You see that? Somebody's out there. I seen a shadow."

"Oh shit," Janine said, pinching out the joint. *It's Tommy's guys.*

"See? There it goes again."

Janine got up, skulked over to the front window, and peeked through the blinds.

"You see something?" Deronda said.

"You know somebody with a little silver car that likes to park across the street?"

"No."

"Somebody's sitting in it, I think he's eating something."

"The fuck they here for?" Deronda said.

They're here for me, Janine thought.

"I know," Deronda said. "They want the food truck!" She strode across the room and disappeared into the hall. "Them muthafuckas be messin' with the wrong sista."

"Deronda?" Janine said. "What are you doing?"

Deronda came back carrying a matte-black pump-action shotgun and a small pistol. "Hard as I work they gonna come here and try to take what's mine? Steal my son's future? Not today, bitches. Not today."

"Anybody ever tell you you were impulsive?" Janine said.

"I'm not impulsive," Deronda said. "I just make up my mind fast. Here." She handed Janine the pistol. "It ain't but a thirty-two but it *will* put a hole in your chest."

"I've never shot a gun," Janine said.

"Ain't nothin' to it. Point and shoot." They heard noises at the back door. "Hide someplace," Deronda said. She turned off the stereo and racked the shotgun. CLACK-CLACK! "Let's party."

Janine went into the foyer and hunched down, holding the pistol with two fingers like there was poison oak on the grip. Deronda was crouched behind the sofa twenty feet away.

"This don't make no sense," Deronda said. "If they want the truck why they coming in here? 'Less they want to rape us."

"Why don't we call the cops?" Janine said.

"I will," Deronda said. "Right after I send these boys a message. Whatever you do in your life do *not* fuck with Deronda." They heard the kitchen door open. "Shit, I forgot to lock it." Two men were arguing in whispers. Deronda peeked over the sofa. "Yeah, come on, you trespassin' muthafuckas. Deronda's got a surprise for your asses."

Janine never sweated but she was sweating now. A poppy field of hives was budding on her arms, her heart throbbing in her throat.

"Get ready," Deronda said. She looked at Janine. "What are you doing? Hold the pistol right." Janine obeyed but didn't put her finger on the trigger. A light went on in the dining room, a dim glow falling on the living room.

"Anybody here?" the guy said.

"Turn the light off," the other guy said.

"Fuck you, Wing."

The intruders split up, the sounds coming from different parts of the house. Janine's leg was asleep and she was afraid she couldn't run. Deronda was squatting on both feet, ready to spring. *Jesus Christ, she's really going to shoot them.* Behind Janine and around the corner was the hallway. *To hell with this, I'm outta here.* She turned and started duck-walking toward it but a light in the hall went on, a man's shadow cast into the foyer. *Don't come in here don't come in here please don't come in here.* The shadow got smaller and sharper. He was coming closer. *Oh shit oh shit!* He stopped. He was right around the corner, Janine could hear him breathing. *Go back go back go back please go back.* She tried to raise the gun, but it weighed a hundred pounds and her hand was trembling. She heard the guy take a step. She could see the tip of his sneaker. *Oh shit oh shit oh shit!*

Deronda jumped up and started shooting toward the dining room. BOOM! CLACK-CLACK! BOOM! CLACK-CLACK! The gun nearly leapt out of her hands, buckshot ripping a light fixture off the ceiling. Janine heard the breakfront shatter. BOOM! CLACK-CLACK! BOOM! CLACK-CLACK! The man in the hallway ran back the way he came. Deronda came around the sofa, waving the shotgun as she moved out of view. "I need to get my aim right." BOOM! CLACK-CLACK! BOOM! CLACK-CLACK! BOOM! Janine heard running footsteps, the guys escaping through the back. BOOM! CLACK-CLACK! BOOM! CLACK-CLACK! BOOM!

Janine went into the living room and looked out the front window. Two Chinese guys came around the side of the house and raced toward the silver car. One was hobbling, a dozen holes in his pants. Deronda ran back into the room.

"What's happening?" she said. A third guy got out of the silver car and started helping the wounded one get in. "Ha HA!" she laughed. "Mess with Deronda and your shit is over!"

"Who's that?" Janine said. Another car pulled up and stopped about forty feet in front of the silver car. The headlights were blinding, the three guys squinting, putting their hands in front of their eyes. A girl got out of the second car, yelling something in Mexican. She had a gun.

"The hell is this?" Deronda said.

The girl started shooting, holding the gun sideways like they do in the movies; bullets shattering the silver car's windshield, blowing off the side mirror and sparking off the asphalt. The wounded guy fell to the ground and rolled under the car. The second guy dived back inside, the third ran around to the back, hunched down, and took a gun out of his pants. The girl kept shooting.

"Shit, that bitch is crazy," Deronda said.

"What's happening?" Janine said. "What's she *doing?*"

"What? What?" the girl screamed. "Fuck your fucking Chink Mob! Come on, you fucking bitches, come on and get some!"

Gunfire flashed beneath the car, the rounds hitting the girl in the shins. She screamed, dropped the gun, and fell to her knees. The guy behind the car stood up and shot her twice. She bucked and slumped over sideways.

"Oh my muthafuckin' God," Deronda said. The guys piled into the car and drove away fast.

"I don't believe this," Janine said. She put her hand over her mouth, her mind connecting her own stupidity with the dead girl lying in the street, the white beams of the headlights reflecting off the pool of blood. It looked like news footage. People were coming out of their houses, shooing their kids back inside and talking on their cells. A couple of the men approached the body, bending forward like they were peering down a well. They looked more puzzled than horrified. The girl was screaming and waving a gun a moment ago. What happened to her? Janine couldn't believe it either. How could the girl's life just disappear and leave behind a lump of skin and bones no more human than a package of ground beef?

"Did you know those guys?" Deronda said.

"No," Janine said.

Deronda glared. "Well, they was after somebody," she said. "And it sho' the fuck wasn't me."

CHAPTER TEN

10-57

Isaiah stood at the kitchen counter eating his Shredded Wheat thinking about his drive around the neighborhood last night. What stuck out in his mind was Manzo's building, the Del Orto. *The best apartments in the hood.* So what? Why did that keep passing through his head? It was nonsensical, but he paid attention to it. Sometimes these random thoughts meant something.

The doorbell rang. As a matter of habit, he picked up the collapsible baton off the coffee table and stuck it in the back of his pants. Peeking through the peephole, he was surprised to see Manzo. Ruffin made people nervous and vice versa, so he sent the dog into the bedroom and told him to stay. Maybe he would, maybe he wouldn't. Isaiah went back to the foyer and opened the door. Manzo stood there, hostile, something definitely wrong.

"You gonna let me in or what?" he said.

Isaiah stepped aside and Manzo entered the living room. He looked around a moment, taking in the polished cement floor and the minimal furniture, probably wondering where the Raiders banner and votive candles were hiding.

"What's up, Manzo?" Isaiah said.

"The hell is wrong with you, ese?" Manzo said. "You go to Frankie's *house?* The guy is sick and you trick him into talking about Loco business? Frankie's like my father, okay? You know your visit messed him up? Ramona had to take him to the doctor."

"I didn't mean for that to happen."

"This is bullshit, Q. I save your fucking ass and this is how you repay me? You don't go screwing around like that. It don't matter who you are."

"I'm sorry, Manzo, I—"

"I don't give a shit if you're sorry," Manzo said. "You stabbed me in the back."

Isaiah knew he was in trouble. Manzo felt betrayed and betrayal was a capital crime in the hood.

"I wasn't thinking," Isaiah said. "It was a mistake."

Manzo had that look of blind, unrestrained malice just like Vicente. A nerve had been touched, a reflexive response to a threat on la familia.

"Fuck your mistake," he said. "Nobody fucks with the Locos. I'm the shot caller," he went on. "Do you know how this makes me look? Do you? You can't disrespect me like that."

Isaiah tried to stay calm. Cowardice was another reason to kick your ass. His mind flashed again: *The best apartments in the hood.* Why did he keep thinking that? "Look, I'm sorry, Manzo. I was trying to find out about my brother."

"Yeah, your fucking brother. You know what? He deserved to get hit."

Isaiah felt his fury billowing up inside him. "What did you say?" he hissed.

"You heard me."

The realization struck Isaiah like he'd been punched in the gut. *The best apartments in the hood.* In one motion, he reached back, grabbed the baton, and snapped it open. Manzo leaned away as Isaiah swung, the metal rod hitting him across the head, the sound like a triple to right field.

"OH SHIT!" Manzo screamed.

Isaiah's fury exploded. All the years he'd spent defined by Marcus's murder, all the years of grief, loneliness, and longing were about to be avenged. "You killed my brother!" he shouted. "YOU KILLED MY BROTHER!" He struck Manzo again and again, the gang leader howling as he staggered away, crashing into the bookshelves, smashing the turntable, LPs spilling to the floor. Isaiah kept swinging. He wasn't going to stop until this motherfucking cocksucking son of a bitch's eyes rolled back in his head and his tongue was hanging out of his mouth. "YOU KILLED MY BROTHER!" he screamed again. He whacked Manzo across the back of the knee. Manzo collapsed, rolled, and came up aiming a gun. He was grimacing in pain, teeth bared like a man-eater, his entire body straining to hold back his trigger finger.

"Motherfucker," he breathed.

At the edge of his peripheral vision, Isaiah saw Ruffin peeking out of the hallway. *Get him, boy, get him!*

"You're dead, Isaiah," Manzo said. "You're fucking dead."

Get him, boy! Get him, goddammit! The dog just stood there like he was considering whether it was worth the risk. *GET HIM, YOU STUPID DOG! FOR GOD'S SAKE GET HIM!*

Manzo got up on one knee, his aim unwavering, blood leaking from his hairline, streams of it snaking down his face. Ruffin was still thinking it over. *FUCKING DOG!*

Isaiah stepped forward. He'd rather die with his hands around Manzo's throat than continue living his stupid, shrunken life.

"Yeah, come on, cabron," Manzo said. "Give me one more reason to kill you."

Ruffin withdrew, huffing dismissively as he did. Manzo turned to look, and Isaiah threw the baton, charging right behind it. The baton hit Manzo in the face. He fired, but the shot went wide. Isaiah threw a lunging punch that knocked Manzo over, the gun falling on the floor. Isaiah sat on his chest and choked him, Manzo trying to pry his wrists apart. "I'm going to kill you," Isaiah snarled, his temples throbbing, his sweat dripping on Manzo's bloody face. "I'm going to fucking kill you."

No one heard the gunshot, or if they did they didn't want to get involved. The gun and baton lay between splotches of blood, dried black on the cement floor. The stereo was hanging over a shelf, the tone arm sticking up like it was waving for help. Ruffin was lying on some album covers, licking the blood off his paws.

It was Manzo who robbed Frankie. The newly inducted shot caller needed capital to start his empire. It was the Locos who would benefit so why not use Loco money? So where had Manzo and Marcus met? *At the best apartments in the hood.* It wasn't hard to imagine Marcus working there, busy, the money and heroin easily slipped into his backpack. It was smart, really, a kind of insurance. If the police found the contraband and word got around, it was solid proof that Marcus was the perpetrator. But why pick on Marcus and not somebody else? It might have been random. He was there in plain sight, he wasn't Latino and had no friends among the Locos. Conveniently, he played basketball at the park every Saturday so Manzo knew where he would be. Sure, a bullet in the head would have been more efficient, but Manzo anticipated the murder investigation that always follows a shooting so he arranged the hit-and-run. An accident, not a homicide. Bottom line, Manzo was the only one who had the means, motive, and wherewithal to pull off something with so many moving parts. And that's why he'd saved Isaiah from a beating outside Beaumont's store. Guilt. Guilt for killing an innocent man with a good heart who'd never hurt anyone in his entire life and left a grieving little brother behind.

Manzo wouldn't go to the hospital so Isaiah patched him up. He knew first aid and had a first aid kit a paramedic would have been proud of. Mini–CPR unit, blood pressure cuff, emergency blanket, ice packs, heat packs, instant glucose, burn gel, blood stop dressing, ammonia inhalant, splinter outs, antiseptics in various forms, twelve different kinds of bandages, and an assortment of other stuff, so much he kept it in a suitcase. In the end, Isaiah couldn't do it. Couldn't strangle a man in cold blood. When Manzo got up, his knees wobbled and he collapsed. Isaiah caught him before he hit the floor and dragged him onto the sofa. When he came to a few moments later, neither of them had the energy to start it up again. Isaiah felt bloodless and blank. The outpouring of rage had exhausted him.

Manzo had a sizeable gash on his head, welts all over him. Isaiah gave him a handful of ibuprofen and rolled him a joint from Raphael's weed. He didn't have enough ice packs to cover all the welts so he used packages of frozen vegetables.

"I'm gonna kill you for this," Manzo groaned.

"You can try," Isaiah said. "If I don't kill you first."

"We'll see what happens."

"I guess we will."

Isaiah's neighbor, Mrs. Marquez, was a nurse, and she'd shown him how to stitch up a wound. Isaiah washed his hands with a surgical prep sponge, put on latex gloves, and drew five ccs of lidocaine into a fourteen-gauge hypodermic.

Manzo was alarmed. "Hey, man," he said. "I hate needles."

"It's the only way unless you want an infection."

"Do you know what you're doing?"

"Yes, I do."

"Fuck it, man, let it go. It'll heal up by itself."

"So the leader of the Sureños Locos 13, who's been shot, stabbed, and beat up who knows how many times, is afraid of a little needle?"

Manzo almost said yes but grumbled under his breath instead. He wouldn't let Isaiah shave the area around the gash so Isaiah did his best to keep the hair out of the way. He numbed the gash, cleaned it, and used a suturing kit to stitch it closed. Manzo gritted his teeth but didn't make a sound.

"You came here to kill me?" Isaiah said.

"No, I came here to scare the shit out of you," Manzo said. "The gun was for show. What was all that shit about killing your brother?"

"Don't play stupid. I know it was you."

"Me? Me personally? You're fucking crazy. The Locos had a hit out on him—what'd you expect us to do? He robbed Frankie."

"No, he didn't. You did."

"The hell are you talking about?" Manzo tried to move, winced, and inhaled through his teeth. "Shit that hurts," he said. "Look, I know your brother did the robbery, okay?"

"How?" Isaiah said, his anger returning. "How do you know? Were you there?"

"I didn't have to be."

"Then how do you know it was Marcus? Did Frankie see him?

How? It was dark out, wasn't it? And the guy had to be wearing a mask. Did Frankie hear his voice? Did Frankie—"

"Shut up for a second, okay?" Manzo said. He sat up, the ice packs and frozen vegetables falling to the floor. He grunted and touched the stitches on his head.

"Don't," Isaiah said. "Let them be. They'll dissolve by themselves in a week or so."

Manzo took a deep breath. "I'm gonna tell you what happened, okay? If you don't believe me, so be it." Isaiah nodded. "So after your brother robbed Frankie—"

"That didn't happen, Manzo," Isaiah said. "He couldn't have—"

Manzo silenced him with a look and started again. "*So after your brother robbed Frankie,* he ran to his car and drove the wrong way, into a dead end. He had to turn around and go back. Frankie saw the car just before he passed out."

"How did he know it was Marcus's car?"

"He didn't, but after he got out of the hospital, I was taking him to physical therapy and he saw the car again, parked right near the hardware store. A dark green Explorer, right? We waited until your brother came out of the store and followed him home."

"So you *did* kill him."

"We would have," Manzo said, "but by the time we got our shit together he was already dead."

Of all the possibilities Isaiah had considered, that wasn't one of them. "How did you know he was dead?"

"We read about it in the newspaper. Jorge saw it on TV. It was an accident. No disrespect, but he was lucky. Vicente wanted to torture him."

Isaiah sat silently. Manzo was telling the truth. "I'm sorry," he whispered. Manzo lay back on the sofa and closed his eyes.

"You owe me, Isaiah," he said. He dozed off.

Isaiah went outside and sat on the stoop. Ruffin sat next to him, laying his chin on Isaiah's knee, maybe apologizing for not attacking Manzo like any other self-respecting pit bull would have done. Isaiah was still incredulous. Marcus robbed Frankie? No. Couldn't happen.

An hour later, Manzo woke up. He went to the bathroom, washed up, and came back. He moved like his entire body was sunburned.

"You want a ride home?" Isaiah said.

"No, I don't want a fucking ride home. Gimme the rest of the weed."

Isaiah stood in the doorway and watched Manzo get in his car, wincing as he slid into the seat. As he drove away, he shot Isaiah a look. "You owe me, Isaiah. You owe me big-time."

Isaiah was numb. He got a beer out of the fridge, lay back in the easy chair, and held the bottle to his cheek. The voice in his head wouldn't shut up. *Did Marcus commit the robbery? Well, did he or didn't he? Why don't you find out? What's the matter? Scared?* He knew he should have settled it earlier, but he'd put it off, hoping the question would somehow settle itself, and Marcus would be vindicated. He didn't like to think about it. Was Marcus everything he believed him to be? Was Marcus living a double life? No, of course not. But *if*—and of course he didn't—but if Marcus had robbed Frankie, the money would be in the storage locker.

The heat wave was tormenting the city. The sidewalks were abandoned, the playgrounds and parks empty. Road-rage fights were reported on every freeway and air-conditioned shelters were provided for old folks. Tune in to any radio station and all you heard was *hydrate hydrate hydrate*. Isaiah went to the locker and burned his fingers on the padlock. He opened the sliding door and got a blast of hot, musty air as repellent as his dread. He did a long, slow scan, his eyes picking their way over the workbench, the trash can, the bins of scrap lumber, the pegboards, tool racks, the drill press, and the lathe. There were some old window frames and a couple of doors leaning against a wall. Unbeknownst to the storage company, Marcus had installed crossbeams near the ceiling so he could store lengths of two-by-four. Six-foot-high metal shelves lined the twenty-foot wall, laden with rows of cardboard cartons and plastic bins with lids marked TAX RECORDS, INVOICES, RECEIPTS, CORRESPONDENCE, BANK STATEMENTS, going back a number of years, as well as Isaiah's school records, awards, and old photos. There were also miscellaneous boxes, piled with a hodgepodge of souvenirs, trophies, favorite toys, things that were meant to be fixed, cassette tapes, fishing equipment, shoes too good to throw away, and a bunch of other stuff you'd find in a typical garage.

Lots of places to hide money. Isaiah considered gridding the locker, go through it systematically like the police would, but that would take a long time. *Okay. So I'm Marcus. Where would I hide the money?* Well, who are you hiding it *from?* A thief, of course, but that was easy to do. No thief would go through the whole place or cart the entire contents of the locker away. The main threat was Isaiah, and if that was the case then where would Marcus *not* hide the money? Sometimes they worked together so it was unlikely to be hidden in or around the tools, the construction materials, or the workbench. The walls and ceiling were corrugated metal so they were out. The floor was cement. That left the cartons and bins. Isaiah had stayed away from Marcus's business. It was boring for a boy in Advanced

Placement classes and Marcus was territorial about his work; that belonged to him. So maybe start with the business records.

Isaiah went down the row, diligently riffling through the cartons one by one. He got impatient and shook the boxes instead to see if he could feel or hear something that wasn't paper. In the box marked TAX RECEIPTS '07, he felt something with some weight to it slide back and forth. *It's nothing. A stapler, something like that.* He opened the carton and underneath a sheaf of file folders was a fireproof box about the size of a dictionary. Clawed hands twisted Isaiah's intestinal tract, his scalp felt like spiders were crawling on it. No, it couldn't be. It was birth certificates, passports, Social Security cards, stuff like that. Isaiah lifted the lid and the smell of old leather mixed with fabric softener wafted out like poison gas. Nothing but money smelled like that.

Crammed in the box were twenty and hundred-dollar bills, rolled into neat bundles and bound with rubber bands. An eyeball count: twenty, forty, fifty—*eighty* grand? Isaiah's first reaction was that it was some *other* kind of money. Marcus had found it or won the lottery or—no, that was ridiculous. There was no other conclusion you could come to. *Marcus robbed Frankie.*

Isaiah shut the box and closed his eyes. It was as if Marcus was dying all over again; Isaiah's perfect image of him hit by a meteor, smashing it to pieces. So Marcus had a hidden side. A side capable of getting a gun and ambushing Frankie and shooting him, however accidentally, and leaving him for dead. But why would he do it? That part was even more bewildering than the robbery itself.

Isaiah went home, put the fireproof box on the coffee table, and flopped down in the easy chair. He stayed there, brooding at the gilded shafts of sunlight coming through the burglar bars. As the sun set, they turned hazy, fading into a pointillist painting of ever-darkening grays, the room dimming into blackness plush as velvet. *Why?* he thought. Marcus wasn't materialistic so it wasn't about buying things. He was a giving person so maybe one of his friends needed an operation or maybe it was for charity. No, that made no sense either. Marcus robbed Frankie so he could pay for a liver transplant or make a donation to the McClarin Park Community Center? No, it was something else. Marcus was a gambling addict? Not possible, Isaiah would have known. Marcus was in debt? To who? For what?

Isaiah remembered when he was in high school. The brothers were having breakfast together. Marcus had his Shredded Wheat and coffee; Isaiah with a raspberry Pop-Tart and milk. They were having an argument they'd had a dozen times before.

"There's lots of other good schools, Marcus," Isaiah said. "UCLA, SC, Davis, Berkeley."

"No. You're going to Harvard."

"What if I'm not accepted to Harvard?"

"You will be."

"What if I'm not?"

"Then you're going anyway. Harvard's the best. Best students, best professors, best everything, and I want you to have the best."

Did Marcus rob Frankie so he could pay the forty grand a year tuition? A sickening thought, Marcus getting killed because his little brother had to have the best. Isaiah made some soup, ate half of it, and gave the rest to Ruffin. By the time he was a senior his GPA was 3.9. He'd scored twenty-two hundred on his SATs and in the thirties on the ACT. He'd won all kinds of awards for academic achievement, was involved in extracurricular activities and community service and had recommendations from counselors, teachers, even a city councilman. There was no doubt in anyone's mind that he was going to get a scholarship wherever he went, including Harvard. The fact was, Isaiah didn't need additional money to go to college. Oh sure, some extra would help but he could work part-time to make his expenses and Marcus would have contributed whatever he could. It made no sense, Marcus risking his life, abandoning his conscience, and maybe going to prison just so Isaiah could have new clothes or a car. It wasn't enough of a reason.

These questions had absolutely no effect on Isaiah's roiling hatred or his determination to find the killer. He wondered if Marcus would approve. Probably not. Marcus was pragmatic. He'd say he was dead after all and couldn't you be doing something more productive with your time? Isaiah wondered if the people who killed their daughters' rapists felt better afterward. He doubted it. Eliminating whoever caused your pain didn't eliminate the pain itself, but that was an intellectual perspective and one that had no effect on his intentions. He would catch the man who took his brother's life and the punishment would be terrible and brutal and oh how that murdering son of a bitch would suffer.

The anger reenergized him. He opened the box again, looked at the money, and closed it. *Okay,* he thought, *start over.* Assuming it wasn't somebody random, the only suspect left was Seb. The tidy man in the glen plaid suit had the intelligence and the means but no motive. Why, of all people, would he kill Marcus? Isaiah couldn't imagine a reason. On the other hand, Seb had been deceptive about knowing Marcus and why would you do that unless you had something to hide? Could have been instinctive. A criminal's response. No, Officer, I didn't see anything, I don't know anything, I don't remember anything. Can I go now?

Isaiah had hit a wall. There was no lead to follow, no evidence to find, not even an idea worth thinking about. Marcus used to say when you're stuck and you feel like there's no way forward, go the other way. Go back to the beginning.

In the morning, Isaiah went back to the corner of Baldwin and Anaheim where Marcus was run down, and the world had changed forever. He took Ruffin with him. Chastened by the girl's comments, he'd speed-read a couple of books on dog training. He'd found an all-positive method that was simple in concept. Reward the behavior you want, ignore the behavior you don't want. A lot better than shouting commands a thousand times, the dog confused. *What was that, Master? Did you just say no? No what? No walk? No pull on the leash? No stand here? No turn? No eat the dog turd? I'm not a mind reader, asshole.* Ruffin always barked at other dogs, so if they were approaching one, Isaiah held a treat in front of his nose to distract him, and when they passed the dog without incident, he got the treat and an enthusiastic *Good boy!* If he barked, Isaiah said nothing, and there was no treat either. The dog picked up on it fast. Same about jumping up. If he did, Isaiah turned away and gave him the cold shoulder. If he approached and immediately sat down, he was rewarded. Sitting had become automatic, the default position, no treats required. Isaiah took Ruffin to the park so he could get used to people, the homeboys admiring him, playing tug-of-war with him. He took the dog to the animal shelter and let him romp with the dogs there.

"You're not such an idiot after all," Harry said.

When Isaiah reached the intersection it was like looking at the photos of the Accord. Everything normal, cars driving by. *Where's the memorial? Why isn't the road closed?* Isaiah shut his eyes and saw the accident happening again. The two of them talking, Marcus asking him what he wanted for dinner as he stepped into the intersection, the car hitting him so hard it was like a cheap special effect. One second he was there, the next he was broken and bleeding and sprawled on the pavement. Isaiah remembered kneeling beside him and screaming for help and telling Marcus everything would be okay and Marcus not moving or saying anything and people telling him an ambulance was on the way.

A cop got there first. He took one look at Marcus and got on his radio. *We've got a 10-57, requesting backup.* Isaiah learned later that a 10-57 was a hit-and-run. Then the paramedics came and told him to stand back and that they'd do everything they could, one of them talking on his radio. *The victim is a male, twenty-five years old, hit-and-run. He has multiple lacerations, impaired breathing, head injuries, fractures to his left arm and leg, and possible internal bleeding.* The paramedic had already decided it was a hit-and-run and so had the cop. Later, an APB had probably gone out for the Accord, but that would have been the extent of the investigation. It wasn't a homicide, and you couldn't assign detectives to look for an individual car in a city choking with them. The conspiracy to kill Marcus had gone off as planned.

But what if the cops *hadn't* bought it? What if they hadn't been so quick to assume that it was an accident and suspected it might be a homicide? What would they have done then? They'd have looked for a *motive.* A struggle with a business rival, a crime of passion, life insurance, revenge. But what did that have to do with Seb? Except for the notation in the workbook, there was no evidence Marcus had ever met Seb, and even if he had, what could he possibly have done to warrant being killed? There had to be a nexus somewhere, but where would you even start looking? Only Seb knew the answers and only Seb could give them up.

CHAPTER ELEVEN

Frankie the Stone

Ramona was in the morgue. Manzo had viewed the body. Neither Frankie nor her mother could deal with it. It was late morning, and the living room was too small for the crowd. People were standing around talking about normal things. What they'd seen on TV. What was on sale. What somebody said about somebody else. Manzo didn't blame them. How much could you say about Ramona?

Frankie was on the couch, his mother clutching him, crying.

"Ella no hace daño a nadie," she sobbed. "Ella era una buena chica."

Did she really believe that? Manzo wondered. That Ramona was a good girl and that she never hurt anybody? Where'd she been all this time? The shooting had only happened last night, but the mantel had already been cleared for Ramona's photograph, two black ribbons crossing the top corners of the frame. It was taken when she was a student at St. Anne's; ten, eleven years old, a tooth missing from her sinless smile, a gold crest on a dark red sweater vest, a prim white collar. Next to the photo, incense sticks were burning in a silver bowl of uncooked rice. Manzo had seen that before but still didn't know what it meant.

Frankie looked like the only survivor on a minefield, the charred bodies of his comrades all around him, their flesh cooking in the flames. Manzo stayed back, not knowing what he'd say to him. It wasn't his fault but he felt guilty anyway. He could have done things differently. Trying to control Ramona had only made her fight back harder and made her look bad to the cholas. He should never have slapped her. He should have talked to her more, not lectured so much. He should have asked Pilar and them to give her a break.

Manzo glanced up and almost flinched. Frankie was staring at him, his eyes splintered with red veins and grief.

"You were supposed to take care of her," he said.

The room went quiet, the people an audience now. A kid came running in and his mother hissed at him.

"She went off on her own, Frankie," Manzo said. "There was nothing I could do."

"I trusted you," Frankie said.

"I know and I'm sorry," Manzo said. "I couldn't be with her all the time."

"Why did you let her do stupid things?"

"I didn't let her, she just did them."

Frankie thought for a moment and then nodded at one of the old ladies. "Tía, cuidar de ella," he said. "I'll be right back, Mom." He got up. "Let's go," he said, people making a wide path for them as they left the room.

They came out of the back door and stood in the yard. "Who did it?" Frankie said, lighting a cigarette.

"Ramona sent me a text before it happened," Manzo said. He got out his phone and read the message. "'Chink Mob in our hood. I got this.'"

"Who the fuck is the Chink Mob?"

"Alphonso said they're from Arcadia," Manzo said. "Look, Frankie, I did my best, okay? It wasn't good enough but I tried."

Frankie smoked and stared at a rusty lawn mower stuck in the weeds. "You know what?" he said. "I'm like throwing the blame on you but it's my fault. I couldn't take her under my wing because I was too sick, too fucked up."

"That's the way she was, Frankie," Manzo said. "You can't blame yourself."

"You see that picture of her, the one in the living room? She was a good girl, she was smart, she was doing good in school and everything." Frankie bowed his head, covered his face with a hand, and wept, his voice hiccupping out of his throat. "She was my sister, man, my little sister. I was supposed to take care of her."

"It's not your fault, Frankie."

"They shot her. They shot my little sister."

Manzo didn't try to comfort him. It felt phony and wrong. He just wanted to get out of there, away from Frankie's conscience, he had his own to deal with.

"I loved her, man," Frankie sobbed. "I loved her."

Did he? Manzo thought. He'd learned a long time ago that people say all kinds of shit but love is what you *do*. Frankie let Ramona hang with the fellas, ditch school, drink, smoke weed, and party all night. He bragged to her about who he'd shot and taught her how to use a gun and flashed thick rolls of cash and drove her around in his lowrider, Cypress Hill blasting out of the Fosgates, Ramona sitting tall, queen of the hood. Was that love? No. That was for yourself. That was ego.

Frankie raised his head, took a long breath, exhaled through his mouth, and smeared the tears off with the heels of his hands. "Come on," he said. There was a stack of junk piled up next to the shed; half sheets of plywood, two-by-fours, stacks of flowerpots, a roll of chicken wire, paint cans, dented rims, rocks, and cinder blocks. "Help me move this stuff," Frankie said.

Frankie worked like Ramona was buried underneath the pile. Pulling things off, tossing them aside, working up a sweat, breathing like a winded dog. A big plastic storage bin was underneath the junk. Frankie pried off the lid. There were five pistols and as many assault rifles. Different makes, different calibers. They were grimy because of the gun oil, patches of rust here and there. Frankie picked up a handgun, opened the ejector, and blew into it. He wasn't stooping anymore; he was standing erect, his shoulders squared. Life was returning to the hollows of his face, and you could feel something moving around in that damaged brain, something with fur and teeth coming out of its den. "Get everybody together," he said. "The park. Now."

His voice was so different Manzo was startled. It was El Piedra's voice. Frankie the Stone. Violence had destroyed him. And violence was bringing him back to life.

"Why?" Manzo said.

"We're going to Arcadia."

Thirty-eight members of the Sureños Locos 13 met in McClarin Park. Frankie made a long, rambling speech, everybody paying attention out of respect. They were going to avenge Ramona, his little sister, who was killed in their own hood. Everybody but Manzo was down for it but he wouldn't say it out loud. One more mission to nowhere that wouldn't do anything except get a few of them killed and a few more locked up for a decade or two.

At eight in the evening, twelve cars full of armed homies caravanned north on the 605 through Downey, Montebello, Temple City, and into Arcadia, the city's hood like any other. Manzo wondered if there was a big factory somewhere that manufactured fucked-up apartment buildings, raggedy houses, liquor stores, and strip malls just for poor people. He stayed well behind. If they wanted to get pulled over, they couldn't have done any better if they'd mounted a machine gun on Alphonso's pumpkin-orange '68 Chevelle, the doorsills two inches off the ground, blasting "Ride of the Valkyries" out of a Crossfire eight-thousand-watt amp and enough subwoofers and speakers to break eardrums in Dodger Stadium. But hey, they looked badass, didn't they?

According to social media, the Chink Mob hung out in an area just off Foothill near the 210. The Locos dispersed and drove around, sometimes passing each other and shrugging. They saw CM gang signs, but there were also tags from Wah Ching and the Four Seas Mafia. Mostly what they saw were a lot of Chinese people minding their own business. Manzo wondered what the fuck they were supposed to be looking for. Some homie carrying a sign that said I BELONG TO THE CHINK MOB?

Manzo parked in a strip mall. If something happened he'd get a text. He got tired of waiting, had a sandwich at Subway, took a nap, waited some more, and finally got a message. It was after midnight when everybody reassembled in the parking lot at Ralphs. Nobody saw any bangers. Frankie made another long, rambling speech, vowing they'd come back and get justice for Ramona. Everybody said they would but at that point, they just wanted to go home.

Frankie had come with someone else and Manzo drove him back

to Long Beach. "Shit, man," Frankie said. "That was really messed up. We'll come back on the weekend."

"Think about it, Frankie," Manzo said. "Do you really want to do that? I mean, what are we gonna do? Come back here and shoot anybody who looks gangster? Ask somebody do they know where the Chink Mob is at? And if we find them, then what? Have a big fucking shootout and we all go to jail?"

Cracks were appearing in El Piedra, the rock face crumbling, chunks falling off, his flesh turning gray as dirt, his body seeming to grow smaller. "Sorry, Frankie," Manzo said. "I didn't mean to bum you out."

"I have to do something for Ramona."

"Ramona's gone, Frankie."

Frankie seemed to be weighing that for the first time. He sat there with his head down like separate dreams were coalescing into one sorrowful nightmare. "Yeah," he whispered. "Ramona's gone."

They drove without speaking, no music, just the thrumming V8. Manzo kept his eyes on the road, he didn't want to look at Frankie anymore. They were almost home before he finally glanced at him. Tears were held in Frankie's eyes. "All the shit I done, man," he said. "How come I'm still here?" He looked mystified down to his core, his stare turned inward for an answer. The tears lost their tension and spilled over; streams of liquid crystal trickling down his old face. "It's not right, man," he said. "It's not right."

No, Manzo thought. It's not.

Leo was really pissed now, chasing all over Vegas for Janine and Benny. What if word got out that he was losing his grip and people started thinking they could skate on him and not feel the consequences? A loan shark might as well be Wells Fargo if a default wasn't punished immediately and with malice of forethought. And who were all these other people? Who were the black dudes? Who were the squinty people? Zar said they were Chinese, like you could tell the difference. Hold one up next to a Korean guy and the most you could say was that the Korean guy had more tickets for reckless driving.

Zar had a thing about the Chinese. They'd be in some fucked-up town looking for a deadbeat, and Zar would somehow come up with a phone book.

"Look at the Hos, Leo!" he'd say, marveling as he turned the pages. "Nancy Ho, Lian Ho, Warren Ho, Zi Ho—"

"Crack ho."

"Look at how many Wongs there are! Bao Wong, Robert Wong, Mee Wong—"

"What's your point, Zar?"

"If you're Chinese you're never alone, eh?"

Leo liked to say he *found* Zar, like he was fishing in Lake Mead and Zar floated by in a reed basket. It happened at Leo's hangout, a bar called Dino's Lounge, a dive on the threadbare end of Las Vegas Boulevard. There was a big sign in the parking lot for a bankruptcy attorney that said BUSTED? on one side and ACCIDENTE? on the other. Leo had grown up in the neighborhood, if you could call it that. Third-rate motels, trash-strewn empty lots, crusty manufacturing plants and old commercial buildings that said DISCOUNT no matter what they were selling.

The Dino's crowd was mostly blue-collar and whatever was below that. The room was smoky and dark, inked-up waitresses, fifties porn playing, white girls painting their toenails. There was a Drunk of the Month contest, the contestants nominated by the bartenders, and if you guessed what suit of cards was under the Pabst Blue Ribbon cap you got a free beer.

Leo loved Fridays, karaoke night, the crowd rowdier and drunker than during the week. He had a decent voice but his specialty was singing falsetto. His rendition of "Stayin' Alive" was always a crowd-pleaser. He'd throw in a few disco moves during the chorus and when he hit that pose—hip cocked, one hand pointing at ten o' clock, the other pointing at four—the bitches went *crr-razy*. He thought about wearing a white suit but decided it was too much.

So it was after his performance, and he was standing at the bar when a guy named Larry approached him. Dockers, rigid polyester tie, a cap that said NATIONAL IRON WORKS that might as well have said SUCKER. Larry said he usually played casino games and didn't know much about sports but his nephew was a towel boy for the Carolina Panthers. They were playing the Tampa Bay Buccaneers in the opener. The towel boy said the Panthers' star quarterback, Cam Newton, was coming off injuries. He'd been sacked a lot, one hundred and eighty-five times. Larry said he wanted to bet Tampa Bay and he wanted to borrow a thousand dollars, and he promised to pay it back right after the game.

"You are one lucky son of a bitch," Leo said, his eyes wide like he'd never met anyone so fortunate. "Hey, I've been doing this for a long time, and let me tell you, the towel boys are the true insiders—wait, did you say a *hundred and eighty-five times?*"

"Yeah, I did," Larry said.

"Cam should be in a wheelchair," Leo said, shaking his head. "Say, do you mind if I bet the game myself?"

Encouraged, Larry upped the loan amount from a thousand to twenty-five hundred. Leo did a quick credit check, confirmed the guy had been in his house for a year, and the deal was done. Leo could have told Larry what would happen. Cam, one of the best quarterbacks in the league, had been sacked a hundred and eighty-five times *over three seasons;* his average for sacks among quarterbacks was about middling, and no one in the press said he wouldn't make it for the opener. The Bucs, on the other hand, were one of the worst teams in the NFL. They'd won four games in the previous season to the Panthers' eleven, and their quarterback, Mike Glennon, was a journeyman. The Panthers won 20 to 14. Predictably, Larry didn't pay after the game, not even the vig, and he didn't answer his phone.

Leo went to visit Larry-boy at his dried-up hacienda in a development called Rio de Oro, Leo thinking the last time there was a *rio* here, dinosaurs were drinking from it, and if there was *oro* around it must look like pea gravel. Surprisingly, Larry opened the door on the first knock.

"Where's my vig, asshole?" Leo said.

"I don't have it," Larry said.

Leo hesitated a moment. He thought he heard some defiance in Larry's voice. He barged past him into the living room. There were a swayback sofa and two big-screen TVs; beer bottles, fast-food debris, and unopened mail scattered around on the smudged shag carpeting. Wife and kiddies had apparently had enough of daddy's gambling away the grocery money.

"I knew you were a loser the minute you walked into the bar," Leo said. "Look at you. You and your stupid cap and crooked glasses and your sweatpants and your—wait, is that a wet spot? Damn, Larry, don't you know you're supposed to shake your dick off before you put it away?"

"It's beer," Larry said, brushing himself with the back of his hand.

"Sure it is," Leo said. "I always drink beer out of my nut sack. Where's my money, asshole?"

"I just said I didn't have it," Larry said, the defiance still in his voice.

Leo held his fist up to Larry's face, his fingers threaded through a brass knuckle-duster. "Then I'm afraid I'll have to make some radical alterations to your appearance, starting with your front teeth." And then an honest-to-God monster came into the room, ducking his head so he wouldn't hit it on the door frame. All he needed were some bolts stuck in the side of his head and he could pass for Frankenstein's big brother. He was wearing cargo shorts that could have carried actual cargo and an old flannel shirt, torn at the elbows and big as a bedspread. The shoestrings on his sneakers were tied at the middle eyelet because they were too short to make it the whole way.

"You don't want to do that, eh?" the monster said. "Larry's my friend."

Most people would have gotten the hell out of there, but Leo the Lionheart had never backed down from anybody in his life except that one time when Misty Love tried to stab him with an ice pick.

"And you think your homo relationship means anything to me?" Leo replied. He gave Larry a shove. "This nonessential drag on the economy owes me money and rule number one is—"

The monster stepped in close, Leo's eyes about level with his nipples, assuming they *were* nipples and not army helmets or hubcaps. Leo thought a moment and said: "Tell me something, Lurch. Have you got a job?"

"A job?" the giant said.

"Yes, a job. You know, you show up somewhere, do something undignified, and they pay you minimum wage."

"Sure, I have a job."

"As what?" A battleship? A mountain? Hoover Dam?

"I'm a bouncer at the Crazy Horse. Don't make fun of me, eh?"

"My apologies. I didn't realize somebody of your magnitude would be sensitive to anything other than hand grenades."

Leo told him he was looking for someone to help him with collections, and Zar had the exact qualifications he was looking for. Leo told him he could ride around in the Mercedes and eat steak and lobster and live someplace where he didn't get his hair caught in the chandeliers, and he'd get him some decent clothes, assuming they could find a tailor who specialized in ogres. By the time Leo was done with his sales pitch, Zar was in.

"That's great, eh?" he said. "Let me get my stuff." Which turned out to be a backpack that fit him like a cupcake stuck on his spine. "Okay, I'm ready."

Leo looked at him, the monster all excited and smiling like a kid going to the water park. The faintest sigh of sadness whispered past Leo's ear and was gone again. "One thing before we leave?" he said.

"What?" Zar said.

"Get the vig from Larry."

Leo called Charlie O and ordered up Misty Love and Renee. He took a shower for Misty's sake and didn't use the cologne she said smelled like overripe bananas. He thought about Janine and Benny, who under no circumstances would be allowed to escape their financial obligations. Didn't matter how long it took or how extreme the measures, rule number one was like the eleventh commandment. The twelfth was *Thou shalt not fuck with Leo the Lionheart*.

The Travel Inn was just off the highway. The traffic noise woke them up. They'd slept longer than they had intended. Dodson made a plane reservation and rushed around packing. Isaiah sat on the bed and talked to Deronda. She told him about the attack and the Chinese guys and the crazy Mexican girl getting shot and killed. Isaiah felt it before he thought it. *Ramona*.

"Was she fifteen-sixteen, pink streaks in her hair?"

"Yeah, how'd you know?"

"Where are you?"

"An undisclosed location, and by the way, who's gonna pay for all the buckshot holes in my daddy's house?"

"Who put them there?"

A slight pause. "That don't matter," Deronda said. "Shit wouldn't have happened if you hadn't sent Janine here."

"Is she all right?" Isaiah asked.

"Yeah, she's fine. She wants to know if Benny and her dad are okay."

"Tell her I don't know yet. You guys stay there. I'll call you back." The call ended.

Dodson was ready to go. "What are you staying for?" he said. "Ain't nothing to do here."

"I start something, I finish it," Isaiah said. He was being an asshole again but couldn't help himself. He didn't want to be left alone.

"I'm not even gonna talk to you," Dodson said.

Dodson was right. There *was* nothing else to do except call the police, but they'd have no better chance of locating Ken and Benny than Isaiah did, and if they somehow managed to find them, Ken would be unmasked as a sex trafficker and go to jail, where he'd be more vulnerable to an attack than if he was walking around on the street. Then the police would question Benny. Why were you kidnapped? What did you do to cause this? Did the kidnappers want something from you? Do you have a girlfriend? What's her name?

Her sister's a lawyer? What's *her* name? Benny would fold like a fresh slice of Wonder Bread.

Embarrassed now, Isaiah said, "I'll take you to the airport."

"That's aight, I know how busy you are," Dodson said. "I'll take a cab."

Isaiah's phone buzzed. A text. No message, just a picture of Ken and Benny seated on the floor. Ken was badly beaten, pulpy face, bleeding split lip, an eye swollen shut, ugly bruises on his face. Benny looked just how anybody would look if they crashed their motorcycle and rolled into the bushes. His head was back against the wall, face screwed up in pain. There was a big rip in his dusty leathers, and his shoulder sagged, broken or dislocated, his arm held against his chest.

"Check this out," Isaiah said, holding up the phone.

"Damn," Dodson said. "They fucked 'em up good."

The phone buzzed again. Unidentified caller, TracFone logo at the top of the screen. A burner.

"How you doing, IQ?" Skinny said, a mocking smile in his voice. "How everything? Everything okay?" Isaiah put the phone on speaker. "How you like the picture, huh?" Skinny said. "I take good one."

"What do you want?" Isaiah said.

"Boss want to meet you. Face-to-face."

"Why?"

"He don't like to talk on phone. Don't worry. No trap."

"Bullshit," Dodson said.

"That's your friend, Dosson, right?" Skinny said.

"How do you know my name?"

"We know ebreting."

In the background, you could hear voices. You couldn't make out the words but the cadence wasn't English. Dishes and silverware were being banged around.

"Hey!" Skinny shouted. "You make too much noise!" But the noise continued unabated.

Isaiah thought a moment, glanced at his watch. "Meet you in an hour at Caesars. I'll text you the exact place."

"No. We pick place."

"Then no meeting."

Skinny had a muffled conversation with someone. "Okay," he said.

"If you're late I'm leaving."

"Sure, sure, no problem."

The call ended.

"What do they want?" Dodson said.

"If I'm Tommy Lau," Isaiah said, "I'm thinking things are getting out of hand. I'd say he wants to make a deal."

"You know they're going to try something."

"There's cameras everywhere, security people, lots of exits."

"What if they follow you?"

"I'll park at a different casino, walk over. They won't have a car." They looked at each other, the eight-hundred-pound gorilla sucking the air out of the room. "Are you coming?" Isaiah said. Dodson heaved a sigh that was almost a groan.

"Aww, man, you can see the fix I'm in," he said.

"It's cool," Isaiah said, so much insincerity in his voice he almost called himself a liar.

"It's the baby, man."

"I know. It's cool."

"Cherise needs me."

"Just go. Really. I'll be fine."

CHAPTER TWELVE

Asian Flower Erotic Massage

Tommy was in Ken's bathroom, retying his red tie. He'd never worn any other color, not for luck, but because he couldn't be bothered choosing ties. He'd sent Tung to Long Beach so Zhi was driving him to Caesars. Some men were already there doing reconnaissance, no surprises. Tommy hated problems like this; something you had to take seriously, but resolving it was tedious and gained you nothing. Liko was running the business now, but he was in over his head. Trafficking was mostly about logistics. Recruiting the people, collecting their fees, laundering the money, bribing the officials, getting transportation, housing and so forth. Over the years, 14K and the triads found easier ways to make money, gradually shifting their interests to gambling, drugs, credit card fraud and other financial crimes, leaving the business largely to the snakeheads. Most were small operations, some family-run, others groups of common criminals. But Tommy realized the triads' lack of interest had left a fortune on the table. Despite its problems, he got back into the business, gradually taking over a substantial part of the market in both California and Nevada. Some of the competition had been absorbed, the rest were visited by the Red Poles and forced to relocate. Tommy made lots of money.

And yet he longed for the old days when it was all about action and audacity. Extortion, kidnapping, armed robberies, gunrunning, drugs, wars with other triads. Twenty-five years ago, he was chief lieutenant for Wan "Broken Tooth" Huok-koi, who ran 14K's operations in Macau. Wan was flashy and arrogant. A real asshole. Custom-made pinstripe suits, cream-colored shoes, and a diamond pinkie ring big as a walnut. Wan modeled himself after John Gotti, but that was a joke. He looked like John Gotti's Chinese pimp. When the police started cracking down on 14K despite all the payoffs, Wan got angry and ordered Tommy to blow up the police chief's car. The chief wasn't hurt, but somebody sitting at a nearby coffee shop was hit by shrapnel and killed. Wan and Tommy were arrested but for racketeering, not the bombing. Wan got fifteen years, Tommy seven, but they continued to run 14K from prison. The guard let them use cell phones, bring in liquor, food, hookers. One of the guards tried to enforce the prison rules and was shot on his day off.

When Tommy was released, he left Macau, moved to Hong Kong and then to San Francisco, bringing some confederates with him and establishing his own branch of 14K. No one was upset, it happened all the time. The triad had no upper management. It was a loose association of splinter groups who helped each other with distribution, resources, enforcement, contacts, and intelligence, and unlike the Italian Mafia, there were no tributes, no paying a cut to the guys upstairs.

In many of the groups, the old initiation rituals had gone by the wayside. Tommy insisted on them. Tradition was important. He himself had gone through them; entering a darkened room under an archway of crossed swords, standing at an altar where the Incense Master recited a triad poem. Tommy was ordered to wash his face and remove his clothes. He was given a white robe and sandals, to cleanse away his past and start anew as a member of 14K. Then he had to read the thirty-six oaths aloud. He remembered a few of them.

If I have caused the arrest of one of my brothers I must release him immediately. If I break this oath I will be killed by five thunderbolts.

I must never reveal triad secrets or signs when speaking to outsiders. If I do so I will be killed by myriads of swords.

If I am arrested after committing an offense I must accept my punishment and not try to place blame on my sworn brothers. If I do so I will be killed by five thunderbolts.

Following the recitation, a cock was killed and its blood drained into a bowl of wine. Yellow paper was burned and its ashes were added to the wine. Tommy drank but didn't know how much was appropriate. He drank most of the bowl and nearly retched. Afterward, Wan laughed at him.

"You only take sip," he said.

The whole ceremony was pure gibberish, but it gave the initiates the idea that they belonged to an ancient fraternity, that they were part of something sacred and bigger than themselves.

Zhi knocked on the door. "It's time to go, boss."

Isaiah parked at Harrah's and from there walked with Dodson to Caesars. He was uncomfortable in places like this, knowing every curve, color, nook, and cranny were designed to manipulate you, make you feel like a high-roller, impressed with yourself for just being there. The lobby was as big as a small lake, with a soaring ceiling and pillars big as redwoods. Roman craftsmen and the set designers from *Star Wars* had apparently joined forces to create the ancient, futuristic chandeliers. The light was the color of an eagle's eye and cast a voluptuous glow over the vast expanses of marble flooring embedded with mosaics and Roman motifs. At the lobby's center, a huge statue of three women wearing togas that exposed one breast stood in a bubbling tiered fountain. Tourists, with their T-shirts, visors, and running shoes, looked lost in all the grandeur and oddly out of place, like they'd gotten off the bus and found themselves at the emperor's summer palace.

The bar Isaiah had chosen was just off the concourse. Small and dim, the ceiling ornate and painted blue. A big aquarium bubbled contentedly, jellyfish drifting like living parachutes. Isaiah and Dodson sat down in a booth. Dumbo and another guy were already seated at the bar. They turned around on their stools and glared. Dumbo's face was bruised from Dodson's rat-tat-tatting.

"Sometime we get together, okay?" Dumbo said. "We see what happen."

"Oh yeah?" Dodson said. "Well, you better bring a firearm, muthafucka, 'cause if you don't shoot me I'll be kicking your ass all over again." Dodson had changed his plane reservation for later in the afternoon. When he told Cherise she hung up on him.

Tommy Lau and a nervous little man who looked like a bean counter arrived promptly at six. The bean counter went to the bar with the others. Tommy sat down in the booth. "Mr. Keen-ta-bee?" he said. "Did I say that correctly?"

"Close enough," Isaiah said.

"And you must be his associate, Mr. Dosson," Tommy said.

"Pleased to make your acquaintance," Dodson said.

Tommy placed a small plastic device on the table, about the size and shape of a Rubik's Cube, tiny buttons on it and a blinking LED. "White noise generator," he said. "You understand, I'm sure. Recording devices are bad for business."

"So why are we here?" Isaiah said.

"Ah yes, Americans get right to the point. The Chinese are very different in that respect. Such candidness is considered bad form. We ease into things, make our proposal indirectly. That way, if the other party should refuse, no one is embarrassed because there was no proposal in the first place. Shall we order something to drink? You are my guests, of course."

Tommy ordered Glenfiddich, Isaiah didn't want anything. Dodson ordered the most expensive thing he could think of, Stoli Elit. "I must admit, I don't like Vegas," Tommy said. "It's so—what is the expression? In your face. I much prefer San Francisco. Unfortunately, I've never been to East Long Beach. I hear it's quite a rough neighborhood."

Sending me a message, Isaiah thought. He knows where I live. "Could we get on with it?" he said.

Tommy took a sip of his drink, the rimless glasses reflecting the multicolored lights from the concourse. He smiled slightly, amused and contemptuous; a warlord deciding the fate of a captive. "All right, if you insist," he said. "We seem to be at an impasse. We both have something the other wants. I wish to speak to Janine. You want to secure her safety and the safety of Ken and Benny. Does that adequately sum up the situation?" Isaiah nodded. "Well, let me assure you," Tommy went on, "we don't want Janine harmed in any way, she is like a daughter to me. All we want to do is talk. If she has copies of the records, she gives them to me, and she can go back to her normal life."

"What about Ken and Benny?"

"We're done with Ken, and as for Benny, he had one copy of our property on a flash drive and another he emailed to himself. Not too smart. Other than that, he knows nothing. If we can come to an agreement about Janine, both shall have their freedom."

"Look, I'm not stupid and neither are you," Isaiah said. "If we turn over Janine, she's dead and so are Ken and Benny."

"The arrangement does require a certain amount of trust."

"I don't have any, and you *do* realize that if Ken and Benny are killed, we'll turn the records over to the police, and if Dodson or myself should accidently be hit by a stray bullet, the same thing will happen. *We* have the leverage, Tommy, so how about this? You hand over Ken and Benny and we don't give your records to the police."

"But what is your leverage really worth?" Tommy said. "If the police close down my business I have others, and I have no direct ties to anything here. Ken will the pay the price, which I am guessing is counter to your mandate. Sarita paid you to extricate him, did she not? Who else could have brought you into this? And if my records should end up with the authorities, you, Mr. Dosson, Janine, Ken, and Benny will be fugitives, on the run for the rest of your lives, and let me assure you, 14K has a long reach." Tommy lit a cigarette and exhaled patiently. "So let us try another approach," he said. He slipped his hand inside his jacket.

The photos of the girls had seared char marks on Isaiah's spirit. He felt the anger buzzing in his ears. "Keep your money," he said. "You think I'm gonna take a payoff from a slave trader? I'd rather put a dead rat in my pocket."

"It's the way of the world," Tommy said, annoyed now. "Don't be naïve."

"Is that what you'd say to your daughter if she was getting fucked by thirty strangers a day? *Don't be naïve, honey, it's the way of the world?* I've met evil sons of bitches like you before, but I still don't understand it. Doesn't it ever bother you that you're a parasite? That you make your living off the suffering of others? That most people would rather spit on you than shake your hand?" Isaiah couldn't think of just the right words to hurt him so he just kept talking. "Did you know that if you died right now, right this minute, people would celebrate and the only thing they'd feel bad about was not getting to torture you before you were gone?"

Tommy looked icebound, his eyes freezer-burned, the warlord smile a hyphen now. "I think that's quite enough, Mr. Keen-ta-bee," he said. Tommy's guys had turned to face the bar, pretending not to hear their boss getting vilified. Maybe they were embarrassed for him, maybe they were glad.

"Tell me something," Isaiah said. "Were you just not smart enough to make it as a legit businessman or were you limited by your lack of character? Was pimping out your own people your only option? You couldn't have done something more honorable, like robbing blind folks or kidnapping babies? What I'm trying to get at is, *what's wrong with you?* Why are you such a freak? Did you live next door to a plutonium mine? Did you *mutate* into a monster? Were you infected by some kind of hyena virus? What happened, Tommy? Tell me, I really want to know."

"This is unwise of you," Tommy said, his voice coming from someplace ancient and covered with blood. "Very unwise."

"That's okay," Isaiah said. "I've been unwise before."

"Maybe one of these days you'll end up in the joint," Dodson said, sipping his Stoli. "Get passed around by the bruthas, see what it's like. Shit. Them muthafuckas will turn your ass into chicken chow mein."

"Was that it, Tommy?" Isaiah said. "Was that your only move, paying me off? Because if it is, go back to whatever shithole you crawled out of and think of something else. I'm done with you."

The warlord was back, and he was going to war. Tommy stood up. The bean counter and the others got up too, relieved it was over. "All right, gentlemen," Tommy said. "Playing chicken with 14K is a very bad idea. We will not have this issue hanging over our heads forever." He glanced at the bean counter.

"Two more hours," the bean counter said, nodding at his watch.

"You have two hours to reconsider your position," Tommy said. "If you do not, Ken and Benny will be eliminated, and if our records should go to the authorities, your leverage will be gone and you will never be safe. *Never.* I am not bluffing, Mr. Keen-ta-bee, and one day we will talk further, in a setting where we can more fully express ourselves." Tommy pocketed the noise generator and strode away, the others hurrying after him.

"You know what?" Dodson said. "That muthafucka didn't pay for the drinks."

Isaiah and Dodson headed back to Harrah's for the car. "He's up to something," Isaiah said. "Remember what the other guy said? Two *more* hours. Like Tommy already has something in the works."

"Like what?" Dodson said.

"I don't know, but when it happens he won't need Ken and Benny anymore." Isaiah thinking, *Tommy needs two more hours because...*

"I know what he's doing," Dodson said. "He's giving us time to think about the money. Like we ain't nothin' but a couple of niggas from the hood. We'll take the payoff sooner or later."

"That's not it," Isaiah snapped. "Two hours is too long. It gives us a chance to come up with something, make a move on him. *Tommy needs two more hours because...*

"There you go again!" Dodson said. "Talking down to me. That shit ain't even necessary, Isaiah. That's why we always going toe-to-toe. Can't you talk and be respectful at the same time?" They crossed an intersection, the fear slamming into Isaiah so hard he nearly stumbled.

"Oh shit!" he shouted.

"What?" Dodson said, annoyed at being behind again.

Isaiah hit the speed dial on his phone and waited for somebody to pick up. "Come on, come *onnn,*" he said.

"Who you calling?" Dodson said. They were in the middle of the street, horns honking. "How 'bout we get our asses over to the sidewalk?"

"Hello?" Sarita said.

"Sarita, it's Isaiah. Get out of your apartment *now.*"

"Why? What's going on?"

"You're in danger. Get your things and get out."

"In danger from who? From what?"

Dodson had a handful of Isaiah's shirt and was pulling him over to the curb.

"Have you got a friend, relative, someplace you can go?" Isaiah said.

"Yes, but why do I have to—"

"Don't ask me any more questions, Sarita, just do it."

"Isaiah, could you please tell me what's—"

"I *said,* no more questions! Get out of your apartment *and get out now!*"

"Okay," she said meekly.

"Text me when you get there."

"I'll call."

"No, text me," he said, knowing he'd be busy. He ended the call.

"So that was it?" Dodson said. "Tommy's guys needed the time to get to LA and kidnap Sarita?"

"Yeah."

"But they can't now, so what's Tommy gonna do about Ken and Benny?"

"He'll kill one of them. Make his point. Probably Ken first. We've got to find them. In two hours."

They sat in the car and looked at the picture of Ken and Benny again. The captives were sitting on the floor between a washing machine and a dryer. Part of a wire rack was visible, bras and panties hanging from it.

"Massage parlor," Isaiah said. "A storefront."

"How do you know it's a storefront?" Dodson said. "That could be a house or an apartment."

"Look at the plumbing," Isaiah said. Behind the washing machine a big chunk of the drywall had been torn away, exposing the studs and plastic pipes, which still had a shine on them. "See there? They had to rip out the drywall to put the plumbing in. They wouldn't have to do that in a house or an apartment building, it would already be there."

"Uh-huh, uh-huh," Dodson said, nodding like he was checking Isaiah's reasoning, making sure it was correct. "Well, I don't see how that helps us. There must be a million massage parlors in Vegas."

"The skinny guy said he took the picture, but he was calling from somewhere else," Isaiah said. "There was a lot of noise in the background." He looked at Dodson as if to say *Well?*

241

"Yeah, I heard all that," Dodson said. "Dammit. I know them sounds, I heard them before."

"The voices weren't in English. The cadence was wrong. It was Chinese."

"That ain't no insight, was a Chinese guy that called us."

"Whoever he was talking to wasn't his crew. When he shouted at them nobody paid any attention. He was in a public place."

"Silverware and dishes!" Dodson said, pleased as a fourth grader with the right answer. "Yeah, you thought you had me, didn't you? Sounded just like the Mandarin Palace. That boy was calling from a Chinese restaurant."

"Took you long enough to figure that out," Isaiah said.

"Yeah, but I'm gaining on you."

"Okay, so he took the picture at a massage parlor but he called us from a restaurant. They couldn't be that far apart."

"How do you know? He could have been picking up takeout and there's Chinese restaurants all over Vegas."

"Chinese restaurants deliver, and if he took the picture he's probably on the crew that's guarding Ken and Benny. He wouldn't have gone far."

"Well, if he could have got a delivery, what's he doing in a restaurant?"

"Would you eat your supper in a massage parlor if you didn't have to?"

"Didn't I just tell you about using that tone with me?"

They used their phones, did some searches and brought up a couple of maps. The first one showed massage parlors in the Vegas area. Dozens of them scattered across the city, Chinese restaurants were the same.

242

"We're looking for massage parlors that are close to a Chinese restaurant," Isaiah said.

"Right, right," Dodson said.

They compared maps. "The majority of massage parlors are right around in here," Isaiah said. "Near the I-15, Sahara Avenue on the north, Tropicana on the south. I'm gonna play the odds, stick to that cluster."

"You just guessing now," Dodson said.

"The area is close to the casinos," Isaiah said. "If I was 14K that's where I'd set up shop. More customers." There were eight massage parlors within walking distance of a restaurant. They called each of them, asking if a nice Korean girl was available. Four said they were Chinese, and Chinese girls were better, more erotic. Isaiah glanced at his watch and started the car. "We've got an hour and fifteen minutes to find them."

The first massage parlor had a neon sign that said FAR EAST MASSAGE in red letters on a background of white. A red-and-yellow Chinese lantern hung over the door, the red drapes drawn, an OPEN sign on the door.

"How do we tell if they in there?" Dodson said, annoyed he had to ask. Isaiah didn't answer. He drove past the place, made a turn and then another, circling the block. He was looking for something.

"The skinny guy's not here," Isaiah said.

"How do you know?" Dodson said. "Did you see something?"

"It's what I *didn't* see."

"You fucking with me now."

"You said you'd help. I can't *help* you help."

Every brain cell in Dodson's skull was firing. *What didn't Isaiah see? Why's he driving around the block? Nothing around here but parked cars.*

Isaiah drove on. "You want me to tell you?" he said.

"I'm getting it, I'm getting it," Dodson said, not getting it at all. *What didn't I see? What's missing?* It was like that time he was in the crack house on Seminole when a storm had dumped too much water on the roof and the whole ceiling came down at once. "I got it!" Dodson said. *"The car.* Skinny boy's car ain't here!"

"You're gonna have to be quicker than that," Isaiah said, with an irritating smile.

"Fuck you, Isaiah."

Skinny's car wasn't at the second place either. The third, Asian Flower Erotic Massage, was right across the street from the Hunan Delight restaurant. Same font of red letters on a background of white, same red-and-yellow Chinese lantern hung over the door. A Tommy Lau franchise. Isaiah drove around to the back of the building. Skinny's BMW was parked in the lot with a clunker that was probably the mama-san's. No customers, that was a plus. Isaiah drove a few doors down and parked, Dodson's brain still whirring. *Okay, they in there but now what?*

Dodson followed Isaiah around to the trunk of the car. The floor panel and the spare tire had been removed, making the compartment extra deep. Plastic storage boxes of various sizes were neatly arranged and labeled. HAND TOOLS. DRILL/CIRC SAW. SOLDER/WELDER. PRY TOOLS. LOCK TOOLS. RESTRAINTS, WEAPONS.

"Damn, Isaiah," Dodson said. "What's all this?"

"Tools of the trade," Isaiah said. Something called the Determinator was in a yellow plastic case.

"What's a Determinator?" Dodson said.

"It's a grenade launcher," Isaiah said.

"Now you talking, son, I'm down with that."

"All I've got are fireworks grenades. They'll burn the whole place down." He opened the SURVEILLANCE box: Binoculars, monocular, variety of hidden cams and listening bugs, long-range mike, night scope, GPS tracker.

"Where'd you get all this?" Dodson said.

"You can get anything on Amazon," Isaiah said. "Did you know they sell a flamethrower?" Isaiah found the WALL BUG: a mike that looked like a suction cup and a set of headphones and small transmitter. "You can listen through concrete with this thing," he said. He crept up to the back door of the massage parlor and put the mike against it. He listened for a few moments and came back to the car. "Skinny and some others are in the back," he said. "Three of them by the sound of it. The TV is on."

"Did you hear Benny and Ken?" Dodson said.

"No, but Skinny lost Benny once already. They're probably close by." Isaiah paused a moment, that faraway look on his face. Dodson knew what that meant. *Shit. I'm running behind,* he thought. *What's next? Oh, I know.* How! *How we gonna get Ken and Benny out of there? Look at him. He's playing it out in his mind.* Frustrated, Dodson didn't even ask.

"Where's Janine's phone?" Isaiah said.

Leo was at the crib, lying on his big round bed, wearing his black silk tuxedo socks and nothing else. He liked to say the black satin sheets were just like Hef's. He was smoking a joint with Misty Love. She was from Eastern Europe somewhere; high cheekbones, glacial blue eyes, fake tits. She always had a look on her face like she was watching C-SPAN cover a golf tournament even when she was on her hands and knees. She once told Leo her last name, and he said: "How can you have a name with no vowels in it?"

"Ven are you goink to marry me, Leo?" she said, passing the joint to him so slowly it was like a sloth climbing a tree. She did everything like that. Leo thought washing her face must take her a day and a half.

"What's that?" Leo replied. "I'm never *goink* to marry you. Leo the Lionheart needs a whole tribe of females to keep him satisfied."

"It's pride."

"Pride? I got pride. I got more pride than that parade they have in West Hollywood. You know me and Zar got stuck in that last year? Yeah, they closed off all the streets and some oiled-up weight lifter with a spray tan hit my car with a sign that said *Queen for a Day,* and Zar grabbed him by his codpiece and—"

"No, Leo, as usual, you are not lisnink correctly. I mean it's a *pride* of lions. Pride means group. Like flock of birds or herd of sheep."

"Or a whole bunch of bitches. Maybe it's different in Slobovia—"

"Lithuania."

"But here in America we don't pay our fiancées before the nuptials. By that time it's more of a barter system. She gives it up and you buy her a car."

They heard Renee in the other room. "Cut it out, Zar, I told you before. Don't you put it in there."

"Marriage is normal, Leo," Misty said. "Vee are perfect together."

"Vee are? Since when?"

Leo handed her the joint back and she took a hit like she was inhaling a noodle that was five feet long.

"Tink about it, Leo," she said. "The screwing is good, yes? Also, I am self-sufficient, I am not botherink you with my problems."

"Well, I gotta give you that. I remember when Charlie O gave you a black eye, and you beat him with that fireplace poker all by yourself."

"Here is bottom line, Leo. You don't luff me, I don't luff you. If we don't luff each other we don't fight. There is nutting to fight about."

"But if we don't luff—"

"Stop it, Leo. It is annoying."

"If we don't love each other why do it?"

"So vee von't be lonely," she said. "It is normal."

Leo's phone buzzed. A text from Janine. broke up with benny just left him at massage parlor getting rocks off. has $$ for vig but won't pay. asian flower massage hurry.

"Hey, Zar?" Leo said, pulling on his black silk boxers. "We gotta go."

"You heard him," Renee said. "Now could you get your sky-scraper ass off of me so I can breathe?"

The back room of the massage parlor had no ventilation and no ceiling fan. Ken and Benny were wedged in the narrow space between the washer and dryer. Benny was semiconscious and leaning on Ken's shoulder. Everybody was sweating, but only Ken seemed to mind, the girls and the Red Poles used to heat and humidity.

"Could we get some water, please?" Ken said.

"You don't need water," Skinny said, grinning. "Pretty soon you never need water again." The three Red Poles laughed.

Ken couldn't believe it. They were really going to kill him. Kill him before he'd lived any kind of life, before he could make it up to his daughters, before he could start over. "Let me speak to Tommy," he said.

"No, Tommy. Too late for that."

"He doesn't need to do this. We're not going to talk to anybody.

Why would we? We'll just disappear. He'll never hear from us again."

"This way he know for sure. You shut up, okay? Or I shoot you right now."

Ken looked at Benny. He was despondent, cradling his broken arm like a baby born dead.

"I wish I could see Janine," Benny said, heaving and blubbering. "Just one more time...tell her...tell her I'm sorry."

"I warned her over and over again that you were a loser but she wouldn't listen," Ken said.

Benny looked at him, the boyish face twisted with rage. "What about you, Mr. Van? I know I'm a loser, but I'm not evil—all those girls. Go to hell, Mr. Van. Go to fucking hell."

Isaiah was rummaging around in the LOCK TOOLS box.

"How're you opening that door?" Dodson said.

"Bump key and the drill are too loud. I've got to pick it."

"You know they got guns in there, don't you?"

"Yeah, I know."

Dodson looked chagrined. "I can't go in there with you."

"What?"

"I said I can't go in there with you. If I get killed, Cherise'll kill me again."

Isaiah looked at him.

"I'm gonna be a daddy, Isaiah. I can't get shot now."

"Fine," Isaiah said. "Look in the weapons box. The red case."

Dodson found the red plastic case. The label said THE HEAT SEEKER. "The hell is this?" he said. He opened it and embedded in the gray foam were parts of a handgun. "Damn, Isaiah. I didn't know you was strappin'."

Picking a lock was one more thing that had no relation to how they did it on TV. Isaiah shook his head when the CIA agent stuck a paper clip in the lock, twisted it around a little, and presto, the lock opened. In reality, you needed to know the mechanics of a lock and practice a thousand times; develop a touch for it because you'll be doing everything blind. Hidalgo, the locksmith, told Isaiah that the people on YouTube who picked a lock in thirty seconds could do it because they were locksmiths. Hidalgo explained that the little peaks and valleys on a key were called cuts. When you put the key into the cylinder, each cut corresponded to a tiny spring-loaded piston, each the size of a large ant. They act as miniature dead bolts and are really what keeps the lock locked. The cuts elevate or lower the pins, aligning them so when you turn the key, they get out of the way and the lock can open. When you pick a lock, you're trying to align the pins just like the key would.

Isaiah inserted a tension wrench first, like an Allen wrench but flat. It kept the pins from springing back into place once they were aligned. Trial and error had taught Isaiah that the weight of one finger was just enough tension. The keyway was narrow so he chose a Deforest diamond pick, thinner than the standard S. He made an exploratory probe and counted five pins. He started with the one at the back, gently nudging and prodding, his eyes closed, visualizing what the pick was doing.

"What's taking you so long?" Dodson said.

"Shut up, okay? I have to concentrate." He found the pin and with a motion no bigger than drawing a grain of rice he felt it slip into place. He went on to the second. He was starting to sweat. He knew the plan was tenuous, reckless and maybe even stupid, but he kept seeing himself lounging on the cream-colored sofa with Sarita, drinking a glass of wine, talking easily, the Modern

Jazz Quartet drifting gently from the stereo, kissing her, stroking her hair...

"You know you got to get this open before Leo gets here," Dodson said.

"Will you *please* shut up?" Isaiah replied. "Load the gun."

Dodson opened the Heat Seeker case and began assembling the components. "Wait a second," he said. "This ain't no real gun."

"It's a pepperball gun."

"Pepperball gun? Did you say *pepper*ball gun?"

"Semiauto, gas-powered, eight shots, sixty-foot range," Isaiah said.

"Them muthafuckas got Glocks," Dodson said. "Semiauto, powered by gunpowder, ten shots, and the range is from here to East Long Beach. Are you crazy? Why don't I just go in there and hit 'em with a salt shaker or a jar of mustard?"

"Load it," Isaiah said. The third pin fell into place.

The Heat Seeker's ammo was in a plastic envelope. Little round red balls. "*This* is what you talking about?" Dodson said, alarmed. "You got a golf club I can hit 'em with?"

"They explode on impact," Isaiah said, probing for the fourth pin. "A habanero pepper is rated at five hundred thousand Scoville units. These are rated at fifteen million."

"Uh-huh," Dodson said. "So how many units is a bullet?"

The white Benz pulled up and parked in front of Asian Flower.

"You know what?" Leo said. "I might have been here before."

He and Zar got out and went up to the front door. It was locked, you had to get buzzed in. He could see the mama-san at the front desk. She had that *what the fuck is that* look on her face like most people had when they saw Zar.

"Sorry, we closed now," she said.

"Then why does that big neon sign say *open?*"

"No more girls. All busy."

"Busy? You mean *forever?* Who are they massaging in there, the National Guard? Open this door, bitch, and open it right fucking now."

"Sorry. We have private party."

"Everybody I know is a liar and you are the absolute worst I've ever heard. Are you gonna open this door or not?"

"Sorry—"

"Sorry what?" Leo said, rattling the doorknob. "There's a flood in the building? You ran out of lube? Open the goddamn door before my friend kicks the shit out of it."

His nickname was *Gujia,* the Chinese word for *skeleton.* It used to bother him, people telling him he was too skinny and to eat more rice, but not anymore. Being hungry all the time gave him an edge. A hungry tiger is more alert than one that's fat and happy. In ten minutes, Tommy would call and give him the go-ahead and then they'd take Ken and the kid out into the desert and shoot them. Gujia used to be bothered by the killing, but now he didn't care; it was more of a chore than anything else, the victim just a floor he had to mop. The only people he could remember actually caring about were his three little sisters; stringy hair and sooty faces, no shoes, playing in the brown puddles on that filthy fucking rooftop. Only one was still alive. The second got sick. It could have been from the raw sewage that ran under their shack or from the water they drank out of a tin bucket or from the spoiled food they ate with their hands. Hard to say. She died without seeing a doctor. The other was a toddler when she fell off the roof. He remembered looking over the edge and seeing people clustered around her body. She was so dirty she blended in with the asphalt. The only thing he cared about now was his status in the triad and that was slipping away fast. He'd fucked up at the Lucky Streak and that wasn't going to happen again.

The alarm buzzer sounded, something was happening in the front. He looked up at the surveillance monitors and saw the giant kick in the door, the glass shattering, the lock ripped out of the doorjamb. The giant came in with the disco guy. The mama-san reached under the counter to get her Beretta, but the giant's arm extended like an old-fashioned car antenna and shoved her into the wall so hard her eyes rolled back into her head as she slid to the floor. There was no other reason for them to be here except to get Benny.

"Let's go," Gujia said. The Red Poles grabbed their weapons and ran into the hallway just as the giant and the disco guy entered from the other end. Everyone stopped and raised their guns; thirty feet away from each other, hard eyes unblinking, not fucking around. The hallway was red-lit and warm. Nobody moved, sweaty seconds going by.

"Well, if it ain't the beanstalk," Disco Guy said. "Anybody ever tell you to eat more rice?"

"You go now or we start shooting," Gujia said.

"I want Benny. Do you want to get him for me, or shall I get him myself?"

"You try. See what happen."

"Do you Charlie Chans know who you're messing with? I'm Leo the Lionheart and I'm not going anywhere unless you got Misty Love standing behind you with an ice pick."

"You bring giant again, huh?" Gujia said. "We not scared of him."

"You should be," Leo said. "Does he look like he's afraid of bullets? We were coming out of Dino's one night, and Ray Santini shot him in the head. Zar didn't even know he'd caught one until blood came out of his ears and fucked up my upholstery."

Gujia thought about Tommy and what he'd say if Ken and Benny got away. "I ready to die," he said. "What about you?"

Dodson was listening with the Wall Bug, Isaiah still picking the lock. "The Red Poles left the room, man, hurry up," Dodson said. "Ain't nobody in there now."

"Will you please leave me alone?" Isaiah said. One of the pins that was already aligned slipped back into its original position. "Dammit, see what you made me do?"

"Stop whining and open the damn thing!"

Isaiah remembered robbing a bicycle store; careening down an alley in reverse, a cop car on its way, Dodson yelling at him just like he was now.

"I can hear 'em arguing with each other," Dodson said. "You gotta get in there *now!*"

"Shut *up,* Dodson!"

Leo's arm was getting tired from holding the gun straight out, and he was getting tired of all this bullshit; in a Mexican standoff with some punk-ass Chinamen who evidently didn't know about Leo the Lionheart. Yeah, okay, he'd given himself the name but it was true. He had a heart as big as a cast-iron lung. Everybody in Vegas was afraid of him except Baby Dewy, the bouncer at the Spearmint Rhino, who had three metal plates in his head; the Klesko brothers, but they were hired killers; Sandoval "Sarin Gas" Gutierrez, a former MMA fighter who was said to live in a cave with his wife, a bighorn sheep; and Elmore the Dwarf, who made his living stealing purses off the backs of chairs. Creepy little dude, with his pudgy hands and oversize head. Say something about his height and he'd whack you in the nuts with a cut-down three-wood.

"Am I ready to die?" Leo said to the skinny guy. "Is that what you said? Are you seriously trying to intimidate *me?* Shit. I been in more gunfights than you wax on–wax off motherfuckers will ever see in your fucked-up Chinatown lives, which might be ending real soon if you don't bring Benny out here. Try and get it through your thick, slant-eyed, undocumented heads that I'm a dedicated, lifelong, unrepentant lawbreaking motherfucker and I play by no one's rules but my own and rule number one is *Pay me my fucking money.*" Leo squeezed the trigger.

Isaiah was working on the last pin, trying to keep his movements small and delicate instead of ripping the fucking doorknob off. He had the flop sweats and couldn't keep his hands dry. He had to wipe them off on his shirt and start all over again. *"Dammit,"* he said. Dodson had finally shut up but you could feel his anxiety growing, about to explode. And then, *gunfire.* Like an artillery barrage. BLAM! BLAM! BLAM! BLAM! BLAM! On and on, deafening even through the door, punctuated by screaming girls and the shouts of the shooters.

No point picking the lock now. Isaiah stood up and kicked the door in. "Gimme the Heat Seeker," he said.

"Fuck it," Dodson said, holding on to it. "Just go."

When the shooting started, Leo leapt sideways into a massage room, Zar too big and slow to do anything but stand there. The

Chinese guys were still shooting, backing out of the hall, two of them hit and staggering.

"Get down, Zar!" Leo shouted. "Why are you standing there like a goddamn high-rise? Get out of the goddamn way!" Leo stuck his gun around the corner and kept shooting. "Zar, did you hear me? Get out of the way!" Zar was looking down like he'd spilled something on himself except it wasn't gravy on his shirt, it was blood. "Zar, can you hear me?" Leo said. "Take cover!" It reminded Leo of an elephant, the way Zar sat down, not bending his knees, his butt going straight to the floor.

"What the fuck, eh?" Zar said. He looked puzzled, like Leo had told him he'd never die so why the fuck was the world turning dark? Then his shoulders went slack and his chin fell on his chest. He was gone. Leo was stunned, and in a rare moment of self-awareness, he realized that Zar was the only person in the world that he could actually call a friend. He slapped in a new clip, roared like a wounded demon and stepped out into the hall.

Isaiah kicked down the door and charged in, Dodson right behind him. The barrage continued. BLAM! BLAM! BLAM! BLAM! BLAM! Bullets coming from the hallway blew up dishes on the counter, punched holes in the microwave. The girls were hysterical, curled up on the car seat, hands up protectively. "Get out, get out!" Isaiah shouted, and they scrambled past him, escaping through the back door. Ken stuck his head out from behind the washing machine.

"Over here!" he said. Isaiah and Dodson rushed over and pulled him and Benny to their feet. "Thank God!" Ken said.

The Red Poles came stumbling into the room, two of them bloody and crawling, Skinny covering their retreat. He saw Isaiah, turned to shoot, and was smacked in the head with something that went *poof!*—white powder covering him like a handful of flour. He screamed and choked, his hands clawing at his eyes, Isaiah and Dodson hustling the captives to the door.

Leo left Zar and went down the hall, realizing only now that he'd been shot. His vision was going on and off like a flashlight with a fading battery. His brain wasn't connected to his legs anymore, and they were moving by rote. He thought about Misty and that as soon as this shit was over with he'd marry her. Maybe she was right about *luff*.

He entered the back room, stepped over the two Charlie Chans, who if they weren't dying already were pretty close to it. Something in the air burned Leo's eyes and scalded his throat. That skinny ass-hole was staggering around screaming. Leo shot him behind his ear and went out the back door. He could feel himself shutting down, a cloak of chain mail weighing on him, everything dimming and getting farther away. He could just make out the black guys help-ing Ken and Benny cross the parking lot. He raised his gun and aimed at Benny. He wanted him to know that he hadn't escaped from Leo the Lionheart. "Hey, Benny," he said. "Pay me my—" He never heard the gunshots or saw the mama-san behind him, scream-ing as she shot him five times in the back.

CHAPTER THIRTEEN
I Am Killing You for Sure.

Isaiah was getting desperate. He had nothing to link Marcus with Seb except a phone number in a work log and that didn't equate to murder or anything else. It was time to take action. It reminded him of the Black the Knife case and trying to kidnap Goliath, the giant killer pit bull. He could either do something dangerous, bordering on stupid, or give up and walk away. He wished Dodson was with him.

At five in the afternoon, Seb came out of the Nyanza Bar. Isaiah followed him to a modest house in Cambodia Town. He was fidgety and apprehensive. If he came up dry here the investigation was over. Seb parked in the driveway and went inside. Isaiah watched from the Audi and did what he should have done a while ago. He got out his phone and did property searches on Seb's addresses. The apartment, the condo, and the house were all owned by a corporation with a PO box for an address. Seb's holding company. There was an IN ESCROW sign posted on Seb's lawn and the Jaguar was brand-new. The previous one was only a couple of years old. New house, new car. Seb was going upscale.

The next morning, Isaiah returned at seven. A little after nine, Seb came out of the house and checked the front door to see if it was locked. He ran his eye over the Jaguar, not admiring it but inspecting, scrutinizing, looking for a dust mote, Isaiah thought. With the suit and cane, the neighbors probably thought he taught African studies at UCLA. Seb drove away but Isaiah waited, wary of Seb's OCD. He might come back to confirm or correct something, and ten minutes later he did, to see if the front door was really locked. Still skeptical, he got back into the car and left again. Isaiah waited another twenty minutes and drove around to the alley behind the house. He got an extension ladder out of the backseat and gathered some tools.

The attenuator box was mounted under an eave. It enclosed the siren or bell that would sound when a motion sensor inside was tripped. Isaiah set the ladder in place and climbed up to it. The box was metal, with ventilation slots and a key lock. Easy to pry apart, but there might be a secondary mechanism that would go off if you forced it open. Isaiah took a can of liquid Styrofoam, put the straw into a slot, and filled the box. The liquid would harden in a couple of minutes and encase the alarm so you could barely hear it.

Isaiah set up at the back door and used a twenty-volt HSS drill with a cobalt bit to drill a hole on either side of the keyhole, cutting the screws that held the locking mechanism in place. As soon as he opened the door, the motion sensors would pick him up and send a distress signal to the monitoring company. They would call Seb to see if it was a false alarm, but he would be twenty minutes away and if the monitoring company called the police it would take a while for them to get there. Isaiah had once made a study of police response times to burglar alarms. Over ninety percent of them were false so they were low priority for the police, especially residential, the response times ranging from forty-five minutes to two days. For a residential alarm call in Cambodia Town the police might never come.

Isaiah slipped inside. He couldn't hear the alarm, the Styrofoam trick had worked. The living room was furnished with expensive white leather furniture. The floors were white, the walls were white, colorful pillows as accents; not a wrinkle, fingerprint, footprint, or speck of anything anywhere Isaiah could see. The hardwood floors were a grayish white. The grain wasn't maple, cherry, or oak. Something else. Bamboo maybe. A jade ashtray, an ornamental lighter, and three coffee table books were laid out on the coffee table in a grid. A sterile arrangement of fake lilies was set on the mirrored mantel, everything in the room *just so*. It was as if Seb had taken a page out of a catalogue, called the company, and said Give me everything in the picture. Yes, the lilies too. African sculptures and masks were placed around without conviction like Seb had thought Well, I suppose I must put up something. Isaiah was starting to feel foolish, wondering what he could possibly find that would link Seb to the murder. A diary? A video of Seb admitting he was the killer? A note to Gahigi to steal a car so they could run down Marcus? The only reason he didn't leave was because he was already here. Shut up and keep looking, he said to himself.

Gahigi was in the basement, lying on his narrow bed. Seb had offered him the second bedroom but Gahigi liked it down here. The impenetrable walls and the damp cement smell. The transom of frosted glass, narrow as a gun slit. The spindly chair. His sparse wardrobe hanging on pegs, his two pairs of sneakers lined up beneath them. Seb said it looked like a jail cell. But to Gahigi, it was a fortress. Come down the staircase and you'd be an open target for the .45 he kept duct-taped to the headboard. Seb wanted to decorate the place but Gahigi refused. This felt right. This was his due. He lit a cigarette. He didn't know what he was going to do today or the next or the next. He thought he should be making a decision, but he didn't know what to decide. When he tried to think of something, all he saw was a long road of red earth leading over a hill into the bright Rwandan sun.

He had a cold. Nothing serious. Sniffles and a slight cough. Seb insisted he stay home. His plans were reaching their conclusion, and the last thing he needed was to get sick. Gahigi was pulling on his pants when he heard the footsteps. He looked up and tracked them across the ceiling. He hadn't heard Seb's car arrive. It was someone else. An intruder.

Isaiah went into the office first, as immaculate as the living room, the smell of cigarettes suppressed with something springtime fresh. He opened a few drawers and cabinets but didn't see anything relevant. There was nothing unusual in the room, the only oddities were copies of *People* and *Los Angeles Magazine,* stacked neatly on a shelf. Again, he wondered, what was he looking for?

In slow motion, Gahigi crept up the staircase, his bare feet going heel to toe, touching the steps like cat's paws, the gun held across his chest, his other hand out in front of him, ready to move a branch or a palm leaf or anything else that might brush against his clothing and give him away. He reached the landing. The doorknob was old and squeaky. He deliberately hadn't oiled it, leaving it as a trip wire to alert him if someone was invading his lair. Ever so gently, he turned the knob in tiny increments, feeling the points where it tightened and easing it through. It was taking a long time, but he wouldn't rush. Stealth, he had learned, was a greater weapon than a gun. He pushed open the door with his fingertips.

Isaiah looked at the framed photographs lining the hallway. There was one of Seb as a boy, sitting on a bare bed, bandages covering the stump where his leg was cut off. He was staring at the camera as if to say *What now?* Another photo showed Seb and Gahigi as boys. Gahigi's scars were fresh and deep; his attacker nearby judging by the look on his face. The boys were dressed in scraps of filthy T-shirts and eating what looked like Cream of Wheat out of aluminum bowls. Another was of Seb in a hospital hallway standing on a prosthetic leg, probably for the first time, the loneliest boy in the world. There was Seb as a young man, posing under a rose arbor with an elderly white couple. Seb's arm was around the woman, the man frowning and standing apart like he was hoping he'd be out of frame. There was another of Seb under the arched entry of an imposing old church. Isaiah guessed fourteenth, fifteenth century, a huge stained-glass window, twin spires, elaborate cornices and reliefs. Seb was wearing a glen plaid suit that was not new and too big for him. Probably a thrift shop purchase, but he seemed immensely pleased with himself. He looked like a servant who'd been given his employer's cast-off clothes.

Without knowing why, Isaiah went down the hall with his camera, taking pictures of the photos. He was halfway along when he noticed that the light in the hallway had changed almost imperceptibly, the smell of cigarettes was slightly stronger. He turned and saw Gahigi standing fifteen feet away, and for the second time in as many days, he was looking down the barrel of a gun.

"Put your hands on de wall," Gahigi said.

"Please don't shoot me," Isaiah said. "I didn't take anything, I was just curious." He shrugged with his palms out like he'd made a stupid mistake.

"Put your hands on de wall," Gahigi said. "You will do dis now."

Isaiah raised his hands chest-high. He tried to work up some tears but couldn't. "Come on, man, please, just let me go, okay? Please?" *Get closer to me,* he thought. He remained stationary, thinking Gahigi was unlikely to shoot him in Seb's house.

"Do what I am telling you!" Gahigi said. "Put your hands on de wall!"

Isaiah tried to look terrified, which wasn't hard to do. Gahigi walked toward him, holding the gun straight out, his eyes like lanced blisters. Isaiah wished he'd practiced the move with Ari more. *Come on, get closer.*

"Do as I say or I am killing you now!" Gahigi shouted.

Okay, close enough. In almost one motion, Isaiah turned sideways, out of the line of fire, grabbing Gahigi's wrist with one hand and the gun barrel with the other. He twisted the barrel upward as Gahigi pulled the trigger, BLAM! The bullet hitting high on the wall. Isaiah wrenched the gun away, but before he could turn it around, Gahigi lunged at him and they crashed to the floor. The gun slid away, and they grappled, Gahigi on top. He was trying to get his hands around Isaiah's throat, but Isaiah straitjacketed him with his arms and legs, holding on like a bear cub on a tree trunk. Gahigi squirmed and torqued his upper body, his chin on Isaiah's shoulder, his hot breath in Isaiah's ear. Gahigi worked an arm free and waggled his body like a swimming snake. Isaiah couldn't see anything but the ceiling, but he knew Gahigi was going for the gun. There was no way to stop him, and getting out from under him would free him up completely. *You must do whatever you can to win. You win or you die!* Isaiah took Ari at his word and bit Gahigi viciously on the neck, tasting salt and then blood. Gahigi screamed. Isaiah bucked him off and scrambled to his feet, kicking the gun away as he ran down the hall.

"You are a woman!" Gahigi shouted. "I am killing you! I am killing you for sure!"

Isaiah sat in his easy chair and tried to get comfortable. Gahigi was strong. The grappling had left bruises and pulled muscles. No one had ever snuck up on him like that. The fight had rattled him. You know you won't live forever, but that's an abstraction. Being helpless, fighting for your life, realizing you could have easily been killed makes you afraid—of your attacker, yes, but the real fear was of mortality. Death was palpable, and you're suddenly aware that you're alive by the thinnest of margins. Cracks appear in the unconscious belief that of all the thousands of people who will die today, you won't be one of them. But now you might. Wrong place, wrong time, an accident of circumstance, and your days on earth were over. You were vulnerable, and like the white rhino or the panda bear, your extinction was out of your control.

Something else was nagging at him. Something he'd seen at Seb's house. A slide show of scenes blinked behind his eyes. *Blink.* Drilling through the door lock. *Blink.* The sterile living room. *Blink.* The ordinary office. *Blink.* The photographs. He lingered on them, visualizing each one. Nothing clicked. He went on with the slide show. *Blink.* Gahigi with the gun. *Blink.* Grappling and falling to the floor. *Blink*—Isaiah sat up. Wait a second—*the floor.*

Excited, he rushed to his office and got Marcus's work log. He found Seb's name and the circle containing the notation: *ISLANDER CHALET 8-47 BAM LT GRY.* That was hardwood flooring. Islander was the brand name, 8-47 the model number, BAM was bamboo, LT GRY was light gray. He got online and looked at samples. They were identical to the flooring in Seb's house. That couldn't be a coincidence. Marcus had installed it. The hardwood was laid throughout the whole house, a big job. Tearing out the old floor, prepping the subfloor, laying down plywood and a moisture barrier, cutting door casements and a dozen other things before installing the actual hardwood. For a man working alone, that was at least two weeks' work. Did Seb really not remember Marcus after seeing him every day for fourteen days, maybe more? And the floor was a reminder every time Seb walked on it. No, Seb remembered Marcus. Bile burned Isaiah's throat. Rage wrapped itself around him, squeezing him until he thought he'd burst. *Calm down,* he thought. *You don't have all the facts yet. You don't know what happened.* It was that exasperating question of motive. If he knew that, he thought, everything else would come together.

Seb took Gahigi to the emergency room, his friend's mood so black it was like a storm cloud in the car. The doctor stitched him up and gave him a tetanus shot.

"You're lucky you didn't sever an artery," she said. "I want to start you on intravenous antibiotics, keep you overnight. How did this happen, anyway?"

"Dis is none of your business," Gahigi said. He got up and left, not bothering with the release forms. By the time he and Seb got in the car, Gahigi's bandages were soaked through with blood. Seb knew better than to say they should go back, a wild look of slaughter and chaos in his old friend's eyes.

"I am killing this woman, Seb," Gahigi said. "I am killing him all de way."

When they got home, Gahigi wanted to clean up the blood in the hallway, but Seb insisted he take a shower and rest. He felt a jab of panic when he saw Isaiah's camera on the floor. He scrolled through the pictures, but they were shots of his old photos, nothing telling, thank goodness. But the pictures of the Accord were a shock. After all these years, Isaiah had actually found the car. How was that possible? The young man was indeed dangerous. Maybe there *was* a way to reconstruct the past. No. That was absurd. There was nothing to reconstruct. It had been eight long years since he'd driven the car into that amiable fool and felt the satisfying crunch of his body breaking apart and somersaulting through the air. There was no evidence, no witnesses, no documents, no videotape, and the police had ruled it an accident. Seb was still uneasy. Isaiah was smart and determined; a risky loose end, and many of his criminal acquaintances had tripped on one and ended up in prison.

Other than that unpleasantness, Seb was happy with the way things were going. He'd closed the deal on the house in Brentwood. Given his desperate beginnings, Seb thought he'd feel victorious signing a seven-figure check. Instead, he felt oddly disconcerted, unable to reconcile the well-dressed man in the real estate office with the emaciated boy with lice in his hair who came from a village where wealth was measured in goats. It didn't seem possible that one had evolved into the other. They were more like separate entities, one remembered, one here and now. How could anyone have come so far and survived?

After the Tutsi man cut Seb's leg off, he left the boy to die in a tall patch of elephant grass. In shock and bleeding, Seb managed to crawl onto the road and was nearly run over by a truck full of French peacekeepers. Seb's father said their mission was to stand around and watch the slaughter. Luckily, Seb was taken to a UN outpost instead of the local hospital, which had become a warehouse for mutilated, flyblown dead bodies.

Seb was eventually sent to an orphanage, where he slept on a dirt floor, ate mashed bananas and boiled sorghum every day, and drank water that smelled like mud. Here Seb met Gahigi. The kinship was immediate, the two boys bonded by their horrific injuries. Seb was thin and weak after months in the hospital, walking on crutches fashioned from tree branches and strips of leather. Gahigi, who was older and tougher, protected Seb from the other boys, who had nothing to do with their anger and despair except purge it on each other. Seb taught Gahigi to read. For the next two years they were inseparable.

Seb was one of the fortunate, adopted by a Christian couple from Northampton, England. Gahigi was stoic when Seb boarded the bus with his new parents, but Seb wept at leaving behind his only friend in the world. His adopted mother, Mrs. McAllister, spent most of her time knitting scarves and mittens for the homeless or baking something inedible for a church function. She introduced Seb to her shocked neighbors as her adopted son from Rwanda, more pleased with herself than with Seb. Mr. McAllister hardly spoke a word to him. If they were in a room together or met each other going in and out of the bathroom, he'd give Seb a look that said *I can't believe it. The gutter monkey is actually in my house.*

Seb was a good student and a dream target for the bullies. *Wha' 'appened to your other leg, mate? Di uh lion bite it off? Why come 'ere, to England, eh? Plenty uh nig-nogs round here already. Whatsat leg made ow uff? Come on, let's 'ave a look a-it.* They tripped him, pushed him down stairs. They threw his books in the street and stole his money. They pinned him to the ground, took off his prosthetic leg, and made him crawl for it. Seb understood cruelty, he'd seen plenty of it, but he did not forgive. The bullies were hit by bricks dropped from rooftops, their lockers smeared with feces, their pets killed.

At university, Seb majored in economics and did well but survival was always foremost in his mind and studying "Macroeconomics and the Global Economic Environment" seemed to ensure nothing. He dealt weed and amphetamines and he gambled. He had lost a leg but his hands were inordinately quick. He learned to cheat. Stacking the deck, palming, false shuffling, false dealing, bottom dealing.

A group of rugby players thought it was great sport to make fun of the African student with one leg; circling him as he limped along, taunting him and throwing rugby balls that whistled past his ears. Sometimes they'd follow him, right on his heels, telling him to hurry on now, or they took the bangers off his tray, chewed them, and spit them back on his plate. Seb slashed their tires and splattered their locker room with black paint and broke their windows with rocks. He hid in the bushes and shot their girlfriends with an air rifle. One girl lost an eye.

The rugby players sought revenge and bulled their way into Seb's flat. The first two through the door were met with Seb's fast hands and a meat cleaver; raw flesh flapping, blood splattering on the walls. The others were horrified and took their mates to the hospital. Seb claimed self-defense and that the meat cleaver was the closest thing at hand, which was true, he kept it on his desk. He narrowly escaped prosecution, his missing leg a key argument in the defense. He was kicked out of school. No matter, he'd have dropped out anyway, he had plans. He sold all his belongings, stole from the McAllisters, borrowed money he would never pay back, and boarded a plane to America, where his passion lay and his destiny awaited.

Years later, Seb made a trip back to Rwanda to find Gahigi, something he knew was impossible. He was delighted to discover his old friend still at the orphanage, working as a custodian. Since their parting as children, Gahigi had also sought revenge, killing Tutsis randomly. He'd only stopped because he'd been arrested on suspicion. The police beat him, but he said nothing and they let him go. Seb hired a lawyer who paid bribes to various officials and got Gahigi travel documents. He flew to America on a 747 wearing the cranberry Members Only jacket and carrying his belongings in a garbage bag. Seb met him at the airport.

Seb cleaned up the blood in the hallway. He threw out his clothes and the cleaning supplies and took a forty-five-minute shower. That evening, he was working at his desk when Gahigi knocked on the door.

"It is me, Seb," he said.

"Come in, Gahigi. I have told you before, you needn't bother knocking."

Gahigi entered. "To be polite is important, Seb."

"Yes, I suppose you're right. Sit down, my friend."

Gahigi remained standing. There was no blood on his T-shirt. Somehow, he must have changed his own bandages. He was somber, which was how he was when he had something important to say.

"What is it, Gahigi?" Seb said.

"Isaiah," Gahigi said. "I am killing him very soon."

"Yes, I know."

"You must not get in trouble, Seb. So I am going. I will stay in a hotel."

"It is not necessary, Gahigi. We have been through much together and we will not separate now."

"No, Seb. This is my business."

"It is mine too," Seb said. "Isaiah threatens us both and he will not give up. He must be dealt with decisively."

"What are you saying, Seb?"

"I am saying, we will kill him together."

This time it would be simple. They'd shoot him and be done with it. This rude, cocky boy who threatened to derail all that Seb had worked so hard for. It was Saturday. They found him playing basketball at McClarin Park. Seb and Gahigi sat in a stolen car parked in front of Kayo Subs. Ironic, Seb thought. Maybe they'd shoot him at the intersection of Baldwin and Anaheim.

They watched him play a full-court game with a group of young men from the neighborhood. They were quite good, quite athletic, all of them bigger and stronger than Isaiah, and yet he seemed to be the leader of his team. He did not shout or curse or complain as the others did. He took only an occasional shot, preferring to pass instead. He was accurate and clever, hitting his man at just the right time for an open shot. His team won six games in a row before they were defeated, more out of fatigue than anything else. Isaiah took his gym bag and went into the restroom.

"Start the car, Gahigi," Seb said. They sat there, the engine idling, waiting for action. All the other players had dispersed, but Isaiah still hadn't appeared.

"We are waiting too long, Seb," Gahigi said.

"Yes, I think you are right. Drive around to the other side. Perhaps there is another exit."

Gahigi was putting the car in gear when Isaiah walked up to Seb's window. "Waiting for me?" he said.

"Isaiah!" Seb said with a surprised laugh. "I was just thinking about you."

Isaiah looked at Gahigi. "Were you the one that ran over my brother? I'm sorry I didn't bite your fucking head off." Glaring, Gahigi moved his shirt aside, a gun tucked into his waistband. He put his hand on the grip.

"Not now, my friend," Seb said. "There are people about." Gahigi reluctantly covered the gun again.

"You are paying a price for dis," he said.

"Oh yeah?" Isaiah said. "Well, you better hurry. You might not be around long enough to collect."

"If you really want to know, I usually drive on our excursions," Seb said. "It relaxes me, although I tend to be inattentive." He lit a cigarette, a cruel glint in his smile. "I've had several near misses over the years, although on one occasion, I did hit a dog." He huffed through his nose. "A useless mongrel, no good to anyone. I ran over it with some pleasure, as I recall. It was better off dead, if you ask me."

Isaiah somehow restrained his fury but couldn't keep his voice from shaking. "Keep talking, Seb. Keep thinking you're safe. I might not cut your leg off, but I'll hurt you. I'll hurt you bad."

"An idle threat, Isaiah," Seb said, suppressing a yawn. "And I will tell you why. You are an honorable man, and however naïve that may be, an honorable man would not persecute someone if he did not have all the facts, and you have nothing. If you did, you would not be breaking into houses taking pictures of things that don't matter to anyone. At this moment, you are but another useless mongrel. Toothless and irrelevant." He flicked his cigarette out of the car. "Now if you will excuse us, we have another appointment." As he rolled up his window he said, "Be careful, Isaiah. The traffic is quite bad around here."

Isaiah watched them drive away, and for the first time in his life, he wished he'd had a gun.

Seb sat in his booth, smoking and sipping tea. He tried to put Isaiah out of his mind. He'd be dealt with soon enough. Thoughts of the future warmed him and brought forth an unaccustomed optimism. He had planned too carefully for his arrangements to fail. Every word of the meeting had been rehearsed, every contingency planned for and countered, even his wardrobe had already been chosen, right down to the pocket hankie and socks. Yes, all would be well.

Gahigi was sitting at the bar. Seb could see his partial reflection in the mirror behind the skyline of liquor bottles. His head was bowed, his hands were around his beer bottle as if he was protecting a baby bird. He looked in mourning—but for who? His loved ones? Those he had killed? Maybe he was lamenting the loss of his soul. Seb's had vanished when he hacked off the leg of the Tutsi militia-man, the blood splashing on his face like a warm rain, the man's screams lost in the mayhem of Seb's fury.

"Gahigi?" Seb said. It was rare that Seb had to call Gahigi twice, the man's hearing like a nocturnal predator's. "Gahigi?" Seb said again. Gahigi looked around sharply as if he'd heard a locked door open.

"Yes, Seb?" he said.

"Come. Sit."

Gahigi brought his beer and sat down in the booth. Seb offered him a cigarette. Resigned, Gahigi took it, and Seb lit it for him.

"You seem troubled, my friend," Seb said. "Is it Isaiah?"

Gahigi finished the beer and turned the beer bottle around like he was unscrewing a lid. "I am thinking I will go home, Seb," he said.

Seb had been afraid of this. Maybe that was what Gahigi was lamenting; the loss of himself. Here, he was a stranger who would always be a stranger; two inches of white sock between his cuffs and his shoes; a jacket that nobody'd worn since the eighties, scars that identified him as either a victim or a victimizer; an African in a land of African-Americans, the two as different as their continents.

"Why, Gahigi?" Seb said. "There is nothing for you in Rwanda."

"There is nothing for me here, Seb."

"How can you say this? We will go on as we always have."

"No, Seb. Your life is changing soon. I am happy for you. But my life is not changing. My life is nothing."

If Seb tried to convince Gahigi otherwise, they'd both know it was a lie. "Rwanda is still dangerous, my friend," Seb said.

"Everywhere is danger, Seb. Everywhere you go is danger."

Flaco Ruiz had been a bystander in the war between the Locos and the Violators, a war Isaiah felt partially responsible for starting. Flaco was ten years old when a gangster's bullet hit him in the head. He was left with a paralyzed leg, halting speech, and a brain that struggled and stuttered. Isaiah dropped in on Flaco twice a week. He was almost nineteen now and living in a condo that Isaiah and Dodson had bought for him.

"Am I interrupting something?" Isaiah said, knocking on the open door. Flaco and his girlfriend Debbie were sitting on the couch, holding hands and watching something on TV. Debbie had Down's syndrome. She had a wide forehead, fat cheeks, and folds under her small eyes, but she was, hands down, the sweetest, kindest girl Isaiah had ever met. Once, he'd watched her pick up a single ant with a Post-it and carry it outside with all the intensity and focus of a diamond cutter. Seeing Debbie and Flaco together made

Isaiah wistful; always murmuring to each other and giggling and holding hands wherever they went.

Isaiah stayed awhile and they ate the pie and ice cream he'd brought. Flaco had been promoted to all-around helper at the pet boutique, and he told Isaiah he was going back to school. Privately, he told Isaiah he was going to ask Debbie to marry him and did he have any advice; a question akin to asking what it was like living on Jupiter.

"I'll get back to you on that," Isaiah said.

On his way home he stopped off at Beaumont's to get some cranberry juice. His cell buzzed, he didn't recognize the number. "Hello?" he said.

"Isaiah, is that you?" A woman's voice.

"Yeah, this is Isaiah."

"It's Sarita."

Isaiah's heart seized up. His tongue was stuck to the roof of his mouth. "It is?" he said. She said she didn't have time to talk, but could they meet up later?

"I know this is short notice," she said, "but how about tomorrow night, around eight? I'll be at the Intercontinental Hotel in Century City. Do you know where that is?"

"No," he said, "but I'll find it."

CHAPTER FOURTEEN

Three for One

Dodson took the wheel on the drive back to LA. Isaiah was too wrung out and hurting and he couldn't keep his eyes open. Ken and Benny were in the back, both of them wrecked like they'd been run over by a train.

When they stopped for gas, Isaiah called Sarita.

"Janine is safe?" Sarita said.

"Yeah, she's fine."

"Benny and my dad?"

"They're banged up some, but they're fine too."

"That's wonderful, that's amazing! Oh, Isaiah, I don't know how to thank you."

"You don't have to," he said.

She said something to someone else and got back on the line. "Are you all right?" she said. "You don't sound so good."

"I'm fine. We've still got problems, you know. The triad will be after them and they won't give up."

"Hmm, yes, but there may be legal remedies for that. We'll talk. Just get here safe. We're going to celebrate big-time."

"I'll look forward to it," Isaiah said. *Cream-colored sofa, here I come.*

Dodson went inside to get snacks and to pee. He knew he shouldn't have gone into that massage parlor. No need to tell Cherise about this. She'd call him foolish and irresponsible and she wouldn't be wrong. He knew what she would say: *Let me see if I understand. You broke into a room full of gangsters with a gun that shoots condiments?*

He was in the bathroom when his phone buzzed. A text. He looked at the photo and almost fell to his knees. He couldn't breathe and started to shake. An acrid mix of terror and fury gushed up from his gut and nearly choked him. The photo was of Cherise. She was sitting in a chair, her hands zip-tied and resting on her belly. Tears and mascara were smeared around her eyes, a fat lip bleeding. Her hair was sticking up every which away, three buttons on her housecoat missing, threads dangling, her collar ripped. Yeah, that girl wasn't going nowhere without a fight. But the expression on her face—anguished but enraged, like all she needed was an opening and she'd jump up and beat her kidnappers to death. Dodson's fear was beyond fear, his anger so deep and primal he could feel himself morphing from human being to beast, vicious and uncontrollable, a drooling werewolf out for blood.

Cherise was looking at the camera, looking at Dodson. *Where were you?* it said. *Why weren't you here to protect us instead of running off to Vegas? They're going to hurt me, Dodson. They're going to hurt our baby.* Dodson's head was about to rocket off his body and smash through the ceiling, the veins in his neck like night crawlers wriggling away from his pounding heartbeat. He looked at the picture again and paced around in a circle, breathing shallow and fast. "Oh, you muthafuckas is dead," he said. "I'm gonna kill every one of you." It was only now he read the message. It said: THREE FOR ONE.

"Three for one?" he said. "The fuck does that mean?" It took a moment before he got it. Trade Janine, Benny, and Ken for Cherise. Three for one. Shit. He didn't even have to think about it. He didn't know those people, they didn't mean any more to him than strangers off the street. If they got killed so be it. That's what they got for being stupid. One way or another, Cherise and Lil' Tupac were coming home.

A man came in and saw Dodson, his eyes gaping and crazed, his mouth in a snarl, a fury coming off him like flames from a blast furnace. "Uh, sorry," the man said, backing out and closing the door. Dodson tried to calm himself down. He threw some water on his face, sucked in some long breaths, and looked at himself in the mirror. He had to keep his head together, think his way through this, stay in control. The shit was going to get deep and the stakes were everything that mattered in his life. He had to keep his cool. He texted back. OK

Dodson drove, everyone else dozing. The air-conditioning was on but sweat had beaded on his upper lip, his insides were whirlpooling, and he was choking the steering wheel so hard his fists were tired. He was glad he was in the Audi, the car doing ninety plus, whipping by other cars like they'd shut off their engines. He considered showing the photo to Isaiah but Isaiah was trying to prove himself to Sarita. He'd take over, do something complicated, try to save everybody and get Cherise and the baby killed. No, Dodson would do it his own way. Simple. No games, no tricks. Three for one and that was it.

It was dark when they crossed the border. Dodson called Deronda. "Where are you?" he said.

"We parked in Nona's backyard, waiting for her to get home from her work," Deronda said.

"Janine okay?"

"Yeah, she's aight. She ain't such a bad egg—for being Chinese." Dodson heard Janine say something in the background. "Girl can eat like Cherise's brother, Jerome. You seen him? On Thanksgiving they had a turkey for the family, and another one just for him."

"Stay there," Dodson said. "We'll meet you."

Isaiah dropped Dodson at his apartment, and he ran into the building without looking back. He vaguely heard Isaiah say something about the baby and good luck. He raced up five flights of stairs to the apartment. The door was closed but unlocked. He went in, hoping there was a Red Pole there he could kill. "Cherise?" he said hopefully. Nothing had been disturbed, but the place couldn't have felt emptier if they had moved out. He went into the bedroom. Covers and sheets twisted up, spots of blood on the pillow, slippers in two different places, a bed table knocked over, a broken lamp, broken glass, and a hardback book on the floor. So she was probably reading when it happened. Two or three of them came in, told her not to make a sound, thinking she'd be scared by the ski masks and guns and wouldn't resist. Knowing Cherise, that didn't happen. She screamed and fought, holding her stomach and kicking with both legs like she was riding a bicycle upside down. They had to yank her out of bed, ripping her robe, and when she wouldn't stop screaming they hit her. The image made Dodson nauseous, his whole body was clenched and trembling. "I'm gonna kill these muthafuckas," he whispered. "I'm gonna kill 'em all." He went to the closet and took a shoe box off the top shelf. He opened it, found the S&W Model 627 .38-caliber revolver with a five-inch barrel. Most revolvers held five or six rounds, the 627 held eight. Even if he missed every other shot he could still kill four of them.

"I'm coming, Cherise," he said as he bounded down the stairs. "I'm coming."

A Chinese man who looked like a boxcar and a couple of punk-ass gangsters had kidnapped her and brought her to a raggedy motel that smelled like mildew and roach powder. They sat her in a chair and zip-tied her hands in front of her. When they arrived, an old man in a suit was waiting for them. He tried to be pleasant but it just made him creepier, like her Uncle Foster, who smiled when he asked her if she'd like to see the bunny rabbit hiding in his pants.

"We will try to make you as comfortable as possible," the old man said politely. "Assuming you behave yourself. But I must warn you, make a disturbance, even a minor one, and we will restrain you completely."

"And I must warn *you*," she said. "Hurt my baby and there won't be a place on the earth, the sun, the moon, or anywhere else where I won't find you and rip the heart out of your chest."

They kept her there, waiting for something, the businessman stepping outside to make phone calls, the others watching TV. One of them was eating from a big bag of popcorn and was so relaxed he could have been at a baseball game. The boxcar man had a crust of blood below his nostrils where she'd kicked him with her bare foot. She was sorry she wasn't wearing stilettos. He glared at her and nodded as if to say *I'll pay you back, bitch.* She lifted her chin and calmly met his gaze. "You want to scare me you'll have to do better than that."

Cherise had always been able to stick up for herself. Early on, she'd learned from her parents and her church to forgive those who trespassed against you but to never submit, never let them take away your dignity. So she would not cower and would not shrink from menace, and somewhere along the line this blockhead son of a bitch was going to lose four or five pounds of flesh. But truth be told, she was terrified. These men hadn't blindfolded her and they weren't wearing masks. They'd kidnapped a pregnant woman and didn't care if she could recognize them, which only meant they were going to kill her. She had to force herself to keep from crying and begging for her life. She'd never see her baby. A baby that was still in her womb but that she loved with every ounce of her being; a baby she'd longed for and prayed for and saw in her dreams. Somehow, she'd get out of this if she had to murder somebody to do it. And speaking of getting out of this, where was Dodson? He and that damn Isaiah had obviously stirred up so much trouble these hoodlums had to kidnap her. She summoned her faith, not in Dodson and Isaiah, but in her Lord and Savior, Jesus Christ. He knew her fear and knew her unborn child was in danger. She prayed. *Save my baby. Take me, Lord, but please save my baby.*

Tommy finished his phone call and came back in the room, the girl still very much defiant. She was unusual, Tommy thought. Not asking where they were or what they were doing; not pleading for her life or her baby's life. She just kept looking at him like she was memorizing every line and contour of his face for future reference.

"Turn her chair around," he said to Tung.

That the girl was pregnant was never a consideration. Tommy had a house on Victoria Peak with a panoramic view of Hong Kong, a six-thousand-square-foot condo in Beijing right next door to the Minister of Agriculture, and a house in the Menlo Park area of San Francisco, where all his neighbors were venture capitalists, internet moguls, or the CEOs of private equity firms, a Bentley parked in all three garages. He drank the best, ate the best, had every conceivable luxury and a string of willing, patient women on three continents. He wasn't about to give that up because of some misplaced twinge of conscience. His primary concern now was getting this over with and leaving no witnesses. He glanced at his watch. "It's time to go," he said to the girl. "Do not call for help, do not try to escape, or there will be severe consequences. Do you understand?"

"Yes, I do," she said quietly.

Isaiah drove down Nona's driveway into her backyard, the food truck parked there. As he helped Ken and Benny get out of the car, Janine burst out of the truck, ran to Benny, and hugged him. He grunted and cringed but hugged her back with his good arm. They cried, blubbering *I love yous* and *I'll never leave yous,* so overwrought and heartfelt, Isaiah was as embarrassed as he was envious. He wondered how Sarita would react when they saw each other. A fraction of that emotion would be heaven.

Ken stood there, hoping, or maybe not hoping, Janine would acknowledge him. He was in tough shape; one eye shut completely, the other one closing, bruises on his cheekbones, a bleeding ear, and a lump on his forehead. There wasn't much room left on his face for humiliation, but you could still see it, like something caustic and unbearable layered over his injuries. Isaiah felt sorry for him but that evaporated when he thought about the girls in the photos.

Janine helped Benny sit down on a lawn chair. "We should get him to the emergency room," she said.

"No," Benny said. "They'll ask questions."

"Questions about what?" Janine said. "You fell off your motor-cycle."

"I'm okay. I just need to lie down."

"Don't be an idiot, Benny, your arm is broken and who knows what else. You're going and that's it." She finally glanced at her father. "Hi," she said evenly. She took no note of his injuries. Ken hesitated a moment, waiting for her to ask if he was all right, but she didn't.

"I'm glad you're okay," he said, but she had already turned her back.

"Can we take Benny now?" she said.

"Ken should go too," Isaiah said.

She sighed like it was a huge pain in the ass. "I've got to get my bag." She crossed to the food truck, Deronda standing at the door with her arms folded. "Thanks for everything," Janine said.

Deronda smiled. "Fuck you." They hugged.

"Fuck you too," Janine said. "And you can't aim for shit."

Isaiah was surprised when Dodson drove Cherise's Prius into the yard. Dodson got out, grim and deliberate. *Something's wrong,* Isaiah thought. "You okay?" he said. "Why aren't you with Cherise?" He knew why when Dodson drew a gun.

"Everybody drop your phones on the ground," Dodson said. "Do it now." Janine and Benny stared with their mouths open, Ken didn't seem to care. Deronda was insulted.

"The hell you doing, Dodson?" she said.

"Shut up, Deronda."

"Tell me what's going on," Isaiah said.

"Shut up, don't ask me shit," Dodson said, and raised the gun, elbow bent, the barrel aimed upward. "I *said* put your muthafuckin' phones on the ground."

"Dang, Dodson," Deronda said. "What's your problem?"

Dodson pointed the gun directly at her. "Put your phone on the ground AND DO IT RIGHT FUCKING NOW!" Deronda couldn't do it fast enough, fumbling around until it jumped out of her hands like a wet bar of soap.

"I don't have one," Janine said, her arms protectively around Benny. "He doesn't either."

"You the one started all this, you dumb-ass bitch," Dodson said. "You and that retarded muthafucka you call a boyfriend." He looked at Ken. "And *you*. Shit. I should shoot your ass for being alive." Ken had his head bowed and looked like he wouldn't mind. "Everybody in the food truck," Dodson said. "Deronda, you're driving."

Everyone gathered at the passenger door. Janine helped Benny in, Ken, right behind her, looking at the back of her head like he was telepathically apologizing.

"Sit on the floor and lace your fingers on top of your head," Dodson said. "Fuck around in there and you die."

Isaiah was last in line. "They've got Cherise, don't they?"

"Get in the truck, Isaiah."

"They want to make a trade."

"That's right, and I'm gonna make one."

Dodson was panting through clenched teeth, each breath a *shhh*, spraying spit, desperation in his eyes, and Isaiah realized, *He'd shoot me, he really would.* He hesitated a moment. Should he play this out or try to take the gun away?

"Yeah," Dodson said, taking a step back. "Go on and try some of that kung fu shit on me and see if I don't put a bullet between your eyes. Now get in the goddamn truck."

Deronda was in the driver's seat. Dodson got in and glared, daring her to start something.

"I ain't said nothing," she said, and started the engine.

Dodson turned halfway around, the gun held close to his chest. Isaiah, Ken, Benny, and Janine were sitting in the aisle, their backs against the cupboards and appliances.

"Do anything but sit there and I *will* shoot you," Dodson said.

"Dodson, we can work something out," Isaiah said.

"Could we drop Benny off at the emergency room?" Janine said.

"I'll go with you," Ken said to Dodson. "Just take me."

"What you need me for?" Deronda said. "Let one of them other people drive."

They were all talking at once, pleading their cases, raising their voices. BLAM! Dodson fired a shot into the ceiling, filling the truck with blue smoke and the acrid smell of cordite, everybody shrinking like sea anemones poked with a stick, their hands over their heads, Janine whimpering *Don't hurt us, don't hurt us.*

"Shut up," Dodson said. "Don't say another damn word." He looked at Isaiah, who was looking back at him. "My woman, my baby," Dodson said. "You ain't got shit to say about it."

"We can work something out," Isaiah said. They looked at each other until Dodson looked away.

Tommy had Tung scout locations for the hostage exchange. He found the perfect spot off Highway 38, between Llano and Piñon Hills, about eighty miles from LA. It was just another isolated, forgettable stretch of the scrubby desert that seemed to take up most of California. Tung found a dirt road that turned off the highway and led to what might have been a parking lot for trucks and earthmovers when they were working on the highway. The lot itself was roughly circular, deep tire tracks in the once-muddy ground, littered with piles of gravel, cinder blocks, and giant sewer pipes and hemmed in by high berms and brushy hills. The headlights on Tung's Cadillac threw a harsh, alien light over the space, the girl in there with one of the gangsters. Ken's Lexus parked next to it.

Dodson would be told where to turn at the last moment, the dirt road the only way in or out. He would be coming from LA, the east, and Tommy had posted pairs of spotters all the way back to the Cajon Pass. If Dodson brought the police, they'd know and tell him to keep driving. Members of the Chink Mob were out there in the dark, all heavily armed. In the unlikely event they needed more firepower, the lookouts could be called in. The wild card was the other black guy, the one they called IQ. He might try something but at this point what could he do? If he approached separately he'd be spotted and dealt with.

That idiot Gujia and the other Red Poles had gotten themselves killed so Tung had brought his cousins in, Longwei and Lok. Not official members of the triad but close associates. They were in the drug business, which Tommy stayed away from. Too much competition, too much heat, he'd said. Longwei was a little taller than Tung, Lok a little shorter, but the square proportions were the same. The cousins were wearing loud Hawaiian shirts and might have been the guys who played the ukulele at the hotel luau if it weren't for their lethal, remorseless eyes and the hands like hockey gloves stuffed with rocks. Tung was frightening all by himself, but the three of them were like comic book villains. Cube Men with black belts in Wing Chun who moved like sumo wrestlers and were experts in hurting people. Tommy had seen Lok punch a guy in the chest so hard he shattered the man's rib cage, crushing his lungs. The man died of asphyxiation.

Tommy had come to the conclusion that IQ and Dodson weren't susceptible to bribes or threats. The only alternative was to turn them against each other. If Dodson came alone, the plan had worked. If IQ was with him, something was up their sleeves and Janine was in a safe house somewhere. Either way, one or both of the men would be tortured until they gave up her location. Tung was good at that.

The only thing Tommy was really worried about was the Chink Mob hiding out there in the dark. Mercenaries were inherently unreliable. For them it was about risk-reward, not loyalty. Tommy had warned them over and over again not to shoot until Janine was well clear of the others. Hurt her and Tung would execute them on the spot.

Tommy was standing near the center of the lot, smoking and talking to Tung. Tung was sitting on a pile of cinder blocks, looking like he was nesting on his offspring. A full moon hung in the vast desert sky like a klieg light waiting for the action to start. It reminded Tommy of a story his mother had once told him. There were once ten suns in the sky, and drought was everywhere, crops withering, people dying. Hou-Yi, a famous archer in Chinese mythology, shot nine of the suns out of the sky and ended the drought. Yi's wife, Chang'e, stole a potion from her husband and flew to the moon, where she became a goddess and is said to be seen dancing during the Full Moon Festival. Tommy might have enjoyed the story if he wasn't starving and his mother wasn't a whore and a heroin addict.

"Everything is prepared?" Tommy said.

"Yes, Tommy," Tung said.

"The girl is secure?"

"Yes, Tommy."

Tommy was satisfied. He was heading back to Vegas. No sense being at the scene of the crime. "I'm going now," he said.

"Don't worry, Tommy," Tung said. "Everything will be okay."

Tung watched Tommy drive away in Ken's car, thinking one day he'd like to give the orders, not giving a shit who got killed as long as it wasn't him. Longwei and Lok came over and joined him, both wielding Uzis with fifty-round clips. They didn't speak, they hardly ever did. What was there to say? We're having a good year in the drug business?

Tung's phone buzzed. One of the lookouts. "Food truck coming," he said.

"Where are you?" Tung said.

"By the overpass."

That was ten miles away. "Cars behind him?" Tung said.

"No. No cars."

Tung raised his hand, a signal. Flashlights winked back from the dark. The Chink Mob was ready. Other lookouts radioed from mile eight, five, two, one, the last one at a quarter of a mile. Tung made the call.

"Yeah?" Dodson answered.

"You make left turn at big yellow sign."

"What about Cherise?"

Tung ended the call and waited. Flashlights winked again. The food truck was turning off the highway. "He's coming," Tung said. He drew his weapon, an S&W .44 Magnum, the Dirty Harry gun. Longwei and Lok racked the slides on their Uzis. They saw the food truck's headlights bump down the dirt road. Dodson was driving, the suspension creaking, cookware rattling, the bumper almost touching the ground as he pulled into the lot. He was alone. Tommy's plan had worked. Still, they had to be cautious.

"Okay," Tung said.

Dodson saw three big Chinese dudes standing out in the open. Behind them, about twenty yards away, a Cadillac was parked with its headlights on. Cherise was probably in there, no other place she could be. Dodson wanted to run the men down and go directly to her but restrained himself. He made a wide turn, stopping with his window facing them, the engine rumbling like a distant storm.

The Chinese guy in the suit stepped forward. "Hello, Missa Dosson," he said. "Thank you for coming."

"Fuck you," Dodson said.

"Turn off your engine."

"Show me Cherise."

The guy gestured at the car. The driver got out, eating something wrapped in foil. He helped Cherise out of the backseat. She looked a mess but didn't seem hurt.

"You okay?" Dodson said.

"Get me and my baby outta here, Dodson," she said, sounding more pissed off than afraid. The driver helped her get back in and returned to the driver's seat, the door locks thunking shut.

"You satisfied, Missa Dosson?" the Chinese guy said. "You make trade now. Fuck around, we shoot you no problem."

"I'll get 'em," Dodson said. "Y'all be cool now, it's a straight-up trade. No bullshit." He turned and clambered back into the truck.

Tung smiled. Stupid guy. Did he actually think this would be on the up-and-up? Tung heard Dodson arguing with someone, shouting going back and forth, maybe with Ken or Benny. Hard to tell over the engine noise. Dodson returned to the cab.

"What's the problem?" Tung said.

"They won't come out and I don't care what you say, I'm not shooting 'em myself."

"You get out," Tung said.

"Don't shoot me now," Dodson said. "I ain't strapping." He got out of the truck with his hands up. He looked over at the Cadillac. "I'm coming, Cherise," he said. "Everything's gonna be all right."

Wing watched from the top of a berm, wondering why he wasn't at home playing *Call of Duty* instead of squatting in the fucking dirt with a gun in his belt and sweating through his T-shirt, his ass hurting from the buckshot wounds. The sky was huge out here. Too huge. Let you know you were nothing in the scheme of things. A pixel in a high-def shot of the universe. Maybe somebody with a giant telescope was watching you from one of those stars and laughing his ass off because you thought you mattered to anybody but yourself.

Wing looked over at Gerald, antsy, grinning like the deranged clown he was. If he racked the slide on his gun one more fucking time Wing was going to take it away and shoot him with it.

"Fuck, man, the shit is going *down*," Gerald said, like it was Christmas morning. For some unknown reason, Huan was Tung's driver, his hands probably sticky with salsa or ketchup or fish sauce, fucking up the steering wheel and stinking up the car. Wing watched the black guy get out of the food truck with his hands up.

"Who's he?" Gerald said.

"Tommy kidnapped his wife. They're exchanging her for—don't you listen to anything?"

Longwei frisked the black guy and made him lie on the ground. Tung said something and Longwei and Lok approached the truck.

"I want to go down there," Gerald said.

"Why?" Wing said.

"I want to get into it. Throw some lead, you know what I'm sayin'?"

"No, I don't," Wing said. "I truly don't."

Longwei opened the truck's door on the passenger side, pointing the Uzi ahead of him. Lok was trying to see in through the service window, tapping his gun barrel on it.

"You come out!" Longwei shouted. "Everybody! Right now or we start shooting!" Nothing happened. "You fuck around we kill you all!" Still nothing. Longwei started climbing into the cab and a burst of gunfire bent him in half and blew him backward. In the same instant, a salvo erupted from the service window, Lok hit multiple times, twisting and falling to the ground. Tung was about to shoot but more gunfire shattered the front windshield, knocking chunks off the cinder blocks. Tung ducked and got behind them.

"I don't know what's going on," Wing said.

"Fuck it, I'm gonna shoot," Gerald said.

"Don't. What if Janine's in there?"

In the next instant, all the truck's doors flew open and men came spilling out, more than you thought possible, most with assault rifles, firing in every direction as they ran for cover. They were Mexican and they were shouting *Venganza por Ramona! Los Locos te destruiran, motherfuckers! Los Locos por siempre, tu putas! Matarlos por Ramona!*

"The fuck?" Gerald said as he started firing at them. "Who are them guys?"

"That girl you shot?" Wing said. "Her people. The Locos, re-member?"

One of the Mexicans threw the black guy a gun as he ran by. He joined the others, who were spreading out, yelling and pointing at where the shooters were, flanking them, racing from rock pile to rock pile. None of that helter-skelter shit. These dudes had a battle plan. *Venganza por Ramona! Matarlos por Ramona!* The Chink Mob was firing back, bursts of white flames and sleeting sparks erupt-ing out of the blackness, the shots so loud they cleaved the night, more coming before the first ones faded, smoke hazing over the headlights' broad beam, silhouettes bent low racing across the alien light.

"Man, I can't hit shit from here," Gerald said. He patted his pockets. "Shit," he said. "Gimme your extra clip. I want to go down there."

"Don't be stupid, Gerald," Wing said. "We should get out of here." The Acura was parked off the road about a half mile down the highway.

"What? I'm not going nowhere," Gerald said. "And who you calling stupid?"

"*You,* okay? You're the stupidest motherfucker I've ever met! How you even stayed alive this long is a fucking mystery."

"Don't disrespect me, Wing," Gerald said, pushing the nerd glasses up and crinkling his nose. "You know I don't take that shit from nobody, not even you."

"If you go down there you're gonna get killed," Wing said. "And for what? Tommy Lau? He doesn't give a shit about you."

"Who's talking about Tommy Lau, man, the *action's* down there. Hey, if you're not going, gimme me your extra clip, will you?"

Wing felt like crying. He felt dumb and afraid and ridiculous, like he was dissolving, a drop of food dye in a glass of water. "Gerald, please, we need to get out of here."

"Why are you being a fucking baby?" Gerald said. "Come on, hurry up, gimme your clip."

"No, forget it."

"Forget it? I'm not playing, Wing. Gimme the fucking clip."

"Gerald, you're gonna get *killed!*"

"No, I'm not."

"Fuck, you're dumb. *Fuck* you're dumb!"

"Shut up, Wing, I swear to God."

"Last time. Are you going down there?"

"Yeah, I'm going!"

Wing shot him. Gerald lurched, blood spurting from the center of his chest, his head wobbling, eyes wide and unseeing as he fell over and tumbled down the berm. Wing scrambled down the other side, got to the highway, and ran, the desert two-dimensional in the silvered darkness, like fleeing into a billboard for a scary movie, his sneakers slapping the asphalt. Wing was terrified he wouldn't find the car. He had no plan except to drive until he ran out of money and then he'd walk until he couldn't walk anymore and he was someplace far away, where he knew nobody and nobody knew him.

Frankie squatted in the food truck with Manzo and a bunch of other Locos, fitted together like chairs thrown in a closet. It was dark, the air feverish, dense with sweat and thundering heartbeats. Frankie felt alive again, like a man again, high on adrenaline, unafraid. El Piedra. Frankie the Stone. When the Chinese guy in the Hawaiian shirt opened the door, Frankie blasted him dead center and jumped out, firing a Glock. "*Venganza por Ramona!*" he screamed. Gunshots popped and flashed, but Frankie didn't stop, yelling *Ramona Ra-mona* as if she was ahead of him, trying to escape. He stumbled over rocks and charged through the brush, thorns catching on his clothes and cutting his hands, the gunshots getting louder, bullets zipping past so close he could feel them ripping holes in the air. Manzo was somewhere behind him yelling *Get down get down* but Frankie kept running.

"Shoot him!" somebody yelled. "Shoot that motherfucker."

Frankie ran on into the blackness, into a volley of bright bursts, his heart thumping like mortar fire, his breathing breakneck and gritty, tearing at his throat—and then he was hit, he couldn't tell where. He staggered but kept going, a warm numbness spreading from the center of his chest, his vision shadowing, his legs too heavy to lift. He was hit again—and again, but he was laughing now, even as the blood spilled from his mouth, even as he fell to his knees and flopped facedown on the rocky desert floor. He was happy because he knew he was going to die.

Manzo threw Dodson a gun as he ran by. Dodson caught it, got up, and started running for the car. "Cherise!" he shouted. "I'm coming, Cherise!" Bullets were singing hornets, cracking sewer pipes and chipping cinder blocks, but he kept running; like a greyhound, low and stretched out, terror and love giving length to his stride. But it wasn't enough. The Chinese guy was already in the car, the tires spinning, throwing up gravel as it roared across the lot. "Cherise!" Dodson screamed. "I'm coming, Cherise!"

Tung looked back and saw Dodson running after them, screaming and waving a gun. The car was on the dirt road now, bumping over the potholes, nearly at the highway. The gun battle was at a standoff, the Chink Mob had to stay whether they liked it or not, Tommy making them park the cars way down the highway. Tung breathed easier, he was getting away. He glanced at the girl. She was staring at him like she had in the motel room.

"Look the other way," Tung said. But she didn't.

"Hey," the driver said. A big SUV with its lights off was coming toward them, blocking the road, some Mexican guys hanging out of the windows, waving guns. Where the hell did they come from? Shit, Tung thought, Tommy isn't so smart after all. The old man had posted lookouts to the east. These guys had gone the long way around. The 385 all the way to Mountain Acres, across to Llano so they could come from the *west*. The SUV kept coming.

"What do I do? What do I do?" the driver said.

"Stop the car! Go in reverse!" Tung shouted. The kid hit the brakes but was too panicked to do anything else. The SUV skidded to a halt, bumping bumpers with the Cadillac. IQ was driving. The Mexican guys piled out and ran off toward the battle. Tung had a moment's relief, and then he saw a pickup truck behind the SUV, more guys jumping out of the cargo bed—no wait, those were *girls*. They rushed over and surrounded the car. They looked like some tribe out of a Mad Max movie, with their black lipstick and red head scarves and hoop earrings and tattoos on their forearms. They pounded on the car, waved guns, and spit on the windows, yelling about Ramona, whoever that was. A big girl with big boobs cupped her hands over her eyes and peered in at Tung.

"Where you going, motherfucker?" she said.

Isaiah got out of the SUV. The girls were dragging the driver out of the Cadillac. They beat on him, stirring up dust, their shoes sliding and scuffling across the dirt. Dodson came running up to the car. "Cherise! Cherise! You all right?"

Tung lowered his window halfway. He had his gun pointed at her. "I shoot her," he said. "You let me go or I shoot her right now!"

Dodson looked like he was going to shoot Tung anyway.

"Easy," Isaiah said.

"You okay, baby?" Dodson said.

Cherise looked more indignant than afraid. "I would be if block-head here pointed that gun away from my baby."

"Let her go and you can drive away," Isaiah said.

"You hurt my fiancée you better say your prayers now," Dodson said. "You won't have the chance after I blow your muthafuckin' brains out."

"Wait," Cherise said. "Did you just say *fiancée?*"

"That's right, baby. It's you and me forever."

"Do you have a ring?" she said like a cop asking for ID.

"Yes, I do."

"You let me go or I shoot her," Tung said, putting the gun to her belly. "I shoot her right now!"

"Get that thing off of my child," Cherise said, slapping the barrel aside. "You want to aim at something aim at me."

"Let her go first," Dodson said.

"No," Tung said. "Me first. I let her go when I get away."

"I've had enough of this," Cherise said. She sidled away from him to the other door and got out of the car.

"Hey!" Tung said. He was flustered a moment and clumsily pointed the gun at Dodson. "See?" he said with a flaccid smile. "She safe now," he said. "You let me go, right?"

"Give up the gun," Isaiah said.

"No," Tung said. "I keep gun."

"What are you gonna do with it?" Dodson said. "Look around." Gun barrels were pointed at Tung through every window, the homegirls grinning, happy to watch him squirm.

Tung took a moment to consider his options, which were none. He swallowed air, turned the gun around, and handed it to Dodson grip first. "Okay, you let me go, right? You promise."

"Promise?" Dodson said. "Did anybody hear me make a promise?"

Cherise came around to Dodson's side of the car. One of the girls produced a knife and cut off the zip tie.

"You sure you ain't hurt?" Dodson said.

"No, I'm not hurt, no thanks to you," she said, "but we'll talk about that later."

"This the one kidnapped you?" Dodson said.

"Uh-huh," Cherise said. "This boxhead muthafucka dragged me out of my bed, hit me, tore my good robe, and endangered my baby."

Dodson hesitated a moment. He'd never heard Cherise swear before. "What do you want me to do?" he said.

"Nothing," Cherise said. "I'll do it myself." She took Dodson's gun and fired into the lower part of the door. BLAM! BLAM! BLAM! BLAM! She would have emptied the clip but Dodson took the gun away. Tung was curled up and groaning, holding his bullet-riddled legs.

"I'll have to check but I think you got him, baby," Dodson said. "Isn't there something in the Bible about leaving vengeance to the Lord?"

"Yes, there is," Cherise said, giving him an unappreciative look. "I'll have to ask Him for forgiveness but under the circumstances I think He'll be all right with it."

The shooting had stopped. Manzo and the Locos arrived. They were hyped and sweating, breathing hard, some smiling, glad they'd made it through. Manzo looked old and sad.

"You guys okay?" Isaiah said.

"Tico and Morales got wounded," Manzo said. The gash in his head hadn't healed over, the sutures still evident. "Lupe's taking them to the hospital. Frankie's dead."

"I'm sorry about that."

Manzo shrugged. "Frankie didn't want to be here no more. If he didn't go out this way it would have been something else."

"Thanks for helping out."

"Had to be done. The homies would have been on the warpath forever." Manzo held Isaiah's gaze a moment. "You still owe me," he said. Then he turned and walked away.

CHAPTER FIFTEEN

Osso Buco

D odson and Cherise's baby was born two days later at the Hurston Community Hospital. Dodson chose to stay in the waiting room during the delivery, telling Cherise if he saw a bloody, slimy baby coming out of her vagina it might turn him off sex forever.

Isaiah came to visit them at the hospital. Cherise had that new-mommy glow, cradling the baby with its big head, munchkin face, and tiny perfect fingers, Dodson about to bust open with love and pride.

"You ever seen a baby that good-looking?" he said. "I might get the boy an agent, put his face on a box of Pampers, let him pay a few bills."

"Did you name him Tupac?" Isaiah said.

"No, we did not," Cherise said. "His name is Micah. From the Book of Micah. There's a verse I love. *What does the Lord require of you? To act justly and to love mercy and to walk humbly with your God.*"

"That's beautiful," he said. Mercy was a rare thing these days when the tiniest slight was seen as disrespect, and if you hit me with a fist I shoot you with an RPG.

"His full name is Micah Isaiah Dodson," Dodson said. "Got a ring to it, don't it?" Isaiah didn't know what to say. "Let's go get some coffee," Dodson said. "You want something, Cherise?"

"No. I have everything I need," she said, lost in the baby's eyes.

They went across the street and got coffee at Starbucks, took it outside, and sat on a bus bench. It was late. A cool, salty breeze was coming off the harbor, empty buses and roving cabs going by. Isaiah was more comfortable with Dodson now, not having to play a role or maintain his position. Something was up with him. He was uneasy but not about the baby. This was different. Something more immediate, something between the two of them.

"How you holding up?" Isaiah said.

"I'm aight," Dodson said. "You know, getting ready to bring the baby home. That shit is dippy, man. *Baby-proofing*. My parents didn't do none of that. My old man said if I hit my head on the corner of the coffee table it'd teach me to look where I'm going."

"You don't look so good," Isaiah said.

"Yeah, I suppose not. It's the food truck."

"I'll help you repair it."

"No, that's not it. Thing is, I shouldn't have gone into it in the first place, but Cherise was on my case about doing something legit. Shit, man, I hate being locked in there all day. You know me. I can't be tied up at the dock. I need to flow with the flow, kick up some waves, be what I be."

"You're not going back to hustling, are you?"

"No, nothing like that." Dodson hesitated. Isaiah was getting nervous. Something was coming and he hated surprises.

"The case in Vegas?" Dodson said. "I don't know what you thought, but I think we did aight, you know, working together."

"Yeah, we did okay," Isaiah said, thinking about all the arguments.

"Yeah, so, I was wondering how you'd feel about—" Dodson took a breath and looked down at the pavement. "Maybe, you know, partnering up."

Isaiah was confounded. It was as if Dodson had told him he was joining the marines. "Partnering up?" he said, hoping he hadn't heard right. "What do you mean?"

"I had your back at the massage parlor, didn't I? And when we was fighting them Red Poles too. And remember back when I saved your ass from Skip? Dropped that roll of tar paper on him?"

"I remember."

Dodson stood up, dumped his coffee into the street. "It's not just the rough-and-tumble," he said. "I could hustle up some bigger cases for you, get some clients with a profile, do some PR, make it a real business, make you a brand."

"I don't know, Dodson," Isaiah said. "That's not what I do."

"You'd still be doing your pro bono thing," Dodson said. "That don't change. But let me ask you something. Do you want to be small-time forever?"

Isaiah had never thought of himself as *small-time*. It was something of a revelation, viewing himself in a wider context.

"And what about Sarita?" Dodson asked.

"What about her?"

"You really think she's gonna be with somebody that lives in the hood and spends all his time busting bums and teenagers? That girl's upscale, Isaiah. What, you think she's gonna live in your world? You know that's not gonna happen. You gonna live in hers, and them people hang on the high side."

Isaiah remembered having the same thoughts himself. At the

party in Century City, he felt like he'd snuck in, like he didn't have a membership card.

Dodson went on. "Maybe I'm off the rails, but I'm guessing you're as bored as me, fucking around all day with petty crime. You need to be working on cases got some scope to 'em, got some *size,* and who's gonna go out there and get 'em for you? You? You gonna blow your own horn? Put yourself on the map? Shit. You got enough trouble just having a conversation."

"Thanks a lot."

"Aight, I said my piece," Dodson said. "If it's wrong for you it's cool. We be straight no matter what."

Isaiah was glad the conversation was over. He was possessive about his work, and the arguments had been distracting. Any number of times he'd wanted to send Dodson home. On the other hand, Dodson had saved his neck and having a friend along was—wait, was that what Dodson was? *A friend?* Isaiah hated this. Another confusing situation he couldn't get a handle on. Maybe stepping out of his isolated life wasn't such a good idea after all. People, it turned out, were a big pain in the ass.

Benny and Ken spent a few days in the hospital. Janine and Sarita had a reunion in the reception area. There were lots of tears and hugs and promises to see each other more often.

"How's Dad?" Sarita said.

"I don't know. I don't know if I'm ready to see him yet," Janine said.

"Me either," Sarita said.

"I'm sorry for all the trouble, sis. I've really been an asshole."

"You won't get any argument from me," Sarita said. "Did I tell you I still have the college fund Dad started for me?"

"You do?" Janine said. "Dad cashed mine in a long time ago."

"Tell you what. You give up gambling, move here, and I'll cover your expenses until you get on your feet."

"You mean break up with Benny."

"If he loves you, he'll join you. If he loves gambling more, well, that's his problem."

Janine thought about that a moment. "I love Benny and he loves me," she said. "Anybody who gives that up is an idiot."

"What if the love is bad for you?" Sarita said.

"What if it is?" Janine said. She kissed Sarita on the cheek. "I'll see you when I see you, sis."

Frankie's memorial service brought out a huge crowd. Extended family, friends, the Locos, the homegirls, their extended families, and people from the neighborhood. Even Frankie's bail bondsman came to pay his respects. Holy Trinity was standing room only. People got up and spoke. Frankie was down for his hood. Frankie was true to the barrio. Frankie never backed down. Frankie was a legend. Frankie will live in our hearts forever.

Manzo sat at the back, a statue of himself. People were surprised when he didn't speak, but what could he honestly say? That Frankie was a killer? That he sold dope, robbed people, extorted them, and didn't care who he hurt? And what did *true to the barrio* mean? That he never tried to be anything but a gangster? Frankie wasn't a legend, he was a mug shot, a rap sheet, a convict in a bright orange jumpsuit. He was shootouts and dead bystanders and bodies lying in the street. Everything else was bullshit.

They buried Frankie next to Ramona. His headstone said: FRANKIE MONTAÑEZ. 1979–2014. NOW YOU ARE IN THE LORD'S ARMS. REST IN PEACE. Manzo stood at the graveside next to Frankie's mother, veiled and weeping over the supermarket bouquets piled on top of the gleaming coffin. What was she thinking about? That Frankie was a good boy and that he'd never hurt anyone? Or maybe that her son was a virus of terror who had infected his sister and many others besides and that death was as good a place as any for him to be. Possible, Manzo thought, but he doubted it.

Manzo looked around at his fellow gang members, their heads bowed, solemn and respectful. They'd all been to funerals like this, one of their own killed in a gun battle. Ask them about it and they'd say *That's the life we live, ese. We got to bang, it's in our blood.* It's in our blood? *It's in our fucking blood?* If *we* say it, why wouldn't white people say it too? That's the kind of stupid shit that makes them want to build a wall and deport eleven million people. Of all the great things about their culture, it was this craziness that kept going, generation after generation. A legacy of waste. He wished Frankie would climb out of that coffin and tell them: *I fucked up my life and I let my sister fuck up hers. Don't do it. Please don't do it.*

Sarita went overseas on business for a few weeks so the celebration was put on hold. Isaiah worked on his cases and did a lot of training with Ruffin. The dog seemed to enjoy the lessons, knowing exactly what Isaiah wanted him to do and getting a liver snack when he did it.

When Sarita came back from her trip she called and asked him to dinner at her apartment. The closest Isaiah had ever come to something like this was coffee at the Coffee Cup or a pizza at Pizza Hut. He was thrilled and terrified, but more than that, he felt like he was running behind; like he'd been held back a couple of grades and everybody else was graduating. He went shopping and bought a charcoal-gray suit from Macy's and Johnston & Murphy cap-toes and took fifteen minutes to tie his tie even after watching the instructions on YouTube three times.

Sarita lived in a glowing tower of sea-green glass overlooking Sunset Boulevard. Isaiah had to say his name twice to the uniformed man in the lobby, the first time it came out like a croak.

When Sarita swung open her apartment door, she smiled and said, "There's my hero."

"Hi," he said with another croak.

She hugged him tight and then took him by the hand. "Well, come on in," she said. The apartment was better than the one he'd imagined. The couch was a dove gray instead of cream, the furniture in different shades of gray, sea green, and beige that somehow blended together. The open kitchen had marble countertops, stainless steel appliances, copper cookware suspended above the stove. Music playing. Something Latin, gentle and arousing. Sarita was dressed casually in that way rich people dress casually. Jeans, ballet slippers, and a cashmere sweater that must have cost more than his suit.

"Would you like a glass of wine?" she said.

"Sure."

"Chardonnay?"

"Yeah, that'd be great."

She went over to the kitchen and poured two glasses. "Enfield Heron Lake, my favorite," she said. "Sit down, Isaiah, relax." He sat down on the edge of the sofa like he'd have to leave soon and wasn't even close to relaxed. She sat down next to him and gave him the wine. "Cheers," she said. She held her glass up. It took him a moment to realize he was supposed to clink it with his. "I can't thank you enough for what you've done," she said. "You were incredible.

I mean you literally saved my whole family. Tell me, are you all right?"

"Yeah, I'm fine."

"You've got bruises on your face," she said, touching his cheek. "And your knuckles are all scraped up." She lifted his hand like she was going to kiss it.

He cleared his throat. "I'm okay. It's nothing."

"Oh, crap, I forgot about the polenta." She got up and went into the kitchen. "I hope you like osso buco. I had it in Italy and went crazy for it."

"Smells good," he said. He'd heard of polenta but osso buco was a mystery. He hoped it wasn't a species of snail or something with tentacles. While Sarita bustled around the kitchen, he settled in, and when he was breathing normally again, he got up and looked around. The room was spacious, with a cathedral ceiling and exposed beams. The floor was black hardwood. Vague, calculated paintings were hung on the walls and there were bright spots of color that took your eye from point A to point B and on into the alphabet. There were precious baubles from different countries and a collection of vases with metallurgic glazes and a bronze crane standing next to a bookshelf full of coffee table books and a coffee table made of reclaimed wood that somehow looked modern. The overall effect was hip and prosperous.

Framed photos were carefully arranged on built-in shelves. There were cap-and-gown pictures of Sarita, high school, college, law school, and pictures of Janine and other relatives. None of Ken. None of Marcus. Isaiah was put out. Wasn't Marcus important enough to be remembered? One photo caught his eye. It was of Sarita at nineteen or twenty. He recognized the clothes. Designer field jacket, lion-colored boots, and the scarf that made her look sophisticated. She was standing on a wide green lawn, smiling, exhilarated to be there, an old majestic building in the background.

"Where was this taken?" Isaiah said.

"That? At Cambridge. Foreign exchange program when I was a sophomore. I had problems over there and came home early. That's when I met Marcus."

Isaiah sat down again and sipped the wine, which smelled better than it tasted. There were other smells too. The food, the spices, vanilla candle wax, the fabrics, the citrus and cypress trees. Together, they smelled like privilege. But there was another scent too. Woodsy, like the fir Marcus used in his carpentry, with a touch of something sweet, lavender maybe, and on top of that a heavier scent. Musk. No, it wasn't perfume. *It was a man's cologne.*

"Isaiah," Kevin said as he came in the door. "Good to see you again."

"Good to see you too," Isaiah said. Kevin was wearing a white shirt, untucked, the sleeves rolled up. Egyptian cotton, the thread count a million plus. His jeans were regular Levi's but he wore driving shoes that looked too soft and supple to be leather. Isaiah suddenly felt like an overdressed bumpkin in his four-hundred-and-thirty-nine-dollar suit, the tie like a choke chain, his collar getting damp.

"I'm sorry about my behavior when we first met," Kevin said, shaking Isaiah's hand. "Can we start over?"

"Sure," Isaiah said. "No problem."

Kevin was carrying a shopping bag and he took it into the kitchen.

"It's about time," Sarita said, and gave him a quick peck on the lips.

"Better late than never," he said.

Isaiah was confused. What was Kevin doing here? Why did he

have a key to the front door? Why did she kiss him? It took a second for him to acknowledge it. *They're a couple.* It was Kevin Sarita was talking to when Isaiah called her from Vegas. Checking with him, seeing what he thought.

Kevin poured himself a glass of wine, came back into the living room, and sat in a chair. He crossed his legs. No socks. He'd replaced the fake Rolex with a real one. Damn, he was good-looking. Where do you get a haircut like that? How come his skin was so smooth? Athletic too. Broad shoulders, deep chest, probably goes to one of those fancy gyms and works on his six-pack abs. He was the reason there were no pictures of Marcus.

"I can't thank you enough for what you've done for Sarita," Kevin said. "Remarkable, really."

"I was glad to do it," Isaiah said.

"I hear you're quite the detective."

"I try," Isaiah said.

"Tell me, how did you come to be doing this line of work?"

"I don't know," Isaiah said, thinking, Why would I tell you? "Fell into it."

"You know, our firm uses investigators all the time. Maybe we could throw some work your way."

"That'd be great."

An empty moment, the tension palpable. Isaiah wanted to get up and run out the door.

"Sarita told me about Marcus," Kevin said, smiling that Billy Dee smile. "He was a wonderful man."

"Yeah, he was," Isaiah said. Anger sucked the moisture out of his mouth and hummed in his head like a power line. What do you know about it, asshole? Sarita to the rescue.

"You guys ready to eat?" she said.

*　　*　　*

They ate dinner, Sarita and Kevin thanking him profusely, toasting him. Osso buco turned out to be baby dairy cow, Isaiah wondering if that was where Kevin's shoes came from. They asked him questions about what happened. He kept his answers brief and general. They seemed satisfied and uninterested in the details, just glad he was okay. They used their knives to push-scoop food onto their forks. They talked about real estate prices and what houses in the neighborhood were going for and Kevin's new Tesla and Sarita's ridiculous shoe collection and how she needed more closet space and Kevin would have to put his clothes on the balcony. They talked about Sarita advancing her career.

"What are your billable hours?" Kevin said in a tone used by people who were senior to you.

"About twenty-two hundred," she said.

"Barely the minimum for a bonus. You'll have to do better."

"I know."

"It's the only way to get noticed. You know, I heard Demco is acquiring Sedgewick International, hostile takeover. That's your bailiwick, isn't it?"

"I would think so. Sedgewick is based in London."

"I'll hint around with Chapman, see if I can get you a leg up."

"That would be helpful. Thank you."

They talked about binge-watching *Breaking Bad* and going to a fundraiser for PETA because a client was involved and Kevin playing tennis with Howie and easing up on him because he was a partner.

"Are you working on any interesting cases, Isaiah?" Sarita said, like she just remembered he was there.

Isaiah hesitated. What would he tell her? That the science club wanted him to get a bully off their backs? That he was on the look-out for Miss Myra's brooch? That on Doris Sattiewhite's birthday, her ex-husband, Mike, sent her a box with a dead mackerel in it? He considered telling them about Marcus's death but it didn't seem to be the right time. "Same old stuff," he said.

"Is it true people pay you with casseroles and discount coupons for carpet cleaning?" Kevin said, like he didn't believe it.

"Some do," Isaiah said.

"How are you able to make a living?"

"I have clients that can pay."

"Well, I commend you for your service to the community," Kevin said. "It's really quite admirable. We need more people who care about something other than themselves."

"That's absolutely true," Sarita said, nodding earnestly. "Really, Isaiah, I'm so proud of you."

As soon as they finished dinner, Isaiah said he had to get going. He had a client to meet who couldn't wait. They looked a little relieved. He thanked them for a great evening. Kevin gave him a manly hug, and Isaiah wanted to hit him. Sarita started to hug him, but he quickly said his goodbyes and left. As soon as he got outside, he ripped off the tie and threw it into the shrubbery. If he wasn't standing on the street he'd have ripped off the suit too.

He drove home, going too slow so he wouldn't go too fast. *Of course* Sarita would be with somebody like Kevin. *Of course* he never had a shot. What was he thinking with his cheap suit from Macy's and his house in the hood and his driveway that would never have a Tesla in it? What did Kevin say? *Maybe we can throw some work your way?* Thanks, asshole, we destitute people in the ghetto would really appreciate it. *I commend you for your service to the community*. Oh, like I need your approval to do my job? Like it's a good thing there are people who serve the community so you don't have to? Fuck you, Kevin. You and your driving shoes and your Egyptian cotton shirt. That Sarita didn't see he was an arrogant asshole said something about her. And what was that Kevin said about Marcus? *He was a wonderful man?* Kevin didn't have the right to speak about Marcus and she didn't have the right to tell him. And she was never going to be a prosecutor or work for an NGO. What she wanted was more room for a shoe collection and a leg up on the Demco case. *Really, Isaiah, I'm so proud of you.* Like he'd finally done something worthy of her praise. Fuck you too, Sarita. Next time she could save her own sister; ask Kevin to drive through Vegas at ninety miles an hour and get beat up and shot at by Chinese gangsters.

The next morning, he went to the wrecking yard with Ruffin. He looked for the girl with the GTI and the pocket watch tattoo but she wasn't there; no reason why she would be. He talked to TK about Sarita, how she was a huge disappointment, how she was nothing like she pretended to be.

"She's not pretending," TK said. "She can't help it if you thought she was something else. That's on you, boy."

"Why are you sticking up for her?" Isaiah said. "You don't even know her."

"Nobody's sticking up for her. I'm just saying she is who she is."

"What's that supposed to mean?"

"You got big holes in your life, boy. All by yourself, no family, no friends, ain't had a girl in a month of Sundays and got no idea where your life is going. Boy's so lonesome he gotta come down here and talk to a broke-down old man like me."

"Look, TK—"

"Hold on now, hold on, let me make my point."

"You mean that wasn't it?"

Seething, Isaiah waited while TK tapped a Pall Mall out of the pack, struck a match, lit it, and sucked down a long drag, squinting as he exhaled.

"You tried to do it the easy way," TK said.

"Do what the easy way?"

"You tried to fill all them holes up in one easy step. Sarita was gonna cure your loneliness, bring some people into your life, give you a family, give you a future. Well, it don't work like that, boy. You want a life you gotta open yourself up, not close yourself down."

"I'm not closed down."

"Well, you coulda fooled me. You ever talk to somebody just to have a conversation? Invite somebody over for a beer, watch the game? Go places to socialize? Bar, pool hall, church, ball field, anywhere where you ain't by yourself? *Do you?*"

"I don't know, sometimes."

"Sometimes? Shit, boy, who you tryin' to kid?" TK said. "And why do you take that goddamn dog with you everywhere you go? To keep folks off of you, that's why. You think a pit bull makes you look more friendly?"

"It's my dog," Isaiah said, shrugging with both shoulders.

Isaiah left the yard, angry and embarrassed. TK didn't know what he was talking about. The old man ran a junkyard. Who was he to be analyzing somebody? Sarita had duped him, got him to risk his life with her hugs and flattery and slender body. And for free too. He should send her a bill and send one to Kevin for being a jerk. He'd been a mark, a sucker, and that was never going to happen again.

Isaiah had dinner at Taco Bell and wondered how many things

you could make out of the same four ingredients. At home, he cut the lawn, mopped the kitchen floor, and played online chess with some hotshot from the Czech Republic and checkmated him in ten moves. He was sitting in the easy chair looking through his emails when he remembered that photo of Sarita, the one he'd looked at in her apartment. He stood up sharply, Ruffin watching him, sensing the change in vibe. Sarita was at Cambridge, standing on the lawn with that magnificent old building in the background. *He'd seen it before.*

"Well, I'll be," he said.

It was the same magnificent old building that was in Seb's photograph, the one where he was wearing the oversize suit, except he was standing in the archway. Seb never said he went to Cambridge but there couldn't be two buildings like that, and he said he'd seen one of his professors panhandling outside the Drummer Street bus station. Isaiah checked. The bus station was five minutes from the Cambridge campus.

A gauzy layer of clouds filtered the evening sun, a thoughtful pewter light cast over the yard. Lonely crickets chirped from their hiding places, the smell of fading leaves in the air. Isaiah sat on the stoop with Ruffin and shared an energy bar, the fingers of his mind carefully assembling the puzzle pieces.

Sarita is a sophomore, doing prelaw at Long Beach State. She's interested in international law and goes to Cambridge on a foreign exchange program. There, she meets Seb, maybe in one of her classes, maybe socially. The timing was right. The lawns in both pictures had the same lush greenness, the same bare patch in the foreground. There was a garden off to the right, flowers blooming identically; a furrow in one photo, its twin in the other. Seb was probably infatuated, who wouldn't be? So he asks her out. She rebuffs him, but he won't take no for an answer. He's an obsessive, after all; dogged in the face of reason. Sending Gahigi back to punish Laquez a second time. Taunting Gahigi repeatedly about smoking. Returning to Rwanda and searching every road into and out of Kigali to find the man who cut off his leg. His spotless booth at the bar needs cleaning again. He returns home to check the front door a second time. The tea set in a grid. Seb wants everything *just so* and he'll keep coming at you until his life is *just so*.

Isaiah imagined a young, awkward Seb, transparent as glass, showing up as Sarita walked to the library or went to London on the train or had a Guinness at the pub with her friends. He saw Seb, fidgeting and smiling sheepishly. *Hello, Sarita, you are looking quite beautiful this evening. Might I join you?* Sarita trying not to cringe, her friends smirking and rolling their eyes. But Seb persists. *Perhaps we might attend a lecture together. Get a bite to eat. A show, perhaps?* Always gracious, she makes excuses. A study group or a test tomorrow or a dental appointment. Seb is not stupid, he gets the message, but what does an obsessive do when they're thwarted? They get more obsessed. He calls her repeatedly, slips notes under her door, peeks in her windows. She changes her schedule, her routes, her hangouts, her friends intervene but he's implacable. Frustrated, and no stranger to confrontation, he gets angry. He tells her he does not forgive and that frightens her. She decides she's had enough and returns home early and meets Marcus.

Still at Cambridge, Seb remains obsessed with Sarita. She's beautiful and intelligent, yes, but more than that, she's optimism, hope, the doorway to a new life for the small African man who is taunted and ridiculed, limps around on one leg and wears thrift shop suits. Isaiah recognized himself in Seb. Vesting his future in a fantasy, planning his life around a pipe dream; a new destiny in one easy step.

Ever determined, Seb leaves school, comes to America and finds Sarita in Long Beach. He has nothing to offer her so he watches and waits. He discovers she's with Marcus. *A handyman*. Laughable, really—but look at them! Fawning over each other like teenagers, it's disgusting. But clearly they're in love. Seb is crushed, his obsession swelling into hatred, but not toward his darling Sarita. Toward the interloper. Seb keeps an eye on the couple while his career transitions from tax preparer to criminal. He hopes they will break up but they don't. Seb can't stand it anymore. He has to see what kind of magic this handyman possesses, what alchemy has turned Sarita's head. But how? Marcus is a handyman, so what if we hire him? The catalogue suggests a light gray bamboo flooring to go along with the white leather furniture, so yes, let's do that. Marcus can replace the flooring. That should keep him around for a while. And what would anyone have seen if they'd hung around Marcus for a while? That he was warm and charming and good-humored; that he was patient and kind and honest. That he was a good man with a good heart. Everything Seb was not and would never be. What now? The answer was simple for someone who hacked off a man's leg and turned it into a walking stick. Marcus had to die.

Marcus, for some unknown reason, needs money, and installing hardwood flooring isn't going to cut it. He learns about the drop; maybe eavesdropping while Seb is on the phone with Frankie working out the details. Marcus intercepts Frankie and robs him, accidentally shooting him in the process. Then he takes the money to the storage locker, puts it in a fireproof box and hides the box in a carton marked TAX RECEIPTS '07. He doesn't know that Frankie saw the car and has identified him. He doesn't know the Locos have put a hit out on him, and he doesn't know that Seb and Gahigi are tracking him, learning his habits, the trails he takes. They discover that Marcus and his little brother play basketball every Saturday at McClarin Park. Good. They have a reliable location but how will they kill him? The method should be something that will not bring in the police. An accident, then, a hit-and-run. But Seb also realizes he must destroy Marcus in Sarita's heart as well or she'll mourn him forever, so while Marcus is busy on that deadly Saturday, Seb plants the drugs and money in the backpack. When the authorities find it they will assume Marcus was involved in drugs, and when Sarita finds out—and Seb would make sure she did—her image of Marcus will be wiped out right along with his physical body.

Marcus and Isaiah play two-on-two with Carlos and Corey while Seb and Gahigi wait in the Accord, parked across the street in front of Kayo's. Seb smokes English Ovals, nonfiltered, the butts would have disintegrated before Isaiah could find them. When Isaiah met Seb in the Nyanza Bar, Gahigi was trying to quit smoking, but what was he smoking eight years ago? An educated guess? Marlboro, the most popular brand in the world. The Carta Blancas? A&J Liquor didn't carry Tusker or any other African brands so they drank the Cartas instead. Seb didn't seem the type to order a submarine sandwich so Gahigi did but only ate half, either because he was nervous or because his lank frame couldn't hold any more.

Having followed the brothers to the park, Seb and Gahigi assumed they'd walk home the same way, crossing Anaheim at Baldwin. They drove around to get west of them, Seb at the wheel. He wanted to make sure it was done right, that there were no mistakes. He gets the car in position, sees Marcus coming off the curb and stomps on the gas, laughing as he slams into his rival, his fractured body flung in the air. Seb's nemesis is gone, but an important part of the plan has failed. The police don't find the heroin and money. Even worse, Sarita goes away to school and then she gets a job in

San Francisco, while Seb has tied his enterprise to East Long Beach. Years pass. Time and distance cool his obsession, but he follows her on social media and learns she's returned to LA.

The obsession reignites. Isaiah remembered the copies of *People* and *Los Angeles Magazine* in Seb's office. Did Seb imagine himself and Sarita in those glossy pages, walking the red carpet and mingling with their glamorous friends? Seb is a wealthy man now. He can reintroduce himself into her life with style and class. He buys a new house and a new Jaguar. All he needs to do now is find an opening, a way to run into her.

So why did Marcus rob Frankie? Isaiah tried to remember what was happening back then. Marcus was agitated and short-tempered and there were all those intense phone calls out on the balcony and the mysterious college brochures left on the coffee table. Only Sarita could have caused such turmoil. Had she broken up with him? Did that account for his upset? Probably. She was going away to Stanford and entering a new phase of her life. She was going to meet new people and make new friends, none of whom would be handymen living in the hood. *Marcus was losing the love of his life.* He had to fight for her but how? What could he give her that would keep her in his arms? *A future.* He had to prove to her that he wouldn't be a handyman forever; go back to school, be an architect or an engineer; show her he was changing and that he was a man worth hanging on to. Marcus collected college brochures but discovered that the tuition would take money he didn't have. He and Isaiah lived hand to mouth. So Marcus robbed Frankie, and he did it because he loved Sarita. The only force powerful enough to push him off the straight and narrow, the only reason great enough to rip away his character and leave him naked and in need. And then Seb killed him.

*   *   *

Isaiah's hatred was a lesion pulsing and oozing pus. It was time for Seb's punishment, but what should that be? Isaiah couldn't kill him, and a beating was temporary. Destroy his business? No. That was numbers on a ledger. It had to be something deeper and more terrible, something to make him suffer until the day he died.

Seb sat in his booth at the Nyanza Bar, feeling nostalgic, smoking and drinking his tea. He wouldn't be around much anymore. Drop in for meetings and such and that would be all. He'd decided where he would run into Sarita. On Fridays after work, she and a few of her colleagues met at the Ten Pound Bar in Beverly Hills, where the glassware was Lalique and the drink minimum was fifty dollars. Seb would stroll in, unassuming, see her, let their eyes meet, then tip his head slightly as if he was recalling her face, and then smile his most charming smile. *Hello! How are you? It's been a long time!* Then they would talk, the problems of the past long forgotten. And what was she doing now? *You're an attorney? Of course, a mind like yours. What am I doing? I'm an investor,* he'd say casually. Equities, real estate, precious metals, that sort of thing, her eyes taking in the six-thousand-dollar Anderson & Sheppard bespoke suit and the two-thousand-dollar Tom Ford oxfords and the eighteen-thousand-dollar Piaget Emperador rose-gold watch, bought on the black market for twelve-five. And then he'd suggest they go to dinner at Bouchon or Spago, and afterward, *How about a nightcap? Well, my house is not far, perhaps we might go there.* By then she would have seen that he'd changed, that he wasn't an awkward college student anymore but a successful and charismatic businessman. Still, the decision would be hers. Seb thought it incongruous, even embarrassing, that a man who always looked for an advantage had given it away to a woman; that she should decide if he was desirable, worthy of love. He got up from the booth, his anxiety and excitement hardly contained. Tonight was the night when his yearning and coveting and frustration would come to an end. Tonight, his new life would begin.

Isaiah entered the bar. The African woman was wailing another lament. The bartender wasn't there, but another soccer game was on TV. Seb was just getting up from a booth.

"Isaiah!" Seb said, his smile warm and mocking. "How are you? Did you come to insult me again?"

"Sarita," Isaiah said.

Seb's smile didn't waver. "Sarita? I don't believe I know anyone by that name."

"I told her it was you. I told her you killed Marcus." Seb went still, the smile held up by two thin threads at the corners of his mouth. "I told her how you did it," Isaiah said. "How you hired Marcus to work at the house and how you planted the money and the heroin and how you waited at the park and ran him down like he was nothing. And I told her you were a criminal. That you laundered money for drug dealers and gangsters and that you bought a new house and a new car to impress her. I told her how you turned a man's leg into a cane."

"You should not have done that, Isaiah," Seb said. He looked stricken.

"She doesn't want to see you, talk to you, or read your fucking handwriting," Isaiah said. "She *hates* you. And you know what she did when I told her you were planning to hook up? *She laughed*. I mean she cracked up! She said, Does that little reptile really think he has a chance with me? That I'd let him *touch* me? He could live in the Taj Mahal and drive a Rolls-Royce and I wouldn't spend five minutes with him if he was the last man left on earth."

"Do not say these things, Isaiah!" Seb seemed to lose his balance, stepping back, leaning more on his cane.

"What was that other thing, I can't remember—oh yeah, she said at Cambridge you used to wear a suit that looked like you'd borrowed it from a grandfather. She said you thought you looked good in it. She used to laugh about it with her friends." Isaiah paused to chuckle and sneer. "And she said you were always pestering her, harassing her, spying on her. She said you were a creep. That's what she called you. A creep. Do you know you're why she left Cambridge?" Seb didn't answer. You could feel his fantasies crashing into reality like the Accord had crashed into Marcus. *"You,"* Isaiah said. "She went home because of *you*."

Seb rapped his cane once on the floor and puffed out his chest. "I do not believe you!"

"Oh, really?" Isaiah said. "Well, did she say goodbye? Leave you a note? Leave you her address? Send you an email? Anything? No, she didn't. She just got the hell out of there. You were such an asshole she didn't just change schools, she had to leave the fucking country."

"Stop! Don't say anymore!" Seb demanded, pounding his cane on the floor like he was trying to kill a rat.

Isaiah grinned. "Did you know that's how she met Marcus? If she hadn't come home early that never would have happened. Funny, huh? How you fucked yourself over? And by the way, she already has a man in her life. An attorney. Good-looking, tall, almost like a model from a magazine. He makes you look like a fucking troll."

"No!" Seb shouted, but he was wilting, curling into himself. "She would not do such a thing!"

Isaiah laughed. "She wouldn't? Why? Because she was hoping you'd come back into her life? The reptile that chased her out of Europe? That annoying little freak that wouldn't take no for an answer?"

Seb covered his face with the back of his forearm. "Please, no more."

But Isaiah couldn't, wouldn't let up. "She said that you were vicious and ridiculous and you murdered someone that was a hundred times better than you'll ever be. She said you were pathetic. She said you weren't even a man."

Seb's lips were trembling like he was frostbitten, a gleaming film over his eyes. He screamed and swung the cane, Isaiah catching it, twisting it away, and jamming it lengthwise under Seb's chin, pushing him into the wall and snarling into his face. "I want you to think about Sarita for the rest of your life. How you will never have her and that she'll always remember you as the pitiful little creep in his grandfather's suit."

Gahigi came rushing out of the hallway, a gun in his hand. Isaiah let go of Seb, kept the cane, and turned to face Gahigi. Seb fell to the floor, coughing and gagging.

"Kill him, Gahigi!" Seb screamed. "Kill him now!"

Gahigi was too far away to strike with the cane and too wary to come closer. The sutures on his neck hadn't healed. He touched them as if to remind himself that Isaiah had put them there. He looked at Isaiah, his weary, despondent eyes searching for something that wasn't there anymore.

"What are you waiting for?" Seb screeched. "Kill him, Gahigi! Kill him!" Gahigi remained still while the bewilderment on Seb's face turned into something that looked like sadness.

"I am not killing him, Seb," Gahigi said. "I am done with

killing. I am done with killing forever." Gahigi ejected the clip and set the gun down on the bar. "I am going now, Seb. I am going home."

Gahigi walked away, two inches of white sock flashing like lane reflectors down the long dark road of the bar. He went out the front door, sunlight exploding, snuffed out again as the door closed behind him.

"You will regret what you have done," Seb said. He was breathing heavily, drool dripping from his chin.

"No, I won't," Isaiah said. "I'll be sorry I didn't kill you."

"You are my enemy now."

"And you're mine."

Isaiah broke the cane across his knee, the snap like a gunshot. He tossed the pieces at Seb, who raised his arm to shield his face, the pieces clattering onto the floor.

"One day, I will come for you, Isaiah," Seb said. "One day very soon."

"You do that, Seb." Isaiah looked down at him; wretched and ruined, like rotten fruit, stepped on and smeared across the sidewalk. "And I won't be an innocent man crossing the street," he said. "I'll be waiting for you."

CHAPTER SIXTEEN
Ruffin, Sit

There are many forms of violence, and stripping away a man's dignity is one of them; more punishing than a beating or taking his belongings or sometimes even death. Isaiah had done it once before, to the hit man. It hadn't registered then, but this time it was so deliberate he had to think about it. He didn't feel victorious or satisfied or unburdened. He felt empty. Like the hatred had scoured out his insides and left him fallow and dry.

The next few weeks went by in a hazy state of apathy. He had to force himself to work on his cases. Cherise's brother, Jerome, coached a middle school football league. Isaiah got him to recruit Rayo, who instantly became a star defensive lineman, venting his aggression on the opposing teams. He sacked one quarterback so many times the kid walked off the field, telling his dad football was stupid and he wanted to play tennis. The science club, grateful to have Rayo off their backs, went searching for Miss Myra's precious brooch. They systematically combed the area around her house and found it tossed in a hedge. Isaiah and Ruffin waited around the Shop 'n Save, and when Doris's ex-husband, Mike, came out, they followed him home and cornered him in his garage; Isaiah and Ruffin standing there, dark silhouettes framed by the sunlight. The dog's amber eyes glowing. He panted slow. *Heh...heh...heh,* Mike thinking he was going to be eaten alive.

"You're going to leave Doris alone from now on, aren't you?" Isaiah said.

"Hey, no problem, man!" Mike said, backing into the wall, his eyes wide as Frisbees. "Swear to God, I won't even *think* about her!"

Isaiah took no new cases, didn't answer his emails and spent his time reading or listening to music or, for the first time in his life, doing nothing at all. Somebody said if you stop moving, the world does too. Gradually, his mood improved, and he started to work again but something had been lost, something that couldn't be replaced.

Isaiah drove down Seventh Street, the unofficial Long Beach railroad tracks; the houses and apartments getting more upscale as you went toward the ocean, more downtrodden if you went in the other direction. He was taking Ruffin to the vet, something wrong with the dog's ear. He was scratching at it all the time, a foul, yeasty smell coming out of it. As usual, Ruffin was sitting in the front seat with the seat belt on. All he needed was a cell phone and he could be on his way to work.

"Say," Isaiah said. "Could you not slobber all over my car?"

He'd come to realize that TK was right. He'd tried to take a shortcut; leapfrog over the messy, uncertain ordeal of starting relationships and making them grow; of filling his life with people and possibilities. The only thing keeping him in the hood was himself. Marcus's murder hadn't condemned him to live how he was living. He could do whatever he wanted. A frightening thought. He'd also come to terms with Sarita. There was nothing wrong with her or her lifestyle. Ambition and a taste for luxury didn't make her a bad person. She'd grown up in the hood and come up the hard way herself. She was someone to admire and appreciate.

She'd called him twice. Once to invite him to a cocktail party, but he made an excuse. The second time, they had coffee. He suspected she knew how he felt that awful night in her apartment and was grateful she didn't bring it up. She told him she'd quit her job and had applied at the Legal Aid Foundation in Long Beach. "I think I have enough shoes," she said. She told him she and Kevin had gotten engaged and she invited him to the wedding and he was sorry he'd given his suit to the Goodwill. He didn't tell her about Seb. Why upset her all these years later?

He thought about Dodson's proposal to partner up. Did he need a partner? Not really. He'd been doing okay on his own for a long time. But then there was that *friend* thing. The closest he'd ever come to having one was Ruffin. Pitiful, when you thought about it, and it *was* reassuring having Dodson around. The bickering aside, he was loyal and fearless and he had a good heart. The experience reminded Isaiah of being with Marcus; going through things together, things nobody else could share. And Dodson had a point about his cases. He *was* getting bored. Stepping out of his comfort zone would be a good thing; take some risks; not like rescuing Ken and Benny, but get out there in the world and make shit happen, see what it's like on the high side. If Kevin had some work for him that would be a start. He'd call Dodson and set something up, maybe invite him over for a beer. He wondered what the shingle would say. QUINTABE AND ASSOCIATE? Dodson would no doubt want it the other way around. They'd have to see about that.

*   *   *

He couldn't keep Marcus's robbery money so he gave it away. Some to repair Deronda's house and pay off the loans on the food truck. Dodson sold his half of the business to Deronda. She and her sister would run it. The rest Isaiah kept for Flaco. The last Isaiah had heard, Janine and Benny were back in Vegas and still gambling. Why wouldn't they? They were debt-free now.

When Ken got out of the hospital, he hid in a motel. He almost committed suicide but hanging yourself was harder than it looked. It was hard to find your courage when you'd never seen it before. Sarita finally demanded that he turn himself in or she'd do it for him. Ken cooperated with the police, giving up Tommy's whole operation. The triad's West Coast string of brothels and massage parlors were shut down. Ken was awaiting sentencing now, his lawyers were trying to settle.

Ken rolled over on the Mountain Master and Tommy fled back to Hong Kong. The police there had been alerted so he fled again to mainland China, only to find that the People's Republic didn't like human traffickers any more than anybody else. Tommy was tried and sentenced to forty years' hard labor at Huaiji Prison in the Guangdong Province, the same place the sick girl was from. He slept on a dirt floor in a space twelve inches wide and near the latrine because he was a new prisoner. He washed up at an outdoor trough shared by his twenty cellmates. His diet consisted mostly of sorghum and corn, ground into a flour and made into bread, and a watery vegetable soup. He was awakened at six a.m., worked in the fields all day, spreading fertilizer made from human shit. Sarita found out through her sources that he'd tried to bribe an official and got forty more years tacked on to what was already a death sentence.

*   *   *

Isaiah turned off Seventh onto Linden and saw the girl from the wrecking yard. What was her name again? Grace, that was it. She was standing in front of an art supply store talking to another girl who was anemically pale. Her jet-black hair was shaved on one side of her head, tats coming out of her tank top like a turtle-neck. Isaiah wondered if TK was right and Grace was a lesbian. Or maybe she had a boyfriend or was married and had kids or maybe she wouldn't recognize him and would think he was some weirdo off the street.

He pulled the car over to the curb and watched in the rearview mirror. He tried to read Grace's body language. Was she friends with the pale girl or was she *friends?* Was she wearing an engagement ring? Was the pale girl wearing one? He couldn't tell. They were laughing now, Grace putting her hand on the other girl's arm. Was that a normal gesture or was she flirting? Isaiah sat there, mired in doubt, the dog looking at him as if to say *What's your problem?*

Okay, Isaiah thought. Make up your mind. Are you going to say hello or not? Not, he decided. This was too off-the-cuff, too spontaneous. He needed time to think about it, come up with a plan. Maybe he'd see her again or meet some other girl. Plenty of opportunities, no need to pressure yourself. He put the car into gear and drove away.

Grace gave Cherokee a hug, said goodbye, and turned for home. She was in a hurry. She had a painting to finish for the art fair in Ojai. A million other artists would be showing their work, but there were rich people up there and she really needed to sell something. Illustrating bilingual workbooks for night school students wasn't exactly a career path. She'd only gone a few steps when she smiled, big and warm and glad. "Hello, friend," she said. The slate-colored pit bull with the fierce amber eyes was bounding toward her. It was nearly on top of her when she heard someone say, "Ruffin, sit," the dog coming to an immediate stop and sitting at her feet.

Acknowledgments

My never-ending gratitude to Esther Newberg and Zoe Sandler for carefully, lovingly guiding my career, and to Josh Kendall, whose unerring editorial eye has made the book better than I ever thought possible. A special thanks to L. F. Monger, whose guidance on a number of issues was indispensable. Sabrina Callahan, Pamela Brown, Alyssa Persons, and Nicky Guerreiro have labored tirelessly to put my work before the public. Their kindness, creativity, and professionalism continue to astound me.